STEALTH GAMBIT

A Cold War Novel Inspired by Actual Events

WES TRUITT

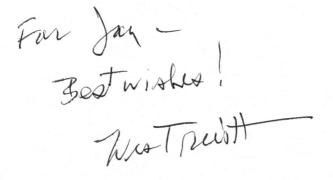

For Jay —
Best wishes !
Wes Truitt

DORRANCE
PUBLISHING CO
EST. 1920
PITTSBURGH, PENNSYLVANIA 15238

The contents of this work, including, but not limited to, the accuracy of events, people, and places depicted; opinions expressed; permission to use previously published materials included; and any advice given or actions advocated are solely the responsibility of the author, who assumes all liability for said work and indemnifies the publisher against any claims stemming from publication of the work.

This is a work of fiction inspired by actual events.

Dorrance Publishing Co
585 Alpha Drive
Suite 103
Pittsburgh, PA 15238
Visit our website at *www.dorrancebookstore.com*

ISBN: 978-1-4809-1928-0
eISBN: 978-1-4809-1905-1

Also by Wesley B. Truitt:

Business Planning: A Comprehensive Framework and Process (Quorum Books, 2002)

What Entrepreneurs Need To Know about Government: A Guide to Rules and Regulations (Praeger Publishers, 2004)

The Corporation (Greenwood Press, 2006)

Power and Policy: Lessons for Leaders in Government and Business (Praeger, 2010)

Contents

Prologue

New York City
April 25, 1974

Two things set the course of Nick Butler's life within an hour after he got off the Broadway subway train at the 116th Street station. He was admitted to Columbia University's graduate school, and he became a CIA agent—destined to play the leading role in a crucial Cold War operation against the Soviet Union's KGB. But he would not know about that for a year.

Going to his admissions interview that morning, he climbed the subway stairs to street level, crossed Broadway, walked through the black iron gates, and stood before the enormous bronze statue of "Alma Mater" in the midst of the magnificent campus of Columbia University, pausing to take in the sight on this sunny spring day.

He continued through the campus to Amsterdam Avenue, turned left to West 118th Street to a block of brownstone townhouses. He entered the third house on the left. A sign on the door read: "Columbia University, Institute of Defense Studies."

"Your name, please?" asked the receptionist, putting her cigarette on the ash tray.

"Nick Butler," replied the ambitious but naive undergraduate.

"Show me your government-issued ID, please," she said in her New York accent. He handed over his Maryland driver's license. Scanning the appointment roster, she found his name and handing back the license said, "Your appointment is with Professor Reynard. Go upstairs one flight. His office is on the left."

He climbed the stairs.

"Are you Nick Butler?" asked a petite woman when he arrived at her desk.

"Yes," he answered with a friendly smile.

"I'm Anna Suzuki, Professor Reynard's secretary," she said, smiling back at the sight of another eager-looking college senior seeking graduate school admission. Though this one seems special, she thought.

"Please go in. Professor Reynard is expecting you."

Opening the door, he entered a dimly-lit musty office that once was the second floor back bedroom of the townhouse. Books lined the walls. An old fashioned goose-neck lamp sat on a corner of the desk illuminating the face of the seated man. As Nick approached the cluttered desk, Reynard looked up, squinted as he adjusted his glasses, then the balding 60-year-old professor brushed aside a wisp of white hair from his forehead, rising to greet his young visitor.

"You're right on time, Nick," said William Reynard. "Alvin Rubin, your senior year advisor at Penn, highly recommended you." While shaking hands, Reynard checked out the clean-cut, six foot, well-built American standing before him and could not resist a smile, pleased with what he saw. His handshake was firm and dry. "Take a seat," Reynard ordered.

Nick took a chair facing the desk expecting the interrogation he supposed perspective first-year students endure before being admitted to an Ivy League graduate school. To his surprise Reynard said nothing at first—he just looked at him, carefully examining his face. Nick steadily returned his gaze. To Reynard, Nick appeared mature beyond his 23 years. After a long few seconds, the professor, the most renowned American scholar in international politics, announced a decision.

"The faculty admissions committee reviewed your application, your undergraduate transcript, and your letters of recommendation. Professor Rubin provided your excellent record in his honors seminar. We have decided to admit you to the graduate school. I hope you'll be happy here in our political science Ph.D. program. I trust this is agreeable?"

Nick was flabbergasted. This was a total surprise. He stammered "yes" to the question and thanked the world-famous professor.

"In addition to admission," Reynard continued, "you will receive a university fellowship to cover tuition, and you will join a special program here at the Institute of Defense Studies, which I chair. That will provide you an extra stipend so you won't have to earn a living during the summers to pay for room and board. You will spend your summers here on the special program. You will of course have to maintain a high grade-point average to ensure annual renewal of your fellowship. Is this also acceptable?"

This spilled out of Professor Reynard with the ease and authority only an older man can extend to a promising protégé.

"Of course I accept. I cannot thank you and the faculty committee enough," the college senior managed to say. "I'm deeply indebted to Professor Rubin. He specifically encouraged me to come to Columbia."

"Good, then that's settled." Reynard informed his new student he would begin work at the Institute in early June, a few weeks away. Student housing would be arranged on campus. Butler eagerly agreed to this. Not having to find a summer job or an apartment was a big relief.

"On your way out Anna will hand you a packet of forms to fill out and mail back to her," Reynard said, dismissing him and returning his attention to the papers on his desk. "Have a good trip back to Philadelphia," Reynard said as Nick left his office.

Butler departed the campus, took the subway to Penn Station, boarded a train to Philadelphia, and returned to his fraternity house on Locust Walk in West Philadelphia—his feet barely touching ground. He'd party that night and tell Dr. Rubin the good news in the morning.

Soon after Butler left, Reynard walked out of his office to ask Anna Suzuki, his Japanese-American secretary, her impression of him.

"I find him very attractive," she responded with uncharacteristic enthusiasm.

"He certainly has all the chops," Reynard observed. "Al Rubin's done it again. Nick's another of his terrific referrals. Let's call Al and thank him."

Anna placed the call. When his phone rang, Rubin was in his office in Stiteler Hall, having just come back from a faculty meeting in College Hall.

"Hello, Al," said Reynard. "I'm calling to thank you for sending Nick Butler to us. We've given him admission and a tuition fellowship, plus a stipend at the Institute."

"Oh, I'm absolutely delighted," Rubin responded. "Nick's a fine young man and in time I think he'll become an exceptionally good spy."

Next, Bill Reynard had Anna dial a number at the Central Intelligence Agency in Langley, Virginia.

"Hello, Bill. How's everything at Columbia?" said the voice at the CIA.

"We're doing all right, Phil," Reynard replied. "I'm calling to let you know I've offered a full fare to another one of Al Rubin's exceptional students. This one's name is Nick Butler. He's a graduating senior from Penn who will join us at the Institute in early June."

"That's good news," replied Philip Myers. "I'll let Susan Samuels know her evaluation of him is corroborated by another astute judge of character. The fellowship is essential, given his family's modest circumstances."

"How do you want to proceed?" Reynard asked.

"Let's wait until he graduates from Penn in a few weeks to begin a protocol," answered Myers. "Meanwhile, I'll have Susan lay out a game-plan tailored for him. Because he's so young and virgin to the service he will not likely be recognized as an agent."

Reynard wanted to confirm the arrangements: "So, as usual, I'll be his control here at Columbia, Susan Samuels will be his Agency control, and the stipend for his work at the Institute will come out of the usual account?"

"Roger that," replied the Vice Admiral.

Thus the arrangements for Nick Butler's life were settled within an hour after he arrived at the 116th Street subway station on Broadway. But he knew only half of it.

How did this come about? To answer that question, we have to go back one year—when it all began.

Chapter One:
The Recruit

University of Pennsylvania
Philadelphia, Pennsylvania
April 10, 1973

Returning to his office after lunch, Professor Alvin Rubin found Susan Samuels, a senior official of the Central Intelligence Agency, waiting for him.

"What a pleasant surprise finding you here, Susan!" exclaimed Rubin with a broad smile and an outstretched hand.

"Nice to see you again, Dr. Rubin," Samuels replied, shaking his hand then closing the office door. "It's been a couple of years since we've seen each other."

"Yes, and it's been about 20 years since you were in my International Relations senior seminar," Rubin said with a chuckle as he took the swivel chair behind his desk. "How's everything at the Agency?"

"The Cold War keeps us busy as usual," she replied as she sat down on a guest chair. "I'm happy to report since I saw you last I've been promoted to Assistant Deputy Director of Operations under Admiral Myers. And I also got married—again."

"Congratulations on both counts," the professor said with a smile. "But I take it this is not a social call," Rubin said getting serious.

"As usual, you're right. I could use your help with something we're doing."

"For you, Susan, I'm delighted to be of assistance," Rubin replied. "How can I help?"

"Over the years you've identified Penn seniors who might be good candidates for the clandestine service. I'm one of them as you well know. I'd be grateful for your help again. Is there anyone who comes to mind?" she asked.

"Hmm, there's no one in the current senior class," replied the 65-year-old professor of International Relations. "The new semester won't start until September as you know. Perhaps someone in the next senior class might be a possibility. Is this urgent?"

"It's more important we find the right person than make a hasty selection," Samuels replied. "The requirements for this candidate are quite specific. What we need is a young man who is highly intelligent and can think on his feet, and he must be physically fit—preferably an athlete—and exceptionally handsome. These attributes are essential for the operation we plan for him."

"I see," muttered the professor, scratching his bearded chin. "You want an All-American boy who looks like a movie star and who's also Rhodes Scholar material. Have I got it?"

"You've got it! Please keep a sharp eye out for Mr. Right and let me know if and when you find him."

"I certainly hope I find him. However," he said with a chuckle, "I think I'll refer him first to my granddaughter who's at Swarthmore."

"Great seeing you again, Dr. Rubin," Samuels said laughing as she rose from her chair and shook his hand. "I hope to hear from you in the coming months."

Central Intelligence Agency
Langley, Virginia
January 14, 1974

The intercom on Susan Samuels' telephone buzzed.

"Professor Rubin is on line one, Mrs. Samuels," her secretary announced.

"I'll take it," Susan replied.

"Hello, Dr. Rubin. Thanks for calling," she said after punching the lighted button on the phone. "After all these months I hope you have good news for me."

"I believe I do," stated the professor. "He's a senior in my International Relations honors seminar who, during the fall semester, demonstrated the intellectual qualities you require. His overall grade point average is 3.9. I've nominated him for Phi Beta Kappa. He also meets your physical requirements to a 'T,' having been the quarterback of Penn's football team last fall. I'm told by the coaches that quarterbacks have to think on their feet! Oh, one more thing, the girls in my seminar practically swoon when he comes into the room."

"Did you call your granddaughter at Swarthmore before calling me?" Samuels joked.

"As always I put my patriotic duty first," the professor chuckled. "Do you want to proceed as usual?"

"Yes. As usual, please put his dossier and photo in a secure pouch and send it directly to me here at Langley. I cannot thank you enough, my old friend, for your help. He sounds ideal for our needs. I'll begin a background check when I receive your package."

Over the next three months at CIA's request, the FBI conducted a full-field investigation of the candidate to determine his eligibility to conduct highly classified work for the Agency. The investigation unearthed no criminal record, no police reports in any jurisdiction he had lived, and strong endorsements from former teachers, neighbors, and associates as to his loyalty to the United States. His fraternity brothers hailed him as a "regular guy" who had everyone's respect, having elected him president of his fraternity his senior year. In short, the investigation resulted in a clean report, clearing him to work for the Agency.

By mid-April Susan Samuels was ready to recommend to Admiral Myers that the candidate be selected and introduced into a protocol to test his skills and qualifications for the important tasks that lay ahead for him in operation "Stealth Gambit."

Making an exception to Agency regulations, it was decided the candidate would be kept unaware of the CIA's involvement with him for the first few assignments. He would perform them in innocence—believing his natural behavior would be his best cover for operational success and for his own protection.

The candidate would not be told that the purpose of this op is to thwart advancements in Soviet military aircraft development by allowing the KGB to steal from him false airplane designs to mislead Soviet aerospace engineers. This would be a classic disinformation operation.

Because the candidate would need to be familiar with the worldwide aviation industry, Samuels decided he should go to graduate school at Columbia University where she knew Dr. David Hammond, an internationally-recognized expert on aviation, was a visiting scholar. To learn the industry, the candidate would become Hammond's Research Assistant at Columbia's Institute of Defense Studies.

The next step was to have Professor Rubin urge him to apply to Columbia's Department of Public Law and Government for admission to graduate school. This recruitment channel had been used for some years. Professor William Reynard, chair of that department and also Director of the Institute of Defense Studies, was the key man for the next phase in the evaluation and training process.

Having made these determinations, Samuels took the elevator to the seventh floor of the CIA building and walked down the corridor to Admiral Myers' office suite. On that April afternoon she briefed CIA's Deputy Director of Operations, outlining her recommendations. Myers approved the selection of the candidate and the protocols for his assessment and training. If he passes his tests, this young man will become the lead player in the clandestine service's operation "Stealth Gambit" to ensure America's continued dominance in military aircraft.

"Finally," Samuels told her boss, "the candidate's name is Nicholas Butler. He's a resident of Silver Spring, Maryland. His widowed mother is an NSA employee at Ft. Meade. Given her clearances, he passed his background checks with flying colors."

As it turned out, Professor Rubin had anticipated the Agency's desire for the candidate to apply to Columbia for admission to their Ph.D. program. At Rubin's urging, Butler had already made the application and had been invited by Professor Reynard to come to New York for an interview in April. During that interview, Reynard informed Butler of his admission to Columbia with a full tuition fellowship.

University of Pennsylvania
Philadelphia, Pennsylvania
June 3, 1974

On this Saturday morning Nicholas M. Butler graduated *cum laude* from the University of Pennsylvania with a B.A. in political science in a moving ceremony at Franklin Field. The young Secretary of Defense, Nathan Hargrove, was the featured speaker, giving a stirring address extolling the virtues of public service. Nick's mother and younger brother attended the ceremony, after which they had lunch at Bookbinder's Restaurant to celebrate. Nick's mother and brother then made the two-hour drive back home to Maryland.

Nick had already packed his belongings at the fraternity house. He boarded a train at 30th Street Station to embark on his new life in New York

City. He couldn't hide the pride he was feeling. He was the first member of his family to graduate from college.

Columbia University
New York City
June 3, 1974

Later that afternoon Butler checked into Columbia's Furnald Hall, the graduate student men's dormitory located on the main campus. Anna Suzuki had made his reservation. He was told this would be his lodging for the summer. Something nicer would be available in September. His single room on the fifth floor overlooked Broadway.

From his window he could see the West End Grill on the other side of Broadway. It looked like the local Smokey Joe's student hangout. He unpacked, went to the grill, and sure enough it was a real campus joint. "Perfect," he thought as he walked in. He took a stool at the bar and ordered a beer and a pastrami sandwich—feeling like a New Yorker.

A few minutes later a good looking young guy sat down on the stool next to Nick. Other stools were available but he chose that one. He ordered a beer. When it arrived he looked at Nick, raised his glass, smiled, and said "cheers!"

"Cheers!" Nick replied, smiling back.

They began talking about the restaurant, the student crowd coming in for dinner, and about life in New York.

"Are you a student here at Columbia?" asked the newcomer.

"I will be on Monday," replied Nick. "I've just been admitted. How about you?" Nick asked politely.

"I was. I graduated last year. Now I work in mid-town but my apartment is on Riverside Drive—right around the corner."

When Nick finished his sandwich and was draining the last of his beer, the stranger said, "Why don't we have another beer up at my apartment? I have a great view of the Hudson River." While saying that, the stranger reached over and put his hand on Nick's thigh, giving him a knowing smile.

Smiling back, Nick said, "I've got to get going. But thanks for the offer." Not needing to be rude, Nick politely rejected this pass as he had others. He left the restaurant alone.

The stranger walked to his apartment and dialed a telephone number in the 202 area code for Washington, D.C.

"Susan?"

"Yes. What's the verdict?"

"He's not gay, that's for sure," said the contract agent.

"Thanks. He passed that test," his Agency control announced and hung up. Yet, Susan Samuels wondered, what kind of man is he? I hope, she thought to herself, he genuinely likes women because we know from experience Yuri Andropov, the cunning chairman of the Soviet Union's powerful KGB, will use women to seduce him for information. For this op that will be just fine with us. And it is essential that it's also fine with Nick Butler.

Monday morning Nick reported for work at the brownstone on West 118th Street. Anna Suzuki sat down with him to review the tasks that lay ahead.

She thanked him for returning the completed application for employment at the Institute of Defense Studies. She told him she forwarded his background data sheet to the Defense Department for a security clearance, and his passport application was being processed at the State Department. She directed him to the university's photo shop to have his picture taken for his university employee badge.

When he returned with his badge, Anna informed him his assignment for the summer would be the Research Assistant to a visiting scholar. She introduced him to Dr. David Hammond, an expert on the world's aviation industry who is a prominent member of the National Defense Analysis Center, a Defense Department think tank in Santa Monica, California. He's here for one year, she said, collaborating with Professor Reynard on a classified project.

Hammond, Nick quickly realized, is a no-nonsense, intense 40-year-old who quickly explained to Nick his research project while at the Institute.

"The National Defense Analysis Center," Hammond said, "has a contract with the U.S. Air Force under which experts at NDAC are performing analyses of the implications of changes in aircraft technology on combat tactics and overall national security strategy. Because military aircraft technology is rapidly evolving, it is vital our armed services constantly reassess their doctrines and tactics to take advantage of these advancements."

Nick was a little bewildered by Hammond's rapid-fire delivery. Hammond sensed his new assistant's sense of inadequacy and reassured him.

"Your tasks will be well within your present capacities. As my Research Assistant you will at first help track developments in aerospace technology by reviewing open sources such as aviation magazines and journals. The really important technology breakthroughs will of course be classified, but I want to know what public sources are reporting. That's what the Soviet Air Force is looking at, too. Once you get a clearance, I'll upgrade the level of data you'll review. Do you follow?"

"Yes sir. When do I start?"

"Right now," Hammond said, taking him into a second floor windowless office. Years earlier the windows in this bedroom were bricked in to make the room secure. "This will be your work station. One more thing: you're not to discuss this work with anyone outside of this building. Is that clear?"

"Very clear, sir. But if I'm asked, what do I say I'm doing?"

"Say as little as possible—only that you're doing academic research for Professor Reynard," instructed Dr. Hammond.

During the next two months, Nick immersed himself in the periodical literature on aerospace. He read cover-to-cover issues of *Aviation Week and Space Technology, Air and Space Magazine,* Naval Institute *Proceedings, Combat Aircraft, Aerospace Daily, Flight International* and a dozen other military/aerospace journals. He rapidly gained an appreciation for the thrilling new frontiers aircraft and space technology were penetrating in the 1970s, picking up insider jargon like leading-edge technology, mach barriers, turbofan engine technology, fly-by-wire controls, and the most intriguing term of all—stealth.

At the close of business one afternoon in mid-August, as he was leaving the brownstone to go to the university's gym for his daily work-out, Anna stopped him at her desk.

"Your Defense Department clearance arrived today," she said. "You are cleared for 'Secret.' Tomorrow you'll be issued a new badge with a red stripe across it to signify that level of clearance. Also your passport arrived from the State Department. Keep it in a safe place." Anna couldn't resist a motherly smile when she added, "In three weeks, you'll need it. You're going to England to attend the Farnborough Air Show."

During June and July, Susan Samuels and Bill Reynard regularly conferred by phone to compare notes on Nick Butler's progress. David Hammond reported to Reynard that Nick was coming along nicely with his research and could hold his own in a general conversation about aviation. Like Nick, Hammond did not know of the CIA's plans for his Research Assistant.

Samuels decided the time had come for another test of the young man and also to introduce him to the international arena. Nick had never been abroad.

Sending him to the Farnborough Air Show in England was chosen to achieve both purposes.

The cover story is he will collect information at the show from companies exhibiting their latest airplane designs and bring the material back for Dr. Hammond's use.

For the trip's underlying purpose Samuels had something special in mind. She asked Admiral Myers to place a call to Sir Nigel Shackelford, Director of MI6, Britain's foreign intelligence service, to make the necessary arrangements.

The day after Anna gave him the news about the trip to England, Reynard and Hammond brought Nick into Reynard's office to brief him on the Farnborough Air Show.

"In the odd-numbered years," Reynard began, "the big air show is in Paris, and in even- numbered years—like 1974—it's held in England at an airfield near London called Farnborough. These are the greatest air shows in the world. Military and commercial airplanes are on static display, some perform flying demonstrations, and their manufacturers have booths loaded with brochures and other information about their products."

Hammond interjected: "The Farnborough Air Show, like the one in Paris, is a cornucopia of data, specifications, and information about the airplanes each manufacturer is currently offering and plans to offer in future years. We want you to collect as much of that information you can and bring it back for analysis."

Nick was told he will be gone for a full week beginning on August 31, all expenses paid by the Institute. He will stay at a Holiday Inn near Farnborough and travel into London on the last day of the show to see the sights. He was instructed to meet as many company executives as possible, both U.S. and foreign. This will not be difficult as all the companies have booths manned by their top people. Simply walk up to each booth and introduce yourself as a vacationing Columbia graduate student who is fascinated by aviation. It will amaze you how much information they will proudly impart.

"Like most people, aerospace executives love to talk about their work," Hammond declared.

Nick was thrilled he was being given this wonderful trip, and, based on his readings so far about airplanes, he couldn't wait to go.

Departure day soon arrived. Nick took the shuttle bus from Manhattan's East Side Airline Terminal to the futuristic-looking TWA terminal at JFK. He boarded the 707, took his seat, fastened his seatbelt, and thanked his lucky stars he was about to the cross the Atlantic Ocean for the first time. He hoped it wouldn't be his last.

London, England
August 31, 1974

Early the next morning, Sunday, he arrived at Heathrow Airport, cleared UK passport control and customs, and took the Holiday Inn van to the hotel at Farnborough about 30 miles away. As he checked in at the reception desk, he did not notice an attractive English girl who was eyeing him from across the lobby. He went to his room and hit the sheets for a serious nap after the long overnight flight.

Later that afternoon he went down to the bar and restaurant. He took a seat at a small booth and ordered a steak, though he was intrigued by a dish call "mixed grill." While eating, he noticed two attractive girls in cute summer dresses enter the restaurant—a brunette and a red head. They were seated at a nearby table. They were deep in conversation so he paid little attention to them. After dinner, he went back up to his room and sacked out for the night.

Farnborough Air Show
Farnborough, England
September 1, 1974

Monday morning the Farnborough Air Show opened, and, though only industry and government people were admitted for the first five days, Hammond had arranged through NDAC to get him a pass. The final weekend of the show was open to the public.

On the show's opening day a torrential rain storm struck Southern England. Butler bought an umbrella, took the courtesy van to the airfield's entrance gate, showed the pass NDAC provided, and hurriedly walked through driving rain into one of the two exhibit halls.

The hall was a cavernous building arrayed with booths put up by the world's major aerospace companies. A poster announced 400 companies from 12 countries had displays. These included British, French, West German, Italian, Canadian, and U.S. companies. The national flag of each country was hung from the ceiling above its booth producing a dazzling array of color.

Within every booth were display tables and in some cases interactive exhibits that advertised that firm's military or civil aircraft. On the tables stacks of glossy brochures and technical drawings of the company's products were available. To Nick, this was one amazing marketing extravaganza.

Butler quickly realized it would take a full day to collect copies of the printed material on display in this hall alone. It might take another day to collect the brochures in the other exhibit hall. Given the terrible weather, no flying demonstrations could be held. He decided to spend the day inside the first hall.

The British Aircraft Company had the largest display. Approaching their booth, he recognized two of the hostesses handing out brochures and talking to prospective customers about BA's products. These were the young women he had seen at dinner the night before. They were wearing uniforms with the British Aircraft logo on the shoulder.

"Hi there," Nick called out as he walked toward the two girls. "Didn't I see you in the Holiday Inn's restaurant last night?"

"We are staying at the Holiday Inn," the brunette volunteered in her soft English accent. "I don't want to crush your ego, Yank, but I don't remember seeing you."

"Well, you're seeing me now," Nick said smiling, trying to recover. "I'm Nick."

"I'm Elizabeth," the brunette said, "and this is Karen." Karen was the redhead.

"What's with the uniforms, Elizabeth?"

"We've been hired by British Aircraft to be hostesses in their salon, but with this nasty weather the salon is closed today. So they assigned us to this indoor booth. They're putting us up at the hotel for the week of the show."

"Nice seeing you AGAIN," Nick added with emphasis, flashing his killer smile as he said it. "Maybe we could get together this evening at the hotel for a drink."

"Maybe," Elizabeth said with a deliberately coquettish giggle, turning away to attend to a customer.

By 6:00 the show was winding down. People were leaving to go to dinner. Nick walked back through the exhibit hall to the main gate to catch the 6:30 shuttle back to the hotel. As he approached the van, he noticed Elizabeth and Karen boarding it. What a nice coincidence, he thought to himself.

Nick climbed aboard and took a seat across the aisle from the girls.

"Fancy meeting you here," Elizabeth said with a smile.

"It's been my lucky day," Nick responded with a grin.

They chatted during the short ride to the hotel, mostly talking about the throngs of people from all over the world who attend the show. Elizabeth asked how he managed to visit the show on an industry day—before the general public is allowed in. Nick responded that a well-connected professor had gotten him a visitor pass. When the van arrived at the hotel, the three young people jumped out, crossed the lobby and entered the elevator.

"What floor?" Nick asked as he prepared to press a button for the girls.

"Five, please," Karen said absently.

Nick pressed five and didn't move.

"Don't tell me you're on five, too?" Karen asked.

As it turned out their rooms were directly across the hall from each other. The girls were sharing a double room. Nick of course had a single.

"Do you have more air show duties tonight?" Nick asked hopefully as they walked down the corridor toward their rooms.

"No," Elizabeth replied. "We're off duty until tomorrow morning."

"Well, in that case how about having drinks together in the bar downstairs?"

"Lovely," Elizabeth answered. "But first we want to freshen up and maybe take a little rest."

"Sounds like a plan," said Nick.

After entering his room, Nick stripped down to his briefs, went into the bathroom and washed his face and upper body with warm water and soap. Then he stretched out on the queen-size bed for a rest. It felt good after being on his feet all day at the show. He didn't go to sleep.

After a while, there was tapping on his door. Reluctantly he got up. Elizabeth asked through the door, "Are you still in there?"

"Coming," Nick answered. He grabbed his khaki pants from the chair, quickly put them on, left off the belt, and thought about putting on a shirt but decided it wasn't necessary. Barefoot and only in pants, he opened the door wide and stood in the center of the door frame. He didn't say anything.

Elizabeth started to say something but stopped before words came out. Standing there, she openly admired the six-foot muscular man from head to toe, her gaze lingered on his six-pack abs. The elastic band of his jockey briefs showed above the waistband of his khakis. He smelled of soap. Nick folded his arms across his chiseled chest—enjoying the admiration the woman was giving him.

In those seconds thoughts cascaded through Nick's mind. At age 23 he felt something new, something different for the first time in his life. With this gorgeous woman admiring his body, he no longer felt like Nick the good boy, or Nick the Eagle Scout, or Nick the scholar, Nick the fraternity president, Nick the quarterback, or Nick the anything—all that was stripped away to something far more basic. For the first time in his life he felt like Nick the man. It was an aphrodisiac sensation.

Elizabeth quickly made up her mind. She turned and called down the hall to Karen, who was approaching the elevator: "Go on ahead. We'll catch up with you later in the bar." She watched Karen board the elevator.

"Were you resting?" Elizabeth asked, her head turning back toward Nick.

"Yes, just stretched out on the bed."

"Well, that sounds pretty good," Elizabeth said. "I didn't get to rest at all. Karen wanted to go for a drink. Do you mind if I join you?"

Nick stood aside to let her come in, then closed the door. She walked over to the bed, sat down, removed her shoes, unbuttoned her blouse tossing it on a chair, slid out of her skirt, and laid down on Nick's bed in only her bra and panties.

Now it was Nick's turn to be speechless. Standing at the foot of the bed, he was struck by her beauty and marveled at her directness in knowing what she wanted and having the gumption to go for it. This was a first for him. With American girls he had to go through the motions of seducing them. Elizabeth was up-front about wanting him.

"You're so beautiful," he muttered as he approached the side of the bed.

Smiling up at him she said sweetly, "Aren't you going to take off your pants?" Nick stripped off the khakis, tossing them on the chair next to Elizabeth's skirt. He laid down on the bed next to her and started to reach for her.

"Why don't we catch our breath for a few minutes," Elizabeth purred. Nick relaxed and laid on his back. The two young adults rested side-by-side for a short time until Nick couldn't stand it any longer. He moved his body closer to hers and began to caress her. She moaned softly. From that moment there was no stopping it. He began making love to her.

Central Intelligence Agency
Langley, Virginia

The next day Susan Samuels was summoned to Admiral Myers' office on the seventh floor. As she entered he handed her a classified cable from MI6 in London. It read:

"My agent, Elizabeth, reports as follows: 'The subject, Nick Butler, is in every respect a healthy, very normal heterosexual male. He makes the assignment a pleasure.'

Shackelford"

"Well, I guess that clears up what kind of man he is," Myers observed.

"More than that," Susan added, "given how quickly he made this happen and the unsolicited comment from the woman, I would say we've got a real lover-boy on our hands. Now that he passed this test we know for certain he's the perfect choice for Stealth Gambit."

Farnborough, England
September 2, 1974

On the second day of the air show the rain let up. Nick took the hotel shuttle to the airport, passed through the main exhibit hall, and walked to the tarmac where airplanes were on static display. There were at least three dozen of them, both commercial airplanes of various sizes, and military planes—jet fighters, transports, helicopters, and one bomber. The stars of the show were the new Anglo-French supersonic Concorde and Lockheed's SR-71 Blackbird, which had arrived the day before from New York setting the speed record for crossing the Atlantic in one hour and 54 minutes.

Facing the line of aircraft and strung out along a wide walkway he saw a dozen enclosed structures—temporary pavilions called salons. The logo of the aircraft company occupying each salon was posted next to their entrance, all of which were guarded by security personnel. Obviously entry into these privileged sanctuaries was by invitation only. Since Nick was not a VIP, he doubted he'd see the inside of any of them.

He decided to hang out in front of the brand new U.S. Air Force YF-15 prototype. After a short while, he observed a group of European air force officers being escorted into that company's salon. A U.S. Air Force general was with them. Hum, thought Nick, the Air Force and the manufacturer are working together to promote the sale of the new F-15 to our NATO allies.

In the distance a small sleek-looking jet fighter caught his eye. He strolled down the fence line to take a closer look. It was Century Aerospace's F-11. A placard hanging on the fence announced this is the number one prototype of a new supersonic fighter being offered by Century Aerospace to America's allies.

Nick wondered how successful they would be with that, given he had just observed the USAF and the manufacturer promoting the F-15 to our allies.

There wasn't much of a crowd in front of the F-11. He could hear a group of men talking near the airplane—about 50 feet away. One of them looked like he might be a test pilot. He waited by the fence. After a while, the man in the flight suit noticed Nick and ambled over to the fence to greet him.

"Hi there, son," he said in a soft Tennessee accent. "You in the Air Force?" he asked.

"Oh no, sir, I'm a graduate student on vacation, but I love airplanes. Can you tell me about this one?"

"Ain't she a beaut! I'll be driving her later today when we get our turn to show-off up there," pointing to the sky.

"Are you a test pilot?" asked Nick.

"Why hell yes I'm a test pilot. I'm Rick Russell."

"Oh, my gosh," Nick gasped. "You're the Air Force's Chief Test pilot!"

"Former Chief Test Pilot," he said with a practiced laugh. Russell couldn't help being impressed with the youngster's knowledge of his claim to fame. "What's your name, boy?"

"Nick Butler."

"What's your career plan after grad school, Nick? You goin' to join the Air Force?" Russell asked seriously. Russell was a Brigadier General in the U.S. Air Force, but he was wearing a flight suit at the time with no insignia.

"My plans are open at the moment, but I'm becoming more and more interested in the aviation industry," Nick replied with sincerity.

Russell looked him over carefully before speaking again.

"Why don't you come back here around 3:00 this afternoon after I put this little beauty through her paces? We can talk further then."

"Thanks. I'd love to do that. See you around 3:00." With that, they went their separate ways.

Shortly before 3:00 Nick returned to the place where the F-11 had been parked earlier. Rick Russell was taxiing the plane back to that spot, having just completed his flying demonstration in the new fighter, which Nick watched in fascination. Russell had performed barrel rolls, inverted flight, a split-S maneuver, gone straight up with smoke trailing behind, and other death-defying maneuvers. It was a great show, and the large industry and military crowd loved it. Knowing it was the famous Rick Russell at the controls added to the excitement.

After Russell climbed down the ladder from the cockpit and accepted the accolades of the Century Aerospace company executives, he noticed Nick leaning on the nearby fence. He took the arm of one of Century Aerospace's executives and walked toward him.

"General Russell, what an awesome demonstration!" Nick called out as Russell and the civilian approached him on the other side of the fence.

"Thank you, son, all in a day's work," Russell said in his nonchalant test pilot way. "Say again your name."

"Nick Butler."

"Well, Nick," said Russell, "I'd like you to meet Walt Gates. He's Century's Senior VP for International Business."

"How do you do, sir," Nick said politely. "Glad to meet you."

"Same here," replied Mr. Gates. "How do you two know each other?"

"We met this mornin'," Russell answered. "This young feller's got a hard-on for airplanes just like we do."

"Well, sir," Nick quickly added, "the truth is I'm just a Columbia grad student who loves aviation."

"Columbia?" asked Walt Gates. "Who are you studying under?"

"Professor William Reynard."

"Well, well," intoned Gates. "I studied under him at Princeton before he was lured away by Columbia. How the hell is the old boy?"

"He's fine." Then Nick took a minute to explain he had only recently begun working under Reynard in preparation for the start of regular classes in the fall.

"Well, I'll be a son of a bitch!" exclaimed Gates.

"You already are," declared Russell, poking Gates on his arm.

Gates ignored the test pilot. "I can't believe this! You and I both having Bill Reynard," Gates exclaimed. Then an extraordinary thing happened. Walter Gates invited Nick Butler to visit Century Aerospace's salon the next afternoon to talk further and to meet some of the other company executives.

"Thank you so much, Mr. Gates," gasped Nick. "What an honor!"

"See you tomorrow," said Gates as he and Russell strolled back to the airplane.

Farnborough, England
September 3, 1974

The next afternoon Nick went to the area where the F-11 was on static display across from Century Aerospace's salon. Nick hoped Walter Gates hadn't forgotten his promise to meet him there. After a short while, Gates came out of the salon and hailed Nick, waiving him to come over to the salon's entrance. Nick brushed past the security guard and shook hands with Gates who greeted him warmly.

Entering the salon, Nick observed it was larger inside than it appeared from the pedestrian walkway. Several small bar-height tables were set up throughout the room, some with barstools. On the tables were trays of peanuts and a small floral piece. At the rear of the room was a hot and cold buffet where two young women acted as servers. A bar was on one side of the room with a bartender. The room was sparsely decorated but in its own way elegant.

"Would you like something to drink?" Gates asked Nick. He declined, not wanting to have his hand encumbered with a glass.

"I'd like you to meet some of the Century folks," said Gates, taking a glass of chilled white wine from one of the servers. Then C. Walter Gates, Corporate Senior Vice President-International Business, guided Nick Butler, graduate student, around the salon introducing him to each company official present. Everyone was in a good mood and was cordial to the young visitor.

Gates saved the best for last. After a certain tall, rather spare gentleman wearing an elegantly tailored grey flannel suit completed his conversation with an Arabian sheik in full robes, Gates steered Nick to him.

"Martin," Gates said, "I'd like you to meet someone. This is Nick Butler, a graduate student at Columbia studying under Bill Reynard. Nick, this is Martin V. Stark, Chairman of the Board and Chief Executive Officer of Century Aerospace." Stark extended his hand. His grip was powerful.

"Very pleased to meet you, sir," Nick stammered, being not a little intimidated by his surroundings and in the presence of one of the world's most famous aerospace company leaders.

"Happy to make your acquaintance, Nick," replied Stark. "How did a grad student get into the Farnborough Air Show on an industry day?" he asked. "The show isn't open to the public until the weekend," Stark added to explain the meaning behind his question.

"I can answer that," volunteered Gates. "Rick Russell introduced Nick to me yesterday. Nick doesn't know it but David Hammond at NDAC had alerted

Rick and me to be on the lookout for Nick, who entered the show on a special pass Hammond arranged for him."

Suddenly Butler realized what appeared as a chance meeting with General Russell had been stage-managed some time earlier.

Stark turned to Gates and asked, "Walt, you're on one of the NDAC advisory boards, aren't you?"

"That's right, Martin. I'm one of the industry reps on NDAC's International Aviation Advisory Board with Rick who's the USAF's representative, and David Hammond is NDAC's staff member assigned to that board. So we all know each other."

"That explains it," Stark said. Nick was thinking the same thing. "Do you have any plans yet after grad school, Nick?"

"Nothing specific yet, sir. I'm going for a Ph.D. in political science with emphasis on international relations. I can't help but wonder if all I'll be equipped for is college teaching, which is something I don't want to do. I'd love to become involved in aviation in some way." Nick thought he was yammering and simply stopped talking.

"Nick," asked Stark, "who do you think buys jet fighters?" Nick drew a blank. "Governments," Stark said helpfully. "Only governments can buy military equipment, so companies that make weapons—like jet fighters—have to market them to governments. Don't political scientists study governments?" Martin Stark asked rhetorically.

"Well, yes sir. And we also study relationships between governments to determine who's a friend and who's not," replied Nick, feeling stupid and out of his depth.

"Century intends to market the new F-11 you saw Rick Russell fly yesterday to allied governments but to make the actual sale *through* the U.S. government using its foreign military sales procedure. Clear so far?" Stark asked, pausing for a second. "Thanks to Bill Reynard and his colleagues at Columbia, you will become an expert on governments—ours and our allies' and that could become a useful, valuable skill in the business world."

"Sir," Nick responded, "that's the most interesting and important reason anyone has ever given me for studying my field and to link it to something tangible in the real world. Thank you so much."

"Walt can explain it to you further. After all, he's in charge of our international marketing team," Stark concluded.

There the discussion ended. Nick's head was spinning. His entire four-year education at Penn and the four years he was about to begin at Columbia finally made practical sense to him. It took a CEO to make the connection, not a professor. And it was linked to aviation, which he was beginning to love.

After thanking Walter Gates profusely, Nick left the Century salon and walked toward the main gate. It was getting late. He didn't want to miss the 6:30 shuttle back to the hotel.

Elizabeth and Karen had already boarded the courtesy van. Nick scrambled on board just in time before the door closed. On the way back to the hotel they chatted about the air acrobatic displays, the girls favoring the Royal Air Force's Red Arrow precision flying team. Nick gave his view that the F-11 with Rick Russell at the controls was the highlight of the show.

Karen asked absently how an American student is able to afford to come to England to attend the air show. Smoothly Nick made up a story that his family, knowing how much he likes airplanes, gave him the trip as a graduation present.

When they arrived at the Holiday Inn, the three young people went to their rooms. Soon there was a tapping on Nick's door. He knew who was there. He opened the door. Elizabeth silently entered the room and walked over to the bed. Nick stripped off his clothes as Elizabeth was doing the same, piling them up on the nearby chair. Words were not needed as they tumbled onto the bed. They made love on-and-off all night.

By the weekend, Nick had gathered the pamphlets, brochures, and technical drawings on military aircraft that were displayed in the two exhibition halls. He packed them in a spare suitcase he brought. His assignment from David Hammond was complete. Moreover, he had met the top executives of one of the United States' most innovative and respected aircraft companies, Century Aerospace, thanks to Hammond and Rick Russell. He wondered what other high-level connections his research supervisor must have.

On Saturday, his last day in England, he had been told he could play tourist. He decided the best way to spend his free day was to go sightseeing in London. He and Elizabeth had agreed to meet at the hotel dining room at 7:30 for drinks and dinner. But when they saw each other they decided to forego that. Knowing this was their last night together, they went straight up to Nick's room to the well-worn queen-size bed for a night of robust love-making.

In the morning Elizabeth asked if he had accomplished everything he'd hoped to while in England.

"Yes," he replied, "and much more. You've been the best surprise of my life."

"I've thoroughly enjoyed every minute of it," Elizabeth admitted. "You're a wonderful lover, my sweet, lusty Yank."

An hour later, Nick boarded the van to Heathrow Airport for his flight to New York. Elizabeth went to the Farnborough railway station and took the train to Waterloo Station in London. From there she took a bus to her flat. Her final message to MI6 simply stated: "Nothing new or different to add to previous report." That message was immediately retransmitted to Langley, Virginia.

Columbia University
New York City
September 8, 1974

The next Monday morning Butler reported for work at the brownstone townhouse on 118th Street, carrying the extra suitcase filled with printed material he collected at the air show. Anna greeted him warmly, asking if he'd had a good time in England.

"Oh, yes," Nick answered with a boyish smirk.

Hammond and Reynard sat down with Nick in the windowless room and began questioning him about the trip. Hammond asked if he had met the Century executives.

"I certainly did, thanks to you," replied Nick. "Everyone was very cordial, especially Walter Gates. He even introduced me to Martin Stark, Century's CEO. Incidentally, Professor Reynard, Mr. Gates said he studied under you at Princeton—before you came to Columbia."

"Yes, he did," said Reynard. "Those relationships with the Century people may well prove beneficial to you as time goes on," he added somewhat mysteriously.

Reynard left Hammond and Nick to plow through the printed material, going down the hall to his office. He asked Anna to place a call to Admiral Myers at Langley. He wanted to know if the CIA had gained any useful insights about Nick from his trip to England.

"Well," Admiral Myers said in response to Reynard's question, "it seems Nick certainly knows how to handle himself. Susan set him up through MI6 with a test situation and he came through with high marks."

"David Hammond did the same with the Century Aerospace executives," Reynard reported. "On all accounts he performed well and made an excellent impression, even on Martin Stark."

"You and Hammond are going to keep that connection operational, aren't you?" asked the Admiral.

"Absolutely," confirmed the professor.

Chapter 2:
The Novice

Columbia University
New York City
September 15, 1974

Regular classes began at Columbia graduate school in mid-September. At that time Nick Butler transitioned from full-time work at the Institute of Defense Studies to full-time work as a graduate student. All his classes were held in Fayerweather Hall, the political science building. He was registered for four courses in the fall semester, and there would be four more in the spring. During his second year, this pattern would be repeated.

In the fall his courses were World Politics with Professor William Anderson, Communism with Professor Vladimir Sovolovski, American Foreign Policy with Professor Allan Warberg, and Political Theory with Professor Francis Hart.

On his last day of work at the Institute Bill Reynard asked him to stop by the office from time to time during the fall just to stay in touch.

True to her word, Anna Suzuki arranged for more appropriate housing for Butler. He moved out of Furnald Hall and moved into a two bedroom furnished apartment on the corner of 120th Street and Amsterdam Avenue—two blocks north of the Institute.

To keep costs manageable, Anna arranged for him to share the apartment with a second year graduate student named Liam Erickson, who also worked at the Institute. Over the summer the two students had become friends and were happy to share the apartment.

During the summer, Liam Erickson was Research Assistant to Professor Leland Hazard, a leading expert on the Soviet Union, especially its armed forces. Hazard hired Liam because of his excellent first year record, but more importantly because he was fluent in Russian which he studied while an undergrad at the University of Wisconsin in Madison. His mother, a native Lithuanian, spoke Russian, the language Liam spoke at home while growing up.

Mrs. Erickson immigrated to the United States as a young woman with Liam's father, a Swede, who died a few years later. Nick knew about Liam's background because they often had lunch together and spoke about their upbringing. Liam's work with Hazard did not require a security clearance.

Late Friday afternoon at the end of the first week of fall classes, Liam and Nick relaxed in the apartment's comfortable living room to compare notes on their classes and professors. Each had immersed himself in his course work and spent the afternoons and evenings studying, having classes in the mornings. By the weekend they were mentally drained.

"Well, Nick-boy," Liam suddenly announced as he rose from his chair, "I'm going over to the cafeteria at the women's dorm at Barnard for dinner. The food's terrible, but it's the best pickup place on campus. I've got to get laid tonight!"

"You shouldn't have any trouble doing that—after all it's the '70s and this is supposed to be the decade of free love," Nick said encouragingly.

"It had better be free," the tall blond man said as he reached the door. "I can't afford to pay for it." Erickson left on his quest to get lucky.

Nick remained in the apartment, made a quick dinner, and hit the books. He was determined not to lose his fellowship by earning poor grades. Later, stripping to the buff and getting in bed, he remembered the advice his mother used to give him: "Never underrate the therapeutic benefits of a good night's sleep." Stretching out his six-foot frame between the sheets, the 23-year-old took that advice.

Liam's and Nick's patterns repeated every week—and weekend—until the semester ended in December.

During Christmas break, both went home to spend the holiday with their families—Liam to Wisconsin and Nick to Maryland. They were proud to report to their mothers they had earned straight A's. It was refreshing to be off campus for a week of almost mindless relaxation. While at home Liam told his mother about Nick and how talented he is, forecasting a brilliant future for his roommate. His mother paid close attention to what her son was telling her about him.

New York City
January 2, 1975

On Sunday, January 2nd, Nick took the train back to New York to resume his student life. He wanted to get a head start on the reading material for his spring semester courses that would begin the following week.

The next morning he walked to the Institute to say Happy New Year. He had dropped by the building from time to time during the fall and was always warmly greeted by Anna Suzuki, Reynard, and Hammond. Hammond's work on international military aerospace developments and their implications for the U.S. Air Force was coming along nicely, he said, and he graciously added he missed Nick's help on the project.

On that Monday morning in January, Reynard appeared distressed. He was happy to see Nick, he said, but he and Leland Hazard had received some bad news. Nick's roommate had phoned Hazard to say he is unable to come to the Institute that week as planned because he had caught the flu and was unable to travel from Wisconsin. He was scheduled to go to France as a courier for Professor Hazard and had been briefed on the security procedure onboard the airplane.

"What a damned shame," Reynard said in an uncharacteristic expression of frustration. "Leland and I need Liam's help this week," Reynard added.

"Is there anything I can do?" Nick asked politely.

"Right now I don't know, but I appreciate your asking," replied Reynard. "Leland and I need to sort this out. Could you come back after lunch?"

Nick left the Institute and walked to Butler Library to check out some of the books he needed for his upcoming courses. He put the books in his carrel, taking time to start reading one of them. Then he had lunch, returning to the Institute at 1:30.

Meanwhile, Reynard and Admiral Myers had a telephone conversation. They were considering their options, now that Erickson was unavailable to travel to France.

What was planned was for Liam to serve as a courier, fly to Paris with a classified document, and deliver it to one of Hazard's colleagues at the Science Po, the great French institute. The French colleague, Professor Jean-Pierre

Capp, was an equally famous Soviet specialist who, like Hazard, was an expert on the Soviet military and was also a consultant to the NATO command in Brussels. Capp was going to study the document and then send it to NATO headquarters with his analysis. The plans for the trip were set with Admiral Myers at the CIA orchestrating the operation. This was the op's cover story.

Its underlying purpose was to set a trap to discover the identity of a Soviet agent. The classified document was the bait. It contained innocuous material along with two items that would be news to the KGB. Both items were false, but no one would know that except the Americans. This sting operation's objective was to expose who at NATO headquarters—or in Paris—was leaking classified information to the Soviet Union. Erickson had not been told anything about the trip's underlying purpose—only that he was to fly to Paris and deliver a package to Professor Capp.

Quickly Admiral Myers made a decision. He instructed Reynard to have Hazard give the package to Nick Butler the next day and have him fly to Paris as previously planned for Erickson. He was the perfect substitute because he, like Liam, was unknown to foreign intelligence services and could handle the mission in innocence. He was just going to be a delivery boy. Besides, thought Myers, this will be a good test of Butler's skills in a real-time op.

When Nick returned to the Institute, Reynard asked him, "How would you like to go to Paris tomorrow?" Reynard quickly explained he would be Erickson's substitute courier. All he would have to do is fly to Paris, deliver a package, spend a day with Leland Hazard's colleague, and then fly back to New York. He will be home Friday.

"Holy shit, Paris!" Nick exclaimed, then quickly apologized for his outburst. Of course he will go, he said. Reynard chuckled at his youthful outburst.

The rest of Monday was spent preparing the classified package, instructing Nick on the procedure he would follow during the flight and after he arrived in Paris, giving him the addresses of the Science Po and his hotel, and getting his tickets. Upon landing in Paris early Wednesday morning, he was instructed to take a taxi directly to Capp's office to deliver the package and to check into his hotel later. He would be flying Air France, taking their 7:10 p.m. overnight flight from JFK to Orly Airport.

Later in the afternoon Nick returned to his apartment and packed for the short trip. He also packed a couple of textbooks he'd planned to read that week in New York. Now he'd read them on the plane.

Leland Hazard sent a cable to Professor Capp telling him of the change of plans—the substitution of Nick Butler for Liam Erickson. He asked Capp to change the Madison Hotel reservation to Butler's name. When it arrived, Capp handed the cable to his secretary, Madam Gardiner, and asked her to change the reservation. Everything about the Air France flight remained the same except the name of the passenger. Capp mentioned to his secretary that Butler would be delivering a package containing "secret" material for use at NATO headquarters.

The next afternoon, Tuesday, was clear and cold in New York. Nick walked the two blocks from his apartment to the Institute carrying his suitcase. Hazard handed Nick a shiny aluminum briefcase with a four-digit combination lock. The briefcase, Hazard told him, is the type airline crews typically use, so it will not appear unusual on the plane. Also, he said this type of briefcase is frequently used to carry classified material. The classified package was already in the briefcase. Nick never saw it. Professor Capp has the combination to the lock.

Nick was instructed to place the briefcase on the empty window seat next to his aisle seat—for which he was issued a separate ticket—and to keep his eye on it at all times. When he had to go to the lavatory, he was instructed to handcuff the handle of the briefcase to the seat using standard-issue New York City Police Department handcuffs. Anna handed him the handcuffs, their tiny key, and an envelope containing U.S. and French currency, traveler's checks, and his tickets. She made sure he had his passport. Anna phoned for a taxi to take him directly to JFK.

At 5:45 Butler's taxi arrived at the international terminal at JFK, having inched its way through Queens Midtown Tunnel in heavy rush-hour traffic. At the Air France ticket counter Nick checked his suitcase and obtained his boarding passes—one for him and one for the empty seat. He took the escalator up to the gate waiting area and sat down. At 6:30 he went over to the boarding gate. The waiting line was not long, given it was winter and only business people were traveling so soon after the holidays.

Boarding the airplane, he walked to the middle of the coach section where he located his seats. He put his overcoat and suit coat in the storage bin above his seat and placed the metal briefcase on the seat next to the window, belting it in. He sat on the aisle seat. The plane was not crowded.

After the typical announcements by the flight crew and the captain, both in French and English, the plane took off. Nick was thrilled that for the second time in six months he was off to Europe, this time to Paris, France no less.

Two chic French stewardesses served the coach section of the Air France 707. When the beverage cart rolled to Nick's seat, one of them asked if he'd like something to drink. He requested a Coke. As she was pouring it she noticed the metallic briefcase lying on the window seat.

"Not a very attractive traveling companion, *oui?*" the stewardess observed with her lilting Parisian accent.

"It's the best looking one I could get," replied Nick, smiling at the pretty young woman.

"Oh, I doubt that, monsieur," she observed, eyeing the good-looking American.

A few hours into the flight, after dinner had been served and cleared away, Nick needed to stretch his legs. The cabin was quiet, the lights were dimmed, and most people were either watching the movie or sleeping. He took out his handcuffs and attached the metal briefcase to the window seat as he was instructed.

He walked to the rear of the plane, passing by non-descript looking businessmen, only two of whom seemed to notice him. They were both middle-age, stocky men in dark suits seated two rows behind Nick on the other side of the aisle. The two stewardesses were working in the galley at the rear of the plane, stowing the remains of the food service. Two restrooms flanked the galley. Nick loitered there for a while, watching the stewardesses.

The one who had spoken to him also served him dinner. She seemed friendly, so Nick struck up a conversation as she was brewing a fresh pot of coffee. The other stewardess soon left the galley pushing a service cart to the far end of the coach section to pick up glasses and coffee cups. She was slowly working her way toward the rear of the plane.

Nick did not know that the stewardess still in the galley was an agent of the *Deuxième Bureau*, France's foreign intelligence service. Admiral Myers had given his opposite number in Paris, Andre Devereaux, the description of his substitute courier. The "stewardess" was posted on Nick's flight to perform a specific task during the flight. She was to distract Nick for a minimum of twenty minutes while he was away from his seat—the metal briefcase being unguarded during that time. This was the bait Myers hoped would attract a prey. It was up to the intelligence agent to determine the best way to keep him away from his seat.

Nick and the stewardess continued making small talk until the coffee brewed. She offered him a cup, which he declined. She positioned herself between Nick and the aisle, blocking his few of his seat. She came up close to

Nick's ear, ostensibly to be heard over the roar of the engines, to tell him her half-hour break was about to start. He could smell her perfume and her warm body was close to his.

"What do you usually do on your breaks?" Nick asked.

"Usually I sit down and read *Paris Match*, but I've already read the current issue."

"Want to do something more interesting?"

"*Mais oui, monsieur,*" she replied softly. "What do you have in mind?"

"Step into my office," Nick proposed, opening the lavatory door.

Looking at the handsome American, she nodded with a smile. She would go in first, she suggested, and he should wait a minute or two before coming in—in case anyone was noticing them. She went in. Nick waited. The other stewardess, far down the aisle, was facing his direction, but she seemed preoccupied with her clean-up duties.

When he opened the lavatory door, the woman was seated on the toilet lid, facing the door. Nick entered, closed and locked it behind him. He turned to face her. Given his height, his waist was at her eye level. Without a word she looked him directly in his eyes as she unbuckled his belt. For the next twenty minutes he wasn't thinking about the briefcase.

Returning to his seat, he found the metal briefcase where he left it. It remained in that position until final approach to Paris when Nick removed the handcuffs and buckled it in for the landing.

While he was in the lavatory, the other stewardess continued collecting cups and glasses, putting them on her service cart. She saw the other stewardess and Nick go into the lavatory. When she got to his row, she slipped onto his seat, took out a tiny key, opened the handcuffs, and lifted the metal briefcase to her lap. She opened a side panel on the service cart and took out an identical metal briefcase and handcuffed it to the seat exactly were Nick had left his. She put Nick's case in the service cart and closed the side panel. She stood up and continued her pick-up duties. The stocky men two rows back observed this.

As Nick exited the plane at Orly Airport, his stewardess was standing at the door saying good-by to the passengers. When Nick approached, she said smiling, "I hope you enjoyed your flight!" Nick grinned back at her saying, "Very much!"

The other stewardess was in the rear galley opening the safety latches to release the service carts for the ground crew to take them off the airplane.

Paris, France
January 5, 1975

Feeling particularly good about himself after the flight, Nick followed the signs through passport control and immigration to baggage claim, retrieved his suitcase, cleared customs, and walked through the terminal building to the taxi area outside to wait his turn for a cab.

It was cold and overcast in Paris. He did not notice another passenger walking behind him—one of the middle-age, stocky men who sat behind him on the flight.

When he got his turn for a taxi, the driver came out and stowed his suitcase in the trunk. Nick carried the metal briefcase into the car with him. He gave the Science Po's address to the driver in French: 27 *Rue Saint-Guillamme, s'il vous-plait.*

The driver said in English/French, "You're going to the Science Po, *n'est-ce pas?*"

"*C'est exact,*" replied Nick.

A black Citroen pulled up to the taxi area. The middle-age man got in the front passenger seat. The driver pulled away from the curb, following Nick's taxi three car-lengths behind.

During his short ride from Orly Airport to the Left Bank, Nick gawked like a regular tourist at the monuments of Paris, passing by the Eiffel Tower, Napoleon's tomb, and near the Cathedral of Notre Dame. It began to snow as the taxi reached the Latin Quarter where the Sorbonne University and the Science Po are located.

The taxi pulled up in front of 27 Rue Saint-Guillamme, the handsome main building of the Paris Institute of Political Science, known the world over simply as the Science Po. The black Citroen stopped down the street at the corner, its motor running.

The taxi driver retrieved the suitcase from the trunk. Nick paid him and entered the building. All three of the large metal gates at the building's entrance were already open. It was 9:00 A.M. The black Citroen drove off, unnoticed by Nick.

In French, he asked the lobby attendant for the office of Professor Jean-Pierre Capp. He was directed to the second floor, turn right, end of the hall on the right. Nick mounted the grand staircase and followed the directions to Capp's office.

"*Bonjour, monsieur,*" said Capp's secretary cheerfully as he entered her office off the main hall. She was a large, late middle-age woman with jet black hair drawn back from her face into a tight bun at the back of her head. She wore red-rimmed glasses that matched the lipstick on her full lips.

"*Bonjour, madam,*" Nick replied, and stated his name.

"I am Madam Gardiner, Professor Capp's secretary," she announced in English. "Professor Capp is expecting you." She ushered him into Capp's office. Professor Capp, an elegantly dressed gentleman in his fifties with salt and pepper hair and a neatly-trimmed Van Dyck, greeted him in English. Madam Gardiner returned to her office and made a telephone call.

"How was your flight?" Capp asked politely.

"Very smooth," replied Nick, as though he was an experienced international traveler. He put down his suitcase and the metal briefcase.

"I'm glad to meet you. Professors Hazard and Reynard speak highly of you," said Capp, shaking his hand after Nick removed his gloves.

Nick thanked him for the compliment, took off his overcoat, and sat down on the chair facing Capp's desk.

"Coffee?" asked Capp.

"I'd love some, thank you. Black, please. No sugar."

Capp picked up the phone and buzzed Madam Gardiner to bring in two coffees.

While waiting for the coffee, the two chatted amiably about Nick's professors in New York and about his classes at Columbia. Nick asked Capp if he taught classes at the Science Po.

"Oh, yes," Capp replied. "It's mandatory to teach at least two courses each semester to qualify for this elegant office," waiving his hand at the posh surroundings. The office was elegant.

Soon the coffee was served. After a few sips, Capp declared it was time to get to business. He took out of a desk drawer a small piece of paper on which was written the combination to the lock on the briefcase. He blocked Nick's view of the combination as he entered the four digits. When the lock disengaged, Capp opened the lid. He took out a manila envelope and brought it over to his desk.

The envelope's flap was sealed with red wax with a red thread through it. The seal was unbroken, as was the red thread.

"I want you to witness that this envelope has not been opened," ordered Professor Capp. Nick agreed the seal was intact. That confirmed, Capp slit the seal and thread with a letter opener and opened the flap. A dozen or so papers were in the envelope, all of which were stamped top and bottom in red with "Secret." A single diagonal red line ran across each page as further notice of the classification level of the document. Because Nick was cleared for "secret," he was permitted to view the document. Capp put the document back in the envelope and placed it in his safe. He told Nick he intended to look over the material later in the day, after teaching a class that was about to begin.

"I'm going to telephone Professor Hazard this afternoon—morning New York time—to report that you and the package arrived safely and intact," stated Professor Capp. "Meanwhile, I suggest you go to the Hotel Le Madison where you have a reservation for tonight and tomorrow night and get some rest. It appears you didn't sleep at all on the plane."

"Sounds good to me," Nick admitted. "When should I plan to return here?"

"Could you come back around 8:00? I'd like to take you to dinner at one of my favorite restaurants. It's the Brasserie Lipp nearby on the Boulevard St. Germaine. It's a traditional French bistro. How does that sound?"

"Wonderful," Nick exclaimed. "Thank you for the invitation. See you at 8:00."

Madam Gardiner telephoned for a taxi. Nick left the building in a driving snow storm. He was not followed.

At the airport, after Nick left for the Science Po, the other stocky man from his flight remained behind—outside the gate where the plane discharged its passengers. He made a quick phone call while waiting for the flight crew to exit the plane after the passengers disembarked. The man knew the crew was based in Paris.

Soon the Air France flight crew came out of the airplane to go home. Among them was the stewardess who switched Nick's briefcase. She was carrying a metal briefcase as were others in the crew. He followed her to the Air France shuttle bus depot from where crew members were driven to a car-park on the periphery of the airport to pick up their cars. A van was waiting for him at the depot and followed the shuttle bus to the car-park. The stewardess exited the bus carrying the briefcase and walked to her red Renault, got in, started the motor, and let it warm up before driving off. It was freezing cold and snowing heavily.

The man following her got out of the van and climbed in a black Citroen that was waiting for him. The stewardess drove to her apartment on the outskirts of the city, followed closely by the two agents. She pulled into the garage beneath the apartment building. One of the agents entered the building's front door and waited to see where the elevator from the garage stopped. It stopped on the third floor. In the lobby the agent wrote down all the names on the apartment mailbox. He went back to the Citroen, handed the list of names to the driver, who then drove into the underground garage. The agent went back into the lobby and waited.

The driver radioed Andre Devereaux at *Deuxième Bureau* headquarters to report what had happened and to give him the names from the mailbox. It appeared the leak was not at NATO headquarters but somewhere else.

Devereaux ordered a cross-check of the names on the apartment mailbox with the names of the Air France crew members on that particular flight. Quickly the name Marie LeBlanc was identified. A background check on the stewardess was begun immediately.

"Very well," Devereaux said to an assistant, "we have identified the pickup courier, but we don't know who she works for or what her purpose is. We don't know who leaked the details of the operation, and we don't know what's in that second briefcase." Despite the hour in Virginia, Devereaux decided to telephone Admiral Myers on a secure line at his home to share this information with him. He woke Myers up.

"The really good news, Admiral," Devereaux said to Myers, "is the bait was taken and it is confirmed we have a security leak somewhere in the system."

"You also have the name of the agent, Marie LeBlanc," Myers added. "We will begin a full-field Agency check on that name to see what comes up at our end."

"Another thing we know," added Devereaux, "is that Nick Butler, though he is only a novice, performed his mission exactly as instructed from start to finish. This is confirmed by my three agents on the flight who were working out of the French Mission to the United Nations—the 'stewardess' and the two heavies."

"I suspect the leak is in Capp's office," Myers observed. "So your side needs to find the link between Marie LeBlanc and someone in Capp's office, maybe Capp himself."

"*D'accord*," responded Devereaux.

About an hour after she returned home from the New York flight, Marie LeBlanc, having changed out of her Air France uniform into casual clothes, left her apartment on the third floor, buzzed for the elevator, and went down to the parking garage.

The agent who had remained in the lobby ran down the stairs to the garage when he saw the elevator engaged from the third floor. In the garage he watched the woman exit the elevator and walk to her Renault. She was carrying the metal briefcase. She put the briefcase on the front passenger seat.

The agent quickly got into the black Citroen, parked in a dark corner of the garage with the other agent at the wheel.

LeBlanc pulled out of the garage and drove into central Paris. She was clearly intent on delivering the briefcase to someone. Mid-morning traffic was light but the snow made driving treacherous. So the agents followed closer than usual to avoid losing her. When she arrived at the Place de la Concorde she pulled over to the curb in front of the Hotel de Crillon.

A man approached the front passenger door, opened it, and took out the briefcase. She drove away as the man hurried into the hotel.

The French intelligence officer in the Citroen's passenger seat followed him into the mammoth hotel. Walking to the mid-point of the lobby, the man grazed by a second man who took the briefcase. The second man walked quickly to the rear of the hotel toward the car-park. The French intelligence officer recognized the second man from his file photo: Alexi Mamanov, the Soviet Union's top spy in France—the KGB *Rezident* in Paris.

At this same time, Nick left Professor Capp's office. Getting in his taxi at the Science Po building, Nick gave the driver his destination in French: *L'Hôtel Le Madison, 143 Boulevard Saint-Germain.*

Acknowledging the destination with a head jerk, the driver engaged the gears and pulled out. It was snowing heavily and the streets were slick, but the driver was expert. Within a few minutes they arrived at the hotel. Nick paid the fare, retrieved his suitcase, and entered the elegant-looking building at 10:00.

At the reception desk he surrendered his passport, as requested, signed the register, took his key, and rode the elevator to his nicely appointed room on the fourth floor. The room faced the Seine and had a partial view of Notre Dame. Nick heaved a sigh of relief knowing he could relax for a few hours before dinner with Professor Capp. He considered taking a shower but realized he was too tired. So he stripped and slid thankfully into bed. He of course did not know the chain of events his trip had set in motion.

At 6:00 Nick woke up. He shaved, took a hot shower, and dressed in the suit he had packed. While showering he couldn't help thinking about his experience in the airplane lavatory with the stewardess. He supposed what had happened did not technically qualify him for membership in the mile-high club, of which he had heard so much while in college. No matter, he thought, it was close enough.

He took a taxi from the hotel to the Science Po, arriving at 8:00. He went up to Professor Capp's office and found him waiting. Madam Gardiner had gone home.

"*Bonsoir*, Nick," Capp greeted him.

"*Bonsoir a vous, mon Professeur.*"

Switching to English, Capp said, "I take it you are fluent in French."

"Not fluent but pretty close."

"Well," said Capp, "I like to practice my English, so if you don't mind we'll stay with that. Okay?"

"Whatever you prefer, *mon professeur*," Nick teased.

Capp chuckled and said, "It's time for dinner, *n'est-ce pas?*"

The two departed the building, taking a taxi to the Brasserie Lipp. Madam Gardiner had made a reservation so their table was waiting.

The ambiance was everything Nick expected in a classic French bistro: gleaming brass rails on a mahogany bar, dazzling white tablecloths and linen napkins, sparkling glassware, flowers on each table, and most of all professional male waiters wearing white shirts, black neck ties, and white aprons.

When a waiter arrived at their table, Capp ordered hors d'oeuvres and a bottle of fine red wine. For the entree, he suggested Nick try the beefsteak and French fries, the traditional bistro meal. Nick took his suggestion.

They enjoyed a relaxing dinner, taking more time to eat and chat than Nick was accustomed to. For him meals were an interruption from studying and were consumed as quickly as possible. He observed no one in the restaurant was in a hurry, including the waiters.

Nick asked if Capp had had a chance to look over the papers he delivered. Capp replied he had taken a fast read through them but wanted to spend tomorrow morning digesting their contents and writing an analysis. He asked Nick to come to his office at 10:00 the next morning to participate in that. Nick of course agreed.

While Nick and the professor were at dinner, Andre Devereaux dispatched two of his agents to the professor's office at the Science Po. As they suspected, the office was empty at that time of evening. They picked the door lock and quickly found the safe. One of the agents was a safecracker. The safe was no challenge to him; he opened it immediately.

The "secret" document was there. In low light they photographed each page with a Minolta mini-camera then returned the papers to the safe exactly as they found them in the manila envelope. They wore plastic gloves so no finger prints were left. They took the camera to the *Deuxième Bureau's* headquarters at 2 bis Avenue de Tourville to develop the film.

At 9:30 P.M. Andre Devereaux telephoned Admiral Philip Myers at his office on the secure line.

"It's been a good day for our intelligence services, *mon ami*," Devereux declared. "The trap we set worked. We now know Marie LeBlanc, the Air France stewardess, is a KGB agent. We also know somewhere between the Institute of Defense Studies in New York and the Institute of Political Science in Paris there is at least one other KGB agent. We have the results of a background check on Madam Gardiner, Professor Capp's secretary, and discovered she was a member of the Maqui, the French Communist underground during World War II. She may still be a Communist. At any rate, she is the prime suspect at our end. There may be another accomplice at your end. We also have photos of the pages in the fake package that LeBlanc planted on the airplane."

"Terrific progress, Andre," agreed Myers. "Have you digested the fake document yet?"

"We're working on it now. We are eager to get Professor Capp's analysis of it, but we're not going to tell him it's specious. What's really needed is for Professor Hazard to see the fake document and compare it with what he sent with Butler. We're transmitting a facsimile of it directly to your office at Langley, bypassing the French Embassy."

"Excellent. As soon as I receive it, I'll forward it to the CIA field office in New York. An agent will take it to Professor Hazard tomorrow to review it."

"We can only wonder at this time," added Devereaux, "what the ever-wily Yuri Andropov wants to mislead us about with this fake document. It appears this is his opening gambit in a new game."

"Let's hope he doesn't catch on that the document he stole from Nick Butler is the opening move in our new game," Myers replied. "After all, this game is played for keeps."

Paris, France
January 6, 1975

At 10:00 the next morning Butler arrived at Capp's office at the Science Po. Capp had already taken the classified document out of the safe and had begun reading it. He handed the first couple of pages to Nick—the ones he already read. The two continued reading in silence for a half hour or so. There were only 12 pages in the package, all stamped "Secret," top and bottom with a red stripe across each page. There was nothing unusual in their appearance.

Nick had never read any of Professor Hazard's reports while at the Institute, but he had learned a great deal about airplanes from his background reading for David Hammond. Capp was used to reading Hazard's analyses of Soviet developments in military equipment, especially aviation. The papers in his hands looked typical of Hazard's work. Neither Capp nor Butler knew the papers they were reading were KGB plants.

What struck Capp about the document was the depth of the information about progress in aircraft design at one of the Soviet design houses—the Mikoyan Design Bureau in Moscow. Given the richness of detail, Capp supposed the CIA had provided Hazard with classified intelligence about advancements in their next generation fighter, the MiG-29.

The impression Butler gained from the document was that the Soviets were far ahead of the U.S. in fighter design and were on the verge of an unnamed major breakthrough giving the Soviet Air Force a decisive advantage in a future air battle with NATO. That is exactly the impression the KGB hoped to achieve.

Capp and Butler wrote a summary of their findings and attached it to the classified report. Capp put the two documents in a secure pouch, sealed it with wax, and gave it to Madam Gardiner to forward to NATO headquarters in Belgium.

Institute of Defense Studies
Columbia University

That same morning in New York, Stephen Dyson, the Chief of Station at the CIA's New York field office, located in the recently-opened World Trade Center, telephoned Professor Leland Hazard at the Institute. Dyson asked to meet with Hazard in his office within the hour on an urgent matter. Hazard of course agreed.

When Dyson arrived at the brownstone, Hazard asked if the Institute's Director, Bill Reynard, could attend the meeting. Dyson, knowing of Reynard's relationship with Admiral Myers, agreed. The three men went into the windowless room. The CIA agent handed Hazard the facsimile copy of the document sent from Paris. He asked a single question: "Is this the document you sent to Paris with your courier?"

Within a few minutes of scanning the pages Hazard declared this is not what he sent to Jean-Pierre Capp. Stephen Dyson already knew that.

Chapter 3:
The Trainee

New York City
January 7, 1975

Stephen Dyson asked Professor Hazard to summarize the document he sent to Paris. As Bill Reynard looked on, Hazard explained his document, prepared at CIA's request, was an attempt to mislead Soviet intelligence into believing U.S. aerospace companies were on the verge of two key breakthroughs in military aviation technology.

"Do you want me to describe the two bogus breakthroughs?" Hazard asked the agent.

"Yes, briefly, and in non-technical language so I can understand," cautioned Dyson.

Hazard explained one research and development effort was designed to perfect turbofan jet engines to enable a jet fighter to achieve super-cruise—the ability to fly supersonically without using afterburners. This would greatly extend the operational range of the aircraft by using less fuel at supersonic speed. The other R&D effort was a navigation breakthrough using space-based satellites to help a pilot navigate his airplane and attack ground targets with great accuracy using precision-guided weapons.

"Neither so-called breakthrough has been accomplished and is years away from happening in the United States," Hazard declared. "We know the Russians are also working on these two areas of technology, and we wanted them to believe we are far ahead of them. We hoped it would dishearten them to think they might not catch up with us in these key technologies, giving us a commanding advantage in combat."

"Thank you, professor. That explanation is very clear. I want you to read this document carefully and give me your summary of it later today or tomorrow. I will be in my office at the World Trade Center." He gave Hazard his business card and left the building.

After Dyson left, Hazard studied the document. Without knowing what Jean-Pierre Capp and Nick Butler had concluded from their analysis of it, Hazard reached the same conclusion—that the Soviet Union was far ahead of the U.S. in certain key areas of fighter aircraft technology. Later in the day he telephoned Dyson to report his finding.

"Thank you for your analysis, professor. Please ask Professor Reynard to secure the document in his safe—not in your safe—and treat it as classified," Dyson instructed. Then he telephoned Admiral Myers at CIA headquarters to report Hazard's finding.

"Well," Myers said to Dyson, "now we know both sides are playing the same game—floating phony reports of fighter technology breakthroughs. The difference is we know the KGB's so-called 'breakthroughs' are bogus. Let's hope they don't find out ours are, too."

Science Po
Paris, France
January 7, 1975

In Paris, Butler and Capp, having finished their report, had a quick lunch together in Capp's office. Madam Gardiner had brought sandwiches and soft drinks from the school café. Over lunch Capp invited Nick to attend his class starting at 1:00. Today he was going to lecture on the topic of how changes in military technology had altered geopolitical relationships throughout history. The lecture would be in French. It sounded fascinating. Nick immediately accepted the invitation.

Capp told him it would be a two-hour class, and at 3:00 Nick would be free to roam around Paris and see the sights, if he wished. His return flight to New York was not until 9:30 the next morning.

A few minutes before 1:00, Capp and Butler went to the lecture hall downstairs in the same building. As they arrived there a strikingly beautiful female student with raven-black hair approached Capp with a question about the day's reading assignment. Capp answered her question then politely introduced her to Nick.

"Mademoiselle Nicole Girard, permit me to introduce you to my American friend, Nick Butler," Capp said in French.

"Enchanted, Monsieur Butler," Nicole said in English, her dark eyes flashing as she gave him an enigmatic smile.

"Enchanted to make your acquaintance, mademoiselle," Nick replied, meaning it.

Then the three entered the lecture hall. Nick asked Miss Girard if he could sit with her during the lecture. Nicole replied, *"Bien sur."*

They took their seats as Capp began his lecture. Nick found it to be a penetrating analysis of how warfare had changed due to technological advancements—the impacts of the longbow, gunpowder, the repeating rifle, the tank, the airplane, and most important of all nuclear weapons. And as weapons changed over time, so did geopolitical relationships between nations.

After the lecture, Nick and Nicole chatted for a while in French. Nick told her he is a first year graduate student at Columbia in New York and is here at the Science Po working briefly with Professor Capp, going back home tomorrow morning. Nicole said she is also a first year graduate student at the Science Po and is a bit overwhelmed by her courses, especially Capp's. Nick offered to compare notes with her.

"Will you have dinner with me this evening?" Nick asked. "I don't know anyone in Paris and my one evening here is open."

"Where would you like to go?"

"There's a famous restaurant on Boulevard Montparnasse called La Closerie des Lilas where Ernest Hemingway is supposed to have written one of his novels. I've read about the place and would love to see it," replied Nick. "Does that interest you?"

"I've certainly heard about it, too, but have never been there. Thank you for the invitation. I'd enjoy going very much."

"Great," Nick said in English. "Err, *tres bien!*" he quickly recovered in French.

They agreed to meet at the restaurant at 8:00. Nick went to Capp's office to say good-by to him and his secretary. He asked Madam Gardiner to make a dinner reservation at the restaurant. Then he went to the Eiffel Tower. He couldn't see much of the city because it was still snowing. Nicole went to another class.

At 7:45 they both arrived at the Montparnasse Metro station, Nick from the Madison Hotel where he had freshened up after his brief sightseeing. Montparnasse was beautiful in the snow, which thankfully had stopped. Some of the holiday lights were still on display, making the walk on this hillside in Paris magical on this unusually cold night.

As they entered the restaurant, Nick asked what perfume she's wearing.

"Do you like it?" she responded.

"Oh, yes, very much. What's it called?"

"It's a new fragrance. It's called '*Oui*'."

"That's my favorite word," Nick said with a devilish grin.

The maître d' showed them to a booth where they settled in for the evening. They had a delicious dinner and a full bottle of wine.

During dinner, Nick asked if Nicole liked airplanes. She said she did and had once attended the Paris Air Show. He told her he'd been to the Farnborough Air Show last summer and enjoyed it immensely. Nicole's French pride showed when she observed that Farnborough has nothing on the Paris Air Show—it's the greatest in the world, she claimed. Nick said he hoped to attend the Paris show some day.

"Well," Nicole suggested, "there's one coming up in June. Why don't you plan to attend?"

"I'd like to but I'm committed to working at the Institute in New York through the summer. But who knows," he said hopefully, "things do have a sudden way of changing."

They left the restaurant and began walking toward the Montparnasse Metro station. Nick wanted to invite her to his hotel room but thought that would be too forward on a first date. Yet, he thought, when would they have a second date?

As they arrived at the Metro station, Nicole asked where he is staying.

"L'Hôtel Le Madison."

"That's not far from my apartment. We can take the same train."

As the train took them to the Saint-Germaine Metro station, Nick decided to make a move. He liked Nicole and she gave every indication of a mutual attraction. As they exited the Metro station, Nicole asked if she remembered correctly he'd said this is his last night in Paris.

"Yes," he replied, "I fly home to New York in the morning. It's been a wonderful evening. You've made it special. Would you like to come up to my room for a cognac?"

She didn't hesitate: "That will be very nice on such a cold night."

They walked the two blocks to the hotel, took the elevator to Nick's room, and removed their coats. Nick opened the mini-bar taking out two miniature cognacs while Nicole went to the bay window to look out at Notre Dame lit-up for the night.

Nick poured the cognacs and brought them to the window. After she took her glass, Nick put his arm around her waist and said "*santé*." They each took a sip.

A moment later, Nick took her cognac and put both glasses on the table by the window. He took her by the shoulders, gently turning her toward him, and kissed her.

"I've wanted to do that all evening," Nick admitted.

"So have I," Nicole said as she kissed him back.

They continued kissing by the window for several minutes. Still kissing, Nick slowly moved them toward the bed where he sat them down. She was as eager as he so after a few more minutes he simply said, "Let's get comfortable."

They took off their clothes. Nick pulled back the bedspread and covers. They slipped under the sheet and blankets.

They forgot about the cognacs until about midnight when they finished them. They slept and loved on-and-off in each other's arms throughout the night.

Nick woke up at 6:30 and roused Nicole. The sun was starting to come up. She looked beautiful in the winter half-light dribbling through the bay window. Propped on his pillow he whispered he had to get up to get ready for his flight.

"Not yet," she purred as she wrapped her body around his. Nick gave in to her and quickly was able to make love to her again.

As soon as they finished, he went into the bathroom to take a shower. When she heard the water running, Nicole jumped out of bed, went to the table where she left her handbag, and took out a small plastic tube. Standing up, she inserted the open end into herself to collect the fresh sample of Nick's sperm. After a minute or so she checked to see if she had enough. Satisfied, she capped the vile and returned it to her handbag.

When Nick finished in the bathroom, Nicole went in, took a quick shower, and returned to the bedroom feeling refreshed and pleased with the way things turned out.

When he boarded the Air France flight to New York, Nick looked around the cabin to see if his favorite stewardess was on board. She wasn't. After the plane took off, he could not stop thinking about Nicole and their night together. He was in an almost constant state of arousal. How fantastic she had been!

Earlier, in his hotel room, after they showered and dressed, they exchanged addresses and phone numbers while munching a Continental breakfast Nick ordered from room service. Nick said he would try to return to Paris in June, if at all possible, to attend the air show. Nicole said she hoped he would. After a final kiss good-by, they left the hotel. Nick got in a taxi to go to Orly Airport. Nicole stood under the hotel's portico waiving good-by as Nick's taxi drove out of sight.

Nicole hailed a taxi. She needed to get to her apartment as quickly as possible. When she arrived there she put the vial in her refrigerator's tiny freezer compartment to preserve the contents, as she had been instructed. Then she carefully removed her diaphragm.

At 12:30 a man dressed in a delivery uniform came to her door carrying a small package containing an insulated bag packed with dry ice. Nicole opened the door and gave the frozen vial to the man, who put it in the insulated bag. He departed at once. He drove directly to the Soviet Embassy.

That afternoon, the vial, packed in a cryogenic case, was put on an Aeroflot flight to East Berlin where it was taken to the headquarters of the Stasi, East Germany's Ministry for State Security, on Karl Marx Square. The Eastern Bloc's center for in-vitro fertilization was near-by.

New York City
January 12, 1975

The following Sunday, both having returned to New York, Nick Butler and Liam Erickson sat on the easy chairs in their apartment's living room. Liam had recovered from the flu, and Nick had spent most of the weekend sacked-out after his brief but intense trip to Paris.

"I hate to say it," Nick said it anyway, "but you're getting the flu last week couldn't have happened at a better time for me."

"How's that, Nick-boy?" Liam asked quizzically.

"I went to Paris in your place," Nick announced to a surprised Liam. Then Nick briefly summarized the series of events that took him to France. He didn't mention the Air France stewardess or Nicole Girard. He didn't think Liam would believe him. He spent most of the time talking about Jean-Pierre Capp and the Science Po. He had been cautioned not to discuss the contents of the classified package.

"Oh, and I also went up in the Eiffel Tower in a snowstorm," Nick added to rub it in a little more.

The next morning the two roommates began their four spring semester classes. They both made occasional visits to the Institute to stay connected.

New York City
March 13, 1975

When spring break arrived in March, Nick and Liam had no plans. On the last Friday of classes, they went to the Institute of Defense Studies—Nick to Reynard's office and Liam to Hazard's. Each asked if there were any tasks that needed to be done during the following week when they would be free of classes. Hazard told Liam he looked like he needed a rest and suggested he fly home to Wisconsin for the week. Liam gratefully departed that afternoon.

Bill Reynard, however, asked Nick to remain in New York the following week and to report to his office on Monday morning for an assignment. Important decisions about Nick Butler had been made at the CIA, and it was time to let him in on the plans for his future.

When Nick arrived at the Institute on Monday morning, Professor Reynard and Stephen Dyson were waiting for him. They went into the windowless room and closed the door.

Reynard introduced Dyson telling Nick he is the CIA's New York Station Chief. Reynard said he invited Dyson to meet Nick with the idea that Nick would make an excellent intelligence agent. Steve Dyson, Reynard said, would like to present Nick with an opportunity to work with the Central Intelligence Agency.

"What we have in mind for you, Nick," explained Dyson, "is not full-time employment with the Agency, but what one might call an association with it. At first you will be a trainee and later you will become a kind of 'sleeper agent'."

"I don't understand what you mean by that. Besides, I'm a long way away from graduating from Columbia with a Ph.D."

"We understand completely," Dyson said. "What we'd like is for you to perform an occasional task for us while you're still a student and perhaps also after you graduate. This will be a great service to your country."

"What kind of tasks would be involved? Would they be anything risky or dangerous?"

"I cannot guarantee the absence of risk or danger. Avoidance of that will largely be a matter of your own skill. Would you say it was dangerous or even unpleasant taking Professor Hazard's package to Paris in January?" Dyson asked with a grin.

"What? Do you mean that was a CIA assignment?" Nick asked, amazed.

"The flight to Paris and the work with Professor Capp was an assignment Professor Reynard organized for you at CIA's request," responded Dyson.

"Well, I'll be damned," Nick muttered. "All I did was sit on an airplane for six hours and deliver a briefcase to the Science Po then help Professor Capp analyze the document in it."

"That's what we wanted you to think," said Dyson as he moved in closer to Nick. Then he said in a low voice: "You did much more than that without knowing it, and you did it remarkably well for an untrained agent. Someday I hope to be authorized to tell you the whole story behind the trip to Paris, if you accept my offer to work with the Agency. Are you interested or not?"

"Yes, I'm interested, but of course I'd like to know more about what I'm getting into."

At that point Dyson outlined a plan for Nick for the next few months. First, he would depart that afternoon to spend the rest of the week at Ft. Holabird, a U.S. Army post in Baltimore, Maryland, where American clandestine agents are given basic training in spy craft. He would return to New York on Saturday. For the rest of the semester he would complete his classes. In June he would go to the Paris Air Show under the auspices of Century Aerospace as their intern, following up on contacts he made last summer at Farnborough. After the air show, he would continue his internship at Century's Washington, D.C. office for the rest of the summer. He would return to Columbia for classes in the fall, as usual.

He was cautioned to discuss none of this with anyone—not his family, his roommate, any girlfriends, no one. He will be given a "Top Secret" security clearance so he can have access to fake advanced aerospace technology to pass to the KGB. That will be his mission.

"Oh my God," Nick exclaimed. "Are you serious about all this?"

"Dead serious," Dyson said with a clenched jaw. "The only people who will know about your new role are Professor Reynard and me, plus my superiors at CIA Headquarters. This role for you has been approved at a high level in the Agency."

"Did you say I'll be going to the Paris Air Show in June?" Nick asked dreamily.

"It's an essential mission for you, and I should think a very pleasant one, don't you agree, Nick?" Dyson asked with a smile. Nick could only wonder if Dyson and the entire CIA knew about his night in Paris with Nicole. For Nick, going back to Paris clinched it.

"I'm in," Nick declared with an outstretched hand to Dyson. He shook it warmly and then Nick and Reynard shook hands.

All Nick could think is "I'm going to be a spy!" As things had turned out, he already was.

Dyson returned to his office and telephoned Susan Samuels at Langley. "He's on board," Dyson told her.

Reynard instructed Nick to return to his apartment, pack casual clothes for five days, and be prepared to leave for LaGuardia Airport on the noon flight to Baltimore. Anna Suzuki would bring your tickets to the apartment in exactly one hour. Nick met Anna in the apartment building's lobby with the tickets. He took her taxi. She walked the two blocks back to the brownstone. It was a chilly, windy March day but at least it was not raining or snowing.

Ft. Holabird
Baltimore, Maryland
March 16, 1975

The flight to Baltimore took less than an hour. When he arrived at Baltimore-Washington International Airport an agent was waiting for him at the gate. The agent simply said to Nick, "Come with me." They picked up his suitcase from baggage claim, walked to the front entrance of the airport, and got in the back seat of a black Chevy with U.S. Government plates waiting at curb-side. Another agent was behind the wheel. They drove into the City of Baltimore— to an industrial area that had seen better days.

The driver pulled up to a closed chain-link entrance gate with razor wire on top. The entire heavily-guarded facility was fenced in with razor wire. A sign on the gate read: U.S. Army, Ft. Holabird. The driver flashed a pass at a uniformed Army MP, who opened the gate. The Chevy drove through stopping at a one-story building.

After entering the building, which looked a like a run-down post office, the agent guided Nick to an inner office and then departed. Seated at a desk was a uniformed Army captain who greeted Nick. The captain asked perfunctorily if he'd had a pleasant flight and gestured to a chair facing the desk. He asked to see Nick's driver's license then returned it.

"Mr. Butler, Ft. Holabird is the name of this Army post. Until last year it was the Army's Center for Intelligence and Counter Intelligence. That Center has now been relocated to Ft. Huachuca in Arizona, but this facility has remained open temporarily for specialty training for CIA agents such as you." The captain paused.

"Any questions so far?" he asked. Nick shook his head no.

The captain continued very slowly and formally: "You will remain within this facility until Saturday at noon when you will return to New York. We have clean but Spartan accommodations—typical of the Army. I believe you will be comfortable and will learn a great deal in a short time. While here, you will be introduced to the basics of spy craft and be given a number of practice lessons. We will provide you with any equipment your instructor judges you may need as you go about your work after your departure. Your training has been specifically tailored to your particular needs and requirements by the CIA. Do you have any questions at this time?"

"Not at this time."

"Very well," the captain said. "During this week you will be under Army regulations and you will be treated as an employee of the U.S. government. Therefore, I now need to administer the oath of allegiance. Please rise and raise your right hand so I can swear you in."

Nick obeyed. The captain stood up and administered the same oath every U.S. government employee takes, swearing true faith and allegiance to the Constitution of the United States.

The captain then picked up the phone and made a call. Within a minute an Army sergeant arrived and walked Nick to a golf cart. His suitcase was stowed in the rear. The sergeant and Nick drove for about five minutes to another one-story building.

"This is the BOQ where you'll be bunked," said the sergeant, who picked up Nick's suitcase. They entered the building. There was a long center hall with private rooms on either side. The sergeant walked to one, opened the door, and to Nick's surprise the room was nicely furnished. There was a TV but no telephone. The bathroom was down the hall.

While the sergeant waited, Nick unpacked. Told to change into casual clothes, he quickly took off his suit and put on a polo shirt, jeans, and sneakers. He asked the sergeant if this was okay. The sergeant's response was "A-OK."

Nick and the sergeant then walked to another building about a block away. Inside was a classroom with several work tables. This, the sergeant said, is where you will spend most of your time.

A grizzled old officer then entered the room. The sergeant braced at attention. The officer said, "Dismissed, sergeant." The sergeant saluted and left immediately.

"I am Colonel Payne. I will be your personal instructor for the week," he said. Nick introduced himself. Colonel Payne immediately began his first lesson. He was a humorless, no-nonsense, serious professional. This was Nick's first appraisal of Payne that did not change all week.

For the next five days, Col. Payne and Nick worked together in the classroom. Nick learned that small things, like a slip of the tongue or a misplaced scrap of paper, can be clues into what another person is thinking or doing or can be a fatal mistake on his part. He learned how to dust for finger prints and was given a travel-size tin of fine-grain powder for dusting. He was taught how to load and operate a Minolta 16mm sub-miniature spy camera to photograph documents even in low light. At the end of the week he was given one of the mini-cameras for future use. At times the lessons were truly fascinating; at other times a real bore. But Nick always showed an eager interest.

One afternoon as a break from the class-work, Col. Payne took Nick to the post's firing range where an instructor taught him how to load and fire an Army-issue .45 caliber pistol. Nick discovered he's a pretty good shot.

For Nick the most interesting part of the week was the time spent learning about other nations' intelligence services—their names, who directs them, how they are organized, and what their principal missions are. The KGB under Yuri Andropov was the most interesting one. He also learned about the numerous U.S. intelligence agencies: the CIA, the National Security Agency, the Office of Naval Intelligence, the FBI, the Secret Service and so forth. Nick realized he was entering into an enormous shadow world filled with international intrigue.

On Saturday at noon, exactly as planned, Nick said good-by to Col. Payne and was driven to BWI Airport where he boarded his flight to LaGuardia. He was exhausted by the intensity of the week's work but nevertheless was grateful to have gained serious, practical skills that would be useful throughout his life.

When he arrived at his apartment, he fell onto his bed fully clothed. He slept for hours that afternoon, mentally drained.

New York City
March 22, 1975

The next day, Sunday, Liam Erickson walked into the apartment, having returned from his week at home in Wisconsin. While there he told his mother more about Nick, mentioning in January Nick substituted for him on a trip to the Science Po in Paris.

"How was your week, Nick-boy?"

"Oh, fine. Just more research for Professor Reynard at the Institute," Nick lied. "Let's go out for a beer," Nick suggested, using a deflecting technique he learned from the colonel.

"Give me a minute to unpack," said Liam, already mentally focused on a cold beer.

Regular classes resumed the next day and continued until the end of May, when final exams were given. Both Liam and Nick did well, earning A's in their four courses. The semester over, both young men reported for work at the Institute. Professor Hazard had already laid out a series of tasks on Soviet aerospace research and development programs for Liam to undertake throughout the summer in his office on the third floor of the brownstone.

Professor Reynard took Nick into the windowless room, his work station on the second floor, to tell him the plans for the coming weeks.

"The Paris Air Show begins on Monday, June 17th and lasts a full week—through the following Sunday," Reynard explained. "You, therefore, have exactly three weeks to prepare for it. As Steve Dyson told you, at the show you will become well acquainted with the Century Aerospace executives, being their summer intern. Are you with me so far, Nick?" asked Reynard.

"Yes, sir. Specifically what should I do to prepare?"

"Look on your desk. There's a stack of Century Aerospace's annual reports for the past ten years and a folder of press clippings about the company Anna put together for you. Read them carefully to gain a deep understanding of Century's products, its progress in aerospace engineering developments, and its financial performance. I want you to become an expert on all aspects of that company."

"Will I have any more work to do for Dr. Hammond before he returns to NDAC in California?"

"Nothing specific," Reynard replied. "But feel free to discuss with him any of Century's programs, such as their new F-11 jet fighter. He knows a lot about the company through his association with their executives on an NDAC advisory board. But you will not reveal your new role with the Agency, as you have been instructed. Hammond knows nothing about that."

All of a sudden it sunk into Nick's conscious mind the complications of the new double life he had embarked upon. He will have to be cautious in all his dealings, as Col. Payne had warned. It's easy to remember the truth, Payne said. It's more difficult to remember the lies—but those are likely to be more important. Try to put a grain of truth in each lie, he suggested, to help you remember.

Over the next weeks, Nick researched deeply into Century's history, its present activities and organization, and current military programs. He came to realize the company did much more than build a jet trainer and the new F-11 jet fighter. There is another part of the company that is heavily into electronics—electrical equipment that goes on airplanes, called avionics. They are also into laser technology and no doubt perform substantial amounts of classified work, he guessed. In many ways the company is an adjunct of the Defense Department, given all its major programs are funded by it. Nick was developing in-depth knowledge of this fascinating aerospace giant.

A few days before his departure for Paris, Nick found Stephen Dyson waiting for him in his office when he arrived for work. Dyson wanted to know how his research into Century Aerospace was coming along.

"I'm learning a lot about the company," replied Nick, "but I suspect there's a whole other part of their activities that's not reported in the press or in their annual reports."

"Your suspicion is correct," Dyson said, "and directly related to your future activities. My superiors met with Martin V. Stark, Century's CEO. They told him about your role with the Agency and asked him to hire you for the summer as an intern. When told you have a Top Secret clearance, he agreed to do that, given the company engages in highly classified Defense Department work. It was helpful you had met him at Farnborough last year. He remembered you as a serious person."

"Will I be working directly for Mr. Stark?"

"Not directly for him but with whomever he designates, especially Walter Gates, the Senior VP for International Business, whom you also know. Only Stark and Gates know of your affiliation with the Agency," Dyson added. "One thing further, have you told anyone you are going to the Paris Air Show?"

"No one," Nick stated truthfully. He had wanted to write to Nicole to tell her about the trip, but he was forbidden to speak about it to anyone.

"Did you not meet a young woman in Paris in Professor Capp's class?"

"Well, yes, but I haven't told her I'll be coming back to Paris," Nick said, wondering how much Dyson knew about his night with Nicole.

"How do you feel about that girl, Nick? Do you like her?"

"Yes, I do," he admitted.

"Very well then, write to her to tell her you're coming to the air show and arrange to meet. That would be the normal and natural thing to do, so I want you to do it," ordered the CIA Station Chief.

"Thanks. I'll get a letter in the air mail today."

"Good. And be sure to take your camera to Paris."

On the afternoon of his departure from New York—it was a Saturday—Anna Suzuki came to the brownstone to give Nick the items needed for his trip to Paris: his airline tickets, an envelope with French and U.S. currency, travelers' checks, and a copy of his reservation at the Hotel Prince de Galles. Nick noted the tickets were for United Airlines, not Air France. She made sure he had his passport and his ID badge showing his Top Secret clearance. He, of course, had already packed his mini-camera, which Anna did not know about.

Later that day Nick took a bus from the East Side Airline Terminal to JFK for the flight to the City of Lights. In his stomach there was an unsettled feeling about this trip. He wasn't an innocent traveler anymore. Now he was a CIA agent on a mission, and he was acutely aware—as Steve Dyson and Col. Payne had told him—that his personal safety was largely dependent on his own skills. Yet, the excitement he was feeling about returning to Paris and especially to Nicole overcame his uneasiness. What an adventure, he thought to himself.

Chapter 4:
The Intern

Paris, France
June 16, 1974

Early the next morning, Sunday, Nick arrived at Orly Airport after an uneventful overnight flight. From his trip there six months earlier he knew the airport routine: immigration, baggage claim, customs, and the taxi queue.

Waiting outside for a taxi was completely different from his experience in January when it was freezing cold. This day the wait was pleasant in warm and balmy June weather. When his turn came to claim a taxi, the driver got out to put his suitcase in the trunk, reentered the car and asked "where to?" in French.

"L'Hôtel Prince de Galles, 33 Avenue George V, *s'il vous-plait.*"

"I know where the Prince de Galles is, *Mon ami,*" the driver said in English/French.

Nick had forgotten for a moment about Gallic pride.

The drive through central Paris was breath taking. On his previous trip it was the dead of winter and snowing. This beautiful day in June was Paris at its best. Everything was blooming and the air smelled fresh. He was in heaven as he drove through the city on his way to the Right Bank—the upper-class part of Paris.

When he arrived at the majestic Hotel Prince de Galles, two uniformed attendants approached the taxi, one to open his door and the other to fetch his luggage from the trunk, which he placed on a hand trolley. The one with the trolley escorted him through the entrance of the stately hotel and led him to the reception desk where he left the suitcase. He tipped his hat at Nick as he walked away. Such elegant service was a new experience for Nick.

He checked in and was assigned a room on the fourth floor. The reception clerk handed Nick an envelope and handed the door key to a bellhop. The bellhop put his suitcase on another hand trolley and led Nick through the grand lobby to an elevator.

When the bellhop opened the door to his room, Nick was amazed at its size. It was enormous. There was an immense king-size bed with a carved wooden headboard that looked like something out of the Versailles Palace. The sitting area had matching upholstered slipper chairs on either side of a round wooden table. Heavy drapes flanked the French window. Nick opened a window and looked out. He discovered the room faced the hotel's interior courtyard. Looking down at the courtyard he saw a garden setting with low trees, banks of flowers, tables and chairs beneath yellow umbrellas, and decorative pools of water. This was a huge cut above the Madison Hotel, which up to that time Nick had considered the height of luxury.

Nick tipped the bellhop, who left immediately, and opened the envelope. It contained a hand-written note from Walter Gates, Century Aerospace's Senior Vice President for International Business. The note read: "Welcome to Paris, Nick. Looking forward to working with you. Please have lunch with me at the hotel's atrium café at noon today. Walt Gates." Now Nick understood why he had been assigned to this elegant hotel—the Century Aerospace people were also staying here. No Hotel Madison for them!

Nick shaved and showered and at noon went down to the atrium café to meet Gates. The café was in the same courtyard he had seen from his window above. On the ground level it was even more impressive. Flowers were everywhere. A glass ceiling high above let in the sunlight but not the elements. The setting was fabulous.

Walter Gates came up behind Nick, who was waiting at the maitre d's desk. He put his hand on Nick's shoulder and said, "Hi, Nick. I'm Walt Gates, remember me?"

"Of course I remember you from the Farnborough Air Show, Mr. Gates. How nice of you to invite me to lunch."

"It's my pleasure. Let's be seated," Gates said. The maitre d' showed them to a table under one of the yellow umbrellas and gave them menus.

"Would you gentlemen like something to drink?" asked a waiter in English.

"Yes, I'd like a martini with an olive," replied Gates.

"I'll have a Perrier," Butler said.

After a little small talk about Professor Reynard, Gates informed Nick the entire Century Aerospace team had arrived the previous day to make sure their arrangements at the air show were to their satisfaction. Most of them are staying at the Prince de Galles, he said.

"Is Mr. Stark also staying here?" Nick asked after the drinks arrived.

"No. Martin Stark prefers to stay with Mrs. Stark at the Plaza Athenee Hotel. But you will see him tomorrow at the air show."

"Is Mrs. Gates with you?"

"There is no Mrs. Gates at the moment. I'm sort of between wives," Gates said with a cynical chuckle.

Gates ordered another martini when the waiter arrived to take their lunch order. Then a serious conversation began. Gates alluded to his knowledge of Nick's other status. He assured him the company would support him in that role and keep his identity secret. Nick thanked him for that reassurance. Gates stated as far as the company is concerned his summer internship begins today. He will be treated as an employee of Century Aerospace, Inc. until September when he will return to Columbia to resume his studies.

Over their food, Gates told Nick a great deal of double-dealing occurs at air shows and some of it has serious consequences. At the last Paris Air Show, in 1973, the consequence of that was fatal. A Soviet Tupolev transport plane, their brand new Tu-144, crashed and killed about a dozen people, including the airplane's entire crew plus people on the ground. It was the first production model of the new airplane.

"I read about it. What a terrible accident," Nick commented.

"Do you want to know what I think caused the 'accident' Nick?"

"I'd be fascinated to know," he replied seriously.

"Well, the press account was that a French Air Force Mirage chase plane got too close to the Tupolev during one of its maneuvers and distracted the Tupolev's pilot who lost control. The plane pitched violently downward and broke up. The behind-the-scenes story was the Mirage pilot was trying get close enough to the Tupolev to get good photographs of its canards as the plane maneuvered—those are the little wings at the front of the fuselage that improve flight stability. It was the first time the Soviets had displayed an airplane in the West of their own design with canards."

"What do *you* think really happened?" Nick asked drawing closer to Gates.

"Canards were invented by the Anglo-French engineers who designed the Concorde, the supersonic passenger airplane that's currently in service with

Air France and British Airways. I think the Anglo-French team suspected the KGB was attempting to steal their canard design. So the Concorde engineers got a little 'careless' and left the key drawings of their canard design lying on a table one night knowing the KGB would try to photograph them. The problem for the Soviets was they didn't know the drawings they photographed had subtle design flaws deliberately put there by the Anglo-French engineers. For that deception more than a dozen people died."

Nick gulped. For him espionage and counter-espionage suddenly took on a new and deadly meaning.

When they finished their meal a waiter cleared away the dishes. Gates then informed Nick about the week's schedule of activities.

"As you know, the air show formally kicks off tomorrow morning at 9:00 at Le Bourget Airport," Gates began. "So the entire Century team will meet in the lobby at 8:00 to board vans to take us to the airport. You will be a member of our official party so be in the lobby at 8:00. At that time Randy Gilmore, Century's PR man, will issue your badge, the type that all industry people must wear around their necks while at the show. Any questions so far?"

"No, sir."

"Each day we will all remain at the show until 5:00 when we'll return to the hotel to dress for dinner. Every night through Saturday we will host a dinner for dignitaries from foreign air forces. You will join us for all of those. You will become acquainted with a great many foreign leaders. Tomorrow night we'll entertain the Chief of Staff of the Imperial Iranian Air Force at Maxim's. We're hoping to ink a contract with them for several squadrons of F-11s. It will be mostly business, but you'll certainly enjoy the food," Gates said wearily.

"What about tonight?" Nick asked as Gates signed the check, charging the lunch to his suite.

"This is your one free night for the week. So enjoy it," Gates said with a smile as he got up from the table.

They walked together into the grand lobby. Gates said he was going shopping on the Champs-Elysees, which is around the corner from the hotel. Nick watched as he left the hotel through the revolving door. Then he walked to the elevator to go to his room for a much needed nap.

As he boarded the elevator a middle-age gentleman in a dark suit boarded the elevator behind him. They were alone. Nick pressed the button for the fourth floor. The other man did not move. As soon as the doors closed the man turned to Butler and said, "Hello, Nick. We have a mutual friend in New York, Stephen Dyson. I'd like to go with you to your room. Ok?"

After entering the room, the gentleman introduced himself and showed his CIA ID.

"My name is Dan Murray. I'm the CIA Chief of Station here in Paris. While you are in France, you will be under my orders and protection."

Nick, though a little shaken by the suddenness of this turn of events, politely invited Murray to take a seat in the sitting area.

Murray explained his presence. "The Century Aerospace people have already told you that you'll be on their team at the air show. That's part of the plan. You'll also dine with them and their foreign guests each night, beginning tomorrow. You already know this from Walter Gates. Am I correct?" Murray asked somewhat rhetorically.

"Yes, sir. That's what Mr. Gates told me over lunch."

"Good," Murray continued. "Now I'm going to give you an assignment that I believe will not be unpleasant for you. Steve Dyson informed me on your January trip to the Science Po you met a young French woman. He suggested you inform her you'll be attending the air show this week. Have you made contact with her yet?"

"Well, I wrote her I'll be coming to the show, but since arriving in Paris this morning I haven't telephoned her yet."

"That's fine. I want you to phone her right away and invite her to dinner tonight—this being your only free evening. Tell her your days will be filled attending the air show and your evenings will be taken up with business dinners. So tonight is your only opportunity to get together. Also when she agrees to have dinner with you, ask her to choose the restaurant given you don't know Paris very well. You can meet here at the hotel or at the restaurant, whichever is convenient."

"Just have dinner with her? That's the assignment?" Nick asked quizzically.

"There's more. Over dinner you will inform her with pride and enthusiasm you've been given a summer internship at Century Aerospace's Washington, D.C. office. Tell her this was arranged through one of your Columbia professors. Also say Century decided you should begin your summer duties here at the air show as part of their delegation. That's the entire story, and it's all perfectly true."

"I understand."

"What you do after dinner is completely up to you. After all, the two of you seem to like each other and it's entirely natural you'd want to renew your acquaintance with her while in Paris."

"Thanks for the assignment," Nick said with a smile, getting the hint. "You're right. I don't think it will be unpleasant."

"When she gives you the name of the restaurant, call me at this number and tell me," Murray instructed, handing him a slip of paper. "Also, I want to exchange mini-cameras with you." Murray pulled a mini-camera from his suit coat pocket and handed it to Nick. "This one has been modified by the Agency's Science and Technology Directorate and has been field-tested. It's an improved model of the one you were given at Ft. Holabird a few months ago, but it operates the same way." Nick took the camera and handed over his.

"Please leave the camera here in the room when you go out to dinner tonight and leave it here each evening when you dine with the Century people. But be sure to take the camera with you each morning to the air show. Is this clear?" the Station Chief asked.

"Very clear, sir."

"On some days at the show," Murray continued, "you will take photographs, some days not. Other people will instruct you at the times pictures will be taken. Always bring the camera back to your room each afternoon and leave it in a drawer before you go out to dinner. On the mornings after you took pictures the previous day go into the pavilion's private room, remove the exposed film, and discreetly hand it to Randy Gilmore, who is a member of the Century team. Don't let anyone notice your doing that. Gilmore will give you a fresh roll of film so go back into the private room and reload the camera. You remember how to do that?"

"Yes, I do."

"Gilmore will quietly hand the exposed film to one of my agents as he walks about the show. I will receive the film later in the day. Good luck with your assignment," Murray said as he shook Nick's hand and departed.

Nick immediately phoned Nicole.

"Hello, Nicole. It's Nick Butler."

"Hello, Nick. I've been expecting your call since I received your letter," she replied. "How in the world did you manage to come to the Paris Air Show?"

"That's a short story I'd love to tell you over dinner. This is my only available evening during my stay in Paris, so I hope you are free tonight?"

"*Bien sur.* I'd love to see you. When and where?"

"I'd better leave that to you since Paris is your home town. I'm staying at the Prince de Galles hotel on the Avenue George V. I can meet you wherever you like."

"This is so sudden. Let me give this some thought. Can I call you back in a little while with a suggestion?"

"Fine with me," Nick said as he gave her the hotel's phone number and his room number. "If I don't answer the phone it's because I've turned off the ringer to take a nap. So just leave a message, and I'll meet you where ever you say. I can't wait to see you."

An hour later, Nicole phoned Nick. He was asleep and had turned off the phone's ringer. Nicole's call was automatically returned to the operator who took her message which a bellman then delivered to his room, slipping an envelope under the door. When he woke up he saw the envelope on the vestibule's floor. The note read: "Meet me at La Grande Cascade Restaurant in the Bois de Boulogne at 8:00. Nicole"

Nick phoned Dan Murray.

The taxi ride to La Grande Cascade Restaurant passed through some of the most beautiful parts of Paris before it entered the woods—the "*bois*"—the large park set in the midst of the city. Approaching the restaurant still in full summer daylight, Nick thought it looked like a small chateau, perhaps a nobleman's former country house, with turrets and high windows. The setting in the woods was amazing.

Entering the restaurant Nick discovered it was filled with flowers. In the center of the main dining room was a tall marble column, perhaps twenty-five feet high, with flowers cascading down from the top, partially covering the length of the dark, highly polished marble. The sight was spectacular.

Nicole arrived a few minutes after Nick. When they saw each other, they rushed to embrace. Nick kissed her lightly on the lips.

"How beautiful you look!" he exclaimed. "Even better than I remembered you."

"*Merci, monsieur.* You look very handsome."

"And you're wearing my favorite perfume—'*Oui*'," he said holding her close.

"I'm wearing it for you, knowing you like it," she said touching his cheek.

Nick gave his name to the maître d', who showed them to a table next to one of the tall windows with a magnificent view of the park outside. The restaurant was beginning to fill up, mostly with tourists, businessmen and a few couples. Two businessmen were already seated at a table near the one where Nick and Nicole were seated.

Over a truly elegant dinner, Nick told Nicole the story Dan Murray had instructed him to say: one of his professors had arranged for him to have a summer internship at Century Aerospace's Washington, D.C. office, and the company decided to begin that internship here in Paris at the air show. "How lucky could I get?" Nick concluded with a big smile.

"You are indeed fortunate," Nicole exclaimed. "But you must have earned the confidence the professor placed in you. So I don't think it was luck. Will you have a chance this week to come to the Science Po to see Professor Capp?"

"I've been told my days will be filled completely by attending the air show at Le Bourget and all my evenings through Saturday will be taken up with business dinners with Century's customers. I fly back to New York on Sunday. So I don't think I'll have any time for Professor Capp, though I'd love to see him again."

Finishing their coffee, Nick asked if she had driven to the restaurant or did she take a taxi.

"I took a taxi. I don't have a car."

"In that case let's share a taxi back to town. I'd love to have a cognac with you in a more comfortable setting," Nick proposed with a grin. He could hardly wait to get his hands on her.

"That sounds lovely," she purred. That understood, they got up from the table and walked to the maître d's desk. Nick asked him to telephone for a taxi.

After they left the table, one of the businessmen from the near-by table got up and walked over to Nick and Nicole's table. He lifted the pepper shaker, slipping it in his pocket. He and his companion left the restaurant, taking with them a small recording devise they had hidden under their table cloth. They were followed out the door by a couple who also sat nearby, after the man lifted a small object from the low floral piece on Nick's table.

When their taxi arrived at the Prince de Galles, Nick and Nicole took the elevator up to his room. Since it was understood what was going to happen next, there was no need for any small talk.

Nick took two cognacs from the mini-bar, poured them into brandy snifters, and handed one to Nicole who was standing by the French window. "Let's drink to the Hotel Madison, of which I have fond memories," he proposed.

"*Moi aussi*," Nicole said. They clinked glasses and took a sip. Repeating exactly what had happened six months before, Nick took her glass, placed it on a table with his, and turned her toward him for a kiss.

"I've wanted to do that all evening," he repeated his line from the Madison.

"So have I," Nicole repeated her line, kissing him back.

Nick departed from the Madison Hotel script. He went over to the huge bed, pulled down the covers, arranged the pillows, and began taking off his clothes. Nicole was ahead of him, having already stripped down to her panties.

They made love until almost 1:00 A.M., at which time Nicole brought Nick to another climax. After he withdrew, Nicole said she should leave so Nick could get some sleep before his big day at the air show. She took her purse into the bathroom, closed the door, and took out a small plastic tube to collect the freshest sample of Nick's sperm, as she had been ordered.

Emerging from the bathroom, she began to dress. He continued lying in bed, enjoying the view as she put on her clothes. When she was ready to leave, Nick got up, still nude, and walked her to the door. They had a final kiss at the door before Nicole left. Nick dropped on the bed, exhausted. He wondered when he would ever see her again.

As Nicole walked through the lobby, she was joined by one of the businessmen who earlier had been at the restaurant and now was waiting for her. They left the hotel together and entered a car parked outside.

A CIA case officer, dressed as a bellhop, was working in the lobby. He observed her leaving with the KGB agent, whom he recognized from his file photo. The couple that had been at the restaurant had already called Dan Murray, having also recognized the two Russian agents.

Once he had the report from the "bellhop," the Station Chief telephoned Admiral Myers at his home in Virginia that Sunday.

"It's confirmed," Murray told his boss. "The girlfriend, Nicole Girard, is a KGB agent. Nick Butler did exactly what we instructed. I have film and audio of their entire dinner conversation during which he delivered his story perfectly. The KGB also recorded it, but I think they only got the audio. Nick and the girl were followed back to the hotel. She left his room at 1:30 A.M. when she was picked up by the Russians."

"Well done, Dan. Now that the KGB has linked up with Butler, we can fully activate the Stealth Gambit op and use him as planned," CIA's Deputy Director of Operations announced. "I'll call Andre Devereaux and ask him to convene a meeting tomorrow at the *Deuxième Bureau* for you and the MI6 Paris Station Chief. I want you to relate to them the status of our agent and his mission to pass false aircraft designs to the KGB. The air show is the perfect venue for this op."

Myers waited until early morning London time to telephone Sir Nigel Shackelford to inform him of the op's start-up and ask him to have his Paris Station Chief attend the meeting with Devereaux and Murray. The head of MI6 said he would give the order. Then Sir Nigel telephoned the Managing-Director of British Aircraft at his hotel in Paris, asking him to meet with his Station Chief at the air show that afternoon on an urgent matter. Of course he agreed.

On Monday morning at 10:00 the three intelligence officers met in a secure room at the *Deuxième Bureau's* headquarters on the Avenue de Tourville: Andre Devereaux, Daniel Murray, and MI6's Paris Station Chief, Pierce Ainsley.

Devereaux asked Murray to inform Ainsley about the role Nick Butler is performing for the U.S. government. Murray handed the two officers the CIA file on Butler that included his photo, his Top Secret clearance authentication, a copy of his Columbia University grades from his first year's classes, the report from Col. Payne about his excellent performance at Ft. Holabird, and a copy of Susan Samuels' clean background check.

"Beginning today," Murray told them, "Butler is on summer vacation from Columbia University working as an intern for Century Aerospace. At CIA's request he is starting those duties here at the air show posing as Century's in-dustrial spy. In this role he will obtain authentic-looking but bogus aircraft technology from three of our companies, thereby establishing the authenticity of that material, making it attractive to the KGB to steal from him. Only two top people at Century know about his CIA role."

"I have assigned two Category-B case officers to Butler," Murray contin-ued. "Both agents are closely monitoring Butler at the Prince de Galle. One is posing as a bellhop; the other established a listening post to monitor activities in Butler's room."

"Last January," Devereaux added, "Butler did a good job of innocently passing false information to the opposition without his knowing it. We will continue using him as a conduit to pass disinformation."

For Ainsley's benefit, Devereaux recounted Butler's role carrying Professor Hazard's fake aerospace report on the Air France flight in January, gave the name of the Air France stewardess who revealed herself to be a KGB agent, and commented on Butler's romantic relationship with Nicole Girard, who is also a KGB agent as confirmed last night by the CIA. She will likely be the contact passing Butler's "stolen" aircraft designs to Yuri Andropov.

"During the January op," Devereaux continued, "we also discovered Madame Gardiner at the Science Po is a KGB spy, having been a committed Communist Party member since the war. The Bureau decided to let Madame Gardiner and the Air France stewardess, Marie LeBlanc, continue in their roles for a while, hoping to net other agents in their ring as we watch them."

Murray then added, "Don't forget we also contained the false KGB report that was planted on Butler during the Air France flight."

"That's right," Devereaux said. "After Professor Capp sent the report to NATO headquarters, we had it isolated where it can do no harm, but we never let on to anyone at NATO we knew the report was a KGB plant."

Pierce Ainsley asked how MI6 can be of service.

"Remember how the Anglo-French Concorde design team planted the false design of the Concorde's canards that the KGB stole for their use on the Tu-144?" Devereaux asked him.

"I remember it well," answered Ainsley. "It was a great success for us, though I'm not supposed to say so. It derailed development of the Tu-144."

"Well," continued Devereaux, "this is going to be a similar operation but on a much wider scale and with even more potential to disrupt Soviet military aircraft developments for a long period of time. This will be a three-party op planting false engineering data from each of our countries to achieve a major Cold War success for NATO. We're hoping to tie in knots Soviet aircraft designers for years. This op is centered on Nick Butler, whose credibility as Century's industrial spy must be established this week at the air show to convince Yuri Andropov the material he steals is genuine."

Ainsley said, "I'll meet with the head of British Aircraft this afternoon and ask for his company's cooperation to provide flawed aircraft designs to mislead both the Mikoyan and the Sukhoi Design Bureaus in Moscow."

"Exactly right," Devereaux agreed. "I'll meet with the top Toulouse Aviation people today to do the same thing."

"And I," said Murray, "will ask General Aerospace, which makes the new F-16, to offer their inputs. We'll have Butler take photos during the day this week at the air show of whatever engineering drawings the three companies provide as though he is working as an industrial spy for Century Aerospace.

He'll leave the camera with the exposed film in his hotel room each evening while he's at dinner with Century's guests, giving the KGB an opportunity to steal the camera to down-load the pictures without Butler detecting any tampering."

"Good show!" exclaimed Ainsley. "I say," he added turning to Murray, "what is Butler's CIA code name? Given the importance of his role, shouldn't we be using that?"

"We haven't issued one for him yet," answered Murray.

"If you don't mind, I have a suggestion for CIA," Ainsley said. "One of our female agents who personally cleared him through some hurdles at the Farnborough show last year—at the request of Admiral Myers, I might add— offered her assessment of his romantic skills and her own code name for him."

"Okay, I'll bite," Murray said with a smile.

"She referred to him as 'my sweet, lusty Yank' and gave him the code name 'Romeo'," Ainsley said. The other two men silently appreciated the flattery to Nick the name implied.

"Done!" Murray announced. "I'll pass that along to Admiral Myers, who ought to get a kick out of it."

The meeting ended. Each of the three heads of their respective intelligence services in France left the building to execute his part of Stealth Gambit.

Chapter 5:
The Enemy

KGB Headquarters
Dzerzhinsky Square
Moscow, U.S.S.R.
January 2, 1975

In Moscow six months earlier, Yuri Vladimirovich Andropov, the sinister and cunning Chairman of the Soviet Union's feared Committee for State Security, the KGB, approved an op in which one of his female agents would collect a sperm sample from an American espionage agent.

Over the next few days Nick Butler's name came up as a possible sperm donor. Madame Gardiner, the KGB agent at the Science Po, informed the KGB *Rezident* in Paris of his impending trip to France as a courier delivering a classified document. This input was collated with information on Butler provided previously from moles living in the United States. Andropov decided Butler was an ideal donor. He sent the order to the *Rezident* at the Soviet Embassy in Paris, Alexi Mamanov, to put the op into play.

As a result, Nick Butler became the leading player in two gambits—one by the KGB and the other by the CIA.

A French KGB agent, who was also an Air France stewardess, was assigned to pick up the classified package Butler was carrying on the Air France flight and substitute it for a disinformation document. Another French KGB agent, Nicole Girard, was tasked to encounter Butler in a way he would think was accidental or at his initiative. Her mission was to collect a sample of his sperm at her earliest opportunity.

The Soviet op unfolded exactly as Andropov ordered. The sperm sample was delivered to the Stasi in East Berlin to implant in an East German woman having physical characteristics similar to the American donor: tall, dark hair, and blue eyes. German women were chosen because they look more like Americans than Russian women.

The Stasi doctors identified five women from the Stasi pool based on dozens of color photographs of Butler taken during his Air France flight, at Orly Airport, at the Science Po, and at a French restaurant. Once they had the sperm, they took a tiny sample of it, defrosted it, and used it to determine the man's blood type. Two of the five East German women had the same blood type as Butler. One was chosen as the recipient.

Her name was Angela Frederick, age 22. She was an orphan who had been left at the door of an East German clinic when she was a few days old. The government raised her and indoctrinated her to become a committed member of the Communist Party. She was shown photos of the handsome sperm donor. She enthusiastically agreed to be the mother. While she ovulated, a doctor artificially inseminated her with Butler's sperm. That occurred on January 10, 1975. Two weeks later she missed her period. She was pregnant with Nick Butler's baby.

Five months later Angela Frederick was ordered to go to the Paris Air Show as part of the Aeroflot delegation. The KGB wanted her to observe Nick Butler first-hand so she could later impart some of his gestures and mannerisms to her child as he or she grew up. She watched him daily at the show, even walking close to him a few times. Clandestine photos and films of Butler were taken constantly while he was at the show, walking into and out of restaurants and various companies' chalets.

Though Angela was five months pregnant, it was of course possible the pregnancy might not go to full term or the baby might be born with defects. Given these possibilities, Andropov wanted a second sperm sample as a backup—to hedge his bet if this pregnancy failed so he could be ready with another. If it was a success, he'd keep the second batch in a cryogenic state for possible future use.

In June when he learned from Nicole Girard that Butler was coming to the Paris Air Show, he ordered her to obtain another sperm sample. She knew the assignment would not be difficult.

By autumn, Angela's pregnancy was progressing nicely. The KGB, the Stasi, and Angela all hoped for a boy. On October 10, 1975 they got their wish.

Angela gave birth to a healthy, tiny version of Nick Butler at an East German clinic. He was named Karl Frederick.

Andropov had big plans for Karl, very long term plans. In a year his mother would take him to the United States via Ottawa, Canada to grow up in a heavily German part of the country—Wisconsin. A Wisconsin birth certificate was forged in Moscow showing him to be a native-born American.

In time it was planned that Nick Butler's son would become the KGB's top agent in the United States—the perfect mole.

These were Andropov's long term plans. Meanwhile, in June, 1975 when Andropov learned Butler was coming to the Paris Air Show as a Century Aerospace intern, he assumed he was being groomed by Century for a major future role. The KGB Chairman decided to watch Butler more closely. For that purpose he assigned one of his best agents, 28-year-old Sergei Malanovsky, to be Nick Butler's shadow while in Paris.

Chapter 6:
The Industrial Spy

Paris, France
June 17, 1975

On Monday morning, opening day of the Paris Air Show, Nick Butler took the elevator down to the lobby of the Prince de Galles Hotel. His mini-camera was in his suit coat pocket. He saw the Century Aerospace executives assembled by the revolving door. He walked up to Walter Gates and said good morning.

"Good morning to you, Nick," Gates said cheerily. "Did you find something fun to do last night?"

"Yes, indeed I did," Nick replied, recalling his love-making with Nicole.

"As you know the rest of the week will be all work and no play, so prepare yourself," Gates said, reminding him of the back-breaking schedule for daytimes at the show and evenings at business dinners. Gates waived Randy Gilmore over.

"Randy, this is Nick Butler, our intern who will be with us during the show and for the summer in D.C. Nick, Randy Gilmore is Century's Public Relations man on the team."

The two shook hands. Gilmore produced Nick's air show badge and hung it around his neck.

"All industry people must wear ID badges to gain admittance to the show and to the various chalets. Take it off only after you return to the hotel this evening to dress for dinner," Gilmore instructed.

The Century team numbered a dozen people, all men. Six boarded each of two vans waiting outside the hotel. Gates steered Nick into the first van and had him sit beside him on the window seat of the first row. After the vans began to roll, Gates stood up in the aisle and introduced Nick Butler, our new intern who will be working for the company for the summer. Everyone hailed with gusto: "Hello, Nick," and gave a cheer. Nick felt very welcome.

The drive to Le Bourget Airport, the venue of the Paris Air Show, took about 35 minutes. As they approached the airport Gates reminded Nick this is the airport where Charles Lindbergh landed "The Spirit of St. Louis" after crossing the Atlantic Ocean solo about half a century ago.

Exiting the vans, the Century team walked through the main gate directly to the flight line pedestrian walkway, on one side of which airplanes were parked and on the other side were the companies' chalets. At Farnborough these pavilions were called salons. In Paris they were called chalets. The overall arrangement was virtually the same as at Farnborough, except this air show was much larger than Farnborough with more airplanes on display and wider international participation. The Soviet Union attended this one.

The location of the chalets was determined first by nationality and then by lottery. The French and British chalets were nearest to the front entrance. The Soviet chalet was next. The Americans were last. Among them were all the major U.S. aerospace companies.

Companies having aircraft on static display parked them in front of their chalets, on the tarmac side of the pedestrian walkway. The walkway and the airplanes were separated by a five-foot-high chain-link fence.

As he walked past the British Aircraft chalet Nick looked for Elizabeth, his lover from the Farnborough Air Show a year ago. He didn't see her.

When the team entered the Century chalet, they immediately went to the rear where a continental breakfast was waiting on a buffet table. Over croissants and coffee, Walter Gates introduced Nick to each of the company's executives. Everyone was in high spirits on the first day of the show. Rick Russell came into the chalet a few minutes later and greeted Nick with a hearty handshake. He retired from the U.S. Air Force after the Farnborough show and became a Century consultant.

At 9:30 Martin V. Stark, Chairman of the Board and CEO of Century Aerospace, entered the chalet. He was smiling and greeted each member of the team individually. When he came to Nick Butler, Gates, standing next to Nick, reintroduced him to the CEO.

"Century Aerospace is pleased to have you on board this summer, Nick. We hope your time with us will be spent productively," Stark said shaking Nick's hand.

"Thank you, Mr. Stark, I'm sure it will. I appreciate very much your permitting me to attend the show as part of your team," Nick replied politely and with genuine feeling.

Before any visitors entered the chalet, Martin Stark asked for silence to address his company's executives. In a brief statement he reminded everyone the company's major objective at the show was to promote the sale of the company's new fighter airplane, the F-11. That airplane is the key—the "vital key" he called it—to the company's future. "Everyone should focus on selling F-11s," he instructed.

As the first day progressed, groups of high-ranking foreign air force officers entered the chalet. During the morning they were from Iran, Morocco, South Korea, and Switzerland. In the afternoon, officers from Singapore, The Philippines, Norway, and Chile came in. Walt Gates and Martin Stark spoke with each visitor. Nick Butler was introduced to every one of them. Some of these countries already flew Century's other aircraft and all were marketing targets for the new F-11.

Nick attended a briefing one of Century's engineers was giving to a Swiss Air Force general summarizing the F-11's major features. He stated it has twin GE afterburning engines enabling it to fly at supersonic speed, it has twin 20-mm cannons, an AIM-9 sidewinder missile rail on each wing-tip, can carry a mix of ordinance on the wings' hard-points, has an auxiliary fuel tank on the center-line, has a speed-break, and range-track radar. The general said he thought the F-11 had no radar and was only a clear air-mass daylight fighter. The engineer assured him it has an advanced radar making it deployable in cloudy conditions and at night. Nick overheard the general say the airplane packs a powerful punch for such a small airframe.

That same afternoon, while Nick was at the Century chalet, Pierce Ainsley, MI6's Paris Station Chief, walked into the British Aircraft chalet. He and the Managing-Director went into the chalet's side room to have a private conversation. The Managing-Director had already spoken with Sir Nigel and had agreed to cooperate. During those few minutes together, Ainsley gave BA's top executive a photo of Nick Butler and told him the op would occur in three days, on Thursday. That should give BA sufficient time to produce some aircraft disinformation and bring it over from London.

Ainsley quickly departed. The Managing-Director summoned BA's Chief Engineer to join him in the side room. The Chief Engineer was given an urgent, special assignment that must be completed in three days. It was all very hush-hush. The Chief Engineer went to a telephone, called London, and passed the assignment to his deputy.

Similarly, that afternoon, Andre Devereaux sent one of the Bureau's agents to the Toulouse Aviation chalet. The same type of meeting took place. The due date for Toulouse was Wednesday. With its headquarters close-by, the intelligence chief felt the French company would need only two days to prepare false designs and deliver them to their chalet.

Dan Murray entered General Aerospace's chalet at 2:00 P.M. the same day. He met with the company's CEO, Seth McCoy, in a private room. He delivered the same message, handed him a photo of Nick Butler, and gave the GA executive until Friday to develop some fictitious designs of the F-16, which had its first flight the previous year. McCoy said this would be no problem because the company had gone through years of trial and error before arriving at the ultimate successful design of their supersonic multirole fighter. Some of those unsuccessful concepts would be easy to locate and bring to Paris by Friday from the factory in Ft. Worth, Texas. Immediately he placed a call to the plant.

At 5:00 P.M. all the chalets closed. Executives from each company walked to the main gate to board their vehicles to return to the city for business dinners. Arriving back at the hotel, Nick went up to his room and put the camera, which had not been used, in the top drawer of the chest of drawers and then stripped down for a short rest. When he got up he showered and put on a different suit for dinner at the famous Maxim's restaurant.

The van was waiting for the Century team, only four of whom boarded it at 7:30. Other Century executives had dinner engagements with customers at other locations. Gates explained that Mr. Stark would go to the restaurant separately.

While Nick was at Maxim's having dinner, Sergei Malanovsky picked the lock and entered Nick's hotel room wearing plastic gloves. He quickly found the mini-camera. He inspected it to see if any film had been exposed. The meter on the outside showed none had. He replaced it exactly where he found it. Then he planted a small microphone behind the bed's wooden headboard and another in the telephone. A listening post had been established in the room next to Butler's where any conversations would be overheard and recorded. Malanovsky left the room and went next door to wait for Nick's return.

Earlier that day the CIA case officer dressed as a "bellhop" had placed a small microphone and transmitter under the round wooden table in the sitting area in Butler's room. Through that he overheard Malanovsky's break-in. He assumed the phone had been tapped. He also discovered from the hotel register the reservation for the adjoining room was under a suspicious name. He phoned Dan Murray, who was pleased the op was developing as planned.

Arriving at Maxim's restaurant, the Century team was shown to an upstairs private dining room. Only five Century people were present: Martin V. Stark, Walter Gates, Rick Russell, Warren Summers, general manager of the company's aircraft division, and Nick Butler. Name cards were at each place-setting on the table. Nick's was next to an Iranian Air Force colonel.

Soon officers from the Imperial Iranian Air Force arrived. There were also five men in that group, headed by General Amir Toufanian. All the Iranians spoke excellent English. Two waiters brought in flutes of champagne and began passing cold Beluga caviar with toast points and a variety of hot hors d'oeuvres while the attendees milled around getting to know each other. Martin Stark and Gates were already well acquainted with General Toufanian.

The dinner was prix-fix. As soon as everyone was seated, waiters began serving food: hors d'oeuvres of *pate de foiegras*, a main course of *canard a l'orange* with princess potatoes, a fresh *salade de maison*, and flaming cherries jubilee for dessert. Champagne continued to be poured throughout the meal. The conversation during dinner was non-business. Over coffee, however, it shifted to business.

Walter Gates asked General Toufanian for his impression of the company's new F-11 jet fighter which he visited at Le Bourget earlier in the day. The general said Rick Russell gave him a guided tour of the aircraft and had seated him in the cockpit while the plane was on static display. His impression, as a pilot, was quite favorable.

"You know, general," Martin Stark stated, "Century is prepared to start full-scale production and ramp-up to ten aircraft per month with a strong lead order. Isn't that right, Warren?" turning to Warren Summers, the Aircraft Division's general manager.

"That's right, Martin," Summers replied. "We have tooling and trained manpower ready to achieve ten deliveries per month after ramp-up. We could begin deliveries to Teheran with the first two F-11s in 26 months and deliver as many as ten per month beginning 36 months from go-ahead."

"How 'strong' a lead order are you talking about, Martin?" Toufanian asked Stark.

"An order of at least 100 aircraft is needed to justify such a steep rate of production build-up," Stark replied. "Of course," he added, "we expect other countries to place orders once a large lead order is announced. We would like to make the announcement of the kick-off order this week here at the show."

Toufanian looked around the table at the members of his staff, seeking any questions or comments from any of them. In the presence of the general no one spoke.

Walt Gates filed the vacuum with a quip—"Don't everyone rush to sign a contract at once!" he said. Everyone laughed, breaking the ice. Gates then added: "We do have with us a draft Letter of Intent for the purchase of 144 F-11s by the Iranian Air Force. This is the number our analysts calculated you will need over the next five years to replace your present aging fleet."

"Let me have the letter," Toufanian requested. "I'll have our contracts people study it, and if all is well we'll sign it before the end of the show, assuming His Majesty approves."

"I propose a toast to the Imperial Iranian Air Force," Martin Stark said, rising from his chair and holding his champagne flute. The Century people rose and said "Here, here!"

The dinner party wound down and soon everyone departed. Butler was amazed at how well things had progressed for Century and felt honored to be present at the critical moment, probably the launch moment, of the new F-11 program on which Century's future depended.

The next day, Tuesday, the same routine resumed at the air show. Nick was armed with his mini-camera. Foreign air force officers streamed through the Century chalet including generals from Indonesia, Venezuela, Mexico, Turkey, Taiwan, and sheiks from Saudi Arabia.

At noon Nick went to a public restaurant in one of the main buildings for lunch. On his way an attractive young woman who appeared to be pregnant nearly bumped into him. She was dressed in an Aeroflot uniform and was accompanied by a man in his late-20s who might be her husband. At the restaurant that couple took a table near Nick from where they observed him. Nick ordered in French. When the food arrived he paid little attention to the couple, enjoying his cheeseburger, fries, and an ice cold Heinekens.

That evening the Century team had a casual dinner with some U.S. Air Force officers at a neighborhood bistro, Le Flandrin on the Place Tattegrain. Nick of course left the camera in his room. The officers were in civilian clothes. One of them was the Commander of U.S. Air Forces within NATO.

Martin Stark and Walt Gates accomplished their mission for the evening, gaining a promise from the Air Force Commander to visit the F-11 sometime during the show. Stark hoped the Air Force would purchase a quantity of F-11s for use in dissimilar aerial combat training by USAF pilots flying F-15s and F-16s. Stark's marketing strategy was this: if the U.S. Air Force bought any number of F-11s, even very few, that would represent an endorsement of the airplane by our own government to reinforce the marketing effort in other countries.

While Nick was at the bistro, Sergei Malanovsky entered his room and discovered no film was exposed that day. He put the camera back in the drawer.

Returning to his hotel room Tuesday night, Nick immediately turned in, wiped out from the intensity of the long day. As he lay in bed he realized air shows are hard work.

At the show on Wednesday something special happened. After lunch, a distinguished-looking older gentleman entered the chalet. Martin Stark and Walter Gates greeted him warmly. His name was Georges Marceau, le Baron d'Artois, a French nobleman who had a red rosette in his jacket lapel. Gates brought the baron over to Nick to introduce him.

"Georges," Gates said very formally, "permit me to introduce you to Nick Butler. Nick is an intern with our company for the summer. He studies political science at Columbia under Bill Reynard and has worked with Jean-Pierre Capp at the Science Po."

"Enchanted to meet you, Monsieur Butler," said the baron in English. "I think we have another mutual friend, Dan Murray." Andre Devereaux, also the baron's friend, had told him to use Murray's name as the identifying cue to Butler.

"It's an honor to make your acquaintance, sir," Butler replied, realizing something was afoot, his having mentioned the name of CIA's Paris Station Chief.

Gates added that Georges Marceau is also a long-time consultant to Century Aerospace.

"The rosette in your lapel is familiar to me, sir. I've seen photos of it, but this is the first one I've seen in person," Nick said. "It's the Legion of Honor of the French Republic, is it not?"

"A-plus, Nick," Gates chimed in. "Georges was a French resistance leader during the war and later, after escaping to England during the Nazi occupation, he joined General De Galle and became a Free French fighter ace. He shot down five Luftwaffe Me-109s. General De Galle awarded the Legion of Honor to him personally after the war."

"Wow," Nick heard himself saying. "What an incredible life you've had, sir."

"Thank you, young man, but I think yours may also be incredible," the baron said mystically, studying Nick's face through his hooded eyes. He turned to Gates and asked, "Is there some place you and I can speak privately with Monsieur Butler?"

"Follow me, please," said Gates, leading them to the private room off the main floor.

The Frenchman began speaking directly to Nick: "I have been invited here today by both Martin Stark and Daniel Murray to assist you with a special task. I will soon escort you to the Toulouse Aviation chalet and introduce you to a few of their top people. The conversation will be in French. One of those men will take you into a private room, much like this one, and leave you alone for about a half hour. There you will find documents lying on a table. You will photograph each of them and rejoin me in the main part of the chalet when you finish. Do you have your camera with you today?" Marceau asked.

"Yes, sir," Nick said, producing the mini-camera from his suit coat pocket.

"Is your task clearly understood?" asked the baron.

"Understood, sir," Nick responded with a catch in his throat.

The Baron d'Artois and Butler left the Century chalet and walked the length of the flight line to the Toulouse chalet, located at the front of the line. On the way they passed by dozens of military and industry people, including one pregnant woman in an Aeroflot uniform and her male companion, who turned in their direction and followed them. The pair watched as they entered the Toulouse chalet. Upon seeing the red rosette in the baron's lapel, the French Air Force guard at the door snapped to attention and saluted the baron as they went in.

The events inside the chalet unfolded exactly as Georges Marceau predicted. Nick was taken into a side room where he saw a small stack of engineering drawings of airplane sections and parts. All the documents were labeled in French "F-2 preliminary design," and all were imprinted with the Toulouse logo. He snapped a photo of each of the dozen drawings. Then he left the room to rejoin Marceau in the main area. They departed the chalet and walked back to Century's, being followed by the same Aeroflot employee and her companion. Nick commented on this to the baron who observed in a world-weary way Russians follow everyone from the West.

Nick and the baron reentered Century's chalet, spending the rest of the afternoon greeting one after another foreign air force officers. At 5:00 the Century team left to board their vans for the trip back to the hotel. The baron had his own car. He proceeded directly to the dinner venue to be certain the preparations were to his satisfaction. He was the host for the evening at his private club on the banks of the Seine.

Returning to his room, Nick placed the camera in the drawer as usual and stretched out on the bed for a little rest. Being on one's feet all day is brutal, even for a now 24-year-old. At 7:00 he freshened up and went down to the lobby to join the others getting into the van.

A KGB agent posted in the lobby observed this and immediately notified Sergei Malanovsky waiting in the room next to Nick's. He went into Nick's room to check on the camera. The camera's meter showed 12 frames of film were exposed. He pocketed the camera, took the elevator to the lobby, and entered a car waiting by the hotel's entrance. The driver went directly to the Embassy of the Soviet Union—about a 15 minute drive. The car entered the underground garage. Malanovsky took the elevator to the third floor where the dark room was located.

The embassy's photography expert took the camera into the dark room. As Malanovsky watched, he removed the film, placed the negatives in a tray and waited for the emulsion to fully develop the pictures. Once that was done, he bathed the film in a clear solution, then clipped the developing film onto a drying rack. The *Rezident*, Alexi Mamanov, was called to view the pictures.

What he saw was astonishing: high quality photos of engineering drawings of portions of Toulouse Aviation's newest model of the F-2, which is in development. The photos were taken earlier that day at Toulouse's chalet by Nick Butler, a fact verified by Malanovsky who had observed Butler entering and leaving that chalet with the Baron d'Artois.

Mamanov called in the Soviet Air Force colonel to evaluate the photos. The air force technical expert agreed these photos are undoubtedly genuine, representing a significant intelligence coup for the KGB. The colonel asked the *Rezident* how they were obtained. The *Rezident* laughed, saying Sergei stole them from an American industrial spy.

The photography expert waited for the pictures to dry completely. He then laid them out on a table, loaded the same camera with the same special type of Fuji film Nick used, and took a photograph of each picture. The camera was then wiped clean of finger prints, returned to Malanovsky, who delivered it back to Nick's room as though it had never left. All this took about two hours. Nick was still at dinner. The CIA "bellhop" monitored the theft. He called Dan Murray to report the op's success.

Murray telephoned Admiral Myers at Langley to inform him Stealth Gambit is under way. He recounted the day's activities, mentioning the code name the British female agent gave Nick at the Farnborough Air Show—"Romeo." He said that code name is being used by all three intelligence services during this op. Myers smiled at the implication of the name and was eager to tell Susan Samuels her suspicion that Butler is a lover-boy was confirmed by MI6.

Wednesday night's dinner party was held at the baron's private club, the Panama Pavilion, located on the Quai Andre Citroen at Point Mirabeau on the left bank of the River Seine. The setting was magnificent, right at the water's edge, with a view up the river of the Isle de la Cite and Notre Dame Cathedral lit up at night.

Floor-to-ceiling sliding glass doors looked out onto the river. One of the sliders was open to let in the fragrant night air. An occasional boat whistle could be heard from the river when a *Bateau Mouche* sailed by.

The Baron d'Artois was a founding member of the club some 25 years earlier and used it regularly for business dinners and family celebrations when he was in town. What he particularly liked was that the club is informal without being casual. The baron's family seat is of course in Artois, but he rarely visits the chateau. Business keeps him in town most of the time.

And tonight is business, Century Aerospace business, and being a consultant to the company he is hosting a dinner party for Martin Stark and his invitees, the Air Chief Marshal of the Indian Air Force, Pravin Singh, and his senior staff.

As the guests arrived the baron welcomed them at the bar. The bartender had laid in plenty of fruit juices for the Hindu contingent as well as champagne for the Americans. On these business occasions the baron always drank Dubonnet red on the rocks. Later, after everyone was acquainted, the baron directed the guests to their table where cold hors d'oeuvres were waiting. The entire pre-ordered meal was vegetarian, honoring Hindu culinary requirements.

Martin Stark was seated next to the Air Chief Marshal. Stark's objective was to assess the Indian Air Force's interest in the F-11 with an eye to establishing a co-production program to jointly produce several hundred of the planes to replace the aging British-built fighters in their inventory. By the end of the evening Stark learned the Indians planned to develop their own new fighter and had no interest in the F-11. Gaining that information was critical to Century, enabling it to discontinue marketing expense toward an unattainable objective.

When Nick returned to his room at the Prince de Galles, he saw nothing amiss. He took off his clothes and got in bed.

Thursday at the Paris Air Show was special. The brand new American YF-16 fighter prototype had a demonstration flight, along with the Soviet's new Sukhoi Su-25 fighter. The flying took place in the morning; everyone went out to the flight line to watch. No business was conducted in the chalets until after lunch.

Before leaving the chalet to watch the aerial acrobatics, Nick went into the private room, opened the camera and removed the film he exposed the day before at the Toulouse chalet. Returning to the main room, he slipped the roll into Randy Gilmore's hand. Gilmore gave Nick a fresh roll of film that he loaded in the camera in the private room. Later that morning, Gilmore passed the exposed film to a CIA agent walking in the crowd. Everyone was looking up watching the flying demonstrations. The pass went unnoticed.

For lunch, each member of the Century team was free to go wherever he wished. Some went into the chalet for the buffet, but Nick, at Walt Gates' suggestion, went to the public restaurant in the main exhibition hall. As he walked past the British Aircraft chalet he spotted Elizabeth coming out the door. This was of course no accidental meeting. Pierce Ainsley had arranged it in coordination with Dan Murray and Gates. Earlier that morning Elizabeth was flown over from London for the purpose of getting Nick into the British Aircraft chalet in a normal-looking manner, knowing he was under KGB surveillance.

"Hello there, Elizabeth," Nick yelled at about twenty paces from her.

"Hi, Nick," Elizabeth yelled back waving at him. "How nice to see you again after so long!" she said as they briefly embraced.

"I see by your uniform you've gotten another temp job with BA," Nick observed.

"Yes, they do dress us well. I think the uniform is very smart. How on earth did you manage to get into this air show—the same well-connected professor?" she asked with a smile.

Quickly recovering from his surprise seeing her, Nick told her the well-connected professor had arranged for him to be a summer intern at Century Aerospace, and they were starting his assignment here at the show.

"What are you doing for lunch?" he asked.

"I was on my way to the restaurant in the main pavilion."

"So was I," he said with a chuckle. "Would you like to join me?"

"Love to," she said smiling at him. She took his arm as they walked to the restaurant.

The pregnant Aeroflot employee and her companion observed this meeting from a discreet distance and followed the couple into the restaurant where they continued to observe them from a nearby table.

After they were seated and lunch was served, Elizabeth invited Nick to come to the British Aircraft chalet on his way back down the flight line. Of course he gratefully accepted her invitation. He was eating a club sandwich with fries. Elizabeth had a salad. As they spoke about their time together at the Farnborough show, Elizabeth occasionally reached over to his plate and plucked one of his French fries. Nick loved this simple expression of intimacy.

Nick said he'd like to repeat their evenings together, but unfortunately he had to spend his evenings at business dinners—all stag at that! Elizabeth said she had the same requirement from her employer acting as a hostess.

After a pleasant lunch, they left the restaurant and went to the British Aircraft chalet, Elizabeth holding Nick's arm as they walked. Elizabeth waived past the guard at the entrance. The two Russian spies watched them going into the chalet.

Elizabeth introduced Nick to the Managing-Director of British Aircraft, who appeared to be waiting for him. He conducted Nick to a private room and closed the door. Elizabeth waited outside. The Managing-Director pointed to a stack of engineering drawings of an experimental attack airplane the company was designing for the Royal Air Force. He told Nick he understood his mission and would wait outside for him to take his photos.

A half hour later, having taken 15 shots of the drawings, Nick left the room. Elizabeth escorted him to the door. She said she was sorry they would not have any private time together during the next few days. He said the same thing, giving her a friendly peck on the cheek as he left the chalet. The Aeroflot employee and her companion were standing outside by the flight-line fence watching. So was a CIA agent.

An hour later, Elizabeth exited the chalet and took a taxi to Orly Airport for her return flight to London.

The rest of the afternoon was filled with meeting more foreign air force officers at the Century chalet. At 5:00 the team left and returned to the hotel. Up in his room Nick deposited the camera in the drawer as usual.

Thursday night's dinner, Butler was surprised to learn when the van arrived there, was at La Grande Cascade in the Bois de Boulogne—the same restaurant where he and Nicole had dined on Sunday. It felt good to be in a somewhat familiar setting. It was as strikingly beautiful as he remembered it.

The guest of honor was Prince Ali Sultan bin Abdulaziz, son of the Minister of Defense of the Kingdom of Saudi Arabia. Prince Ali was Chief of the Royal Saudi Air Force. The Saudis wore Western civilian clothes perfectly tailored on Savile Row. To honor the kingdom's Muslim requirements, Martin Stark had instructed no alcohol be served at the table. This was a particular hardship for Walt Gates who was deeply devoted to champagne. He would have to make do with Perrier.

Once again the business purpose of the dinner was to persuade this potential customer to purchase a quantity of Century's F-11s. This was done not-so-subtlety by Stark and Gates, each working off the other in a well rehearsed script extolling the virtues of the plane. Prince Ali appeared to listen intently, and near the close of the dinner over strong espresso he requested a Century team come to Riyadh to discuss the operational capabilities of the airplane with his staff. Martin Stark gave the order to Gates.

Meanwhile at the hotel Sergei Malanovsky entered Nick's room and found 15 frames had been exposed in the camera. He pocketed the camera, went down the elevator, got in the waiting car, and went to the Soviet Embassy. When the film was developed, the *Rezident* was once again impressed with the quality of the documents—engineering drawings of a powerful new attack aircraft being developed at the direction of the RAF by British Aircraft at a factory in the North of England. The authenticity of the material was unquestioned, as confirmed by the Soviet Air Force technical expert and by Malanovsky, who had personally observed Butler going into and out of the British Aircraft chalet earlier that day. The KGB Station Chief had a growing admiration for this young American industrial spy.

Malanovsky returned the camera, now fully loaded with fresh photos of the photos, to the drawer in Butler's room. The CIA "bellhop" observed his coming and going. He called Murray to report.

On Friday morning at 7:30, Walter Gates telephoned Nick in his room. Gates informed him there was a change of plans for Saturday night's dinner. Nick would not be needed to attend as Martin Stark and Gates had just arranged a private dinner meeting with a high-ranking guest whose name he couldn't reveal. No one else on the Century team would be present, so don't take it personally, Gates said as a joke. He wanted Nick to have this heads-up, he said, so he could make his own plans for the next evening—his last in Paris.

Unknown to Nick, Gates made the call at Dan Murray's request so the KGB listening post next to Nick's room would hear it through their phone tap as an authentic development. Murray coached Gates on how to phrase the conversation to set-up the KGB. Nicole Girard was going to be entrapped and Nick was going to be the bait. There was no "high-ranking guest." But this fabrication would appear legitimate to the KGB. Hearing this conversation, Malanovsky immediately reported it to the *Rezident*.

A half hour later the Century team assembled in the lobby and entered the vans. The routine was getting old for everyone. Upon arrival at the chalet, Nick went into the private room, removed the exposed film and palmed it to Randy Gilmore, who passed him a fresh roll of film, which Nick loaded in the camera. The rest of the morning was spent at the chalet like the others with one foreign air force team after another coming in for a talk or in some cases for a formal briefing on the F-11.

Right after they finished their buffet lunches, the team was surprised by the unexpected arrival of General Amir Toufanian, Chief of the Imperial Iranian Air Force. The general asked to meet with Martin Stark privately. They went into the side room. Their meeting lasted only a few minutes when Stark opened the door and asked Walt Gates and Randy Gilmore, the PR man, to come into the room. Stark asked Toufanian to repeat to the others what he had said.

The general spoke very formally: "His Imperial Majesty, the Shah of Iran, has given his approval for me to sign your Letter of Intent for 144 F-11 aircraft to be purchased by the Imperial government of Iran. He also authorized your company to issue a press release today to that effect." Stark and Gates rushed to shake the general's hand. Martin Stark stated his hope for a long and happy relationship between our company and your country. The general handed the signed Letter of Intent to Stark, dated that day. Stark ordered Gilmore to prepare a brief press release to announce the agreement exactly as General Toufanian just stated it. Stark ordered Gates to prepare to go to Teheran with a contract team to finalize the deal.

The four men then opened the side room's door. The entire Century team was waiting expectantly for an announcement. Martin Stark stated the government of Iran has committed to purchase 144 F-11 aircraft, representing the launch order for the entire production run. A cheer went up from the Americans, who realized their careers at Century had just been secured. Randy Gilmore was already at his typewriter.

About an hour later, after the celebrating simmered down, Rick Russell came over to where Butler was standing. Russell said he wanted to tell his former Air Force colleagues who now worked at General Aerospace the news about the Iranian order. Would Nick like to go with him to the GA chalet?

"Absolutely, General Russell."

Unknown to Nick, Martin Stark, acting on Dan Murray's request, had instructed Russell earlier in the day to find a way to get Butler into the GA chalet without causing a commotion. The Iranian news provided the opportunity.

It was a short walk to GA's chalet, located next to Century's. Nick noticed the pregnant Aeroflot woman and her companion watching them go in.

Once inside, Russell sought out GA's CEO, Seth McCoy. Russell introduced Nick to him. The CEO recognized Nick from the photo the CIA had given him. After a minute or two of polite conversation about Century's Iran deal, McCoy asked to speak privately with Nick, taking him into a separate room.

Closing the door behind them, McCoy pointed to a stack of engineering drawings lying on a table. He said he understood Nick's mission and GA was happy to assist. These documents had arrived that morning from the plant in Ft. Worth, Texas. The CEO left the room, leaving Nick to his task.

There were 20 engineering drawings. Each had the General Aerospace logo and was stamped "U.S. Air Force Secret" top and bottom. They appeared to be drawings of parts of the F-16, the USAF's new multirole supersonic fighter. Nick took a photo of each document, and then left the room, his camera in his pocket. Russell and Butler departed the GA chalet and returned to

Century's. The Aeroflot woman and her companion were watching. A *Deuxième Bureau* agent was watching them.

At 5:00 all the chalets shut down. Everyone headed to the main gate for their rides back to town. When Nick arrived at his room, he deposited the camera in the drawer as usual and fell on the bed, fully clothed, wondering what in the hell he was getting into. Oh well, he thought, not to worry. It's being done at the direction of the U.S. government.

At 7:00, now refreshed and in a different suit, Nick took the elevator to the lobby of the Prince de Galles. Gates was waiting with Warren Summers and Randy Gilmore. Gates told them the dinner that evening would be held at the hotel next door, the George V. A private dining room was reserved to entertain the delegation from the Republic of China, Taiwan. This would be an elegant and very Chinese dinner for Century's most important potential customer for the F-11.

As they walked along Avenue George V to the hotel of the same name, Gates told them preliminary discussions had been held in Taipei with the Taiwan ministry of defense, which expressed interest in co-producing a large number of F-11s for their air force. Now that the launch order from Iran was secured, Gates and Stark believed Taiwan might now be willing to make their own purchase. Tonight's dinner was with the commanding general of the Taiwan air force. Gates said this as the four men arrived at the front entrance of the grandest hotel in Paris. Martin Stark, getting out of his limo, joined them under the portico.

The Century team walked through the magnificent lobby to the hotel's main dining room. A maitre d' in white tie and tails led them to a nearby private dining room. The Chinese guests had already arrived and were drinking Scotch whiskey. They were wearing business clothes. Stark knew the Commander of the Republic of China Air Force, General "Stony" Lee, so he introduced his team. Like a lot of Chinese officers, General Lee had adopted an American nick-name. He introduced the four other members of his team. Everyone immediately found his place card at the round dining table and sat down, according to Chinese custom.

A liveried waiter brought in a round serving tray with ten individual tall shot glasses that looked like mini-beakers. Each glass was in an individual holder on the tray. The waiter filled each glass half way from a bottle of Johnny Walker Black, the favorite Scotch whiskey of all East Asians. The waiter placed the tray in the middle of the round table and stood by holding the bottle.

Martin Stark reached for the glass nearest him and invited the commander to do the same. Everyone at the table followed suit. Stark turned to the commander, on his right, and holding the middle of the glass in his right hand and his left hand supporting the bottom of the glass, spoke the traditional Chinese toast in the ceremonial manner, looking directly at his guest: "To your very good health, General Lee."

The general, holding his glass the same way, replied: "To your very good health, Mr. Stark."

Each man drained his glass.

Everyone at the table toasted the man on his right the same way using the same words, according to Chinese custom. The empty glasses were replaced in the round serving tray. The waiter immediately refilled them.

Stark wasted no time getting down to business. He announced to the Taiwanese leader that Iran had just that day committed to the purchase of 144 F-11s, enabling Century to begin a production run of the airplanes immediately.

The Taiwan commander reached for his shot glass and toasted Mr. Stark on his immense success. Stark toasted him back in thanks for his gracious comment. They drained their glasses, as did everyone else. The waiter immediately refilled the glasses. Nick realized this was going to be a very long night!

Stark told General Lee that Century would like to revise its offer to his air force in light of this major new development. He asked the general's permission to send a contract and production team to Taiwan in the near future with new and improved pricing and scheduling, based on the Iranian order.

"Our hope, General Lee," Stark concluded, "is that the Republic of China Air Force and Century Aerospace will be authorized by your government to build a manufacturing and assembly facility at CCK Airport to co-produce 300 F-11s over the next five years to strengthen your country's air defenses."

"I will gladly receive your team in Taipei in approximately two weeks. When I return to my hotel, I will telex Taipei and give the order," General Lee replied, nodding to one of his aides.

Stark then toasted General Lee for that important decision. The general toasted him back by saying, "Mr. Stark, you are a Friend of China, our country's highest compliment." All the Chinese officers stood and toasted Mr. Stark, saying "A Friend of China." The glasses were drained and refilled.

Walter Gates gave a signal to the waiter to begin serving food. The toasting continued throughout the meal.

Sergei Malanovsky continued his routine. He entered Nick's room, saw that film was exposed, and took the camera to the Soviet Embassy. After the pictures were developed, Alexi Mamanov once again was amazed at the richness of the material he was getting from this remarkable industrial spy, the authenticity of which was unquestioned. This was the third night of gaining technical data of the utmost importance from the Soviet Union's three most powerful Western enemies—France, Britain, and the United States.

It was clear to him the young American spy had accomplices assisting him inside each of these aerospace companies. He was more successful penetrating these companies than the KGB had been in years. Now Mamanov wanted to find out how many additional companies the man's network included and who his agents were.

To accomplish that he decided to put Nicole Girard back to work. Saturday evening would be a perfect opportunity for her to gain this information and hopefully penetrate his network.

Malanovsky returned the reloaded camera to Nick's room. A staff member took the Soviet Embassy's diplomatic pouch to Orly Airport, placing it on an Aeroflot flight to Moscow. The photos were in a sealed envelope inside the pouch. The envelope was addressed to Yuri Andropov, Chairman of the Committee of State Security, Dzerzhinsky Square, Moscow.

About midnight, Butler, Gates, Summers, and Gilmore returned to the Prince de Galles following dinner with the Chinese. They walked. The fresh night air was a blessing, sobering them up a little. After a dozen toasts throughout the evening, all with straight Scotch, Nick was more inebriated than at any time in his life, even at college fraternity parties. When he got to his room, he stripped, took two aspirin, and fell in bed.

Saturday morning arrived with a hangover. Nick took two more aspirin, pocketed the camera, and walked to the elevator, wondering what shape Gates, Summers, and Gilmore were in. He found out when he arrived in the lobby. They were amazingly okay and chuckled, looking at Nick's greenish complexion. Ah youth, the older men were thinking—they can't take it. As they boarded the van, a hotel waiter handed each man a paper cup filled with hot black coffee. Gates thought of everything.

This was scheduled to be the top executives' last day at the Paris Air Show. The senior people were returning to the States the next morning. Nick was glad he was being treated as a top-level member of the team so he could leave a day early. He was also glad he had no company dinner to attend that night.

Arriving at the chalet, he took the camera into the side room and removed the exposed film. As usual, he palmed it to Gilmore and took a fresh roll to reload in the camera.

The day turned out to be pretty boring except for a few spectacular flight demonstrations by the French and Russians. At no time during the day was Nick escorted to another chalet to take photos.

When 5:00 rolled around, everyone was more than ready to pack it in and head for the vans. For Nick it was a relief to have no commitments until his United Airlines flight to New York the next day at 1:00 P.M.

Chapter 7:
The Recruiter

Paris, France
June 21, 1975

Back now in his room at the Prince de Galles, Nick deposited the camera in the drawer, took off his clothes, and got in bed for a serious nap. About an hour later he woke up and took a hot shower. As he emerged from the bathroom, still nude, he heard a knock on the door. He grabbed the hotel-provided terrycloth bathrobe from the armoire and put it on. To his immense surprise it was Nicole. She was dressed casually in a skirt and blouse.

"Surprise!" she said, "glad to see me?"

"Well yes, very glad, and also surprised," he stammered. "How did you know I'd be here and not at a business dinner?"

"I didn't," she lied. "On the spur of the moment I took a chance you might be free for your last night in Paris."

"Well, you and I are both in luck. I was excused from tonight's dinner. I'm free for the evening."

"I'm so glad," she said smiling.

He led her to one of the chairs in the sitting area. He took the other chair and arranged the bathrobe around him. The chairs were upholstered, soft and comfortable, and had no arm rests.

"Would you like a drink?" he asked.

"Yes I would. But you stay there. I'll get the drinks this time." She went to the mini bar and took out two cognac miniatures and two snifters. She brought them to the table and poured the drinks.

"I can't get over seeing you again," Nick confessed as he raised his glass to her and took a sip. "Is there some special reason you took a chance to come see me tonight?"

She put down her drink, rose from her chair and stood in front of Nick, quite close.

"Yes, there are three special reasons," she purred. "I missed this," she said as she took his face in her two hands and held it for a minute, peering into his cobalt-blue eyes. "And I missed this," she said before kissing him on his lips. "And mostly I missed this," she said as she opened the robe and wrapped her hand around him.

"I missed this," Nick said with a catch in his voice as he slid his hand up her skirt. Without another word, he carried her to the bed.

The CIA case officer listening through the bug under the sitting area table called Dan Murray at the American Embassy: "Nicole showed up as we hoped and Romeo just scored with her. The plan is working."

"That was fantastic," Nick said still breathing heavily. "*You* were fantastic."

Nicole went into the bathroom, used the bidet, then returned to the bed. A few minutes later, he went into the bathroom and closed the door. Nicole rushed to the dresser drawer where she was told the camera was always kept. She found it and observed that none of the film had been exposed. She dashed back to the bed and whispered to the wooden headboard: "No film was exposed." Sergei Malanovsky next door heard her. So did the CIA agent, further confirming her status as a KGB spy. Both agents were recording everything.

Nick returned to the bed. They lay side-by-side for a little while without speaking. It was about 8:00.

"Are you hungry?" he asked.

"Famished. But I don't feel like getting dressed and going out. Do you?"

"No way. Why don't I order a plate of cold sandwiches and a couple of beers from room service?"

"Sounds wonderful."

Nick picked up the phone and placed the order. Malanovsky heard the call through the bug in the phone. The CIA case officer heard it, too. He immediately alerted the CIA "bellhop" of the opportunity to be the room service waiter and called Dan Murray.

When the food was ready in the hotel kitchen, the CIA "bellhop" delivered the tray to Nick's room. On the tray was a folded piece of paper with

Nick's name on the outside. Inside was a note Murray had dictated. The note read: "Nicole believes you are an industrial spy working for Century. Try to persuade her to become a member of your spy team. Dan Murray."

Nick and Nicole had gotten out of bed to prepare to receive the room service waiter. He put on the hotel robe. Nicole took the other robe from the armoire into the bathroom. Out of feigned modesty, she said she did not want to be seen by the waiter.

Shortly, Nick answered the knock on the door, letting the "bellhop" enter with a large tray. He went straight to the sitting area table, put down two place settings with napkins, then placed at the center of the table a large platter filled with a variety of cold sandwiches, each sliced into quarters. He asked Nick if he should open the bottles of beer. Nick said yes as he sat down on one of the chairs.

The "bellhop" slipped the note onto Nick's plate while Nick was signing the check. When Nick saw the note, the "bellhop" put his finger across his lips, indicating he should say nothing. Nick unfolded the paper and read the note. He looked at the "bellhop" with dismay but understood the message. He immediately realized the CIA was monitoring the activities in his room. He wondered why the CIA considered Nicole to be so important. His mind was swirling with questions as the "bellhop" took the note out of his hand, put it in his pocket, and left the room.

Nicole emerged from the bathroom wearing her robe and sat down on the chair facing Nick. She was smiling at him as she took a sandwich from the platter. He did the same, his mind reeling from the implications of the secret note he just read. Suddenly he felt exposed, naked, realizing that others had been watching or listening to his love-making with this woman. Yet, the message was clear. He had his orders directly from the CIA Station Chief himself: try to recruit Nicole to become an industrial spy for Century.

Nick shook himself out of his mental wandering and realized he had said nothing since Nicole sat down. He poured the two beers and, returning to his previous attitude, he toasted the most beautiful girl in Paris! Nicole almost blushed as they clinked their glasses across the table. They spent the next few minutes in idle chatter as they devoured a couple of sandwiches.

It was Nicole who opened the serious conversation with a casual question: "Did you learn a lot at the air show?"

He thought to himself, she did *not* ask if I had a good time at the show, the typical question, but did I *learn* anything at the show. This, he thought, was a good opening for him to work on his new assignment. But he realized he would have to proceed cautiously.

"Oh yes," he replied. "I met quite a few foreign air force leaders at the Century chalet and at the various dinners. Century even cinched a big order for their new F-11 with the Iranian government. I suppose you read about it in today's paper."

"Yes, that's wonderful news for your employer. Did you meet any of Century's competitors at the show?" she asked, knowing very well the answer having been briefed by the pregnant Aeroflot employee and by Sergei Malanovsky. This was a test on her part to see if he would open up to his real role at the show.

"As a matter of fact I did," he answered truthfully.

"Who did you meet?" she asked boldly.

"Oh, I was taken to the Toulouse chalet and a couple of others," he replied as he took another bite of sandwich.

"What others?" she inquired somewhat absently.

"British Aircraft and General Aerospace also let me into their chalets through some friends."

Nicole knew this information was truthful, Nick being open about his activities. So she pressed on, hesitantly.

"You must have some high-ranking friends to get into those forbidden territories," she said as a matter of fact, not as a question.

"Well, only if you consider a temp hostess at the BA chalet a high-ranking friend," he responded with a laugh. "She's someone I met a year ago at the Farnborough show where she also was a hostess for BA. We encountered each other here quite by accident and she invited me to see their chalet."

"How fortunate you happened to encounter each other," she said rather quizzically, concealing her knowledge of the truth of this statement as confirmed by Malanovsky. "How did you get into the General Aerospace chalet? Aren't they Century's arch enemy?"

"General Rick Russell wanted to share the news about Century's new deal with the Iranians with some of his old Air Force buddies who work there, so he took me along to their chalet."

Nicole was amazed at the easy way he was handling this conversation that recounted the most daring and successful industrial espionage she had ever heard of. She knew from Malanovsky that Nick's report of his comings and goings to the other chalets was genuine, but she did not believe for one minute the motives he stated. The real motive was industrial espionage. She decided to ease off from her interrogation.

Believing his open-faced recounting of his activities had convinced her of their innocent nature, he now saw an opening to begin recruiting her for Century.

"What are you planning to do with your degree from the Science Po?" he asked, changing the subject.

"Oh, I suppose I'll go to work for the French government in some capacity. That's what our graduates usually do. I'm not really sure what I'll do next."

"I don't want to get too personal, but can you make any real money working for the government?"

"Not really. But it's enough to keep body and soul together, I suppose."

"Have you considered working in the private sector? You seem to be interested in airplanes. What would you think about going to work for Toulouse or Dassault or one of the other French aerospace companies? Wouldn't they pay better than the government?"

"I've never really considered that as a career, though it is interesting to think about."

"That's my focus," he said honestly. "I'm really grateful I've had an opportunity to become acquainted with the top executives at Century Aerospace. I hope to join them on a permanent basis after graduation. As you know, this summer I'll work for them as an intern in their Washington, D.C. office."

"You seem to do very well for them."

"Oh, you don't know the half of it," Nick said with a grin.

"What do you mean by that?" she asked after a hesitation.

"I'm only an intern at the moment, but I've been given responsibilities that go beyond that—way beyond," he said with pride. "What I've been doing for Century here in Paris requires a lot of help from other people in other companies. What I'm telling you is very confidential, you understand."

"Of course I understand," she said moving forward in her chair. She was thinking her mission was about to be fulfilled—finding out the network he had working with him.

"At the moment I'm only a courier for the company. I pick up information that's been collected by others and deliver it to Century, but some day I hope to establish my own team of people working inside other companies."

"Oh, my God," Nicole exclaimed with false surprise. "You're some kind of spy!"

"No, I'm not a spy. I'm just a courier."

She didn't believe that for a minute but let on she did. "Isn't that danger-ous? I mean couldn't you get in a lot of trouble if you're caught?" she wondered aloud, trying to express concern for him.

"Not if you're careful and have the right people working with you." After a pause he asked, "Are you interested?"

This question was completely unexpected, taking Nicole by surprise. It was a vague job offer to spy for Century Aerospace.

"Well, I don't know," she stumbled to get some words out, not having any prior instructions from the *Rezident*. "I'd have to think about that."

"Well, think fast," Nick said, becoming assertive. "I leave for New York tomorrow and it would be helpful to know your answer before I takeoff at 1:00."

"Exactly what do you have in mind for me?" she asked tentatively.

"You will complete your education at the Science Po next year, as sched-uled," he began, rolling out a plan he was making-up on the spot. "During the coming year you should apply for a position at Matra, the big French missile company, or Thomson, the French electronics giant, and hope to be hired next June when you graduate."

"Why not Toulouse, Century's most important European competitor?"

"That's already covered," he replied mysteriously. "Century also makes missiles and airborne electronics equipment, so Matra or Thomson would be ideal."

"Well, I don't really know what to say," she replied honestly not having had any instructions for this sudden turn of events. She was impressed with the cool and professional way Nick was conducting this unexpected recruiting session that clearly put her on the spot.

They finished the sandwiches and beers during this part of the conversa-tion. Nick got up from his chair, very much the man-in-charge, and stepped over to her chair. He put his arm around her and lifted her from the chair.

"Why don't you sleep on it—with me?" he murmured as he pulled the robe off her and kissed her shoulder, her neck, behind her ear, and then her mouth. Kissing this gorgeous woman and feeling her warm body next to his, his hormones took control. He didn't care if the CIA was listening or watching. He was going to have her again.

While Nick and Nicole were making love for the second time that evening, Sergei Malanovsky in the next room telephoned Alexi Mamanov at the Soviet

Embassy to report the latest development: Nicole was being recruited by Butler to become one of his industrial spies. She had not given him an answer.

The *Rezident* was delighted with this sudden turn of events: he would order her to accept the offer. That would put her in the network that was being so incredibly successful penetrating industrial giants such as British Aircraft, General Aerospace, and Toulouse. Butler had specifically mentioned he needed agents at Matra and Thomson. That meant he was receiving no information from those two major French military contractors. Well, he thought, Nicole would be able to obtain their inside information—for the KGB as well as for Century Aerospace. Moreover, she would be in a position to funnel highly credible *dis*information to one of those firms and to Century and—this would be the great prize—through Century to the U.S. government whenever that proved to be useful to the Soviet Union.

All in all, he concluded, this was a most fortunate turn of events. We could fool the Americans and the French for years, he chuckled to himself. Nicole had suddenly become a highly valuable asset. The *Rezident* immediately telephoned Yuri Andropov in Moscow to report this immensely important news.

At the same time, the CIA case officer at the hotel's listening post phoned Dan Murray to report. He told Murray that Butler had been ingenious in handling the situation without any prior warning or direction. He made Nicole an offer to be one of his industrial spies at Matra or Thomson, and she's thinking it over. He said he wants her answer before he leaves for New York tomorrow afternoon.

"What's the current status?" Murray asked.

The agent put one of the earphones to his ear and listened for a few seconds. The sounds from the room were unmistakable. "At the moment," he answered, "Romeo is scoring again with Nicole."

"Okay," Murray said. "We've got to find a way for Nicole to get out of his room, even for a little while, so she can receive an order from her KGB superior to accept the job offer."

"Maybe she or the KGB will create that opportunity," the agent wondered.

"Or maybe Romeo will," Murray said. "If she's not out of the room within the next hour or so, we'll have to find a way for her to gracefully exit the scene."

Then Murray telephoned Andre Devereaux to relate the news. Devereaux was impressed with Romeo's skillful handling of the situation, creating a first-class opportunity to use a KGB agent for his own purposes. She would become a credible conduit for years planting disinformation into the Soviet Union at the highest level. He congratulated Murray on this achievement. He said he expected the KGB would order her to accept the job offer.

"When Nicole accepts Romeo's offer," Devereaux asked, "how do you propose to handle her activities in the future?"

"I think French Intelligence should take over using someone in Romeo's so-called network as her handler," Murray replied. "Wouldn't the Baron d'Artois be the perfect control for her?"

"Excellent suggestion!" Devereaux exclaimed. "When Nicole accepts the offer, we'll have Romeo tell her to come back to his hotel room in the morning to meet someone. He'll hand her off to the baron at that time within ear-shot of the KGB. Meanwhile I'll call the baron tonight and give him the game-plan. I'm certain he'll agree to do it. After all, he's a Hero of the French Republic and this will be an important new opportunity for him to help both France and his Century Aerospace employer."

Nick and Nicole finished their love-making and relaxed into each other's arms. Her mind was starting to come to grip with the need to communicate with her KGB superiors—to accept Nick's offer or not. She had to get out of his room, she realized, but he wanted her to spend the night. On a personal level, she wanted to stay, too.

Nick, on the other hand, was calmly basking in the sexual after-glow. He was satisfied with the way he had executed Murray's order to recruit Nicole. It was now her problem, but he decided to help her solve it.

He looked at the clock by the bed. It was 10:30.

"It's getting late, Nicole," he whispered into her ear. "And I've got to get up early to do some final Century business and get ready for my flight home. What do you say we turn out the light and get some sleep?"

She saw the opening he had given her. "Why don't I let you get a good night's sleep—by yourself," she murmured sweetly in his ear. "I'd love to stay the night, but you need your rest. Besides, I've got a lot of thinking to do before you go to the airport." She kissed him tenderly, holding his face in her hands. It was a kiss she didn't want him to forget. She got up, went into the bathroom, then returned to the bedroom and dressed.

"Will you call me in the morning?" he asked.

"Of course I will. What would be a good time?'

"8:30 or 9:00 would be good," he answered. By now she finished dressing and was walking toward the door. Nick got up and walked with her. It was the same scene as last Sunday night after their dinner date: her dressed and him nude, saying good-by at the door. He kissed her tenderly and said good night. He closed the door behind her.

Nicole walked down the hall to the adjoining room. Sergei Malanovsky was waiting with the door open. She entered unseen. Malanovsky had the *Rezident* on the telephone. Mamanov ordered her to accept Nick's job offer when she phoned him in the morning. With that decided, she went to her apartment.

Nick quickly put on some clothes and quietly left his room. He took the elevator to the lobby and used a pay telephone to call Dan Murray at the Embassy for instructions. Murray was relieved Nick had thought to avoid using the phone in his room and quickly informed him it had been bugged by the KGB. Nick said he'd suspected that. Murray congratulated Nick on his artful handling of the recruitment and assured him Nicole would telephone in the morning to accept his offer.

"What do I do then?"

"In the morning when Nicole phones," Murray instructed, "ask her to return to your room at 10:00 for instructions. She will agree to do this. I want the conversation to take place in your room because the KGB will be listening and the discussion must be credible to them."

"I understand," Nick said, now realizing the KGB had also listened to this love-making with Nicole.

"There's more." Murray added, "Do you remember the Baron d'Artois?"

"Of course."

"The baron is going to come to your room also. He will arrive just before 10:00. You will introduce him to Nicole as a member of Century's industrial espionage network, working within Toulouse. Tell her the baron will be her contact in Paris during your absence. Tell her he reports to Century at a high level and will be the one who gives her instructions."

"Okay," Nick said.

"The baron will leave your room first and Nicole second—so you can give Nicole a final kiss good-by alone with her. Is everything clear, Nick?"

"I've got it," Nick said as he hung up. The "bellhop" case officer working in the lobby observed Nick talking on the phone and also observed no one else was watching. He called Murray to tell him that.

The next morning unfolded exactly as Murray predicted. Nicole called Nick at 8:30 to accept his offer. He asked her to come to his room at 10:00 for instructions. At 9:45 the Baron d'Artois knocked on Nick's door. Nick and he had a carefully worded conversation in the room, knowing the KGB was listening. At 10:00 Nicole arrived. Opening the door, Nick gave her a little kiss and ushered her in.

"Nicole," Nick said with great formality in French, "permit me to introduce you to Georges Marceau, the Baron d'Artois. The baron is the head of the Century Aerospace team here in Paris. Monsieur le Baron, this is Nicole Girard."

Nicole said, *"Enchante, monsieur le baron,"* extending her hand. She recognized him from photos the KGB took of Nick and him entering and leaving the Toulouse chalet at the air show.

"Enchante, mademoiselle," the baron said kissing her hand.

Switching to English so the KGB listeners would be sure to understand it, Nick said: "I've just been telling the baron about your willingness to work undercover for Century Aerospace after you graduate from the Science Po, assuming you get employment with a major French defense company."

"Yes. I would like to do that. Is there a particular company that would be most appropriate?" she asked the baron.

"Well, mademoiselle," the baron replied, "I suppose Thomson would be the most interesting one, given their product line in military electronics is in direct competition with part of Century's. Does that interest you?"

"Very much. Their offices are in Paris and I prefer to remain here."

"I've given the baron your telephone number so he can be in touch with you from time to time to give you instructions," Nick said to Nicole. "In my absence from France, he will be your contact. He may also be helpful getting you a job at Thomson next spring. He's personal friends with their top people." The baron handed her his business card.

"Please feel free to phone me if there is anything I can do to assist you, mademoiselle," the baron said. The baron then said how much he was looking forward to his association with Nicole. He said bon voyage to Nick and left the room.

"You will enjoy working with Georges," Nick said as he closed the door. "He's very well connected as you can imagine."

"I noticed the rosette of the Legion of Honor in his lapel," she said. "He's a French hero, so how does he justify working for a foreign company, I wonder?"

"Like everyone else, he has to make a living and Century provides a very good one, as you will find out."

"I certainly am grateful to you, Nick," leaning forward giving him a kiss. "This has been an amazing week for me getting to know more about you. When do you have to leave for the airport?"

"In about a half hour."

"Well, in that case, I've heard of an American expression and wonder what it means. Could you take a moment to explain it to me?" she asked innocently as she held him by the waist.

"I'll try. What's the expression?"

"A quickie," saying it with a straight face. Nick doubled over with laughter. Nicole went directly to the foot of the bed, pulled up her skirt, and took off her panties. Nick was still laughing as he dropped his pants in front of her. A minute later the American explained a 'quickie' to the French girl.

The CIA agent at the listening post roared with laughter as Romeo scored again. Sergei Malanovsky learned the meaning of a new American term.

At Orly Airport, Nick checked in at the United Airlines ticket counter. Walking toward the departure gate, an American gentleman in a dark suit began walking beside him.

"Nick," he said, "will you please come with me. Dan Murray wants to speak with you."

Nick and the agent entered a secure area of the airport and walked down a long corridor to a metal door. The agent knocked. The door opened. Murray was standing there with a Frenchman.

"Nick," Murray said, "I want to congratulate you on your brilliant work this week. And my colleague here also wants to congratulate you. This is Andre Devereaux, head of the French intelligence bureau. We've been working together all week on this operation."

"Nick," Devereaux said shaking his hand, "I am personally delighted to meet you. Your performance this week was first class. You have done much to improve the future security of France, the United States, and all of NATO."

"I'm flattered. Thank you for your compliments. During most of the week all I knew was to obey Mr. Murray's orders, but I certainly didn't know *why*."

"Your innocence made your performance highly credible, Nick," Murray explained. "This week you firmly established in the KGB's mind that you are Century's industrial spy. The airplanes you photographed were bogus designs from the three leading NATO countries. You don't know it but the KGB lifted those films from your room and duplicated them for use by the Russian design bureaus."

"So that's why I was taking photos of airplane parts," Nick realized.

"That's exactly right, Nick. Those false designs will disrupt their work for many years. At any rate," Murray concluded, "Andre and I wanted to thank you personally for your excellent work in a very important operation. We also suspect it wasn't a total hardship for you."

Nick almost blushed with the knowledge that Murray and perhaps also Devereaux were listening to his love-making. "You're right, Mr. Murray, part of it was a pleasure."

"I'll relieve you of your mini-camera now, Nick. You'll be issued another one in D.C. if it's needed." Nick handed it over.

The secret meeting ended. Nick boarded his flight to New York after an unforgettable week in Paris.

Chapter 8:
The Apprentice

Moscow, U.S.S.R.
June 21, 1975

High up in his office in the Lubyanka Building on Dzerzhinsky Square in Moscow, Yuri Vladimirovich Andropov finished studying the reports and the Russian language translations of the tapes sent by his *Rezident* at the Soviet Embassy in Paris. He was pleased with the week's successes at the air show where he gained a bonanza of highly important aircraft information from three major Western companies. His professional respect for the young American industrial spy deepened as he read the dialogue of his recruitment of one of his own agents.

This was perhaps the greatest achievement of the week: having a KGB agent planted inside a major French defense company. The flow through this woman of valuable information and the counter-flow of bogus intelligence could last for years. This fortuitous turn of events reinforced his belief that women are the best spies, being able to manipulate men almost at will. Nicole Girard was highly adept in her handling of Butler.

He walked over to the window to look out on the square below, admiring the hulking bronze statue of "Iron Felix" in the center of the square. He thought to himself how much the KGB had grown in importance since Felix Dzerzhinsky headed the forerunner of today's KGB.

While standing there, Andropov arrived at a decision. He would order the Stasi to artificially inseminate the other East German woman with the second batch of Nick Butler's sperm. Andropov wanted another person to inherit Butler's natural espionage skills to grow up to become a KGB agent. This child would be brought to the Soviet Union to be raised under his direction at the state orphanage near Leningrad. Nick's first child was already scheduled to grow up in the United States to become a sleeper agent for him.

Returning to his desk, Andropov made another decision. He ordered the start of an op using his top double-agent in the United States, an American under the control of the *Rezident* at the Soviet Embassy in Washington, Anastas Kamarovski. He ordered Kamarovski to have "inside channel," the double-agent's code name, initiate contact with Nick Butler while he is working this summer in Washington as a Century Aerospace intern. Knowing now that women are Butler's vulnerability, he directed the *Rezident* to have "inside channel" use an attractive young woman mole as the contact to steal more aerospace intelligence from this excellent industrial spy.

He also decided not to send Sergei Malanovsky to Washington to continue shadowing Butler. He knew "inside channel" had enough resources already.

Thus, the KGB's op and CIA's Stealth Gambit both now centered on Nick Butler as he returned to the United States from Paris.

New York City
June 23, 1975

Butler's United Airlines flight landed at JFK early on Sunday evening. He took the shuttle bus to the East Side Airline Terminal in Manhattan, and from there he took a cab to his apartment on 120th Street. It was good to be home, among familiar things. Liam Erickson was in his room studying when Nick walked in.

"Hi Liam," Nick said as he came through the door, "I'm home."

"Well, well, the prodigal son returns," Liam said getting up from his desk and clapping his hands around his roommate's shoulders. "How was your trip, Nick-boy?"

"Fascinating," he replied as he walked down the hall to his room to unpack.

A few minutes later Liam came into Nick's room and suggested going out for dinner.

"Great idea. I've come to detest airplane food. I didn't eat anything on the plane. Let's go."

The two friends had a pleasant meal at their favorite inexpensive restaurant. Over dinner Nick recounted the many foreign air force and industry people he met at the Century chalet and at the five business dinners. This impressed Liam no end. Nick never mentioned Nicole or Dan Murray.

The next day, Monday morning, Nick reported for work at the Institute as usual. He was greeted warmly by Anna Suzuki and Bill Reynard, who asked how he enjoyed the Paris Air Show. He said it was the thrill of a lifetime he would never forget and that the Century people couldn't have been nicer—including him in everything even though he was only an intern.

They were chatting for about a half hour when Stephen Dyson and a conservatively dressed, serious-looking middle-age woman arrived at Reynard's office. Dyson ushered Nick and Reynard into the windowless room. He closed the door. Then he introduced Nick to Mrs. Susan Samuels, Assistant Deputy Director of Operations, Central Intelligence Agency. Reynard already knew Samuels.

After everyone took a seat in the crowded room, Dyson said the Agency was very pleased—no, highly impressed—with Nick's performance in Paris. He turned the meeting over to Susan Samuels.

"Nick," she opened, "all of us at the Agency appreciate the work you did in Paris. It was first-rate in every respect. Your handling of the bogus aircraft designs from the three aerospace companies was excellent, but your recruitment of Nicole Girard was masterful, given the fact you had no prior warning of the need to do that. You certainly can think on your feet!" she said.

"Well, I just did what Dan Murray told me to do," Nick replied modestly.

"You did it with great credibility because you did not know that Nicole Girard is a KGB agent," Samuels stated. "That information was deliberately kept from you to help you maintain your innocent appearance."

"Well I'll be damned," Nick murmured. "Nicole's a Russian spy! I can hardly believe it. She was so genuine—so real—to me. There was nothing fake about her."

"Yes, she is a superbly trained agent," observed the CIA senior executive. Samuels went on to give Nick an appreciation of the importance of that recruitment. Nicole will be a credible conduit for many years of disinformation from French Intelligence to the KGB. French Intelligence will of course be in charge of this operation. She told him his recruitment of Nicole was a major Cold War success as she thanked him again.

"Wow," Nick said, feeling very proud.

"Now before discussing the next phase of your assignment, I want to emphasize the vital importance of your continuing to appear to the KGB as Century

Aerospace's industrial spy," Samuels cautioned. "That cover story provides your best assurance of performing the upcoming tasks successfully and, more importantly, of ensuring your personal safety. The KGB must never get even a hint you work for us and not for Century. Otherwise the risk to you is very great. Do I make myself absolutely clear on this point?"

"Yes ma'am," Butler replied with a lump in his throat.

"Very well," she continued. "Later this week you will move to Washington, D.C. to continue your internship at Century Aerospace. We expect Nicole will be sent to D.C. at some point during the summer on one pretext or another to resume contact with you. That's why I told you who she works for. You will need to remain very convincing to her about your role as Century's industrial spy. Never let on you know who she works for and that you work for the Agency. Is this understood?" she demanded.

"I understand," Nick said, feeling more threatened than at any time in his life.

"I certainly hope so. During the summer your assignment will be to provide the KGB with disinformation about U.S. companies' technical advancements. We will provide you with the documents we want them to have from a highly credible source, namely you. Are you very sure you're okay continuing in this role?"

"I'm okay with it," Nick replied, feeling ill-at-ease and looking shaky.

Samuels handed him a slip of paper with nothing on it but a phone number. "Check in with me periodically at this number. Call any time day or night from anywhere in the U.S.," she directed. "Identify yourself with the code name 'Romeo'."

After Samuels and Dyson left the brownstone and got into the waiting Agency car, Samuels said she certainly hopes Butler will remain convincing with the industrial spy pretense because if the KGB discovers he's an Agency asset, Yuri Andropov would disregard all the disinformation material Nick funneled to him and would undoubtedly take revenge against him for the deception.

"How serious is the risk to Butler if his Agency role is discovered?" asked Dyson.

"Knowing Andropov's ruthlessness, it would be fatal for Butler," she replied. "You remember how savagely he put down the Hungarian Revolution. Because Nick's very life is at risk we must keep a close watch on him to be certain he continues to perform in D.C. as well as he did in Paris."

Washington, D.C.
June 28, 1975

On Friday of that week Nick relocated to Washington, D.C. Liam Erickson, who was continuing to work with Professor Hazard for the summer and knowing of Nick's internship in Washington, had sublet Nick's furnished room for the summer to a college buddy from Wisconsin who was interning at a company in New York. Nick was relieved he would not have to pay double rent for the next three months.

Arriving at Washington's Union Station on a muggy Friday afternoon, Nick took a taxi to the Arlington Hyatt where Century was putting him up for a week until he found an apartment. The hotel was a couple of blocks from Century's office building on Wilson Boulevard in Rosslyn, Virginia, on the south side of the Potomac River across from Georgetown.

After he unpacked, Nick walked across Francis Scott Key Bridge into Georgetown, familiar territory for him having been raised in suburban Maryland and having high school friends who went to college at Georgetown University. Hoping to get lucky that night, he knew the best Georgetown hangouts for picking up girls. He went straight to the "1789," a French restaurant. The main floor of the restaurant was a formal dining room. The basement level was a bistro that was, as the college kids called it, a real meat market.

Though the university was closed for the summer, the bistro was crowded with college-age students. He found a vacant bar stool and ordered a beer. Surveying the room through the cigarette smoke and noise, he saw any number of cute young women seated at tables with their girl friends. How nice it was to be back in his home territory. The guy seated next to him got up to join friends who came down the stairs and took a table.

The bar stool didn't stay vacant for long. A pretty brunette about his age, probably a graduate student like himself, came through the door, surveyed the scene, walked over to the bar, and sat down on the empty stool next to Nick. She ordered a manhattan on the rocks and lit up a cigarette.

"You know those aren't good for you," Nick said to her, taking a sip of his beer.

"I know, but I like to smoke," she said without being defensive.

"Oh, I was referring to the manhattan," Nick said with a grin.

She had to chuckle at this obvious pickup line as she turned to look at him.

"Do you have much success with that line?" she asked.

"Only if the girl has a sense of humor. And it appears you do. You're talking with me."

"So I am," she said, smiling. "I'm Sonja."

"I'm Nick."

"Well, Nick," she said as she carefully looked him over and liked what she saw, "what's the next line: 'your place or mine?'"

"Am I that obvious?" he asked with feigned embarrassment.

"Well, it certainly would cut through a lot of useless BS."

"Your place or mine?" Nick asked, flashing his killer smile. She had to laugh.

"Okay. Mine is on O Street, just a few blocks away. Where's yours?"

"I'm staying at the Arlington Hyatt in Rosslyn."

"That settles it. Mine's closer," she announced as she finished her drink and reached for her handbag to pay her check. Nick had already put money on the bar to cover both checks. He slid off his bar stool and helped her off hers. They headed to the door after less than five minutes of conversation.

After they had sex, they lay together quietly on her king-size bed. She asked if he was just traveling through D.C., staying at a hotel. He told her he was interning for the summer at an office in Rosslyn and needed to find an apartment. She suggested trying for a sublet in Georgetown. Many graduate students were looking for temporary tenants for the summer. Go to the student housing office at the university and check the bulletin board, she suggested.

They continued chatting for a while. Neither was in a hurry. She was giving him time to recover, waiting to see if he was up for another round. To find out, she nestled closer to him, resting her hand on his muscular chest. After a minute or so, she slowly slid her hand across his washboard abs and down. He was ready.

Before Nick left her apartment, she gave him her phone number and asked him to call anytime. She liked his directness, she told him.

The next day Nick walked from the hotel back to Georgetown, going to the university's student housing office as Sonja suggested. More than a dozen 3x5 cards were stapled to the bulletin board advertising summer sublets. The ones near the university he wrote down. This part of Georgetown had always appealed to him.

After checking out a few apartments that had already been rented, he struck pay-dirt. It was a nicely furnished studio apartment in a small building on N Street, half a block from one of his favorite restaurants during his college years, Martin's Tavern on the corner of N Street and Wisconsin Avenue. He figured he'd stay in Georgetown and walk across Key Bridge everyday to the Century office in Rosslyn. It was only a mile and he needed the exercise. Besides, the apartment was a block away from Sonja's on O Street. He moved in early Sunday morning.

Nick continued to feel unnerved by the dire warning Susan Samuels gave him at their meeting in New York. He needed to do something about that feeling—to restore his self-confidence for his own safety. Though not a religious person, he walked the two blocks from his new apartment up the hill to P Street where he remembered there was a church. He entered Georgetown Presbyterian Church in time for their Sunday 11:00 A.M. service and prayed for God's help and protection in his new more dangerous Agency assignment.

After the service, he found a pay phone and called his mother, asking her to come into town for dinner with him that evening at Martin's Tavern. She was happy he'd called and said she was eager to see him after such a long time. She brought his younger brother. They had a delightful evening as Nick regaled them about his time in Paris. His mother was especially interested in the restaurants and the food; his brother asked a lot of questions about the airplanes.

That same day in East Berlin, the Stasi obeyed Andropov's orders. The second East German woman was artificially inseminated with the second batch of Nick Butler's sperm. Her name was Brigitte Schaeffer, age 23. The following March she gave birth to a healthy boy she named Stefan Schaeffer. A year later he was taken from his mother to a state orphanage near Leningrad to be raised to become a KGB agent. Unknown to him, Nick Butler now had two sons, both destined to become Soviet spies.

Century Aerospace's Washington Office
Rosslyn, Virginia

Early Monday morning Nick left his new Georgetown apartment, walked across Key Bridge to Rosslyn, and entered the high-rise office building at 1000 Wilson Boulevard where Century Aerospace has its Washington, D.C. office. The building directory listed Century on the 14th floor. Other aerospace companies' offices were also listed on the directory. He took the elevator up and was greeted at the 14th floor's reception desk by a cheerful young secretary with a thick southern accent. He gave his name.

"Oh yes, Mr. Butler," she acknowledged. "Mr. Gates is waitin' for you in Mr. Stanley Ebersol's office. Just go down this hall all the way to the end to the double doors," she said, pointing in that direction.

He walked down a long corridor past a series of offices that faced the outside of the building. All the offices had glass doors off the hall. At the far end of the corridor was a glass double door. As he approached the doors he saw Walter Gates talking with another man. He knocked and opened one of the doors.

"Hello Nick," Gates turned and greeted him with a hearty handshake. "How's the boy?"

"I'm fine, Mr. Gates, thank you."

"Nick," Gates said turning to the other man, "this is Stan Ebersol. He's the Corporate Vice President in charge of Century's Washington Office. Stan, meet Nick Butler."

"Pleased to meet you, sir," Nick said to the heavy-set, bald man in his early 60s.

"My pleasure, I assure you, Nick," Ebersol replied. "Walt told me about your attendance at the Paris Air Show two weeks ago. You made quite an impression on him and Martin Stark."

"Thank you, sir."

Ebersol waived Nick to a chair in the sitting area where the three sat down. Coffee was brought in by a secretary. Ebersol took over the meeting.

"Walt informs me you will be an intern for the summer here in Century's Washington Office," Ebersol stated. "This is a decision Martin Stark himself has made. That's fine with me. While you are here you will work under my direction as my assistant. No one in the office will give you assignments but me. Understood?"

"Yes sir."

Ebersol went on to say: "I also understand you will have a special role, performing tasks a little unusual for a typical Century intern. That's also okay with me. All I need to know about those activities is when you come and go. I have a company obligation to be cognizant of my employees' whereabouts. I don't need to know the substance of the work you will be doing. Is this understood?"

"Yes sir."

"Good. Now my secretary, Gladys, will show you to your office for the summer. It's next door to mine. She will also be your secretary." He buzzed for Gladys to come in. She escorted Nick back through the glass doors into the adjoining office.

Gladys gave him a company badge, showed him how to use the phone, and made sure pads of paper and pens were already in the desk. She left him alone to get comfortable in his new, luxurious surroundings. In the credenza behind a cabinet door, Nick discovered he had a safe with a combination lock.

The office had an outstanding view of Washington, D.C., looking down across the Potomac River at the Lincoln Memorial, the Mall, the Washington Monument, and in the distance the Capitol Building. The sight was truly breathtaking.

Minutes later, Gates walked into Nick's office, shut the door and sat down.

"Stan does not know of your connection with the Agency," Gates said. "He was told you will be performing some extracurricular activities for the company under Martin Stark's personal direction. We have to keep it that way by direction of the Agency. Only Martin and I know your real role."

"I'm happy to be here and will do whatever I'm asked," Nick responded, feeling a little mysterious and not knowing what else to say.

"Your Century duties begin today with a bang," Gates then said. "You and I are going to the State Department right away for a 10:30 meeting with the Assistant Secretary of State for Near East and South Asian Affairs. We need State's approval for our sale of 144 F-11s to Iran. We've requested an export license to negotiate a formal contract in Teheran next week. Since you were present in Paris when Gen. Toufanian announced the Shah's approval of the sale, I thought you should be in on the U.S. government part of the transaction. Okay with you?"

"More than okay with me," Nick replied enthusiastically. "I've never been to the State Department."

"Well, get used to it. You're going to go there a lot. In fact, this afternoon at 3:00 we have another appointment there. That one's with the Assistant Secretary of State for East Asian and Pacific Affairs. We need his approval to renegotiate the Taiwan F-11 co-production deal you heard about in Paris at the George V dinner with General Lee."

Gates checked his watch, got up from his chair, and said, "Let's go."

A company car and driver were waiting for Gates and Butler by the elevator in the building's garage. The motor was running in the black Ford Crown Victoria. Another man from the Washington Office was already in the front passenger seat. As they sat down in the back seat Gates introduced Nick to Graham Wolf.

"Graham is the Washington Office's liaison with the U.S. Departments of State and Defense," Gates told Nick. Graham leaned over the seat and shook Nick's hand. "Graham, as you already know, this is Nick Butler, our summer intern."

Each man said to the other, "Pleased to meet you."

The drive across the Potomac River on the Theodore Roosevelt Bridge into Foggy Bottom took only ten minutes. During that time Nick asked Gates about Stan Ebersol's background. Gates told him Stan is the former Comptroller of the Defense Department and before that he was Staff Director of the Senate Armed Services Committee. Needless to say he's very well connected politically, added Gates.

They arrived at the C Street entrance of the block-long, non-descript building. The driver pulled onto the curved driveway where the three men got out at what is officially named the State Department's Diplomatic Entrance. Graham Wolf led the way into the building and up to the reception desk.

Department of State
Washington, D.C.

The reception area is a large, two-story-high room the interior side of which has a glass wall facing an open-air courtyard enclosed by the four sides of the building. Flags of the nations with which the U.S. has diplomatic relations hang from the top of the glass wall. Nick had seen the room many times on TV news shows, being a favorite backdrop for reporters interviewing foreign dignitaries.

Graham Wolf flashed his permanent government ID card and asked for two visitor badges for Gates and Butler. Seeing they were both Americans, the receptionist asked for their drivers' licenses and then recorded their names and license numbers in her log book. Non-U.S. citizens are required to present their passports, Wolf told Butler.

After passing through security and walking toward an elevator, Gates informed Nick that Graham Wolf is a retired U.S. Army colonel whose career was in military intelligence. "He speaks three foreign languages fluently: French, German, and Arabic." Gates added with a chuckle, "His English is pretty good, too."

Nick was impressed and said so to Col. Wolf. Nick commented that for his Columbia Ph.D. he has only a two foreign language requirement; for him they are French and Italian.

The elevator took them to the sixth floor where the office of the Assistant Secretary of State for Near East and South Asian Affairs is located, directly below the office of the Secretary of State on the seventh floor.

Wolf spoke to the receptionist at the center of a large suite of offices. She buzzed the Assistant Secretary. The three visitors were escorted through a series of inner offices until they arrived at the Assistant Secretary's office on the corner of the building. Wilfred Gerlach, the Assistant Secretary of State, rose from his desk to greet them.

"Hello, Graham," Gerlach said, extending his hand.

"Hello, Mr. Secretary," Wolf said. "You remember Walter Gates, Century's Senior Vice President for International Business."

"Of course, hello Walt," Gerlach said, shaking Gates' hand.

"And may I introduce Century's summer intern, Nick Butler, a Columbia grad student?" said Wolf.

"How do you do, Nick," Gerlach said extending his hand.

"Pleasure to meet you, Mr. Secretary," shaking his hand.

"Please take a seat, gentlemen," Gerlach said as he indicated the sitting area that surrounded a large coffee table. An aide entered the room and took a seat behind Gerlach. "What can I do for you today, Graham?" the Assistant Secretary asked.

Graham Wolf began his prepared speech: "Century Aerospace has been honored by the Imperial Government of Iran with an invitation to Tehran to negotiate a contract for 144 of our new F-11 jet fighters. That government signed a Letter of Intent at the Paris Air Show, a copy of which is in your office, and we now seek an export license to go to Tehran to negotiate the final contractual terms and conditions. Last week we filed the request for the license with your office. Walt Gates is prepared to lead a team there next week with the Department's approval."

Gates immediately added: "The Iranian purchase is the kick-off order for us to go into full-scale production of the new airplane. Other governments are also interested in the F-11 and are waiting for us to finalize the Iranian order before they commit to their own purchases."

"Can you tell me who the other governments are?"

"Taiwan will likely be the next olive out of the bottle," Gates announced. "Korea or Saudi Arabia may come after them, though we are a ways away from a deal with those countries."

"Taiwan and Korea are both in the East Asia Bureau's domain, as you know Graham," Secretary Gerlach observed. "Yet, the consequence of the Iranian order on an impending deal with Taiwan is germane to my decision. I'm pleased to learn this. Will you brief the EA Bureau on this prospect, which I personally consider to be a positive development for the United States?"

"At 3:00 this afternoon we will brief EA," Wolf answered.

The Assistant Secretary then stated to Graham Wolf: "My office has already coordinated your export license request with the Department's Bureau of Politico-Military Affairs and the Office of Munitions Control. They approved the license. The coordination with the Defense Department resulted in a 'no objection,' which as you know is their way of granting approval. When you brief my colleagues in the East Asia Bureau, you can inform them that the Near East and South Asian Affairs Bureau granted Century Aerospace an export license to negotiate your contract with Tehran," Gerlach announced as he gave a signal to the aide.

"We are most grateful, Mr. Secretary," Wolf and Gates said almost in unison.

Secretary Gerlach concluded the meeting: "The start of production of this new, inexpensive, yet high performance jet fighter is a major development. It will be a powerful new addition to our foreign policy tool kit. This bureau is pleased to be in at the launch. Thank you, gentlemen, for coming in today. I wish you success in Tehran, Walt."

As the three men walked out of the Secretary's office, the aide said to Wolf the formal export license will be ready this afternoon. He can stop by and pick it up after his meeting with the EA Bureau.

They left the building. Wolf waived to the driver who was parked down a side street facing the building's entrance. The car quickly arrived at the curved driveway where the three got in. Once inside the car, Gates and Wolf let out a war whoop. They realized with this production go-ahead their careers at Century are now secure for the next 20 years!

Gates told the driver not to go back to the office in Rosslyn but to go to The Palm Restaurant off Connecticut Avenue. He wanted to celebrate. He said lunch is on me. Graham Wolf got on the car phone calling Stan Ebersol at the Washington Office to give him the good news. He knew Ebersol would immediately phone Martin Stark at Century's headquarters in Los Angeles to report this all-important positive development.

Arriving at The Palm, Gates told Graham and Nick this will have to be a one-martini lunch given the fact they have the 3:00 appointment back at the State Department with the East Asia Bureau. When they were seated, Gates ordered a round of martinis. When they arrived, Gates toasted the F-11: "Long may it be in production!" They clinked glasses. Everyone ordered a steak and salad, The Palm lunch specialty. Nick wondered if every day would be so terrific.

At 2:45 they arrived back at the State Department's Diplomatic Entrance. They went through the same check-in routine and took the elevator to the sixth floor where the office of the Assistant Secretary of State for East Asian and Pacific Affairs is located, around the corner of the building from where they had been earlier.

After they sat down with the Assistant Secretary, Graham Wolf informed him the Near East Bureau had granted the export license for Iran—Secretary Gerlach having asked him to deliver that message. The Assistant Secretary said he appreciated that information and was likewise prepared to grant Century an export license to negotiate the co-production contract with the Taiwan government. All necessary coordination had been completed with no objections. That license would be ready for pick up tomorrow.

Gates and Wolf thanked the Assistant Secretary and left his office. They walked down the hall to the Near East Bureau and picked up the signed export license for Iran. All in all, this was a red-letter day for Century Aerospace.

Century Aerospace
Rosslyn, Virginia

Upon their return to the Century office, the three men were congratulated by Stan Ebersol, who told them Martin Stark was very pleased. Gates phoned Stark, his direct boss, in Los Angeles and told him he had already organized a contract negotiation team and was prepared to fly to Tehran the following Sunday to begin negotiations.

Stark told him he called General Toufanian to pass along the export license news and to prepare to receive Gates and his team. Stark said he also instructed Randy Gilmore to issue a press release stating that Century and the government of Iran were in negotiations for the purchase of a large quantity of F-11s with the approval of the U.S. Government. Stark speculated the company's stock would get a bump up the next day.

"When you return from Tehran, Walt," Stark said finishing the phone conversation, "I want you organize another team to go to Taiwan right away to cut the co-production deal with General Lee. It looks like your passport is going to get a workout!"

When he hung up, Gates related to Ebersol and Butler what Stark said. He concluded by saying the company is on a roll. Stan and Nick couldn't have agreed more.

Ebersol ordered everyone in the Washington Office to come to the large conference room for a major announcement. He told Gladys to break out the champagne he had stocked for this occasion. Celebrating continued through the rest of the afternoon.

Before he left the office at 5:00, Nick phoned Sonja to ask for a dinner date at Martin's Tavern at 7:30. He said he has some late-breaking news to celebrate.

"See you there," she said.

Georgetown
Washington, D.C.

It was hot and muggy that June day in Washington. Walking across Key Bridge was a real effort. When he arrived at his apartment, Nick stripped off his damp clothes and took a cool shower to freshen up for his date with Sonja. He dressed casually in a Navy blue short-sleeve polo shirt, khaki pants, and sneakers.

They arrived at Martin's entrance on Wisconsin Avenue at the same time. She was wearing a cool-looking sleeveless tan blouse and matching skirt.

"You look terrific," he told her.

"You don't look so bad yourself," she said, admiring his muscular arms.

They decided it was too hot to sit on the outdoor patio facing N Street, so they went into the restaurant through its two sets of double doors and immediately appreciated the air conditioning. The restaurant, at the corner of N Street and Wisconsin Avenue, had window booths facing both streets and tables situated in the middle of the room. A long mahogany bar took up the interior wall space. The atmosphere was that of a neighborhood Irish pub—casual and friendly.

A waiter conducted them to a window booth. He told them this is the "proposal booth." It's where John F. Kennedy proposed marriage to Jacqueline

Bouvier. The waiter added with a smile looking at Nick: "Not to put any pressure on you, sir!" They sat down facing each other across the narrow wooden table with high wooden backs to the benches. It was very private. The waiter asked what they want to drink.

"A manhattan on the rocks please," Sonja answered.

"The same for me please," Nick said. The waiter walked over to the bar to place the order. Nick asked if she'd like an hors d'oeuvre. He said Martin's serves particularly good Chesapeake Bay oysters on the half-shell, and their Little Neck clams on the half-shell are also excellent. Sonja said she prefers clams.

When the waiter brought the manhattans, Nick ordered the clams and oysters. They settled back in their booth with their drinks for their first real date. Nick thanked her for the suggestion to go to the student housing office. He found a nice studio apartment half a block away on N Street.

"You said on the phone you wanted to celebrate. Okay, what are we celebrating?" she asked.

"Today I was at the State Department with my boss at Century Aerospace when the government approved the company's export of its new jet fighter," Nick cheerfully told her. "This is a huge success for Century that launches production start-up of the new airplane."

"Let's drink to Century Aerospace," Sonja proposed, raising her glass.

"To Century," Nick said. After they took a sip, Nick continued: "The really interesting thing about this approval today is that I was in on the start of the Iran deal at the Paris Air Show two weeks ago." Nick told her in general about the dinner at Maxim's with the Iranians. "Today was the second installment of that story. I find the business fascinating and feel really fortunate to be in the midst of it," he admitted to his date.

"Well, then, here's to you," Sonja said, raising her glass.

"Thanks," Nick said with a chuckle as the waiter served the hors d'oeuvres. He ordered another round of drinks along with their dinner order. Both asked for the grilled fish.

After a little pause, he said, "You know, Sonja, we have not formally introduced ourselves. I don't know your last name. Mine is Butler. What's yours?"

"It's Dahl," she answered. "It's spelled D-A-H-L."

"It's a fairly unusual name, but I've heard of it before. There's a famous political science professor at Harvard, Robert Dahl. Is he your father?"

"No. My father's name is Richard. He lives in Chicago."

"Are you a political scientist?" he asked.

"Well, I sort of am. My undergrad degree was in political science at Northwestern. Now I'm studying in the Foreign Service masters program here at Georgetown."

"My undergrad degree was also in political science—at Penn. Are you planning a career in the Foreign Service?"

"That's the plan at the moment," she answered with a worried look. "I don't really know how things will turn out."

At that moment the waiter arrived to clear away the hors d'oeuvres plates and serve their dinners. They both ate quietly for a few moments and then continued their conversation about their careers and how well political science prepares them for whatever they finally do. Nick mentioned that Martin Stark, Century's CEO, had pointed out to him that governments are customers for many companies' products, and political scientists are experts at understanding governments. Working in industry might be another career path for her, he suggested, as he hopes it will be for him.

As the conversation and the dinner came to an end, each sensed the other was ready to move on to the next event. Nick asked for the check, paid it, and they got up from the booth. At the double door, he turned to her and once again asked with a smile, "Your place or mine?"

"They're about the same distance, N Street and O Street. What size bed is in the studio apartment?"

"It's a single bed."

"Then it's my king-size bed again," she declared as they began walking toward O Street and her apartment.

She had left the air conditioner on in her apartment, so when they arrived it was pleasantly cool after their muggy walk. As soon as she closed the door behind them, Nick took her in his arms and began kissing her. After a few minutes, they fell onto the king-size bed.

Century Aerospace
Rosslyn, Virginia

The next morning, as Nick walked down the hall to his office, Stan Ebersol waived at him through the double glass doors to come into his office. He had some news.

"On Saturday evening there will be a black tie dinner at the Mayflower Hotel's grand ballroom," Ebersol announced. "This is the annual bash of the international aerospace community. It's an elegant affair with senior representatives of the world's leading aerospace companies in attendance. I want you to go with me as part of the Century team."

"Thank you, sir," Nick replied. "It'll be an honor."

"You'll need to rent a tux if you don't have one," Stan added. "So you might want to go to a tux shop today and get fitted. Normally Walt Gates would go with me, being the international VP, but he'll be leaving for Tehran the next day from Los Angeles, so he won't be available. Oh, also you can bring a date, if you know anyone you'd like to bring. Mrs. Ebersol will be with me."

"I do know someone. I'll ask her if she's free Saturday night," Nick replied as he left to go into his office to call Sonja. She immediately accepted his invitation and confessed she will have to start shopping like mad for a proper evening dress.

When he hung up from Sonja, Graham Wolf knocked on his glass door. "Want to tag along with me to State, Nick?" he asked. "I'm going to pick up the Taiwan export license from the EA bureau."

"You bet," Nick replied walking out the door to join Wolf.

Department of State
Washington, D.C.

A KGB agent observed Butler and Wolf entering and leaving the Department of State. An agent's car was always parked on 21st Street, a side street facing the State Department, from which the agent could observe people entering and leaving the building's Diplomatic Entrance. This was the third time in two days the young man had been marked. The agent knew who Wolf was but the man with him was new.

Telephotos of him were taken, later developed at the Soviet Embassy on 16th Street, and then put in the diplomatic pouch going to Paris on the overnight Air France flight. In Paris the pouch was transferred to an Aeroflot flight to Moscow where the photos were taken to KGB headquarters on Dzerzhinsky Square. There they were matched with other photos already on file. The man in the photos was quickly identified as Nick Butler, industrial spy for Century Aerospace. This was the first time he had surfaced since the Paris Air Show.

Yuri Andropov ordered Anastas Kamarovski, his *Rezident* at the Soviet Embassy in Washington, to track him and to be certain that "inside channel" had assigned one of his female agents to connect with him. Kamarovski assured him he had. He assigned an agent to tail Butler to further develop the file. The agent went to Century's office building in Rosslyn, waiting for Butler to emerge at the end of the day.

At 5:15, Butler came out of the building and walked to Key Bridge. The agent followed at a distance. He tailed him to a Georgetown apartment building on N Street where Butler entered. He watched the windows from the street and shortly Butler was seen at a window on the second floor pulling closed a drape. The number of the apartment was easily identified from the names on the lobby mailboxes. The agent returned to the Soviet Embassy to file his report, giving Nick's address and apartment number. The *Rezident* ordered a phone tap installed there the next day while Butler was at work.

Century Aerospace
Rosslyn, Virginia

When Butler and Wolf returned from the State Department to the Century office, Nick dialed the number Susan Samuels gave him the previous week in New York. He felt it was time to update her on his activities. A male voice answered with the words "code in." He hesitated a second and the voice repeated "code in." Then Nick remembered to say "code in: Romeo."

"One moment," the voice said. The line went dead for about a minute.

"Hello Nick," Susan Samuels said as she turned on a recording device and a speaker phone in her office at CIA Headquarters.

"Hello, Mrs. Samuels," Nick said. "I'm calling to give you an update on my activities since arriving in D.C. last Friday."

"I've been expecting your call. Go ahead."

"First of all I moved into an apartment in Georgetown," giving the address. "I've been to the State Department with Graham Wolf three times and on the first two visits also with Walter Gates. We've obtained export licenses for Iran and Taiwan for the F-11 airplane."

"You've been to State three times?" she wanted to confirm.

"That's right. Twice yesterday and again this morning."

"Go on," she ordered.

"Mr. Ebersol invited me to attend the International Aerospace Association's ball at the Mayflower Hotel on Saturday night. It's black tie."

"I know about the ball," she said. "All the major companies will be present, as well as senior military and Administration officials. Will you take a date?"

"Yes."

"What's her name?"

"Sonja Dahl, spelled D-A-H-L," he replied.

"Have you known her for a long time?"

"No. I met her Friday night at a college hangout, the '1789'."

"How did you meet her? Were you introduced by a friend?"

"No. She sat next to me at the bar and we started talking." At this point Samuels both admired Nick's pickup skills—but feared he had been marked.

"Have you seen her since then?"

"Yes, we had dinner together last night. And today I invited her to the ball at the Mayflower."

"And she accepted?"

"Yes."

"What do you know about her? For example, where is she from?"

"She's from Chicago. Her father's name is Richard. He lives in Chicago. She graduated from Northwestern with a major in political science. She's enrolled in the Foreign Service masters program at Georgetown."

"She sounds interesting," Mrs. Samuels observed guardedly. "This is an excellent report. You've made great progress in only a few days. I want you to call me again at 5:15 this afternoon from a telephone other than the one in your office. Incidentally, have you installed a telephone in your apartment?"

"It's being installed this afternoon. The landlady is going to let the phone company in."

"Excellent. Call me at 5:15." She hung up.

CIA Headquarters
Langley, Virginia

Samuels turned to the two agents who had been listening to the phone conversation.

"What do you think? Was he marked by this Sonja Dahl?" she asked them.

"It's certainly possible, but at the same time he might have been living up to his code name," a male agent observed.

The other agent was more skeptical. She suspected Dahl is an agent, having accepted an invitation to a formal ball after having only two dates with Butler. "That's an expensive commitment for a woman that none of my girl friends would have agreed to after only two dates."

"I want a full background check on Sonja Dahl," Samuels ordered. "This is high priority. I want to know who she's working for. It's certainly not us. If she's working for the KGB, how did she know he arrived in D.C. as of last Friday? I want his phone tapped today. Please alert the FBI to get on it. Tell them it's a national security priority so we won't have to wait for a court order."

"Given the fact he's been to the State Department three times, there's no doubt the KGB has marked him," observed the male agent.

"This is in fact good news for us," Samuels said. "We can keep playing the same game we did in Paris using Romeo as the conduit to Andropov. Let's get a game-plan ready for Romeo for the ball on Saturday night," she ordered. "I think Wilshire Aerospace should have a turn to provide disinformation for the next installment of Stealth Gambit."

Samuels took the elevator up to the seventh floor to Admiral Philip Myers' office. She quickly explained to her boss the opportunity before them to plant more bogus aerospace technical information in the KGB's hands through what they believe is a credible source, the industrial spy Nick Butler. It's time, she thought, to provide them with a major prize—a stealth design. The drop will be made Saturday night at the aerospace ball. For this op she needs Wilshire's help.

Myers readily approved the plan and asked his secretary to place a call to Robert Grossman, Wilshire Aerospace's CEO at his office in Burbank, California.

Grossman's secretary answered the call and buzzed him: "Admiral Myers, Deputy Director of the Central Intelligence Agency, is on line one, Mr. Grossman." He picked up the receiver, punched the lighted button on the phone, and said, "Hello."

"Hello, sir," Myers said into the phone, being careful not to use a name. "Before you say anything I want to be certain we are on a secure line."

"We are not," Grossman replied. "I'll call you back immediately on my red phone. I have your number." Both men hung up. Seconds later Myers' red phone rang.

"Hello," said Myers, following security protocol.

"This is Robert Grossman," the other man said. "I'm on a secure line. What can I do for you, Admiral?"

"We need Wilshire's help with a classified activity we are undertaking. It involves providing disinformation to our friends on the other side that looks credible but is in fact false and misleading. We hope to send their fighter aircraft designers down a blind alley that will tie them up for years. At the same time we would also like to convince them American industry is way ahead of them in a key area of aircraft technology. We need your help ginning up such data. Are you with me, sir," Myers asked.

"I follow you very clearly," replied Grossman. "It will be our pleasure to provide expert technical material that will meet your twin objectives: credible looking advanced technology that is false and misleading."

"Correct. Thank you for your cooperation," Myers said. "We will need that technical data in the form of a roll of film from a Minolta mini-camera. The roll of film will be passed by one of your people to my agent at the aerospace ball on Saturday evening at the Mayflower Hotel in Washington. Our man will get it into the bad guy's hands soon afterward."

"Understood," said Grossman. "I'm planning to attend the ball myself. How will my man know your agent?"

"He will be introduced to you at the ball by someone known to you. My agent's name is Nick Butler. Be sure your man with the film recognizes Nick Butler."

"Very well," said Grossman, jotting down the name. "Is there any particular type of fighter design you prefer?"

"Yes," said the Admiral. "We particularly want to mislead them with respect to stealth technology. I'll leave the details entirely in your hands, Mr. Grossman. After all, you are the expert."

"Some rather intriguing thoughts are already coming to mind. I'll meet with my design staff immediately. I'm certain our chief engineer will come up with something useful for your purposes. Good-by, Admiral."

Century Aerospace
Rosslyn, Virginia

At 5:15 Nick dialed Samuels' number from a phone in another office. He said, "code in: Romeo" when the voice answered.

"Hello, Nick," Susan Samuels said after a short pause. "Here's what I want you to do. Tonight after you get home from work I want you to telephone Sonja Dahl and chat. Use the telephone in your apartment that was installed today and give her your new phone number. Reconfirm your date for the aerospace ball and give her some logistics, like what time you'll pick her up in a taxi and so forth. Also while chatting, you should mention an idea for an outing on Sunday afternoon—something that will keep you out of your apartment for several hours with her. Have you got it?"

"I've got it. That won't be a problem."

"While you're at the ball on Saturday night, someone from Wilshire Aerospace will slip a roll of film in your pocket or will hand it to you discreetly. This will be done in the men's room. Ask Sonja to excuse you from your table to use the men's room at some point during the dinner. When you go there linger over a wash basin. The Wilshire man will silently approach you and make the pass. Understood?"

"Sounds easy and I already know what to do on Sunday afternoon. We'll go boating if the weather's nice."

"When you return to your apartment Saturday night, put the roll of film in a drawer, just like in Paris. When you go boating Sunday, leave the film in the apartment. On Monday, when you go to work at Century, take the film with you to the office. Someone will pick it up. One more thing, Nick, the KGB is no doubt aware you are here in D.C. and probably has bugged your apartment phone. So have I. So be aware of that as you use it."

"Thanks for the warning," he said with a gulp.

Georgetown
Washington, D.C.

At 5:30 Nick left the office and walked to his apartment. He dialed Sonja's number on his new telephone.

"Hi Sonja," he said. "It's Nick. I'm calling on my new telephone. It was installed in my apartment today. Can I give you the number?"

"Of course, what is it?" she replied, getting a pencil and paper. He gave the number.

"I'd like to thank you again for going with me to the aerospace ball Saturday night at the Mayflower. Did you find a dress today?"

"I looked in two shops but nothing seemed right. So I'll go out again tomorrow. I'm sure I'll find something nice."

"I'm sure you will," he said encouragingly. "Incidentally, I'll pick you up on Saturday in a cab at 7:00. Is that okay with you?"

"That's fine. I'll be ready."

"Oh, by the way, I have an idea for Sunday if you're still speaking to me after the ball on Saturday night," he said with a chuckle.

"Oh, I imagine we'll still be speaking on Sunday," she said with feigned seriousness. "What's the idea?"

"Do you like to go boating?"

"Boating? What kind of boating?"

"Well, I thought on Sunday afternoon we'd rent a canoe at Fletcher's Boat House and paddle around on the Potomac for a few hours. It's a great way to work on our tans. I'll pick up some drinks and sandwiches and we'll have a little picnic at a neat spot I know up the river. We'll probably be out all afternoon. How does that sound?"

"It sounds lovely," she said enthusiastically.

"Good, then it's a date?" he asked seriously.

"It's definitely a date," she said laughing.

The KGB took note that Butler would attend the aerospace ball at the Mayflower Hotel on Saturday evening and that the apartment would be empty on Sunday afternoon. Kamarovski assigned a male and a female agent to attend the ball as part of the Sukhoi Design Bureau's delegation. He reported by coded telex to Andropov in Moscow.

Mayflower Hotel
Washington, D.C.

Nick was swamped with Century work that week, and so he didn't have a chance to see Sonja until the following Saturday when he picked her up at 7:00 to go to the ball. The taxi waited as he went up the steps to her building and rang the bell at her door. She opened the door immediately.

She was ready. She stood inside the doorway and slowly twirled a full circle to model her chic new dress. When she completed her spin to face him, she smiled and asked "How Do I Look?" repeating Audrey Hepburn's famous line from "Breakfast at Tiffany's."

Her evening dress was fabulous: sleeveless black silk with thin silk cords over the shoulders holding up a gathered bodice and a partly bare back. The dress was taken in at the waist to show off her perfect figure and cut just below the knee. Her brunette hair was artfully swept up high on her head. A pair of large gold hoop earrings framed her face. She looked "stunning," which is exactly the word he used to answer her question as she reached to pick up her black lace wrap and a tiny black purse that matched her peau de soie shoes. Smiling, he leaned over to kiss her lightly on the cheek, then handed her an orchid for her wrist.

"You look pretty good yourself, Nick," she said, admiring him in his rented tux. They went down the building's front steps and got in the cab for the short ride to the Mayflower on Connecticut Avenue.

At the hotel a doorman opened the taxi door for Sonja while Nick paid the driver. Entering the hotel, they walked down a long carpeted corridor until they arrived at the grand ballroom. An orchestra was playing dance music as waiters circulated among the hundreds of guests with trays of cocktails. The setting was elegant. A full-scale replica of the Wright Brothers' airplane was suspended from the ceiling, and flags of the nations represented at the ball were arrayed behind the head table. Low bouquets of flowers decorated each round table of eight, giving the room splashes of color.

Nick sighted Stan Ebersol and steered Sonja, holding his arm, toward him.

"Hello Mr. Ebersol, may I introduce my friend, Sonja Dahl. Sonja, this is my boss at Century Aerospace, Mr. Stanley Ebersol."

"I'm delighted to meet you, Sonja," Stan said meaning it as he admired the strikingly beautiful young woman in front of him. "May I introduce my wife, Sarah," Stan said to Sonja. The women shook hands. "And this, my dear, is the famous Nick Butler, the young man I've told you about from the Paris Air Show who is now my summer intern."

"I'm happy to know you, Nick," Mrs. Ebersol said, admiring his good looks.

"I'm happy to meet you, Mrs. Ebersol," Nick replied. Nick then offered to buy everyone a cocktail as a waiter passed by.

"Thanks anyway, Nick, but tonight is on Century Aerospace. What would you like to drink?" Stan asked them. They both ordered manhattans. The Ebersols ordered white wine.

The foursome continued chatting when Seth McCoy, the CEO of General Aerospace, walked over to them. He recognized Nick from his chalet at the Paris Air Show and of course he'd known Ebersol for years.

"Nice to see you again, young man," McCoy said to Nick shaking his hand. Turning to Ebersol he said, "This young fellow made a brief but powerful impression on me at our chalet in Paris. Any chance I can steal him away from Century?"

"No chance," Ebersol said with a laugh. "He's mine." The General Aerospace CEO chuckled and moved on to his table, joining his associates.

"That was a very nice compliment to you, Nick," Sarah Ebersol observed.

"It certainly was," agreed Stan.

Ebersol noticed the Wilshire Aerospace party entering the ballroom. The day before Ebersol had received a phone call from Walter Gates in Los Angeles asking him to introduce Nick to Wilshire's CEO while at the ball.

Remembering that, Ebersol asked the ladies to excuse Nick and him for a moment. He said he wanted to introduce Nick to the famous Robert Grossman. The two walked over to Grossman, who was accompanied by several gentlemen on the Wilshire team. Ebersol and Grossman were old friends. Stan shook hands with Grossman and introduced his intern, Nick Butler.

"How do you do, Mr. Butler?" said the ever-formal Grossman, recognizing Butler's name from Admiral Myers' phone call.

Robert Grossman was the dean of American aerospace executives, having served as Wilshire's chief executive longer than any other company's CEO. Wilshire was also the largest aerospace company in the world. Grossman's manners were impeccable, as was his tailor-made Savile Row tuxedo. He was as close to being an English lord as an American could get.

"How do you do, Mr. Grossman?" Nick replied formally.

Grossman then introduced Nick to each of his associates, all stag. They shook hands. Nick wondered which of these men would rendezvous with him later in the restroom.

Ebersol and Nick returned to the ladies and sat down at Century's table. Four other people joined them shortly: two U.S. Air Force generals with their wives. Century, it seemed to Nick, is always in a marketing mode. How shrewd of them, he thought.

The typical banquet routine soon began. An MC welcomed everyone on behalf of the International Aerospace Association. A Boy Scout led the pledge of allegiance, which of course only the Americans were expected to make. A pastor offered a brief invocation prayer, and then dinner was served. The orchestra played throughout. To Nick, the food was fine but nothing like what he'd had in Paris.

After dessert was cleared away, the speeches began. During a break between speakers, Nick asked to be excused. He got up from the table and slowly walked to the men's room. He noticed a Wilshire Aerospace man got up from his table.

In the men's room, Nick stood before one of the dozen or so sinks and slowly washed his hands. When the Wilshire man arrived, he went to the sink next to Nick. Nick took a cloth towel from the attendant. The Wilshire man took one also and turned facing Nick, putting his back to the attendant. He dropped a roll of film onto Nick's towel. Nick palmed it and put it in his tux jacket pocket in one smooth move. It seemed no one noticed the pass.

Each man returned to his table. The KGB couple at a table in the rear of the ballroom noticed the coming and going of Nick and the Wilshire man. They suspected a drop had been made. The CIA agent knew the drop was made. He had been in the men's room watching.

When the banquet ended, Nick and Sonja left the ballroom and walked down the hotel's main corridor to the Town and Country Bar, the famous watering hole at the Mayflower, for a night cap. The room was crowded with the after-dinner crowd but they found two bar stools together. Nick ordered cognacs. They chatted about the dinner and enjoyed their drinks. After about a half hour, Nick said he thought taxis would have become available again after the earlier crush. They strolled to the main entrance and asked the doorman for a taxi. He blew his whistle; a Yellow Cab drove up. Nick gave the driver Sonja's address as they got in.

Georgetown
Washington, D.C.

Arriving at her apartment, they embraced for the first time that evening. They hadn't made love since Monday and both were eager to get started. Sonja declined his offer to help with her dress, saying it was a little complicated. She had it off in about 30 seconds.

He had started to undress, having pulled off his shoes and socks. His jacket was already hanging on the back of a chair. Sitting on the side of the bed, he was taking out the shirt's cuff links. In bra and panties she came over to help him. She slipped the suspenders off his shoulders, untied the bow tie, took the studs out of his tux shirt and helped him out of it. He pulled off the T-shirt. They were more than ready as they fell on the king-size bed. Nick spent the night.

Sonja woke up first, around 9:30 on Sunday morning. She let Nick sleep a little longer. She put on a robe and went to the kitchen to start the coffeemaker. The coffee smell woke him up. She came to the bed, gave him a sweet kiss, and went into the bathroom. He lay there for a while, then got up, found his briefs, and went to the kitchen for coffee. She joined him shortly, sitting at her little kitchen table.

"How about some bacon and eggs?" she suggested.

"All that and you cook, too?" he teased.

"I'm a pretty good cook as long as the meal is simple, like bacon and eggs."

"Sounds good to me. I'm famished."

After breakfast, Nick said he needed to go to his apartment to shower and dress for their canoe trip. He put on the tux pants and T-shirt for the short walk. He gathered up the rest of the tux outfit and gave her a little peck good-by.

"I'll be back around 11:30 or so," he said as he left. He checked: the film was in the tux jacket pocket.

As he approached his apartment building on N Street, he noticed a white van parked across the street. He remembered seeing it for the past few days.

He entered the building and went up to his apartment. He placed the film in the bureau's top drawer. He shaved, showered, put on fresh briefs, tan shorts, and a light-weight red T-shirt. He laid down on the bed for a few minutes to figure out how he should handle the next move, given he was under surveillance by two first-class intelligence agencies. That thought gave him the creeps.

He decided to use his new phone, knowing who was listening, to reconfirm for the KGB the arrangements for the afternoon. On the phone he asked Sonja if she was ready to go boating. She said she'd be ready in about 15 minutes. He reminded her they would be on the water for several hours. He told her there's some serious sunshine out there today so she should bring sunscreen.

Then he picked up the throw from the bed and put it in a shopping bag. It would be the ground cloth for their picnic. He put on his sneakers without socks and his red Philadelphia Phillies baseball cap. He'd been a Phillies fan since entering Penn, given his home town, Washington, had no baseball team. He left the building for the short walk back to O Street. An FBI agent followed. His task was to find out Sonja Dahl's address and take photographs of her.

A few minutes later a KGB agent got out of the white van, entered Nick's building, picked the lock on his apartment door, and took the roll of film. The agent drove the van to the Soviet Embassy to process the film, just like in Paris. Two hours later the photos of the photos were back in Nick's bureau. The prints were put in the Soviet Embassy's diplomatic pouch and taken to Dulles Airport for an afternoon flight to Europe. Stealth Gambit was underway again.

Sonja opened her door dressed in pink shorts, a matching pink halter top, and sneakers—perfect boating attire. The FBI agent photographed her as she came out of the building and went down the front steps. The couple walked south on 34th Street toward the Potomac River, making a stop on M Street at a deli to pick up sandwiches and a cold six-pack of Cokes. Then they made their way down the hill, across the C&O Canal to the river's edge where Fletcher's Boat House was located, next to the boat house of Georgetown University's crew.

Nick rented an aluminum canoe and a Styrofoam chest which the boat house manager filled with ice to keep their lunch cold. Nick and the manager moved the canoe to the edge of the floating wooden landing. Sonja got in and sat on the forward seat. Nick and the manager pushed the canoe further into the water. Nick jumped aboard. He sat on the rear seat, facing Sonja. The manager shoved them off. Nick began paddling down river.

It was a perfect summer afternoon. The temperature was in the mid-80s, the humidity was unusually low, and the sky was clear except for a few white puffy clouds. The river was calm. Sonja looked fresh and beautiful sitting in front of him. Occasionally she dipped her hand in the water as Nick expertly steered the canoe. They passed under the high arches of Key Bridge and floated down river to Roosevelt Island. As they drew parallel to the island, now a national park, they looked above them at Roosevelt Bridge, which connects Rosslyn to Washington.

"A lot of people think the bridge and the island are named for FDR," Nick said. "In fact both are named for Teddy Roosevelt. Do you know why?"

"I have a feeling you're going to tell me," she said teasingly.

"It's because on hot summer afternoons President Theodore Roosevelt and his close friend the French ambassador—his name was Jusserand—used to ride their horses down to the river's edge over there," he said pointing to a sandy area on the shoreline, "take off their clothes and skinny dip over to this island to cool off."

"I suppose that was the equivalent of air conditioning in those days," she observed. "You sure know your history, don't you?"

"Well, I was born here and a lot of history just sort of seeped in."

Nick steered the canoe around Roosevelt Island and turned up river. Now he had to paddle more aggressively going against the current. After a few minutes he began to sweat. He put the paddle down, took off his cap and pulled off the T-shirt, tossing it into the shopping bag. He put the hat back on. As he resumed paddling, Sonja watched his muscles ripple with each stroke of the paddle. She enjoyed the sight of his fabulous body that she knew so well. Seeing it in broad daylight was a whole new experience. It was turning her on.

They continued up river for about an hour until they arrived at a place just below Great Falls—an isolated cove on the Maryland side of the tree-lined river.

Nick steered the canoe directly onto a sandy bank shaded by the overhang of a large tree. The front end of the canoe lifted out of the water. He stepped past Sonja and jumped onto the shore. From there he pulled the canoe half way out of the water. He effortlessly lifted her 115-pound body out of the canoe onto dry land. Then he pulled the canoe completely out of the water so it wouldn't drift away.

Sonja realized this was the neat spot he had mentioned on the phone. It was secluded, tree-shaded, and inviting. No one was around. She heard the sound of the waterfalls in the distance and birds chirping in the surrounding woods.

"When I was a Boy Scout," he said, "my troop used to canoe on the river. We found this spot by accident one day and always returned to it. We used to build a camp fire over there," pointing to a sort of fire pit formation in the rocks. He pulled the throw from the shopping bag, spread it out on a grassy area, and then brought the cooler from the canoe, placing it beside the throw. They stretched out on the throw to have lunch.

Sonja, still enjoying the sight of his bare upper body, moved close to him on the throw. He reached for the cooler.

"First things first," she said kissing him while stroking his upper body. Nick got the message. They made love in the warm open air under the canopy of a blue summer sky. Nick's Boy Scout dream came true.

KGB Headquarters
Moscow

When Yuri Andropov saw the pictures of Wilshire's technical drawings, all marked Top Secret, he gasped. This could be one of the great intelligence achievements of his career, he thought to himself. He called for his Soviet Air Force technical advisor to come into his office to give his assessment. After studying the photos, the colonel stated in a thick voice, "The Americans are developing stealth aircraft."

"What does that mean? Does that give them an advantage?" demanded the ruthless Chairman of the KGB.

"If they are able to build aircraft with stealth capability," the colonel stated, "our radar will not be able to detect them as they penetrate the Motherland's air space. They will have an overwhelming advantage in air combat."

"Do you mean our air defense radars and our anti-aircraft missile systems that we just completed at a cost of tens of billions of rubles will be nullified?" a horrified Andropov demanded.

"That is exactly what I mean, comrade Chairman."

"Then we must learn more about the Americans' intentions for using this technology. Finding out their operational plans is now our highest priority. Meanwhile, turn these drawings over to the Sukhoi Design Bureau to get started on our own stealth airplane," ordered Andropov.

Century Aerospace
Rosslyn, Virginia

On Sunday mornings a cleaning company sends a crew of char women to Century Aerospace's office suite in Rosslyn. They perform the usual tasks: emptying trash, vacuuming carpets, dusting furniture, and so forth. One of the women was a substitute for a regular who had become ill that morning. The substitute was assigned the cleaning duties in the executive suite, Ebersol's office and the ones next to it. In the office adjacent to Ebersol's she saw a name plate on the desk. It read "Nick Butler." She discovered the office has a safe in the credenza.

Without being obvious she took a tiny microphone out of her cleaning cart and inserted it in the phone on that desk. Later, she put a small transmitting device in the rear of the janitorial closet behind a stack of paper towels. That device would pick up the signal from the phone bug and transmit it to a listening post the KGB established in a neighboring office building.

Later that day she reported to Anastas Kamarovski that the bug was in place. She also reported that Nick Butler must be very important to Century Aerospace because his office is closest to that of the Vice President in charge. This added to Butler's credibility in the eyes of the *Rezident*. To the Russian, office locations are a sure indicator of one's level of importance.

On Monday morning Nick arrived at Century's office at the usual time, 9:00. At 10:00 the receptionist buzzed him. She said in her charming Southern accent that a messenger has a package for him that requires his signature. Nick told her to send him to his office. The messenger walked down the hall. Nick saw him coming toward him through the glass door.

The messenger waited in the hall, indicating Nick should come out of his office. After the messenger closed the door behind Nick, he handed him a manila envelope and asked him to sign for it. As Nick was signing the receipt, the man said, "Susan Samuels asked me to say hello. Do you have something for her?" Nick reached in his pocket and produced the roll of Wilshire film, handing it and the signed receipt to the man. The messenger departed without another word.

The envelope contained a single piece of plain paper. Typed on it was the following: "Your office telephone has been bugged by the KGB and there may be additional listening devices in your office. Be careful what you say. Phone me at 3:00 today from another office. Destroy this piece of paper." The message didn't need to be signed.

Chapter 9:
The Double-Agent

Century Aerospace
Rosslyn, Virginia

At 3:00 Butler dialed Susan Samuels' number from an empty Century office down the hall from his. A voice said: "Code in."

Nick hesitated for a second then remembered to say: "Code in: Romeo." When Samuels came on the line, she directed him to meet her after work. Her instructions were precise: leave the Century building at 5:00, take your usual route toward the Key Bridge Marriott, walk up the driveway and enter the hotel. Go through the hotel to the rear parking structure and exit on the second level where a black car will be waiting. The driver will be the delivery man from this morning. Get in the front passenger seat. He will take it from there.

"Would you recognize the delivery man from this morning?" she asked.

"Yes."

"Good. He's my assistant. His name is Elliott Peterson. See you later."

At precisely 5:00 Nick left the office and followed her instructions. Two men who looked like they might be CIA agents were in the Marriott lobby watching to see if he was followed. He wasn't. Nick went to the parking structure's second level and found the black car waiting with its motor running. He recognized the driver, Elliott Peterson. As soon as he closed his door, the car started moving.

Elliott maneuvered the car out of the parking structure, entering Lee Highway going west. Soon he merged onto George Washington Parkway. After a few miles he pulled into a parking area with a scenic view overlooking the Potomac. At that hour of day there were no sightseers. The lot was deserted except for a single black sedan. Elliott parked next to it. He told Nick to get in the other car—enter the back seat behind the driver. "Susan Samuels is waiting for you in the back seat," he said.

"Hello, Nick," she said after he sat down and closed the door.

"Hello, Mrs. Samuels."

"I'm sorry for the cloak and dagger routine," she said, "but it's necessary. You must not be seen with me by the KGB as that would blow your cover story and endanger you. We have much to discuss and I didn't want to put you at risk or jeopardize the operation by using a phone that might be tapped. We're perfectly secure in this car."

"I'm happy to see you again," Nick replied lamely, feeling far from at ease.

"First, I want you to know you handled the Wilshire film drop very professionally. You were flawless. I can tell you the film will disrupt Soviet aerospace designers for at least a decade, probably more. Have you heard of stealth?"

"Yes, I read about it in *Aviation Week* some time ago, but it sounded too far-fetched to be believed."

"At the moment it almost is, but developmental work at Wilshire and another company is showing signs of progress. What the Wilshire film communicated to the Soviets is that engineers at Wilshire's classified design center have made a breakthrough in stealth technology that will render Soviet air defenses useless. That should dispirit them because they recently spent about $20 billion—dollars, not rubles—on a new generation of radar and anti-aircraft missiles that will be unable to detect our stealth planes as they penetrate Soviet air space. Stealth will give the U.S. a decisive advantage for years to come."

Nick's eyes flew open with the realization he had been instrumental in making this happen. He was speechless.

She continued: "The Wilshire film contained technical designs that have already proven to be useless or failures. If they use those designs, the Sukhoi Design Bureau will be going up blind alleys for years and years achieving nothing. Through trial and error, the U.S. is at least 10 and perhaps 20 years ahead of the Russians and this film will waste their time even more. I'm telling you this because I want you to appreciate how important your role has been in helping to maintain the security of the United States."

"Thank you for telling me. I do appreciate knowing."

She paused for a moment while Nick took in that information. Her face became tense.

"Now I come to a difficult item," she said coldly. "It concerns Sonja Dahl. You told me she had told you her father, Richard, lives in Chicago. Am I correct?"

"That's what she told me at dinner last Monday night at Martin's Tavern."

"We've checked into this thoroughly. Richard Dahl lived in Chicago but he was killed-in-action during the Korean War in 1951. She did graduate from Northwestern, but she is not registered at Georgetown University's School of Foreign Service."

"Oh my God," Nick said under his breath. "She's been lying to me."

"The one thing we do know for sure is what she is *not*," declared CIA's Assistant Deputy Director of Operations. "What we *don't* know is who she is— and more importantly who she's working for."

Nick took a deep breath before asking, "How can I help?"

"We're counting on you to gain some hard information about her. We are aware you spent the night at her apartment after the aerospace ball. Am I right?"

"Yes, I did," he admitted.

"We want you to continue seeing her as if you hadn't learned what I just told you. Without arousing suspicion, gently probe for more information about her background and personal history. In particular, when you are in her apartment and have the opportunity, look at her driver's license and take down any data on it—date of birth, address, and especially her name. We suspect the license is forged, but it might give us a clue. Does she have a passport?"

"I don't know," he answered truthfully.

"If she does, check it out and take down any information on it. It's probably forged also, but it may also give us clues."

"Who do you think she works for and why would she spend so much time with me?"

"The answer to the first question is what we have to find out, and as to the second," she paused and with a crooked smile looked him up and down the way only an older, experienced woman could, "you might not fully appreciate your masculine charms."

Nick actually blushed.

"There's one last item," she added quickly, having evaded his question and wanting to change the subject. "Next month the International Studies Association will hold its annual convention here in D.C. at the Washington Hilton. Scholars from all over the world will attend to read papers and conduct panel discussions and generally schmooze with old friends. You're going to attend that convention. Century will send you as their representative. How does that sound to you?"

"It sounds great. I've never been to an ISA convention but have wanted to."

"You remember Dr. David Hammond from the National Defense Analysis Center?"

"Yes, of course, I worked with him last summer at the Institute."

"I know. Hammond will present an important paper at the ISA meeting on implications of advancements in military technology on national security policy. That's the subject you assisted him with last summer. This topic will attract a large audience, including the Soviets. I want you to fly to Los Angeles and spend a few days with Dr. Hammond at NDAC's Santa Monica headquarters to help him prepare that speech. Are you willing to do that?"

"Absolutely!" he replied, looking forward to his first trip to California.

"Make a date with Sonja sometime this week and over a meal tell her that Hammond requested you to assist him in L.A. with his technical paper. Be very proud of this. Tell her Century is paying your way. Don't discuss this with her on any telephone, the one in your office or the one in your apartment. Do it in person and continue to be very careful."

With that instruction, Samuels signaled to her driver the meeting had concluded. He waived to Elliott who had been standing guard. He opened Nick's door. Nick got back in the other car, and Elliott drove him to the Marriott's parking structure. Nick's head was spinning as he walked across Key Bridge to his apartment with the realization he was getting deeper and deeper into dangerous territory.

The next afternoon, Tuesday, at his Century office Nick telephoned Sonja and asked her for a dinner date for the following evening. He said he would pick her up at her apartment at 7:00. Was that okay with her? She said, "Of course." He deliberately did not tell her where they would go for dinner. She would assume Martin's Tavern.

Next, he went to a pay phone in the building's lobby and dialed the special number for Susan Samuels. He told her he had a dinner date with Sonja for the next evening at 7:00 and he had not mentioned the name of the restaurant. He said it will be at Clyde's in Georgetown on M Street—in the rear patio. She thanked him for the information.

When they hung up, Samuels called in her staff to give them her plan to entrap Sonja Dahl—to find out who she works for. CIA will ask the FBI to arrange with Clyde's maitre d' to seat Nick and Sonja at a particular table the FBI will bug. They will also ask the FBI to stakeout an agent at her apartment to track her activities after she returns home from dinner.

Georgetown
Washington, D.C.

At 7:00 the following evening Nick picked up Sonja at her apartment. They walked east on O Street to Wisconsin Avenue, turned south and kept walking past Martin's to M Street. Half a block later they arrived in front of Clyde's, a popular Georgetown restaurant. He asked if Clyde's is okay with her. She said it's one of her favorites.

They entered the double doors. Nick gave his name and asked the maitre d' for a table on the outdoor patio at the rear of the restaurant. It's a pleasant evening so it would be nice to be outside, he suggested. Sonja agreed.

They were seated at a table for two under a lighted vine-covered trellis. Nick ordered manhattans on the rocks. She told him how much she had enjoyed their canoe trip on Sunday, especially the picnic. He smiled and said the same. They were a little pink from sunburn, but it wasn't painful. A waiter delivered the drinks.

"I've got some really great news that I'm bursting to tell you," Nick exclaimed.

"Well don't burst, tell me!" she demanded with a smile.

"Century is sending me to Los Angeles to work with Dr. David Hammond at the National Defense Analysis Center's headquarters in Santa Monica. I worked with Hammond last summer at the Institute and he asked for my help again to prepare a major paper he will deliver at the International Studies Association's annual convention next month here in D.C. I feel truly honored to be asked for my help by this top-notch expert."

"My goodness," she exclaimed. "That really is big news! You must have impressed Dr. Hammond with your work to be asked to do this. Is Century paying your way?"

"Yes. I suppose Century sees this as a way to contribute to NDAC, which is the Air Force's most important think tank. I imagine they can score some points with the government that way. Plus the topic of the paper is right up Century's alley."

"Well don't keep me in suspense, what is it?"

"It's on the ramifications of military technological advancements on national security policy."

"My, my, that sounds heavy," she observed.

"It certainly is. I suspect there will be two versions of the paper—one unclassified for the ISA speech and one classified for the Defense Department. Since I'm cleared for Top Secret, I expect I'll be helping with both versions."

"How very interesting," Sonja commented. "When do you leave for L.A.?"

"Next Monday. I imagine I'll be gone all week."

At this moment the waiter returned and asked for their dinner order. Nick ordered another round of manhattans while they studied the menus.

After dinner, Nick walked Sonja back to her apartment. They were in a happy mood and were enjoying the warm summer evening. The streets of Georgetown were clogged with tourists and summer school college students. When they arrived at the steps of her apartment building, Nick paused, waiting for an invitation. She was surprised at his hesitation.

"Don't you want to come in?"

"Yes, I do, very much. I was trying to be polite, waiting for an invitation."

"Oh, silly. I want you as much as I suspect you want me."

That settled, they charged up the steps to her door and then to her king-size bed.

After sex, Sonja got up and went into the bathroom, closing the door behind her. Nick moved swiftly to the table where she left her purse. The driver's license was there. He had a slip of paper and pen in the pocket of his shirt which he picked up from the floor and quickly noted the vital statistics on the State of Illinois license: No. C9772435, Name: Sonja Rebecca Dahl, DOB: October 12, 1950, Hair: Brown, Height: 5' 6", Weight: 115 lbs., Eyes: Hazel, Address: 1221 Lake Shore Drive, Chicago, Illinois.

He returned the license to the purse and the pen and paper to his shirt, tossing it back on the floor. He got back in bed just before she emerged from the bathroom. He'd have to look for a passport another time.

Nick told her he had an early meeting at Century the next day and should probably be going to his place to get some sleep. She said she was sorry he had to leave so soon but hoped to see him again before leaving on his trip to California next week. Let's plan on it, he told her. He got up, dressed, and left—after a lingering kiss at the door.

Outside, walking down the dark tree-lined street, Nick did not notice an FBI agent lurking in the shadows across the street from Sonja's apartment building. Nick continued on to his apartment on N Street where he did notice the same white van parked in front of his building. He went in. He'd have to get up an hour earlier than usual to make the fabricated meeting appear genuine in case anyone was watching. He put the slip of paper he'd used in his wallet, hidden between some dollar bills, just as Col. Payne had taught him.

The next morning, Thursday, Nick left his apartment early, walked across Key Bridge and entered the Marriott. He planned to have breakfast in their coffee shop—as he often did. But first he went to a bank of pay phones off the lobby and dialed Susan Samuels' number.

"Code in."

"Romeo."

Samuels quickly came on the line. Nick reported the information on Nicole's driver's license. She thanked him. She added that she appreciated the way he handled the dinner conversation.

"You overheard it?" he asked.

"No. The FBI recorded it. I listened to the tape last night. You conveyed the information perfectly about your up-coming trip to L.A. and the ISA paper Hammond is working on."

"Thanks for the compliment."

"The information you gave Sonja had the effect we expected. After you left her apartment, she also went out. She walked to M Street to a pay phone. An FBI agent followed her. She talked for about five minutes before returning to her apartment. She was obviously reporting to her superior what you told her at dinner."

"Who is her superior?"

"We're working on that right now," she said. "The Chesapeake & Potomac Telephone Company is cooperating with the FBI to determine the phone numbers called from that particular pay phone around 11:00 last night. Once they get the phone number, they'll also have the address. It shouldn't take them long. Why don't you call me again this afternoon? We should have more information by then."

Century Aerospace Office
Rosslyn, Virginia

Just before noon the phone on Nick's desk at Century buzzed. The receptionist informed him Dr. Hammond was on line one. Nick pushed the lighted button.

"Nick Butler speaking."

"Hello Nick. This is David Hammond calling. How are you?"

"Doing great, Dr. Hammond, thank you."

"Well, Nick, by now you've been told I need your help with the paper I'm writing for the International Studies Association convention next month. Century agreed to my request and will fund your trip to L.A. Am I right?"

"Yes sir. I'm happy to help and I'm looking forward to it," Nick replied enthusiastically.

"Good. I want you to fly to Los Angeles International Airport next Monday and plan to spend the week with me in L.A. NDAC made a hotel reservation for you. I doubt you'll have much free time, but in case you do you might want to pack a bathing suit if you'd like to take a dip in the Pacific Ocean. Sound good?"

"Yes, sir!" he replied with gusto.

"Meanwhile, I need some technical information to include in the paper. It will be made available to you at the Pentagon in the office of the Chief of Staff of the U.S. Air Force. Part of it is unclassified material on our aircraft inventories, but most of it is classified—the parts relating to military doctrine and tactics. Do you think you'll have time to gather this information for me?"

"Yes I do. But how do I get into the Pentagon?"

"Graham Wolf has access to the Defense Department with his government clearance. He will escort you and handle the logistics. I've already spoken with Stanley Ebersol about it," Hammond said. "After you obtain the material, I want you to digest it as best you can and write a memorandum of your findings on the implications of technological changes on the USAF's force structure and operational strategy. Do you think you can handle all that?"

"Yes, sir," Nick replied, looking forward to this fascinating new assignment.

The KGB of course recorded the telephone conversation, exactly as Susan Samuels planned. The Soviet Union's interest in Butler would be heightened even more hearing this news. Hammond read his script perfectly and Nick sounded youthful and enthusiastic as she knew he would. The name of the hotel where he'd be staying in California was deliberately not mentioned. This opening move in a new chapter of Stealth Gambit was starting nicely.

After hanging up with Hammond, Nick walked down the hall to Graham Wolf's office. Through the glass door Nick could see he was reading a folder of classified material. When Nick tapped on his door, Wolf quickly closed the folder.

"Come in, Nick. I've been expecting you."

"Dr. David Hammond and I just had a phone conversation about my traveling to L.A. next week to carry material from the Air Force. I take it you're already aware of this?"

"Yes, I am. We have an appointment this afternoon at 3:00 in the E Ring of the Pentagon. That's where the Service Chiefs and the top-level DOD officials have their offices. I've been waiting for Hammond to close the loop with you on this assignment."

"Well, the loop is closed and I'm really excited to get going on this. There isn't much time left before I go to Los Angeles on Monday."

"You're right. Let's go downstairs and grab a quick bite at the café while I fill you in on the procedures," Wolf said as he put the classified document in his safe. "You have your driver's license with you? You'll need it for check-in at the Pentagon."

"I've got it," Nick answered as they walked down the hall toward the elevator.

FBI Headquarters
Washington, D.C.

The Chesapeake & Potomac Telephone Company completed its check of calls from the M Street pay phone. At 11:00 P.M. the previous night a call was made to a residential phone number. At 11:10 another call was made to a number at FBI Headquarters on Pennsylvania Avenue—to the FBI agent's own phone. He made that call to mark the call Sonja Dahl made immediately before.

Sonja's call was to a residence in Washington, D.C. Phone company records identified the name and address of the subscriber. A senior C&P security official phoned the FBI agent running the case and gave him that information. FBI Special Agent Lamar Williams instantly recognized the name. He nearly fell off his chair. He asked for an immediate appointment with the Director of the Federal Bureau of Investigation, Samuel Dean.

He was granted the appointment. When he entered the Director's office, he shut the door, walked to the side of the Director's chair, and leaned over to whisper.

"The C&P phone company reported at 11:00 last night Sonja Dahl telephoned the home of Harvey Walker, Deputy Director for Counter-Intelligence of the FBI," Special Agent Williams told Director Dean.

The Director and the Special Agent looked at each other while the Director digested this startling information. The Nick Butler op suddenly took on a whole new level of importance, striking at the very heart of the FBI itself.

Then Director Dean rose from his chair and walked out of his office, accompanied by the Special Agent, down the hall toward the secure room. On the way he told his secretary to summon the Deputy Director of the FBI and the FBI's General Counsel to that room. Minutes later the four men gathered in the sound proof room and shut the door.

Director Dean asked Special Agent Williams to repeat what the C&P official had said. The other two men gasped at the implication of that information.

"Gentlemen," Director Dean said, "it appears we have a double-agent within our midst. Harvey Walker has access to all the agents the FBI operates for counter-intelligence against the Soviet Union and every other nation that threatens the United States. Who knows how many outside agents he's running on his own? It appears Sonja Dahl is one of them. As of this minute the FBI's highest priority task is to penetrate Walker's operation, find out who he's working for, how many assets he has in his network, and as quickly as possible roll up this espionage ring before it does more damage to our country."

"Sam," the Deputy Director chimed in, "we'll need to coordinate this operation with the CIA since they are running the asset, Nick Butler."

"You're right," the Director replied, reaching for a phone.

"There's a problem with that," the General Counsel cautioned. "By Executive Order, our two agencies are prohibited from working joint domestic operations without a Presidential waiver."

"Very well," Director Dean said, "I'll call the President's Assistant for National Security Affairs and request a meeting at the White House this afternoon to authorize a waiver. I'll ask him to invite Admiral Myers and his Assistant Deputy, Susan Samuels. She's the person running Mr. Butler." The Director made the call. An appointment was set for 4:00 at the White House.

The President's Assistant for National Security Affairs, Dr. Burk Singleton, telephoned Admiral Philip Myers at CIA Headquarters at Langley, Virginia.

"Phil," he announced, "we have a high priority action item that emerged from the FBI this morning. Director Dean requests a meeting here with you and your Assistant Deputy, Susan Samuels. It concerns one of your assets. I'd like you two to come to the Situation Room at 4:00. Can you make it?"

"Of course, Burk, we'll be there," replied the Admiral. Myers notified Samuels and ordered his car for a 3:30 departure. Then he buzzed the Director of Central Intelligence and asked to meet with him at once on an urgent White House matter.

The Pentagon
Arlington, Virginia

At 2:50 Nick Butler and Graham Wolf walked into the Pentagon through the River Entrance. Wolf showed the receptionist, a female Marine sergeant, his government ID and asked for a visitor pass for Butler. Nick handed the sergeant his Maryland driver's license. She entered the information in her log. Wolf declined an escort saying he knows the way to the Chief's office.

The two walked about a city block to a ramp, went up the ramp to the second floor of the E Ring to a part of the massive building that faces the Potomac River. This is where the suite of offices of the high command of the United States Air Force is located.

They walked down the gray concrete corridor until they arrived at a wood-framed double door flanked by the American and Air Force flags. Two armed Air Policemen stood guard. Nick quickly saw why. A sign on the door read: Chief of Staff, U.S. Air Force. Wolf showed his badge and said good afternoon to the guards, who opened the door to the spacious reception area.

"Good afternoon, Col. Wolf," said the civilian receptionist with a cheerful smile. "The Assistant Chief is expecting you. Please go right in." She waived toward a door on her left.

"Thank you, Mildred," Wolf replied with a smile.

They entered a large wood-paneled office decorated with Air Force unit flags with combat ribbons flowing from them. Paintings of airplanes in various wars hung from the walls. The room, carpeted in deep blue, had a large wooden conference table and a sitting area with a leather couch and two leather chairs facing it. The other side of the room was dominated by a huge wooden desk situated in front of a massive window overlooking the Potomac. Behind the desk sat a three-star general wearing an Air Force summer uniform.

"Hello Graham," the general said rising from his chair.

"Good afternoon, General Montgomery," Graham Wolf replied. "I'd like to introduce Century's summer intern, Nick Butler. He's the person we spoke about who's doing research for David Hammond at NDAC."

"Pleased to meet you, Nick," the lieutenant general said as he shook Nick's hand.

"It's an honor, sir," Nick replied, admiring the campaign ribbons and decorations on his chest.

"Please take a seat," General Montgomery said, pointing to the couch. The general then buzzed his secretary, asking to have Major Lawrence join them. "Would you gentlemen like some coffee?" he asked. Nick and Graham declined.

General Montgomery went to the sitting area and took a chair. He explained Major James Lawrence had been assigned to prepare material for Dr. Hammond's report on the impacts of changing aerospace technologies on force structure and air combat strategy. The major would work with Butler for the next couple of days here at the Pentagon.

When Major Lawrence entered the room, the general made the introductions. The major appeared to be in his early 30s, tanned and very fit, looking every inch like a tough fighter pilot.

The general repeated the essence of the assignment to Nick and the major—to support Dr. Hammond's work at NDAC by helping him prepare a major speech at the International Studies Association meeting next month. That would be the unclassified work product. There would also be a classified deliverable—a formal report—for use inside the Air Force and NDAC, the USAF's principal think tank. He said the resources of the Air Force are at your disposal for these critically important studies that the USAF contracted with NDAC to perform.

Montgomery reminded Lawrence that Butler has a Top Secret clearance and will transport their report to Los Angeles next Monday. The major should check him out on Air Force procedures for handling classified material on commercial air. He asked if there are any questions.

"No sir," replied Major Lawrence and Nick Butler at the same time.

"Very well, gentlemen," General Montgomery said rising from his chair, "start your engines." The others stood up. The major saluted the general and turned toward the door. Nick and Graham Wolf shook the general's hand and followed Lawrence out of the room.

The three walked through the Chief of Staff's reception room and entered the main E Ring corridor. About five doors down the hall on the interior side of the building Major Lawrence stopped, used his access code on a security lock, and entered a room. Wolf and Butler followed.

The room had no windows, appeared to have lead-lined walls and ceiling, a concrete floor, and a wooden conference table in the center. The walls were lined with gray file cabinets with locked steel bars down the front of the drawers. The three sat down at a corner of the conference table.

"Nick, please call me Jim," said Major Lawrence. "The same goes for you, Col. Wolf."

"I'm Graham," replied Wolf with a smile.

"I'd like to get started on this assignment right away given the short fuse we have to work with," said Lawrence. "I've assembled a folder of unclassified material I'd like you to take with you to study tonight, Nick. I'll need your full-time attention on this project starting tomorrow, Friday, to properly prepare for your trip to NDAC on Monday. Can you come to this room at 8:00 tomorrow and remain until at least 5:00, maybe later. We will need to work Saturday and perhaps Sunday. Your evenings will be free, however."

Nick looked at Graham for any sign of disapproval. Seeing none, he agreed to the schedule.

Lawrence continued: "I'm going to walk you down to the Air Force security office and get you fitted with a Top Secret government ID badge so you won't have to sign in as you enter the building. That badge will give you access to almost the entire building, but our work will mostly be in this room. As you see, it has the ambiance of a bank vault, but what it lacks in décor it makes up for in security. In here we're safe from prying eyes and ears." Lawrence handed Nick a manila folder marked "unclassified." The three left the room to go to the security office.

The White House
Washington, D.C.

On the other side of the Potomac the meeting in the White House Situation Room began at 4:00. Dr. Burk Singleton, Assistant to the President for National Security Affairs, asked everyone to take a seat at the narrow rectangular table set in the middle of the small room in the basement of the White House.

He opened the meeting by making sure the attendees knew each other. He had invited his deputy, Dr. Edith Garland. The five attendees were Singleton and Garland from the White House, Myers and Samuels from the CIA, and Dean from the FBI. Dr. Singleton asked FBI Director Samuel Dean to state the reason for this urgent interagency conference.

Dean briefly recounted the events. He reported the FBI, at CIA's request, had staked out Sonja Dahl's apartment in a sting operation. Last night, shortly after Nick Butler left her apartment, so did Sonja. She walked to M Street and at 11:00 placed a call from a pay telephone and then returned to her apartment. The FBI agent tailing her observed this. Our Special Agent in charge of this op asked the Chesapeake & Potomac Telephone Company to trace the call to determine the phone number she called. This morning the phone company completed the trace and reported their finding to our Special Agent.

"Last night Sonja Dahl telephoned the home of Harvey Walker, Deputy Director for Counter-Intelligence of the FBI," he stated. Myers and Samuels were stunned. So were Drs. Singleton and Garland, all of whom immediately understood the implication of this information: Walker, the man in charge of America's counter-espionage, is himself a KGB agent who is running his own spies.

After a brief pause, Director Dean turned to the President's Assistant for National Security Affairs and formally requested a Presidential waiver to authorize an interagency investigation of this matter.

"CIA joins the FBI in requesting the waiver," Admiral Myers stated.

"I'm going to authorize the waiver in the President's name," Dr. Singleton declared formally, turning to his deputy who made a note.

"I have directed the FBI to put the Walker matter front-and-center," said Dean. "As of today it is the FBI's number one priority."

"The President will want this matter to be CIA's number one priority also," Dr. Singleton stated, looking at Admiral Myers. "This is a serious threat to the security of the United States and the President will want all our national security resources focused on it."

"Aye, aye, sir," the Admiral responded.

"Director Dean, please tell us what prompted Miss Dahl to make that telephone call," requested Singleton.

"Again at CIA's request," Dean stated, "we recorded a dinner conversation between Dahl and CIA's asset, Nick Butler, in which Butler conveyed pre-approved information to Dahl that would likely stimulate her to take some action."

"Susan," asked Singleton, "please fill us in on the nature of this op."

Susan Samuels responded: "Nick Butler is a summer intern at Century Aerospace's Washington Office. We have convinced the KGB he is Century's industrial spy to enable us to credibly pass through him to the Russians high value aerospace disinformation. Last weekend Butler passed to the KGB a false stealth fighter design Wilshire Aerospace prepared at our request."

"What about Sonja Dahl?" Singleton asked.

"We suspected Sonja Dahl is a KGB sleeper agent," Samuels answered. "Last night our asset told her he's participating in a classified air power study with the Air Force and with NDAC's Dr. David Hammond. He said he'll fly to Los Angeles on Monday carrying classified material to work on the project. She obviously concluded that information was important enough to pass to her handler."

"Tell us about the asset, Susan," requested Dr. Edith Garland.

"He's a handsome 24-year-old Columbia grad student who just ended his first year there under Bill Reynard. He was originally identified to us by Al Rubin at Penn where he was an undergrad. Reynard agreed he'd make a good asset for us. We gave him a crash course at Ft. Holabird. He's undertaken two foreign assignments for us. One as a courier whose disinformation documents were 'stolen' by the KGB and the other acting as an industrial spy for Century at the Paris Air Show where he performed beautifully, passing disinformation from three countries' major aerospace firms. This was a tri-service op with French and British intelligence. His KGB contact in Paris was a female whom he recruited to be an industrial spy for Century but she will in fact be controlled by the *Deuxième Bureau*."

"He recruited a KGB spy to work for him?" Dr. Garland asked, surprised. "He's really that good?"

"Dr. Garland, Nick Butler could charm the panties right off you!" replied Susan Samuels. Everyone had a good laugh. "To underscore that point, the female MI6 agent who tested him for us last year at Farnborough gave him the code name 'Romeo.' We're using that code name."

"As you may know," Admiral Myers interjected, "Yuri Andropov believes females make the best agents. Well, we have a male asset who outdid one of his female assets big time."

Everyone at the table—except Samuels, who had met him—instantly wanted to meet this suave Casanova, but they realized such a meeting might compromise his non-CIA status and thus compromise the ongoing op.

"Very well," Dr. Singleton said clearing his throat and regaining control of the meeting, "moving forward from here," he said, looking at Dean and Myers, "what do either of you have in mind to ensnare Harvey Walker?"

"Given this is an op within the United States, I think the FBI should have operational control of the mission to catch one of our own," stated Director Dean.

"I concur," added CIA's Deputy Director of Operations. "And CIA will provide our asset and other resources as needed, Director Dean."

Dean stated: "I will inform the Attorney General of the situation and fill him in on our plan. We need the AG's approval to request court orders for surveillance authority."

"I agree with this approach," said the National Security Advisor. "In the short span of time you've known of this situation, have you formulated a game-plan?"

Dean replied: "I believe the key is to keep Romeo in touch with Dahl and give her more information regarding his travel plans and hotel arrangements. Walker may have assets in Los Angeles. With Romeo as bait, we might catch one. If Romeo could convey a compelling piece of intelligence to Dahl before he departs, this may stimulate another phone call to Walker. We're putting a tap on the pay phone on M Street. Dahl obviously will not use her home phone so a tap there is pointless."

"We'll provide something compelling for Romeo to tell her about his Air Force work," Susan Samuels said. "Tomorrow night or Saturday night he'll convey it."

"I have one more piece of the puzzle to share with you," added the FBI Director. "Since this morning when we received the driver's license information on Sonja Dahl from CIA, our Special Agent in Charge of the FBI's Chicago office did some checking. He found the Chicago address on the license is non-existent; it's on Lake Shore Drive but on the beach side of Lake Michigan where there are no buildings. Also there is no record in the Cook County Records Office of a live birth of a female by that name having occurred on the date shown on the license. We also know from previous information she supplied to Romeo she lied about her father and about being a grad student at Georgetown University. She is not registered there."

For a moment there was dead silence in the room while this news was digested.

Director Dean continued: "I'm putting a close watch on Walker, and we'll put some false information in front of him to see what he does with it."

"As far as contacts are concerned," Samuels observed, "we know the KGB tapped Romeo's telephones at his Century office and his apartment where the FBI also has a tap. So we'll want to use those phones carefully. Yesterday I gave Romeo instructions to speak with Dahl only face-to-face at a location she did not know of in advance."

"It goes without saying I'll request a court order for a wire tap on Walker's home phone," Dean stated. "But he's a professional counter-espionage agent so I doubt he'll use that phone for out-going calls. Most likely he uses dead drop locations. I'm putting a tail on him beginning today to find them."

The interagency op had been approved by the White House, and everyone now had their assignments. The meeting ended at 5:00 in an atmosphere filled with apprehension for the nation's security.

All five attendees climbed the stairs up from the Situation Room to the main floor of the West Wing. Four of the five turned left toward the outside door on West Executive Drive. There, Myers and Samuels got in their car and Dean into his. Dr. Garland walked across West Executive Drive and entered the Old Executive Office Building, going to her office to prepare the formal Presidential waiver authorizing the interagency op.

Dr. Singleton turned right at the main hallway and walked to the President's secretary's desk. He requested an immediate meeting with the President. While he waited for her to get his response, the President's friendly golden retriever, Freedom, trotted over to him. Singleton gave the beautiful dog a few pets. The secretary said he could go in.

Entering the Oval Office and approaching the man seated behind the famous desk made from the timbers of *HMS Resolute* and given to America's presidents by Queen Victoria, Dr. Burk Singleton announced to Dillon Reed: "Mr. President, there's a problem at the FBI."

Century Aerospace
Rosslyn, Virginia

At 5:00 Nick Butler, having returned from the Pentagon, telephoned Susan Samuels' number from a pay phone in the lobby of Century's building.

"Code in."

"Romeo."

The line went silent for a moment.

"Call again at 6:00," said the voice and hung up. Samuels was leaving the White House and would be back in her office at Langley in an hour, given heavy rush hour traffic on George Washington Parkway.

Butler took the elevator up to the 14th floor. Walking down the hall to his office, he noticed everyone had gone home for the day except Gladys, his secretary, who was still at her desk. She called him over and handed him a large manila envelope.

"Mr. Butler," she said, "your airline tickets to and from Los Angeles are in here, along with a confirmation slip of your hotel reservation NDAC made for you at the Santa Monica Holiday Inn. There's $2,000 in traveler's checks you should sign immediately. A printed itinerary of your trip and a form for reporting expenses when you return are also enclosed for your convenience. If you have any questions, I'll be here for a little while to answer them. I understand I will not see you tomorrow. Mr. Wolf tells me you'll be at the Pentagon all day."

"Thanks, Gladys," Nick responded as he went into his office to check out the contents of the envelope. The airline ticket was for a United flight on Monday morning at 9:15 and the return ticket was for the following Friday departing L.A. at 1:00 P.M. He signed the top portion of each traveler's check. Everything was in order. He sealed the envelope and buzzed Gladys, telling her to go home if she was otherwise ready to leave. She thanked him and left.

He opened the large manila envelope Major Lawrence gave him. It contained U.S. Air Force data on each type of combat airplane in service with the USAF—airplane type, range, speed, armament, manufacturer, date of initial operational capability, and so forth. Nick began studying the data, focusing first on fighter aircraft.

At 6:00 Nick left the office for the day, taking the two envelopes with him. He went to a pay phone in the building's lobby and dialed Samuels' number.

"Code in."

"Romeo."

"Hello, Nick," Susan said. "How was your afternoon at the Pentagon?"

"Very interesting. It was my first visit there. Graham Wolf certainly knows his way around that labyrinth. I've got my work cut out for me for the next couple of days."

"You'll do fine, I'm sure," she responded encouragingly.

"Do you have any new information on Sonja from the driver's license data I gave you this morning?"

"I'm afraid not," she lied, betraying her promise to keep him informed. She did not want him to become too concerned about who and what Sonja Dahl is. "What we do know is we need to continue to be very cautious around her until we learn more. Here's what I want you to do: tomorrow afternoon I'd like you to phone her from the Pentagon and make a dinner date for Saturday evening—a farewell before your trip to L.A. on Monday. Do not tell her the name of the restaurant. Will you do that?"

"Sure."

"During the day on Saturday, I know you'll still be working at the Pentagon. I want you to call me from there around 1:00. That's when I'll give you further instructions."

"Okay."

FBI Headquarters
Washington, D.C.

At 5:30 P.M., having returned from the White House, Director Dean convened a meeting of the FBI's Senior Staff in the sound-proof conference room of the recently-built J. Edgar Hoover Building. Harvey Walker was not invited. Dean announced the start of a new, top priority operation: find out who Harvey Walker works for and who works for him. Ordinarily leadership for this counter-espionage op would go to the FBI's Deputy Director for Counter-Intelligence. But since Walker, who holds that job, is the suspect, Director Dean had to assign the lead role to someone else.

Dean announced he was assigning leadership of the op and all appropriate FBI resources to the Special Agent in Charge of the Washington, D.C. area, Lamar Williams. It was Williams who had supervised the stakeout at Dahl's apartment and had obtained the C&P phone company information about Walker. Williams was just handed the biggest assignment of his career—the FBI's most important operation. The Senior Staff rose and applauded the appointee.

Lamar Williams was the highest-ranking black agent in the entire FBI. He knew the Washington, D.C. area very well, having grown up in the city and having graduated from one of its top public schools, Coolidge High, and then graduated from Howard University. He studied criminal law at Georgetown University's Law Center and passed the D.C. Bar. Williams immediately joined the FBI, wanting a career in law enforcement. Despite being a minority, he rose rapidly in the ranks of the mostly white FBI.

The minute Director Dean gave him the assignment, Special Agent Williams went into action. He requested the FBI's General Counsel obtain a court order putting Walker under surveillance—a tap on his home phone, a tail, and an examination of his bank records.

As Special Agent Williams continued to orchestrate the op, Director Dean left the room. He had a 6:00 appointment with the Attorney General at the Justice Department building across Pennsylvania Avenue to brief him on this counter-espionage operation against Walker.

Thus, within two hours from the onset of the meeting in the Situation Room, the wheels were set in motion throughout Executive Branch of the federal government to snare Harvey Walker, presumably the Soviet Union's top double-agent in the United States.

The Pentagon
Arlington, Virginia

The next morning, Friday, at 8:00 Butler knocked on the door of the secure conference room in the Pentagon. Major Jim Lawrence let him in. Lawrence had brought coffee from the cafeteria. The two men settled in for a long day to analyze the implications of technological advancements on Air Force operational strategy and their impacts on overall U.S. national security policy.

"Based on my reading of the material you gave me to study last night," Nick summarized, "it appears to me the pivotal technological innovation that could fundamentally alter the outcome of an air war is stealth. This could be a change in the balance of power as important as was going from propeller-powered aircraft to jets."

"I agree with you. Our focus should be on stealth," Major Lawrence said. "Yet, we need to go beyond that assumption to develop a mission concept for each stealthy aircraft type. For example, should the Air Force focus its stealth R&D on fighter aircraft or ground attack birds or bombers or reconnaissance aircraft or some entirely new type that will maximize the value of stealth technology?"

"I see what you mean," Nick said rubbing his chin. "This analysis should make the assumption that stealth technology exists—or can be brought into existence—and our job is to find the best application for it from an operational standpoint. Do I have a correct reading of our mission?"

"You read it five-by-five," replied Major Lawrence. "For a civilian puke, you're really with it!"

"I hope that's a compliment," Nick asked with a smile.

"It certainly is—Air Force style. Now listen to this. Dr. Hammond out at NDAC is well along with his estimate of the optimal stealth application. He's already concluded that ground attack aircraft using an entirely new design should be our highest priority. This will be a jet-powered airplane carrying a minimum of ordinance. The plane will be capable of penetrating heavily defended air space, such as European Russia, attacking air defense installations to neutralize them before waves of non-stealthy heavy attack birds and bombers are launched."

"Assuming a high rate of survivability because of their stealth feature, we won't need many of these silver bullets will we, Kemosabe?" asked Butler.

"Right again, Tonto," said Lawrence. "Hammond estimates about 100 planes should do the job."

"What do *you* think, Jim?" Nick asked the major.

"I have no reason to doubt Hammond's estimate," he replied. "What's worrying me is what should be the next application of stealth—beyond light attack aircraft. Should it be a bomber or fighters? In time I suspect the Air Force will need all three—light attack, bombers, and fighters, all stealthy. We don't have the resources to build all of them at one time, and—even worse—we don't know yet if the technology will actually work in combat situations."

"What do you say we do some primitive modeling of our operational needs based on two or three combat scenarios?" Nick suggested.

"Okay with me," Lawrence said, leaning forward. "How would you proceed?"

"Scenario No. 1 would be an all-out attack by the Soviet Union and the Warsaw Pact on our European-based NATO armed forces. What order of battle—that's the right term, isn't it, Jim—would NATO need to blunt such an attack?"

"That scenario has been war-gamed to death in this building and at NATO HQ. But I see your point—how would a fleet of stealthy birds change the outcome? Okay, what's the next scenario?" asked Lawrence.

"Let's go to the opposite end of the combat spectrum for this scenario," Nick suggested. "Let's assume a low-level penetration of some place in the West by the Russians. It could be another choke-hold on Berlin, it could be para-military infiltration into some remote spot such as eastern Turkey, or maybe it could be a proxy penetration by say Cuba of a Central American republic. In this scenario stealthy air power might not be directly needed but the very existence of it might forestall the Kremlin from taking larger-scale action."

"I'm writing these down, Nick. Don't stop. You're on a roll," Lawrence said.

"Okay, scenario number three is a middle-level one," Nick continued. "Let's hypothesize that the Red Army openly invades a bordering country, say Afghanistan. How would our having any stealthy aircraft types help us in such a scenario? The U.S. would have to be a combatant in such a situation to commit assets as valuable as stealth aircraft. We certainly wouldn't lend them or sell them to another nation for its use, would we?"

"Highly unlikely," Lawrence agreed. "Yet it is likely there would be middle-level combat situations the U.S. would be directly involved in where such assets would be used, perhaps decisively."

"You're thinking of something between World War II and World War III? Something like Korea or Vietnam where the U.S. is directly involved, right?"

"Exactly," replied Lawrence. "The likelihood of another middle-level war is the one that most of our war games are based on. It's the most probable type of warfare in the future. Stealth aircraft would be a game-changing asset in any of those mid-level scenarios involving the U.S."

The two analysts decided to flesh out their three scenarios of future combat situations for the rest of the day. To each scenario they assigned a number of stealth aircraft of each combat type. Attack aircraft always emerged as the most important type in the initial phase of combat.

At 1:00 Nick left the conference room, walked to a public area, and dialed Sonja's number from a pay phone, as Samuels had directed the day before.

"Hi Sonja, it's Nick. How are you?"

"I'm fine. How about yourself?"

"Fine, thanks. I'm at the Pentagon working on some things in preparation for my trip to L.A. I was thinking we should get together for dinner tomorrow night—sort of a farewell before I leave on Monday. Are you interested?"

"Dinner with you tomorrow night? That sounds great."

"I'll pick you up around 7:00. Okay?"

"It certainly is okay!"

Immediately following that call, Nick dialed Susan Samuels' number.

"Code in."

"Romeo."

"Hello Nick," Susan Samuels answered. "You're right on time."

"Thanks. I'm at the Pentagon as you know working with Major Jim Lawrence. Boy is he sharp!"

"I can imagine. Everyone on the Air Staff is. Have you made a dinner date with Sonja for tomorrow night?"

"Yes, I just hung up with her. I'll pick her up at 7:00. I did not mention the name of the restaurant."

"Good. Do you know yet where you'll take her?"

"I was thinking of Mr. Smith's restaurant on M Street in Georgetown. They have an open air patio like Clyde's. If it's a nice evening—not too hot—it would be pleasant to be outside. How does that sound to you?"

"It's perfect. Plan on it," she replied. "Now listen carefully. During dinner, you should generally discuss your experience at the Pentagon but do not mention any specifics about your work except that it's very interesting and probably extraordinarily important for U.S. national security. On the walk back to her apartment, I want you to return to the Pentagon topic and in a casual way mention you'll be carrying Top Secret Air Force material to NDAC in Santa Monica and that you'll be staying at the Santa Monica Holiday Inn. Also say the word "stealth." No specifics, just stealth—like it slipped out. Got it?"

"I've got it," he replied, knowing better than to ask why.

"Call me on Sunday when you get a chance. I'd like to know how it went."

At 8:00 the next day, Saturday, Nick and Major Lawrence reconvened in the Pentagon's conference room to complete writing their report. Nick brought the coffee. They both looked a little haggard after the intense day they had on Friday.

"You look like you'd rather be in a cockpit than a conference room, Jim," Nick said to the young major.

"Man, you just said a cotton pickin' mouthful."

"What type of airplanes do you fly, Jim—cargo planes?" Nick asked the pilot.

"Me? Fly trash-haulers? Never! I fly F-4s," Lawrence responded with feigned indignation.

"Excuse me!" Nick said backing off. "I didn't mean to offend you." Both were laughing.

"Well, let's get at it," Lawrence said, pulling up his chair to focus on the work at hand.

By early afternoon, they completed their report. It was 20 pages, single-spaced on U.S. Air Force stationary. They took it to the Air Force security office, which is always open.

Lawrence asked the officer in charge to classify the report Top Secret. He did so, stamping each page top and bottom with those words in red ink and putting two red ink lines diagonally across each page. The report was then duplicated. One copy was to be kept at the Pentagon, and the original was put in a messenger envelope, also stamped Top Secret. A red wax seal was placed across the flap; a red thread was put under the seal. The envelope was now tamper-proof.

"Okay, Nick. We're done," Major Lawrence announced. "I'll keep both copies in the safe in the conference room until Monday morning. An Air Policeman—that's what we call MPs—and I will bring the original to you at Dulles Airport at 8:00 on Monday in a sealed metal container with a combination lock. I'll handcuff it to you for the trip. The AP will escort you through airport security and onto the plane. When you arrive at NDAC's office in Santa Monica, the security chief there will open the handcuffs. Dr. Hammond has the combination to the lock. Understood?"

"Understood," Nick replied.

"It's been a pleasure working with you, Nick," said Lawrence with a smile and a handshake.

"Likewise," replied Nick, trying to sound military. "I'll see you Monday morning at Dulles." They parted. Nick went to his apartment in a taxi.

FBI Headquarters
Washington, D.C.

At FBI Headquarters on Saturday morning Special Agent Lamar Williams convened a meeting of his Walker team in the secure conference room. Members of the team reported that court orders had been obtained for surveillance of Harvey Walker's home—phone tap and stakeout. The phone tap would be installed whenever the family left the residence. The court also approved a search warrant for Sonja Dahl's apartment. The pay phone on M Street was tapped during the night. C&P phone company security was advised of the tap, complying with a requirement of the court order. Williams said he received a phone call from CIA the day before to arrange the next step in baiting the trap.

What Samuels told him was Romeo would take the suspect, Sonja Dahl, to dinner at Mr. Smith's restaurant on M Street in Georgetown, beginning after 7:00 tonight. They would sit in the patio area. Her apartment would be empty during the next few hours. After they return to the apartment, prepare to tail her after Romeo leaves. That might be a few hours later. Williams could imagine why.

Samuels then phoned Dr. Singleton at the White House to update him, as he requested.

Georgetown
Washington, D.C.

At 7:00 Sonja opened the door. She was dressed casually as was Nick. They walked to Mr. Smith's restaurant, a block further down M Street from Clyde's. The maitre d' said it would be a short wait for a table and could he have the gentleman's name. Nick gave it and requested a patio table. Moments later they were seated at a table for two on the restaurant's rear patio, still in summer daylight. The evening air was fresh and pleasant. Nick ordered manhattans, as usual.

"So how was your day at the Pentagon?" Sonja asked casually.

"Actually it was my *two* days there—all of yesterday and most of today. It was quite an experience being inside the world's largest office building. I didn't see much of it, only the Air Force portion, and even then only a small part of their operation."

"Were you working alone?"

"No. An Air Force major and I worked together. He's an expert in his subject matter. The work, frankly, was quite difficult but at the same time fascinating. I believe it's really important to U.S. national security."

"Can you tell me anything about it?" she probed a little deeper.

"Not really. The work is classified. All I can say is that it's very far-reaching in its importance to the government, especially to the Air Force."

The waiter brought their manhattans at this point and Nick suggested they look at the menus. There was no further discussion of the Pentagon work while they were at the table.

At about 9:15 they finished dinner and left the restaurant. They walked slowly through the crowd of summer tourists on Wisconsin Avenue and then turned left on O Street toward Sonja's apartment. That residential tree-covered street was quiet and dark. Walking on the brick sidewalk in front of historic Federal period townhouses was romantic on this warm summer evening.

"The trees rustling in a gentle breeze sound nice don't they," she said taking his arm.

"Yes indeed. I'm going to miss this next week while I'm in L.A. It's going to be all work and no play out there. "

"The same kind of difficult work you were doing at the Pentagon?"

"Oh yes, more of the same. I'll be carrying Top Secret material to NDAC for more Air Force research. It's stealth. They're putting me up at the Santa Monica Holiday Inn."

They continued walking without speaking. When they arrived at Sonja's door, she invited him in. Neither noticed the FBI stakeout in the shadows across the street.

Once inside, Nick, reaching for her, said how much he'd missed her since their canoe trip a week ago. She said the same but seemed distant, like she had something on her mind.

"Is something wrong?" he asked tentatively, taking her by the waist.

"No, not really. I guess I'm just a little tired."

"I was really looking forward to being with you tonight," he said, feeling disappointed.

"So was I, but I suppose I'm not up to it."

"Do you want me to leave?"

"I think it would be best."

Reluctantly, Nick left her apartment and walked toward his own, feeling let down. A week had gone by since they had sex. Then he got to thinking her mood changed abruptly during the walk to her place right after he mentioned the Top Secret assignment and Samuels' key word "stealth." He decided to go to Martin's Tavern to try to pickup someone new.

At Martin's he sat at the bar and ordered a beer. On this Saturday night, like most, the restaurant was crowded. There were a lot of couples in the booths and a few tables of all guys or gals. No single girls appeared. After about a half hour he decided to give it up and go to bed.

As he walked into his apartment the phone was ringing. He picked it up. Sonja was on the line.

"I'm so sorry for the way I behaved, Nick," she said. "I don't know what came over me. You were a perfect gentleman and left but I wish you hadn't. I think I was feeling sad that I hadn't seen you for a week and I won't see you again for another week. Maybe I was punishing you or something."

"Why don't you get some rest," he suggested, cutting through the girlie chatter. "That's what I'm going to do."

"Won't you please come back to my apartment?" she pleaded.

"Not tonight. I'm completely turned off," he said and hung up.

Listening in, the KGB assumed this was a lover's spat. The FBI knew better.

Earlier, within minutes after Butler left her apartment, Sonja also went out. She hurried down 34ᵗʰ Street to the pay phone on M Street. The FBI agent tailed her. At 9:55 she dialed a number and spoke for about five minutes. Then she returned to her apartment and started frantically dialing Nick's number. There was no answer there for about 40 minutes. Finally Nick did answer. She pleaded with him to come back to her place. He brushed her off.

FBI Headquarters
Washington, D.C.

Special Agent Williams heard Sonja's call through the pay phone wire tap while it was being recorded. She had dialed the same number—Harvey Walker's residence—and reported that her mark revealed he would be carrying Top Secret Air Force documents to NDAC in Los Angeles on Monday, staying at the Holiday Inn in Santa Monica. She said he mentioned the word "stealth." Walker ordered her to resume the conversation immediately and try to obtain more information about the documents and his assignment.

"Get him in bed and get him talking," he ordered Sonja in his high-pitched, reedy voice.

A short while later Special Agent Williams enjoyed listening to Sonja's pleading with Nick through the tap on his apartment phone. He understood the desperation she was feeling at failing to fulfill Walker's order to get him to return to her apartment. Nick did not need to return. Unknown to him, his task was accomplished by stimulating Dahl to call Walker.

Williams telephoned Director Dean and Susan Samuels to report the events of the last hour. They were conclusive: Nick Butler laid the bait in the trap, the suspect took it, and she irrefutably marked Walker as a double-agent and herself as his accomplice.

Chapter 10:
The Sting

Georgetown
Washington, D.C.

On Saturday evening, while Nick and Sonja were having dinner at Mr. Smith's restaurant, a plumber's van pulled up in front of Sonja's apartment building. Three men dressed in plumbers uniforms got out of the van and entered her building. They went to her door, picked the lock, and went into her apartment. They were FBI agents armed with a court order to break and enter—having shown a federal judge probable cause that Dahl was a threat to the United States. The three agents were looking for any type of evidence that might indict her.

The agents were experts at their work. They knew exactly where to look for items an occupant wants no one to find: in a dresser drawer under lingerie, in a shoe box, inside a toilet tank, under a lamp, in a sugar bowl, and so forth. An agent found a small key taped behind a loose baseboard. The name Riggs and a number were stamped on the key. It was obviously a safe deposit box key for the Riggs National Bank. The agent made a wax impression of the key, photographed it, and replaced it exactly where he found it. Nothing else of interest was discovered in the apartment. After lifting several sets of finger prints, the agents left and reported to Special Agent Williams.

Sunday morning Nick telephoned Susan Samuels from a Georgetown pay phone as she requested. She had already read the transcript of the dinner table conversation at Mr. Smith's and was pleased. Now she was eager to hear

Romeo tell her exactly what he said on the walk back to Sonja's apartment that stimulated her to phone Walker.

"I brought up the Pentagon work again, as you wanted me to," he reported, "and told her the work I'll be doing at NDAC is more of the same, and that I'll be staying at the Holiday Inn in Santa Monica. I mentioned I'll be carrying Top Secret Air Force material on the plane. After saying that I simply said 'it's stealth.' When we got to her apartment, it was as though she was a different person. She basically threw me out."

"Perfect, Nick. You did it perfectly," she complimented him. "I can tell you she was anxious to get you out of the way so she could report to someone what you told her. You triggered the reaction from her I expected."

"Well, that's a relief," he admitted. "For a while there I thought I'd lost my touch."

"Nick, you'll never lose your touch," the woman said admiringly. "Now here's the main point: only Sonja Dahl knew you'd be traveling to L.A. with Top Secret material and where you'd be staying. We've kept that critical information from the KGB; they only know you'll be carrying classified material. So now we'll wait to see if someone approaches you to learn more about your work—either on the plane or in Santa Monica. Be watchful as you travel and let me know if you are approached, as I expect you will."

On Monday morning, an FBI attorney went to the same Federal District judge to request a court order to open Sonja's safe deposit box. Having been shown probable cause of espionage, the court granted the order. An hour later, Special Agent Williams and the FBI attorney went to the Riggs bank branch in Georgetown at the corner of M Street and Wisconsin Avenue and presented the order to the branch manager. The manager escorted the two federal agents to the vault, produced the bank's duplicate key, and watched Williams insert the new key the FBI made from the wax impression. The two keys opened the lock. The manager removed the box from the vault and sat it on a table.

Special Agent Williams opened the lid. Inside the box they found two passports, a wad of U.S. currency, and a loaded Colt .38 revolver. One passport was U.S. in the name of Sonja Rebecca Dahl with the same Chicago address as on her driver's license. The other passport was Canadian in the name of Angela Schmidt with an address in Ottawa, Canada. The photos in the two passports were the same. The agents photographed the passports and counted the currency. There was $50,000 in $100 bills. The entire contents of the box were photographed. The FBI attorney asked the bank manager to type up an inventory of the contents, sign the inventory, and make a copy for the bank's records. The FBI attorney took the original to be used later as evidence, if needed. The box and its contents were replaced in the vault.

Returning to FBI Headquarters, Lamar Williams asked to see Director Dean immediately in the secure conference room. Director Dean, Special Agent Williams, the FBI attorney, and the FBI General Counsel entered the sound proof room. Agent Williams presented the findings of the apartment break-in Saturday night and the inventory of the safe deposit box. Of particular interest were the Canadian passport and the money. A finger print check was underway.

Director Dean telephoned Admiral Myers at CIA headquarters on the secure line. After learning about the Canadian passport and the money, he suggested a meeting at the White House with Dr. Singleton. This case had now taken a new and more ominous turn. It was possible that Angela Schmidt is Canadian but, Myers speculated, she is more likely a Stasi sleeper agent from East Germany. Moreover, Sonja's urgent call to Walker Saturday night to report what Butler said was evidence she was a conspirator against the United States.

The White House
Washington, D.C.

The meeting at the White House Situation Room convened at 1:00. The attendees were Admiral Myers, Susan Samuels, Director Dean, Special Agent Williams, the FBI General Counsel, and Drs. Singleton and Garland. Special Agent Williams recounted the events since Saturday night so everyone would be on the same page. After he finished, the speculation began.

"Do you think the large quantity of cash suggests that Dahl/Schmidt is spying for money?" Singleton asked Director Dean.

"Not necessarily," replied Dean. "The cash could be get-away money in the event her role is found out. The gun being in the safe deposit box also indicates she is not expected to use it unless she faces a threatening situation."

"The phone call by Dahl to Walker on Saturday night after Romeo laid the bait is convincing that Walker is the boss," stated Dr. Garland.

"There's no doubt she works for Walker," Dean stated. "Yet, the key question remains: who does Harvey Walker work for?"

"Romeo told only Sonja Dahl about traveling with Top Secret Air Force material to NDAC in Santa Monica and the name of the hotel where he'll be staying," Samuels reported. "If he is approached there, it's because Walker ordered it, not the KGB."

"I'd like to have our COS in Ottawa begin an investigation there into Angela Schmidt," said Myers.

"What's a COS?" Singleton asked.

"Sorry for the acronym," Myers apologized. "It means Chief of Station."

"A preliminary investigation only at this point," Singleton cautioned. "Before we go very far with this in Canada, I'll need to bring the State Department into this matter."

"Do you think Romeo is in any danger?" Samuels asked the FBI Director. "After all he is the bait and he's transporting some awfully tempting material on an airplane as we speak."

"He's being protected all the way without knowing it," Dean stated. "I've had two agents tailing him since he left his apartment this morning. They're on the airplane with him now, and after he lands they will tail him to the front door of NDAC in Santa Monica. His safety is assured."

"What are you doing about Walker at his office?" Singleton asked Director Dean.

"We're watching him closely without tipping him off that he's under suspicion," replied Dean. "Special Agent Williams assigned an agent from outside his area to begin working with him as sort of a trainee, learning from the master so to speak. As soon as his wife leaves their house today, we will enter the residence to conduct a search and tap his telephone. We have a court order authorizing that."

"Excellent," commented Singleton. "As soon as your Station Chief has anything to report from Ottawa, Phil, I want to know it."

"Affirmative," the Admiral replied.

The meeting ended. Drs. Singleton and Garland went to the Oval Office to report to the President on the enormous danger to U.S. national security that a graduate student summer intern at an aerospace company was instrumental in exposing.

National Defense Analysis Center
Santa Monica, California

Nick Butler's United Airlines flight landed at Los Angeles International Airport at 2:30 P.M. Pacific Daylight time. He deplaned with the aluminum combination lock brief case handcuffed to his left wrist. It had never left him since Major Lawrence attached it at Dulles Airport that morning.

Nick was met at the gate by a uniformed security officer from NDAC. He was easy to spot carrying the briefcase. Two men in dark suits followed him off the plane, along the concourse, and down the escalator to the baggage claim area. Nick picked up his suitcase from the baggage carousel, then he and the NDAC security officer walked outside where a black Chevy was waiting curbside. The security officer put the suitcase in the trunk and held the rear door open for Nick, before joining the driver in the front seat.

Another black Chevy with U.S. government plates pulled out behind them with the two FBI agents and the driver. The two cars exited the airport, turned north, and then northwest on Lincoln Boulevard. At that time of day traffic was light. Twenty minutes later they pulled up at the entrance to NDAC on Main Street in Santa Monica.

When Nick and the security officer were safely inside the building, the other black Chevy drove off. Inside the lobby, Nick identified himself to the receptionist and put his government ID badge around his neck. She telephoned the chief of security and Dr. David Hammond. A few minutes later both men arrived in the lobby.

The security chief, Captain Sullivan, unlocked the handcuffs and took them away. Dr. Hammond greeted Nick warmly, shook hands, and escorted him through the security door to the building's main hallway. They went to a secure room well inside the building where Hammond put the brief case on a table and opened the combination lock. He lifted the lid and took out the manila envelope.

"I'm glad to see you again, Nick," Hammond said smiling. "It's been about a year, hasn't it, since we worked together in New York at the Institute?"

"Yes, sir. It was last June."

"Major Jim Lawrence telephoned to say what a significant contribution you made in only two days to this analytical work we at NDAC and the Air Force are doing together," Hammond said.

"I appreciate the compliment, but Jim is one hell of an analyst himself."

"I know," Hammond said. "That's why he's on the study team. Yet he tells me it was your idea to construct combat scenarios of varying levels of intensity to assess the airplane types that would optimally benefit from the stealth feature in each situation."

"It's an idea you gave me last summer when you were telling me about Herman Cole's pioneering work here at NDAC," Butler said. "He's the godfather of scenario-building, and I simply picked up on that concept."

"It's going to take some time for me to digest the report you and Lawrence prepared," Hammond said as he slit open the manila envelope's wax seal and took out the report. "Why don't you knock off for the rest of the day and go check in at the Holiday Inn and relax. I'd like to see you here tomorrow at 9:00. Dress casually. We'll really get into it then. After all, we have all week to finalize the two reports—one classified for the Air Force and one unclassified I'll use in two weeks for my speech to the International Studies Association."

"Sounds good to me. How do I get to the hotel?'

"Walk back to the lobby and tell the receptionist to have the same car take you. Your luggage is still in the trunk. Tomorrow you can walk here from the hotel. It's only two blocks away."

Santa Monica Beach

After checking in at the hotel and going to his room, Nick discovered he had a view of Santa Monica Pier and the Pacific Ocean. The water looked inviting. He took off his suit, put on his swimming trunks, a T-shirt, sneakers, and his red Phillies cap. He grabbed a hotel towel and walked to the beach on the other side of Ocean Avenue.

It was a warm late June day. The sky was crystal clear. He could see all along the shore line up to Malibu and out to Catalina Island in the distance. He thought how lucky can I get—going to the beach in California. A Beach Boys song started playing in his head "Wish they all could be California girls." He saw at least a dozen of the tanned blond beauties as he crossed the sand and arrived at the water's edge.

The water was surprisingly chilly as he waded into the surf. He didn't mind. He was going to have his first swim in the Pacific Ocean. He plunged head first into a rolling breaker. He swam for about 10 minutes, then returned to the place where he left his towel and cap. After drying off, he laid down on the towel. The Southern California sunshine felt wonderful.

Later, when he sat up, he noticed a well-tanned blond beach bunny in a yellow bikini sitting alone not far from him. She noticed him. He smiled at her. She smiled back. He picked up his towel and T-shirt, put on his cap and walked toward her. He stopped about ten feet from her, struck by her beauty.

"What are you looking at?" she asked.

"I'm looking at you," he answered with a lusty smile.

"Is there something the matter with me?"

"Not that I can see. Mind if I sit with you?"

"It's a public beach," she said, smiling up at the handsome young man now standing over her.

"I'm Nick," he said as he spread out his towel and sat beside the gorgeous girl.

"I'm Natalie. Nice to meet you, Nick." They sat quietly for a few minutes watching the waves and some volley ball players further down the beach.

"What brings you to the beach on a Monday afternoon aside from the obvious desire to continue working on your fabulous tan?" Nick asked, admiring her body.

"You're tan could use a little work," she commented as she looked him over.

"I agree. That's why I'm here."

"To answer your question, this morning I turned in a major paper to my professor at UCLA. I came down here to decompress. What brings you out on a weekday afternoon?"

"I just arrived in town and had the afternoon to kill before going to work tomorrow."

"What kind of work do you do?"

"I'm a grad student intern at an aerospace company. I'm here for the week helping to write a report at NDAC."

"That sounds important."

"I suppose it is, but right now I'd rather not think about it. After a long flight this morning from the East Coast I thought I'd come down to the beach to decompress also."

"Where are you staying, Nick?"

"Right up there at the Holiday Inn," he said, pointing to the hotel on the bluff above. After a pause he added, flashing his killer smile: "The beach is one way to decompress, but I know another way that's even better."

"Why don't you show me how it works?" she replied, getting up and gathering her things. They went to his hotel room.

Later he turned to her in bed and asked, "If you don't have any plans, will you have dinner with me? I don't know anyone in L.A. and I hate to eat alone."

"I don't have any plans. I'd enjoy having dinner with you, Nick."

"Since you know the town and I don't, why don't you pick the restaurant? It has to be within walking distance because I don't have a rental car."

"No problem. My car is parked at the beach parking lot. Do you like sea food?"

"Yes, very much."

"Then let's drive out to the Charthouse in Malibu. It's one of my favorite places. The restaurant sits above the water's edge on a pile of rocks. The view from Malibu is fabulous."

"Deal. Do you want to shower here or at your place?"

"I'll need a change of clothes so I'll shower and dress at my apartment. It's not far from here. You go ahead and shower. I'll rest here for a little while."

Nick got up and padded to the bathroom. He closed the door and turned on the shower but did not get in. He was thinking there's something peculiar about the way this happened so fast. It reminded him of Nicole and Sonja. It was too easy, he thought.

After a minute, he carefully turned the door knob and peeked out through a crack in the door. Natalie had gotten up and gone to the dresser. Her back was toward him. She was going through his wallet. She found the slip of paper with Susan Samuels' phone number between the dollar bills. She was writing the number on the hotel telephone pad. Nick closed the door silently and stepped into the shower.

Now he knew: it *had* been too easy! She was some kind of spy. Susan Samuels had warned him he might be approached by someone while on this trip.

He showered, dried off, and put on a sport shirt and jeans. He asked if that was too casual for the Charthouse. She said it's perfect. He put on his sneakers. They left to reclaim her car at the beach parking lot to drive to her apartment.

It was about a mile away in a residential section of Santa Monica. He made a mental note of the address, using the association technique Col. Payne taught him. The apartment was neat and clean but rather bare. She showered and put on jeans, a cute blouse, and sandals. She looked awesome.

Malibu, California

Leaving the apartment, she drove to Ocean Avenue and then down the face of the palisades on the California Incline to Pacific Coast Highway. It was twilight and the lights rimming Santa Monica Bay were coming alive. The view was breathtaking. The radio was playing a Mamas and Papas tune—"California Dreamin'." They drove a few miles along the water's edge to the restaurant and left the car with the valet.

The Charthouse was perched on pilings above the shoreline. Breakers were crashing on the rocks below. The entire sight was spectacular for an East Coast boy. He thought to himself: Wow! I've just had sex and now I'm in Malibu, California with a gorgeous girl!

The hostess seated them at a window table overlooking Santa Monica Bay. Nick ordered margaritas and two jumbo shrimp cocktails. After they studied the menu, Natalie decided on the halibut; Nick chose the snapper. When the drinks and shrimp arrived, Nick excused himself to go to the john.

Inside the men's room was a pay telephone. He dialed Susan Samuels' toll-free number.

"Code in," said the voice.

"Romeo."

Instantly Samuels came on the line. "How's it going in California?"

"Very well," he answered. "I only have a minute. I'm in a restaurant in Malibu called the Charthouse. This afternoon a woman named Natalie made contact with me. I met her on the beach below the Holiday Inn. She said she's a student at UCLA. Later in my hotel room I saw her going through my wallet while I was in the bathroom peeking out. She wrote down this phone number. The address of her apartment is 711 5th Street, apartment 201, Santa Monica. I can call you later but that's the essence of it."

"I'm glad you called, Nick," she said with no surprise in her voice. "I want you to keep the contact going with this woman; pretend you didn't see her snooping. Let everything go normally. Over your meal mention you're working at NDAC on a classified Air Force project and you'll be meeting with Century Aerospace's top people during the week. That should keep her interested."

"I'll be meeting with Century's executives?" he asked, surprised.

"Yes, you will. That's been planned. Hammond was going to tell you tomorrow. But tonight is even better. Any problem with that?"

"None. I'd better go. Call you again tomorrow."

He returned to the table and devoured his six shrimp, not until then realizing how hungry he was. Swimming and sex sure work up an appetite, he thought to himself. Soon the waiter brought their entrées.

"What are you doing here this week?" she asked. "You mentioned something on the beach but I forget what you said."

"I'm participating in a study at NDAC for the U.S. Air Force," he replied as Samuels had instructed. "It's a classified national security project and I feel honored to be part of it. Later this week I'll be meeting with the top people at Century Aerospace."

"My goodness. You must really be something! You're a grad student intern doing all that high-level stuff."

Nick noted to himself she remembered he'd said on the beach he was a grad student intern and yet she pretended to forget the NDAC part of the conversation.

They finished their meal, Nick paid, then they got her car from the valet. As they drove along Pacific Coast Highway back to the Holiday Inn, he asked if he could see her again tomorrow night. She said she'd love to see him again. He took down her phone number. At the portico of the hotel, he gave her a good-night kiss and got out of the car. She thanked him for a lovely dinner. As he got in the elevator, he realized they didn't know each other's last names.

CIA Headquarters
Langley, Virginia

Hanging up from Romeo, Susan Samuels immediately went up to Admiral Myers' office to report on his phone call from Malibu. Both were working late. It was clear to them Nick's casual-appearing encounter with "Natalie" was no accident and that she was most likely part of Harvey Walker's network. She couldn't be KGB because they did not know about Romeo's hotel in Santa Monica. Only Sonja Dahl knew and had reported it to Walker.

Myers telephoned Director Dean to inform him Romeo had once again been the bait and had caught another prey. Myers asked Dean to begin an investigation of Natalie. He gave Natalie's address and that she's a student at UCLA. Dean asked Myers to have Romeo obtain Natalie's last name and a set of her finger prints the next day, if possible. Myers then telephoned Dr. Singleton to report the news.

At the FBI everyone was also working late on the Walker case. Director Dean summoned Special Agent Williams to his office and debriefed him, speculating that Walker's network may be more far-flung than previously believed. Williams telephoned the Special Agent in Charge of the Los Angeles FBI office ordering him to begin an investigation of "Natalie." This is FBI priority number one, he told the agent.

National Defense Analysis Center
Santa Monica, California

At 8:45 the next morning, Tuesday, Butler left the hotel and walked across the bridge above the western end of Interstate-10, the Christopher Columbus Transcontinental Highway. The NDAC office campus was on his right.

He went in the entrance facing Main Street where he had been the day before. He showed his badge to the receptionist, who telephoned Dr. Hammond to escort him in. Hammond arrived in a few minutes and the two walked to the same secure room.

Hammond said he had studied the report Nick and Major Lawrence prepared.

"It's excellent work, Nick. You and Jim Lawrence did a terrific job sorting out the options and arriving at a set of highly justifiable conclusions."

"Thanks, Dr. Hammond. That's high praise coming from you."

"Now," Hammond went on, "our next step is to take the scenarios you and Lawrence identified and factor into them another layer of complexity. We're going to overlay on each scenario what force levels the Russians could put against our forces during various phases of combat. Once we do that we can estimate the exchange ratios."

"Exchange ratios?"

"That's a term of art within the Air Force community," Hammond explained. "It means how many of our aircraft would we lose vs. the enemy's losses. With some number of stealthy aircraft in our order of battle and assuming they have none in theirs the result should come out with us way ahead. I'm expecting at minimum a three-to-one win ratio in favor of our side."

"Do you think we can accomplish all that this week?"

"We certainly can finish the most likely scenario. The less likely ones can wait until after the International Studies Association meeting. I especially want to complete the mid-level scenario you and Lawrence identified as the most likely. For my formal paper to the Chief of Staff I want to report our study concludes that the Soviet Air Force doesn't have a prayer against the U.S. Air Force in a direct face-off or in a proxy war with each of us supplying equipment to the combatants."

"Can you give me an example?"

"Sure. A proxy example would be an Israel vs. Egypt war with Israel having our equipment and Egypt having Soviet armaments. The classified version of our report for the Air Force will incorporate the stealth factor on the Israeli side, indicating the exact number of airplanes by type and our estimate of the resulting exchange ratio. My hunch is the Israeli Air Force with its well-trained pilots using our first-line equipment will probably have a five-to-one kill ratio against the Egyptians."

"It sounds like we'll be doing some serious modeling this week."

"You've got that right. Our computer people are standing by to provide technical support for us throughout the week."

"That's a relief," Nick sighed.

"There's something else we're going to do this week," Hammond said, changing the subject. "I'm going to take you to Century Aerospace's factory to meet some of their senior people. Since you're cleared for Top Secret, I can tell you that only two aerospace companies have U.S. Air Force contracts to investigate the application of stealth technology to military aircraft. Wilshire Aerospace is one and Century is the other. Each is approaching the task in a different way, and the Air Force asked NDAC to help evaluate which approach is best."

"That's fascinating," Nick responded. "When will we go there?"

"Our appointment is set for tomorrow afternoon at their plant in El Segundo, which is south of LAX."

An hour later, Butler and Hammond took a break. Nick asked to use a telephone. Hammond took him to his office and left him alone while Nick dialed Susan Samuels' number.

"Hello," said the voice.

"Code in: Romeo," Nick responded.

Samuels immediately came on the line.

"The answering response," she informed him, "was simply 'hello' because Natalie had doubtless given Walker this phone number. We don't want him to suspect you're working for the CIA. So we changed the number. Please take it down." She gave him the new number.

"You mentioned Walker." Nick asked, "Who's that?"

"He's the person we think Natalie and Sonja Dahl are working for."

"Is he KGB?"

"We're not sure who he's working for, and that's why we want you to continue your relationship with Natalie—so we can learn more about him through her. Did you give her the script I gave you last night at the restaurant?"

"Yes. I gave it exactly as you dictated it. And I have a dinner date with her tonight."

"Good," she said. "Now this may be a little tricky, but I'd like you to try to obtain one of her finger prints. Do you remember how to lift prints from your training with Col. Payne?"

"Yes, I remember, but what will I do when I get them?"

"You'll call me and I'll give you instructions. I also need to know her last name."

Nick returned to the secure room. He and Hammond continued their work through the rest of the day. At 5:30 Hammond told Nick to knock off and go relax.

"Be sure to wear a suit tomorrow for our meeting at Century," Hammond said.

U.S. Embassy
Ottawa, Canada

The CIA Station Chief in Ottawa telephoned Admiral Myers to report on his investigation of Angela Schmidt aka Sonja Dahl. The address shown on her Canadian passport was an apartment building in an area of the city inhabited mostly by East European immigrants. The apartment number shown on the passport was currently occupied by someone with a name other than either Schmidt or Dahl. The agent checked with the apartment manager who stated Angela Schmidt lived in the unit until last year when she moved out. He recognized her photo from the passport and identified her as Angela Schmidt. She left no forwarding address.

Finger prints taken from the Georgetown apartment were checked with Canadian police. Because she had no Canadian criminal record, there was no match in their files.

Admiral Myers passed this information to Susan Samuels and Director Dean. Dean said he would begin a finger print check through Interpol. Dean added, "At least we now know her real name is Angela Schmidt."

Santa Monica, California

Back now at his hotel room, Nick telephoned Natalie. He asked where she would like to have dinner. She said she'd figure it out and pick him up at the hotel entrance in an hour, if that was okay with him. It was.

He took a quick shower to freshen up and put on clean clothes—a fresh casual shirt and khaki pants. He put a small roll of clear tape and a tissue filled with fine-grain power in his pocket. Col. Payne had given him the powder in a travel-size tin labeled "talcum powder."

Natalie drove up to the hotel at 6:30. Nick was waiting at the entrance and jumped in the car. She suggested going to The Warehouse restaurant in Marina del Rey. She said they have great steaks and sea food and an awesome view of the world's largest man-made marina. He said it sounds terrific.

During the short drive down Pacific Avenue through Venice Beach, Nick asked for her last name.

"It's Thompson," she replied. "What's yours?"

"Butler," he answered.

They pulled into the restaurant's parking lot and left the car with the valet. Walking on wooden planks above an enormous Koi pond, they entered the restaurant.

The hostess showed them to a window table overlooking the harbor. The sight of the marina was fantastic. There must be 5,000 sail boats docked there, Nick estimated.

A waiter brought menus and two glasses of water. They both ordered margaritas. Nick suggested they order hors d'oeuvres. She chose shrimp cocktail again; he asked for six oysters on the half-shell. When the hors d'oeuvres arrived, each ordered the house specialty: steaks, rare, with baked potatoes, sour cream, and chives.

The conversation was inconsequential until they finished the hors d'oeuvres and margaritas. That's when Natalie asked how his day had been at NDAC.

"It's hard work, but very important national security work," he said. "I wish I could tell you about it but it's Top Secret. I can say the people at NDAC are first-rate. Tomorrow afternoon they're taking me to one of Century Aerospace's factories for a meeting. I can't wait to see what they're doing."

As she reflected on what he said, she reached for her water glass and took a sip. Putting it down, she excused herself to go to the ladies' room. When she left, he reached across the table and picked up her water glass by its rim with his cloth napkin. He took out his powder and tape. He lightly powdered the glass, exposing finger prints. He placed a strip of clear tape on each print. He removed the tape from the glass and attached the strips to a piece of white paper he had folded in his pocket, just as Col. Payne had taught him. He cleaned the powder off the glass with his napkin and put it back. She returned to the table a few minutes later.

Nick suspected she made a phone call while she was away from the table. His guess was correct; she had—to Walker. The FBI wire tap in Walker's home phone picked up the call. Natalie told Walker the target, named Nick Butler, is working at NDAC on an important Top Secret national security project and will be visiting Century Aerospace tomorrow afternoon. Walker told her to learn more about the work at NDAC tonight, but more importantly probe for information tomorrow night about the Century visit. He said pay attention to the word "stealth" should he use it. That's the key to the assignment.

The FBI agent monitoring the call immediately telephoned Special Agent Williams and reported the call. Williams asked him to play the tape. Then Williams called Director Dean and reported the suspect, Natalie, had called Walker, who directed her activities for the rest of the evening and for the following day. This phone call established Natalie as a member of Walker's espionage ring and confirmed her as a suspect.

Dean had Williams call Susan Samuels to play the tape for her. Samuels knew what to expect. Once again, Romeo had repeated her script perfectly and had further confirmed Harvey Walker as a double-agent. Dean had already informed Dr. Singleton at the White House. All this took place in Washington while Nick and Natalie were having dinner in Marina del Rey, California.

After Nick and Natalie finished dinner, they took a stroll along the pedestrian walkway bordering the marina to get a closer look at the sail boats. It was an unusually warm night for Southern California in late June. The air was fresh with a breeze off the ocean. Returning to the car, Nick asked Natalie, "What would you like to do now?"

She didn't reply. She simply wrapped her arms around his neck and kissed him. Words were not needed.

An hour later, Natalie left his room and drove back to her apartment. While they were at dinner, the FBI tapped her apartment telephone and collected several sets of finger prints. The prints Nick collected would be used to identify her prints from others in the apartment.

The next morning, Wednesday, Nick dressed in a suit for his visit to Century. He walked to the NDAC building and was escorted to the secure room. Hammond was already there writing the report. Later in the morning Nick asked to use the phone. He dialed Samuels' new number. The voice said "code in."

"Romeo," he said.

"Good morning, Nick," Samuels said immediately. "How was your date last night?"

"Everything went according to plan. I lifted a set of her finger prints. Also she told me her last name is Thompson."

"Well done. Did she leave the table for a few minutes during dinner?"

"Yeah. I suspected she made a phone call."

"Indeed she did. She called Walker and reported what you said at dinner, including the visit to Century today. Did she probe for more information later in the evening?"

"She did, but I found a way to deflect it." She could imagine how.

"Please go to the NDAC Security Office and meet with Captain Sullivan. Give him the set of prints you lifted. Someone from the FBI will pick them up from Sullivan later today."

"Understood."

Century Aerospace
El Segundo, California

At 1:00 P.M. Hammond and Butler arrived at Century's factory in El Segundo, directly south of Los Angeles International Airport. This enormous industrial complex appeared to be a mile in length. Leaving the highway, they drove across a railroad spur, parked in a visitor's space, and went in the main entrance. A security guard checked their IDs, signed them in, and made a phone call. A short time later an executive joined them in the reception area.

"Gentlemen," he said, "welcome to Century. I'm Ivo Espy, Vice President for Special Projects here at Century's Military Aircraft Systems Division."

"I'm David Hammond and this is Nick Butler, who's an intern at Century's Washington office." Everyone shook hands. Espy inspected their badges, noting both visitors had a Top Secret clearance.

Espy opened the inside security door that led down a long corridor finally opening into the high-bay part of the factory. There they saw a production line of aft-ends of fighter aircraft. Espy told them they're F/A-18s, the U.S. Navy's new fighter/attack airplane. Passing beyond the production line, they walked across an area open to the sky between factory buildings. Finally they arrived at a large windowless building painted black. Two armed guards stood at the door. Espy opened the door with a pass code as the guards inspected the visitors' badges.

"This is the Special Projects area," Espy announced as they went inside and walked down a corridor. "Let's go to the conference room where I'll explain a few things." Arriving there, everyone took a seat. A project engineer joined them. He was carrying a manila envelope.

"Last week," Espy began, "Century's CEO, Mr. Martin Stark, received a request from the government to assist you, Mr. Butler, with a project you have underway. Mr. Stark agreed Century would provide that assistance."

"I'm grateful for Mr. Stark's cooperation, Mr. Espy," Nick said.

Espy took the package from the engineer, who left the room.

"This package," Espy said handing it to Nick, "contains information the government requested. The document inside is stamped 'Top Secret, Special Access Required.' The Air Force granted you temporary 'Special Access' in addition to your Top Secret clearance so you could receive this package. You are to do with it as you have been instructed or soon will be. Do you have any questions?"

"No, sir," Nick replied.

"Very well," Espy shifted gears, "now let's talk about what you came to see us about, Dr. Hammond. Century is engaged in an investigation of stealth applications to military aircraft. We have been informed by the government that Wilshire Aerospace is similarly engaged. We were told our approach is quite different from Wilshire's and that's what's interesting to the Air Force and to NDAC, which is helping the Air Force with the evaluation. But you already know this, right?"

"Correct," Hammond replied, moving to the edge of his seat.

Espy continued: "We believe it is possible to design an airplane that will be resistant to radar detection. No presently flying airplane can accomplish this because of its inherent nature. A stealthy airplane has to be designed from scratch—entirely new in its basic design to achieve what we call 'low observable.' We are presently designing such an airplane. It is well along and may be flight tested within the next few years, as I suspect Wilshire's will. If either design is successful in evading radar detection, the Air Force will have achieved the breakthrough it has long sought—virtual invisibility. Soviet air defenses will be useless against such an attack force and they know it. We will have won the Cold War without firing a shot."

"Once again American technology will triumph—this time peacefully!" Hammond observed. Then he asked hesitantly: "Are you permitted to tell us what type of stealth airplane Century is designing?"

"I am permitted to tell you we are designing a bomber," replied Espy.

Hammond and Butler whistled through their teeth as they fell back in their chairs, not expecting such a dramatic announcement. This was stunning news, portending a decisive shift in the global balance of power in favor of the United States.

"If its flight tests are successful, it will go into production immediately. This information is of course Top Secret," Espy added.

"Do you know what type of stealth aircraft Wilshire Aerospace is designing?" asked Hammond.

"You'll have to get that information from Wilshire or the Air Force," Espy responded. "We at Century have not been told, but I personally suspect it's *not* a bomber."

"The work you and Wilshire are doing right now is the single most important undertaking within the United States to enhance our national security," Hammond declared. "The consequences of your success, we at NDAC agree with you, will be the game-changer in the Cold War. We are eager to help the Air Force with the technical evaluations."

"Thank you, Dr. Hammond, for that comment," Espy said. "It helps me to know that NDAC also recognizes that we are in the midst of a sea-change in military technology that has far-reaching consequences—all for our nation's benefit. Is there anything else I can do for you gentlemen today?"

"Not today," Hammond replied. "We've already taken up too much of your valuable time. Thank you for your information."

Espy reached for a telephone. He said the engineer whom they had seen earlier would escort them out of the building. When the engineer arrived, everyone shook hands. The visitors departed the Special Projects area.

National Defense Analysis Center
Santa Monica, California

Arriving back at NDAC, Nick asked Hammond to let him use his telephone. In Hammond's office Nick dialed Samuels' new number.

"How was the Century visit?" she asked.

"Beyond fascinating," Romeo replied. "Mr. Ivo Espy gave me a manila envelope he said contains highly classified information the government requested. He was careful not to say in front of Dr. Hammond it was requested by the CIA. The envelope is not sealed."

"That's according to plan. Here's what I want you to do with that package. Call Natalie Thompson right away and ask for a date for tonight. She will accept. Tell her you're tired of eating in restaurants and suggest a take-out to have at her apartment. Tell her you're carrying a package you'll have to bring along for safe-keeping. I want you to spend some time there this evening. Clear so far?"

"Yes."

"Good. While you're in her apartment find an excuse to let her see the contents of the package without you observing her doing that. I expect she'll secretly photograph its contents. That's what I want her to do. It's vital she not see you observe her doing it. Can you find a way to make that happen?"

"I'll think of something."

"Call me in the morning from a pay phone and let me know what happened," she ordered.

Nick dialed Natalie's number. She asked how his day is going.

"It's been fabulous," he replied, prattling like a teenager. "My visit to Century was incredible. I learned so much. Their manufacturing complex is enormous. I've never been in an airplane factory. It was amazing!"

"Well, well," she murmured. "I'd like to hear more about it."

"I'd like to tell you more about it. How about over dinner tonight?"

"Terrific. Where do you want to go?"

"You know, I'm tired of restaurants. How about we pick up a Chinese take-out and have it at your place?"

"I have a better idea," she said. "I'll cook for you, if you're not afraid of ptomaine poisoning?"

"I'm sure you're a great cook. Could you pick me up at NDAC about 5:30 and we'll take it from there? I have a Century package I'll have to bring along for safe-keeping."

"Deal," she replied.

Santa Monica, California

Natalie immediately telephoned Walker to report on the evening's plans, saying that Butler will be carrying a Century package. Walker told her he will have another agent standing by outside her apartment with a camera. He ordered her to find a way to remove Butler from the scene while the package is photographed.

An FBI agent listened to the call through the wire tap on Walker's home phone and reported to Special Agent Williams. He phoned Samuels and the Special Agent in Charge in L.A., who confirmed the call from his tap on Natalie's phone.

At 5:30 Natalie picked up Nick in front of the NDAC building and drove directly to her apartment. She noticed he was carrying a manila envelope. She expected to see him in a business suit, given he was at a meeting at Century. After they entered her apartment, she handed him a pair of jeans in his size—32x36.

"I expected you'd want to change into something more comfortable, so I bought these for you this afternoon after we talked," she said. "I hope you like them."

"Thanks. They're just what I wanted and"—after he looked at the tag—"exactly my size," he said as he started to remove his suit. He laid the envelope on the dining table and began piling up his business clothes on a chair next to it. "On second thought," he said, "what I'd really like to do is take a shower to freshen up before I put on your jeans. Do you mind if I use your shower?"

"Not at all," she replied, realizing he had solved her problem. "I'll get you a towel."

Nick took off the rest of his clothes, went into the bathroom and shut the door. He stepped into the tub, closed the shower curtain, and turned on the water, planning to take an extra long shower to give Natalie ample time to photograph the contents of the package. After about ten minutes, he turned off the water, opened the shower curtain and began to towel off, still standing in the tub.

When Nick first went into the bathroom, Natalie opened the apartment door and let in an agent. He had a mini-camera. He opened the Century package, laid the engineering drawings on the dining table and began taking photos. There were a great many drawings to shoot. He had not finished when the shower water went off. Natalie thought of a way to buy more time for the agent. She stripped and entered the bathroom.

After their shower together, Nick and Natalie dried each other off. When they left the bathroom, everything in the apartment appeared normal. The agent had left with his camera loaded with 20 photos of the 20 engineering drawings in the Century package. He had replaced the drawings in the envelope.

Nick put on the new jeans without bothering with his briefs or his T-shirt and padded barefoot into the kitchen to make their drinks. Natalie dressed in shorts and a tank-top. Nick assumed she had taken the photos because she was relaxed and seemed indifferent to the package lying on the table. She joined him in the kitchen and started to fix dinner.

After the agent left Natalie's apartment, he walked directly to a pay telephone on 3rd Street to call Harvey Walker. He reported he had photographed the Century classified material without being observed by the target. Walker ordered him to take an overnight flight to Washington, D.C. and put the film in the previously designated dead drop. The FBI of course recorded this conversation.

Earlier, Special Agent Williams had directed the FBI's Los Angeles office to stake out Natalie's apartment. When Walker's agent left, an FBI agent tailed him to the pay phone. While he was on the phone, the FBI agent photographed him. Finishing his call, Walker's photographer got in his car and drove to LAX. The FBI agent tailed him. He watched as the suspect went to the American Airlines ticket counter. He purchased a roundtrip ticket to Dulles Airport, departing LAX at 11:10 P.M.

The FBI agent phoned his supervisor to report. The supervisor dispatched another FBI agent to the airport to pick up the camera and bring it to headquarters to develop the film. The supervisor ordered the first agent to purchase a ticket for the same flight and keep the suspect under surveillance. The supervisor reported all this to Williams in Washington.

Special Agent Williams ordered two FBI agents to meet the flight when it arrived at Dulles at 6:50 A.M. to link-up with the incoming FBI agent to identify the suspect. These D.C.-based agents would then tail the photographer to the dead drop. If Walker goes to the drop and picks up the classified film, he will be indicted for treason.

The next morning, Thursday, Nick called Susan Samuels from a pay telephone in the hotel lobby. He told her he believed Natalie photographed the Century package's contents.

"Actually," Samuels stated, "*she* didn't. An accomplice of hers did."

Oh, Nick thought to himself, that's why she came into the shower.

"Well," Nick said to Samuels, "at least the job got done."

"You never saw the accomplice last night and he never saw you?"

"That's right."

"Well, how in the world did you manage that?" she asked, disbelievingly.

"I was in the shower with Natalie," he reluctantly admitted. Samuels nearly burst out laughing. Romeo had done it again, she thought to herself.

"Okay," she said, recovering her composure. "You did very well last night. The FBI is tracking the accomplice and we hope he will lead us to Walker. I have one more task for you. Do you have the Century package with you?"

"Yes."

"Please take it to Captain Sullivan at NDAC's Security Office. In front of him I want you to seal the flap of the envelope and sign your name across the flap. Do not print your name—sign it. The FBI will pick it up later today."

"Okay."

"As far as Agency work is concerned," she continued, "your task in L.A. is finished. If you want to see Natalie again, that's up to you. At any rate, you should return to D.C. tomorrow as scheduled. Call me when you arrive at Dulles." She hung up and burst out laughing: "In the shower with Natalie! What a guy!" she said out loud.

Nick walked over to Captain Sullivan's office in the NDAC building. He sealed and signed the envelope in Sullivan's presence.

Then he returned to the secure room to continue writing the report with Hammond. The speech Hammond would give at the ISA meeting was well along and would be finished later in the day. The classified report to the Air Force was also coming along nicely. Hammond said he would complete it the following week. At 2:00 Hammond told Nick to take the rest of the day off, as well as the next morning, Friday.

"Why don't you get out of here and see something of Los Angeles. You deserve a break from this work," Hammond said. "Your help has been invaluable, and I appreciate it very much."

"Thanks, Dr. Hammond. I'll see you in Washington at the ISA meeting."

Nick walked out of the building and back to his hotel room. While he was changing into his swimming trunks, he phoned Natalie and suggested they spend the rest of the afternoon on the beach where they first met. She said she couldn't wait.

Chapter 11:
The Traitors

Washington, D.C.

American Airlines' red-eye flight arrived at Dulles Airport Friday morning at 6:50. Two FBI agents were waiting at the gate in the main terminal building. They had a facsimile copy of the suspect's photo the L.A. field office transmitted during the night and a photo of the FBI agent tailing the suspect. When the two men came through the gate, they recognized both. The L.A. FBI agent marked the suspect by pointing at him and then wandered off into the crowd. After the hand-off, the D.C.-based agents resumed the tail.

The suspect walked to the front of the terminal building to the taxi loading area. He waited his turn for an Airport Flyer cab. The FBI agents had a car waiting in the loading zone. They got in and the driver followed the taxi at a distance. The taxi went into Washington across Key Bridge, down the Whitehurst Freeway, and then to Connecticut Avenue where it turned north. The agents followed more closely now, being in morning rush hour traffic.

The taxi went to the D.C. side of Chevy Chase where it turned off Connecticut Avenue into an up-scale residential neighborhood. Soon it arrived at Tennyson Street, which on one side has expensive-looking single-family homes. Facing the homes on the other side was a densely wooded park. The taxi stopped in front of 2930 Tennyson Street, N.W. The FBI car parked at the end of the block. The passenger got out of the taxi and began walking slowly toward the house. After the taxi disappeared around the corner, the suspect turned around, crossed the street and vanished into the thick woods.

The FBI agents waited in their car. A few minutes later the suspect emerged from the woods and walked down the street away from the FBI car. At the end of the block he stopped and waited. Several minutes later a different taxi arrived and picked him up. It was a Yellow cab. Using binoculars, the agents took down the license plate number and the taxi's number.

The lead FBI agent used the car radio to report to Special Agent Williams what had happened. When he told Williams the address where the taxi had stopped, Williams whistled through his teeth. He knew Harvey Walker's house was at 2900 Tennyson Street. He ordered the agents to remain in place and watch for Walker to come out of his house at 2900 Tennyson. Photograph him but do not arrest him. Williams dispatched a second FBI team to drive to the opposite end of Tennyson Street and wait there.

"We want to know what he'll do next with the film," he told the agents.

Williams telephoned Director Dean to report the latest events. Dean told Williams to keep the surveillance teams in place until Walker appeared and then follow him. No doubt there was another dead drop he'd use if he's working for the KGB.

A half hour later the garage door at 2900 Tennyson opened. Harvey Walker, dressed in a suit, walked out through the open garage, down his driveway and across Tennyson Street. He disappeared into the woods. In a few minutes he came out and returned to his garage. Seconds later he drove off in his black Ford Crown Victoria.

He headed toward the second FBI agents' car parked at the far end of the street around the corner. Those agents watched Walker drive past. Before long he entered Rock Creek Park. The lead agent radioed Williams to report. Williams ordered both cars to continue the tail.

Rock Creek Park is a large, forested area in the northwest part of the city bordering the creek for which it is named. Walker drove about a mile into the park then pulled off the road into a clearing, a picnic area's unpaved parking lot. It was deserted at that hour of the morning. He got out of the car, looked around, seeing no one, then walked past the picnic tables to an abandoned metal BBQ, opened the rusted-out lid and put a small package inside. He closed the lid, scratched a horizontal white chalk mark on the side of the BBQ facing the road, then returned to his car and drove off.

This entire activity was photographed and filmed from concealed locations by the FBI agents using telephoto lenses. They were parked off the road some distance away behind trees and bushes. The agents radioed Williams to report.

Williams ordered one of the cars to drive beyond the picnic area to another camouflaged location and wait. Now agents were parked out of sight at both ends of the picnic area.

About a half hour later a black Buick with D.C. Diplomatic plates drove into the picnic area and stopped. Anastas Kamarovski got out of the car. He was alone. The FBI agents recognized him from his file photo as the KGB *Rezident* at the Soviet Embassy. The agents photographed and filmed every step of his walk to the BBQ, photographed him removing the package, smudging the chalk mark, returning to his car, and driving away with the package.

The agents radioed Williams. He ordered the agents in both cars to come immediately to FBI Headquarters to develop their film. Williams asked to see Director Dean.

FBI Headquarters
Washington, D.C.

After his debrief with Williams, Director Dean summoned his Senior Staff to the secure conference room. He asked Special Agent Williams to summarize the past two day's activities, beginning with the photographer taking pictures of Century's Top Secret material in Natalie Thompson's apartment in Santa Monica. While Williams was giving his report, Dean phoned Admiral Myers.

"It looks like we've caught a double-agent this morning," Dean stated to the Admiral. He recounted the picnic area events that proved conclusively Walker was working for the KGB. "The *Rezident* himself picked up the film shortly after Walker placed it in the dead drop."

"What's your plan now?" Myers asked.

"I'm going to arrest Walker as soon as he arrives at his office, which should be at 9:00."

"What about Sonja Dahl and Natalie Thompson?"

"I plan to arrest them at 9:30, along with the photographer. He's on his way to Dulles according to the Yellow cab dispatcher. I'll have him arrested there and charged as an accessory to commit treason. We're rolling up this spy ring today."

Dean then phoned the Attorney General and Dr. Singleton at the White House to convey the same information. Singleton congratulated the FBI on their excellent counter-espionage work.

"Thanks very much," Dean said. "But none of this could have happened if it hadn't been for Romeo. We owe that young fellow a great debt."

"I agree," said the Assistant to the President. "I'll inform the President at once."

At 9:00 A.M. Harvey Walker arrived at FBI Headquarters to begin his day's work. As usual he parked in his reserved space in the building's underground garage and took the elevator up to his office—Deputy Director, Counter-Intelligence.

His secretary informed him Director Dean had called a meeting of the Senior Staff and wanted him immediately in the secure conference room. Walker went to the conference room. As he entered he saw the FBI's Senior Staff members already assembled. No one was speaking. Walker took a seat, assuming something important was about to be announced.

Special Agent Lamar Williams walked over to where Walker was seated and stood before him.

"Harvey Walker," Williams stated, "you are under arrest for the crime of high treason against the United States." Walker said nothing. He just stared vacuously at Williams through his close-set, wolf-gray eyes.

Two well-built FBI agents standing in the back of the room immediately came forward and handcuffed Walker. One of the agents read his Miranda rights. Williams had already removed Walker's ID badge and checked for a weapon. He was not armed. The two agents took him out of the room to the elevator, each agent holding him firmly by an arm. At the basement level he was locked in a holding cell. Walker uttered not a single word except "yes" to the Miranda question.

Director Dean congratulated Lamar Williams on his excellent handling of the case. The entire Senior Staff stood and applauded Williams. The telephone rang. Director Dean picked it up. Dr. Singleton was on the line. He said the President wanted to congratulate him and the FBI on capturing this most heinous criminal. Dean said the congratulations should be given to Special Agent Williams. Singleton agreed. Dean handed him the phone.

"Special Agent Williams," President Reed said, "on behalf of the American people I want to thank you and your entire team for your excellent work ridding our nation of this despicable traitor. You have my heartfelt thanks."

"Thank you, Mr. President," Williams replied. "I appreciate your kind words."

Georgetown
Washington, D.C.

At 9:30 A.M. Sonja Dahl was still asleep in her Georgetown apartment. The ringing of the door bell awakened her. The ringing continued. She reluctantly got out of bed, put on a robe, and went to the door.

"Who's there?" she asked through the door.

"Federal Agents," was the reply. "Open up!"

She opened the door to be confronted by two serious-looking men in dark suits.

"Are you Sonja Dahl?" one of the men asked, showing his FBI ID.

"Yes, I am. What's the matter?"

"Sonja Dahl," the agent stated, "you are under arrest for the crime of conspiracy to commit high treason against the United States. You will come with us to FBI Headquarters."

"I don't understand," she stammered. "I never did anything."

Before she could say anything more, the agent read her Miranda rights. "Do you understand these rights?" he demanded.

"Well, yes I do, but there must be some mistake. I never committed treason," she babbled.

"There's no mistake, miss. You can put on street clothes before we take you in or you can come dressed as you are. It's your choice."

"Come in," she said. "I'll get dressed." The agents watched her carefully as she dressed.

Ten minutes later the agents handcuffed Sonja Dahl and put her in the back seat of their car. When they arrived at FBI Headquarters she was taken to a holding cell on the lower level. Though they were only twenty feet apart, she and Walker did not see each other.

Santa Monica, California

The previous afternoon in Santa Monica Nick Butler and Natalie Thompson met on the beach. It was a warm summer day and the sun felt great. Natalie was in her yellow bikini; Nick was in his swimming trunks and his Phillies cap. They lay side-by-side on towels absorbing the Southern California sunshine.

"So you were sprung early from your work at NDAC?" she asked rhetorically.

"Yes," he replied with a grin. "I suppose my boss felt I'd done enough damage to the project so he let me go early," he said with a chuckle. "My work here is finished. I'll leave for D.C. tomorrow at noon."

"And you wanted to spend your last day in California with me. How sweet."

"You bet. And I'm glad you wanted to be with me, too," he said as he leaned over to give her a kiss.

As the afternoon faded the air began to get chilly as usual. Nick asked if she was free for the rest of the evening. She replied she's free until the morning.

"In that case," Nick said, "why don't we get started? My hotel room is closest."

"Sounds good to me," she said picking up her things.

They walked up the hill to his room at the Holiday Inn. He turned down the bed. They took off their bathing suits and got in. They made love twice before they decided they needed some food. Natalie suggested they take a quick shower, get dressed and go to her apartment, picking up a take-out on the way.

At her apartment and after eating Chinese, they got in Natalie's bed and made love again. Eventually the young lovers fell asleep in each other's arms.

The next morning, Friday, at 6:30 A.M. there was a loud rapping on Natalie's apartment door. The rapping continued. Nick and Natalie woke up startled. She got out of bed, put on a robe and went to the door. He stayed in bed.

"Who's there?" she asked through the door.

"Federal Agents," was the reply. "Open up!"

She opened the door to be confronted by two men in dark suits.

"Are you Natalie Thompson?" one of the agents demanded as he showed his FBI ID.

"Yes."

"Natalie Thompson, you are under arrest for the crime of conspiracy to commit high treason against the United States," he announced. The other agent presented his FBI identification and read her Miranda rights.

"What are you talking about? I haven't committed treason!"

"Do you understand your rights?"

"Yes, but. . ." she stammered.

"You will come with us dressed as you are or you can put on clothes."

"I'll get dressed," she said as she turned back into the apartment. The agents followed her into the bedroom. Nick sat up in bed. He was nude but partly under the covers.

"What's going on?" Nick asked. "Who are you?"

"Sir," an agent replied, "this does not concern you. This is FBI business. Miss Thompson is coming with us."

"Going with you where?" Nick demanded.

"To the Federal Courthouse," the agent replied. "She's under arrest."

"Under arrest? For what?" Nick almost shouted.

"Conspiracy to commit treason against the United States."

Nick got out of bed and put on his jeans. The agents watched Natalie closely as she dressed in jeans, a blouse and sandals. They handcuffed her and took her out the door, each agent holding her by an arm. Nick followed with a bewildered look on his face. Natalie was put in the back seat of the sedan between the two agents. Nick was standing at the curb with his mouth agape, watching as they drove away.

Nick returned to the apartment and started to use Natalie's telephone to call Susan Samuels, but just in time he remembered the phone was probably bugged by the FBI and perhaps also the KGB. He put on his T-shirt and sneakers, gathered up his business clothes and the Century package, and left the apartment to find a pay phone to call Susan Samuels. He found one two blocks away on 3rd Street.

"What the hell is going on?" he shouted into the phone when Samuels came on the line.

"What are you talking about?" she responded, startled by his tone of voice.

"What am I talking about? Are you serious? The FBI just arrested Natalie right in front of me—for treason, for God's sake! They took her away. They said to the Federal Courthouse."

"That's right," Samuels said. "She participated in the theft of classified documents from you and passed them to Walker, who passed them to the KGB. The FBI rounded up the entire spy ring this morning, including Natalie."

"What do you mean—the entire spy ring? Who else was arrested?"

"Sonja Dahl was also arrested this morning at her apartment, along with Walker himself."

"What? How in the hell. . . ." Stunned by this news, Nick was at a loss for words. Two women in his life were arrested. He tried to say more but words wouldn't come out. He was reeling.

"Nick," Samuels spoke in a calm voice, trying to put his mind at ease, "you have been the key instrument in a sting operation that caught the most destructive double-agents in modern U.S. history—Harvey Walker and his accomplices Sonja Dahl and Natalie Thompson. You should be proud of yourself."

All of a sudden he felt sick at his stomach. It wasn't fun and games anymore. He was responsible for this—putting his lovers in jail, for God's sake! Samuels had used him to betray these women. Guilt for doing that and anger at Samuels for manipulating him welled up inside him. When he finally managed to speak, he erupted—spitting out his fury: "Go screw yourself," he shouted in the phone and slammed down the receiver.

Soviet Embassy
Washington, D.C.

Looking at the developed film he lifted that morning from the dead drop in Rock Creek Park, Anastas Kamarovski congratulated himself. This, along with Wilshire Aerospace's stealth engineering drawings he previously obtained, is my greatest intelligence achievement. He hoped these two triumphs would earn him the Order of Lenin.

The technical advisor at the embassy, a Soviet Air Force colonel, gave his opinion that these Century engineering drawings would save the Sukhoi Design Bureau at least a decade of trial-and-error design work and testing, enabling the Soviet Air Force to field operational stealth aircraft almost as soon as the United States. Kamarovski put the developed pictures in the embassy's diplomatic pouch to send to KGB Headquarters that afternoon.

The *Rezident* phoned Yuri Andropov on the secure line.

"Comrade Chairman," Kamarovski began proudly, "this morning we achieved a second major intelligence coup against the United States. I am sending in the pouch 20 high quality photographs of Top Secret engineering designs of a stealth airplane from Century Aerospace's Special Projects area."

"Congratulations, Comrade *Rezident*," Andropov said. "I am eager to see the photos. What was the method you used to obtain this information?"

"The 'inside channel' we recruited years ago obtained it. He has performed brilliantly. A female member of his network lifted the documents from the industrial spy Nick Butler without his knowing it happened."

"He deserves a bonus to share with his network," the Chairman declared. After all, Andropov thought to himself, "inside channel" was no committed

Communist. Walker made it clear from the beginning he was working only for money. To Andropov, this success further confirmed his theory is correct—female agents produce the best results once they secure a relationship with a target through easy, regular sex. "Put one hundred thousand U.S. dollars in the dead drop, in addition to his regular monthly payment of $10,000."

"Right away, Comrade Chairman."

Sitting alone in his office, Andropov reflected on the two stealth airplane designs his agents had obtained. Not to diminish the importance of engineering drawings, he realized he did not know how the Americans planned to use these warplanes—what their operational strategy would be for them. This technology breakthrough would arm the U.S. with a first-strike capability. To enable the Soviet Air Force to counter this terrible threat, he realized he now needed to obtain the U.S. Air Force's operational plans. He knew those plans would be in David Hammond's classified report. He must have that report to learn the Americans' intentions. Obtaining it just became the KGB's top priority.

Santa Monica, California

Still in a daze from witnessing Natalie's arrest and furious at Susan Samuels, Nick decided to walk to the Holiday Inn to try to figure out what to do next. It would take him about a half hour. He hoped the cool early morning breeze off the ocean would clear his head.

Walking on Ocean Avenue along the palisades overlooking the Pacific, he tried to come to grips with what had happened—and with what he had done. To be honest, he thought to himself, he had known from Samuels that Sonja was a foreign agent. He also knew from the way Samuels used him to set Sonja up with information he was entrapping her. Yet, when the trap shut—as it did this morning at her apartment in Georgetown—the shock of it hit him like a ton of bricks.

He also realized what he knew about Natalie Thompson was less clear. He did know she was some sort of spy, but he had never been told by Samuels she was a KGB agent, only that she worked for Walker. That person must be a KGB agent to have been arrested this morning. Nick knew nothing about Walker except he must be the center of the spy ring. Who is that person? he wondered.

What was troubling him above everything else, he began to realize as he continued his walk, was that he had been manipulated. Samuels even called him an "instrument." He felt like a tool! He was kept totally in the dark about *why* he was doing some of the things she told him to do, and he was kept blind to the consequences of the things he did. All his adult life he was used to being in control, but in this situation he was under Samuels' control. Yet, he had to admit to himself he had known all along what he was being told to do was no game. It was serious and it was real!

The most shocking moment was when the FBI came into Natalie's bedroom and right in front of him arrested her. He was literally naked, powerless to help his lover. Yet, *she* had used him, too. Now he understood why she came into the shower—to buy time for an accomplice to photograph the Century package in the next room. How crude is that! Yet, that's exactly what Samuels wanted.

The events of the past weeks were muddling his brain as he arrived at the hotel early that Friday morning. As he took the elevator up to his room what stood out from everything that happened was that he had been used—played like a damned puppet on a string. And Samuels pulled the strings. He'd had enough! He was ready to quit.

Chapter 12:
The Moles

CIA Headquarters
Langley, Virginia

Immediately after hanging up with Romeo, Susan Samuels took the elevator to the seventh floor of CIA Headquarters and rushed into Philip Myers' office.

"We have a serious problem with Romeo," she nervously stated to the Admiral as she closed the door. "He's behaving erratically, which is highly unusual for him. In fact, I'm afraid I've lost control of him."

"How do you mean—'erratically'?" her boss asked.

"He was upset witnessing the arrest of Natalie Thompson this morning. And when I told him the FBI also arrested Dahl and Walker, he became furious. He cursed at me and slammed down the phone."

"I see," the Admiral muttered, rubbing his face deeply-lined from years at sea. "This *is* troubling. We cannot lose control of Romeo. He's the critical player in Stealth Gambit as well as the FBI's prosecution of Walker's espionage network."

"I know how vital he is and that's why I fear I mishandled him and may have lost him," Samuels confessed to her boss.

"Well, let me think out loud," Myers said trying to calm his Assistant Deputy. "The arrest of Natalie Thompson occurred at 9:30 A.M. Washington time. The FBI planned to make all three arrests at about the same time— Walker's, Dahl's, and Thompson's. In Santa Monica that was 6:30 A.M. And you say Romeo witnessed Thompson's arrest?"

"That's what he just told me."

"That means at that hour of the morning he was in bed with her in her apartment, obviously having spent the night," Myers concluded. "No wonder he was upset. He was startled by a knock on the door in the early hours, watched as his lover was handcuffed and taken away, and no doubt felt like his world had crashed down around him."

"I didn't know he would be with her," Samuels admitted. "But I did tell him yesterday he could see her again if he wanted to. I also told him his work for us in Santa Monica was finished."

"From what we know about his prior behavior there is no way that young man would not want to spend his last night in L.A. with that woman. It was the shock of seeing her arrested that caused him to blow up."

"I think it was that and something more. I think he felt I had manipulated him," Samuels speculated. "Perhaps I needed to tell him about the importance of trapping Walker's network and what a critical role he was playing in that op. After all, that was a different assignment from Stealth Gambit. For the Walker counter-espionage op he was operating blind."

"I think you have a point," Myers said. "What's vitally important in the Walker case is the prosecutors will need Romeo's testimony at the trial of the three traitors. He will be the key witness. For our part, we absolutely need Romeo to continue our Stealth Gambit disinformation op with the KGB. The Walker matter is incidental to our op—important though it is in and of itself. Yet, nothing must be allowed to derail Stealth Gambit, which is moving along so successfully. So for the sake of *both* ops what it boils down to is this: we have to rehabilitate Butler and bring him back under control." To accomplish exactly that, CIA's Deputy Director of Operations gave his Assistant Deputy some very specific instructions.

Holiday Inn
Santa Monica, California

By the time Nick arrived at his room at the Holiday Inn he concluded, regardless of what had happened, he is finished in L.A. and needed to get back to his apartment in Georgetown and to his job at Century Aerospace. Yet, his heart wasn't in it.

Feeling like a zombie, he showered, put on a T-shirt, the jeans Natalie had bought, and sneakers. He packed his other clothes and the Century package for the flight to Washington.

He checked out of the hotel, took a cab to LAX, and checked in at the United Airlines counter. He took the escalator up to the concourse, walked to his departure gate, and slumped down on a seat in the boarding area to wait for the flight to D.C. to be called. The flight was scheduled to arrive at Dulles that evening at 8:40.

He was dispirited, mentally adrift—in a surreal dream-state disconnected from reality. But mostly he was bitter—disgusted at himself for failing to realize he was being played and infuriated at Samuels for jerking him around.

FBI Headquarters
Washington, D.C.

During the day on Friday, FBI Director Dean telephoned Admiral Myers at Langley.

"The finger print check with Interpol on Angela Schmidt, aka Sonja Dahl, produced no match," Dean stated. "We're at the end of a blind alley, I fear, as far as checking criminal records are concerned. She has no criminal record so our official sources are unable to identify her."

"Thanks for that information," Myers said. "However, we have some fresh intelligence from one of our sources. We have verified Angela Schmidt was born in East Germany and taken as a child by the Stasi to Ottawa, Canada to be raised there. This is the typical route the KGB uses to introduce moles into the United States. There is no doubt she is a trained KGB agent posing as Sonja Dahl."

"That's exactly what Susan Samuels had guessed," Dean observed. "And now it is absolutely confirmed?" he asked, knowing he could not inquire how the CIA had come by this intel.

"Absolutely confirmed." A CIA double-agent in East Germany made the confirmation.

"Do you have any additional information on Natalie Thompson at this time?"

"Nothing definite yet. We suspect she is also a Stasi/KGB-trained mole. This is the pattern Yuri Andropov has used any number of times."

"So your theory is Andropov's op was to supply Harvey Walker with trained KGB female agents posing as Americans to facilitate his double-agent role to obtain classified aerospace technology?" asked Dean.

"That's right. And a further tip-off is both of these agents are females. As you know, Andropov believes women make the best spies."

"We can only wonder how many more men these women have seduced to gain valuable intelligence for Walker to pass to the KGB," speculated the FBI Director.

"For Andropov, the usual targets for these women are married men. They seduce them, taking photos or film to prove it," said Myers. "Then someone in the KGB threatens the man with exposure to his wife or his employer unless he plays ball. This blackmail usually works. For our Stealth Gambit op we chose Nick Butler partly because he's a bachelor and a proven ladies' man so blackmail wouldn't work on him. He enthusiastically enjoyed having sex with Walker's agents without fear of later exposure. He was proud of his sexual exploits in the mistaken belief he initiated and controlled them."

"Butler's real achievement was to extend your Stealth Gambit op into my counter-intelligence op," Dean concluded. "Butler linked the two ops for us, giving each of us a successful outcome. His performance was masterful, and, based on what you just said, he apparently enjoyed himself doing it."

Dulles Airport
Washington, D.C.

When Butler's flight landed at Dulles Airport that evening at 8:40 it was met with lightning and thunder. Torrents of rain splattered against the windows as the mobile lounge traveled from the mid-field terminal across the tarmac to the main terminal building.

The fierce weather matched his foul mood. Nick couldn't get it out of his mind how he had been given not one shred of information about Walker's spy ring and how Samuels had played him. He felt like a sucker.

When he arrived at the gate inside the ultramodern terminal building, he was surprised to be met by Elliott Peterson—the same CIA agent who had delivered the message to him at the Century Aerospace office and who had driven him to meet Samuels.

"Good evening, sir," the young well-dressed agent said to Butler. It took Nick a second to recognize the man.

"Good evening to you," Butler replied with a startled look.

"Sir, will you please come with me? I have a car waiting for you."

CIA Headquarters
Langley, Virginia

Earlier in the day, after Samuels left Admiral Myers' office to carry out his instructions, she returned to her office to begin orchestrating Romeo's rehabilitation program.

First she arranged for him to be picked up at Dulles by an agent he would recognize—Elliott Peterson. The agent was instructed to drive Romeo to CIA Headquarters entering the grounds by the back road off George Washington Parkway. Using that heavily wooded entrance, Romeo would not likely be spotted by the KGB, especially in a driving rain. Elliott was told to park the car in the secure area under the building and take the Director's private elevator to the seventh floor to Myers' office.

Second, she telephoned FBI Director Dean, asking him to send Special Agent Williams to CIA Headquarters at 9:00 that evening to meet Romeo and inform him how important his role has been rounding up Walker's spy ring. When Dean informed Williams of Samuels' request, he agreed to go. Williams was eager to meet this amazing spy anyway.

The officials assembled at 9:00 in Admiral Myers' office waiting for Butler to be brought from the airport. Each was prepared to do his part to keep him operational. Myers was in his three-star Admiral's uniform.

At 9:30, Butler, escorted by Elliott Peterson, entered Myers' office looking haggard. Elliott departed immediately. Standing alone by the door, Nick saw three important-looking people. The only one he recognized was Susan Samuels, toward whom he was furious. She walked to the door and greeted him warmly.

"Come in, Nick," she said taking his hand. "I hope your flight was pleasant."

"It was okay," he muttered in a surly way, suspicious about what was happening to him and not sure he liked it one bit. What's she up to now? he wondered.

"Nick," Samuels said, "we brought you here to fill you in on the importance of the work you've been doing for us. To help do that, I want you to meet the people who have been working on the same task you have. This is the leadership team that brought down the most dangerous double-agent in modern times."

Nick's anger was beginning to fade at being greeted so graciously, but he felt awkward standing in this beautifully-appointed office wearing jeans and a T-shirt. The others were in business clothes.

"First," said Samuels, "this is my boss: Admiral Philip Myers, CIA's Deputy Director of Operations. Admiral Myers, please meet Nick Butler."

"Nick," said Myers, "I'm proud to meet you. Your work for the Agency has been superb. Thank you for what you've done for our country." The two men shook hands.

"You're welcome," Nick replied unenthusiastically.

"Next," said Samuels, "I'd like to introduce FBI Special Agent Lamar Williams. Agent Williams headed the FBI team that caught the Walker spy ring. Special Agent Williams, please meet Nick Butler."

"Mr. Butler," Williams said, "on behalf of the FBI it is an honor to meet you and thank you for a job well done." They shook hands. Lamar Williams continued, "The FBI and CIA team could not have penetrated this spy ring without your help. You were the critical factor in this operation's success."

"Thank you," Nick responded to Williams, starting to feel better about what was happening.

"Please take a seat everyone," Myers said as he moved toward the sitting area. "Nick, please sit by me," said the 6'2" Admiral as he put his arm around the younger man's shoulders guiding him to a chair.

After everyone was seated, Myers asked Special Agent Williams to explain who Walker is and what he had done.

"Mr. Butler," Williams started, looking at Nick, "you have a need to know that Harvey Walker was the most dangerous double-agent in the recent history of the United States. His position was FBI Deputy Director for Counter-Intelligence, reporting to the Director of the FBI. For years he had access to the most sensitive information about the FBI's pursuit of KGB agents operating in the United States and American agents operating abroad. He literally knew everything. It is now clear he provided that information to the Soviets for money."

"Please inform Mr. Butler of the latest events, Mr. Williams," directed Myers.

"The Top Secret material you obtained from Century Aerospace," Williams stated, "was the final nail in Walker's coffin. A member of his network, Natalie Thompson, had the contents of that package photographed by another of Walker's agents. The photographer brought the film to D.C. and put it in a dead drop where Walker picked it up. Our agents tailed Walker to another dead drop in Rock Creek Park where he left the package. A short while later, the KGB's top man at the Soviet Embassy came to the drop, picked up the film, and took it to the Soviet Embassy. From there it was no doubt flown to Moscow in the embassy's diplomatic pouch. Later in the day, the *Rezident* returned to the same dead drop and placed a package there. It contained $110,000 in cash. We confiscated the money. Walker has no doubt been in the pay of the KGB for many years, and it is likely he passed to them not only industrial secrets but also the identities of American agents operating in the Soviet Union, a number of whom have been murdered."

Nick didn't speak but the expression on his face said volumes—he was astonished.

"Now Nick," said Myers, "Susan Samuels will tell you about Sonja Dahl."

"We had suspected she was a KGB agent operating under cover," Samuels began. "That suspicion was recently confirmed. She was born in East Germany and brought to the United States to be a sleeper agent for the Soviet Union. She was assigned to the Walker spy ring to assist him with his espionage work for the KGB. Her real name is Angela Schmidt. Her father does not live in Chicago. She lied to you about that, as well as being a student at Georgetown. That was her cover story. She is an East German orphan trained by the KGB to be a spy."

"What do we know about Natalie Thompson, Mr. Williams?" asked Myers.

"Our investigation into that woman's background is continuing. Thus far we have not confirmed her origin. What we do know is she also lied to you, Mr. Butler. She is not registered at UCLA. She was in constant contact with Walker during the times you were with her conveying the stories Mrs. Samuels gave you to tell her. She had an accomplice photograph the Century classified package, which is the hard evidence we needed to indict her and Walker."

"We suspect Natalie Thompson is also an alias," Samuels interjected. "We further suspect she is an East German sleeper agent."

"What happens next?" Myers asked, looking at Williams.

"Walker will be indicted for the crime of high treason against the United States," said Williams. "Dahl and Thompson will be indicted for the crime of conspiracy to commit treason. The photographer/courier will be indicted as an accessory to commit treason. There will be trials on each of these criminal charges. The Department of Justice will provide the evidence we gathered to the U.S. Attorney to prosecute all four of them in Federal Court. If convicted, Walker will likely be sentenced to life in prison. The two women, if convicted, will likely serve long prison terms, as will the photographer."

"Oh my God," Nick muttered under his breath.

"Mr. Butler," Williams said, "we will need you to testify at these trials. Your role in this matter was the key to obtaining indictments, and your testimony will be the key to obtaining convictions. The government owed you this information to assure you your performance has been exemplary and in every respect honorable. You can be proud of yourself."

Nick heaved a heavy sigh of relief. He felt his guilt and anger lifted from him.

"Also, Nick," Samuels joined in, "your cover story as Century Aerospace's industrial spy will continue to be vitally important. Using that cover story, you have helped us misdirect the Soviet Union's aircraft design work—particularly stealth—for many, many years. We cannot let the KGB know your true role as a CIA agent. That would nullify the good work you achieved at the Paris Air Show and with the Wilshire and Century bogus designs."

Letting that information sink in with a pause, Admiral Myers, leaning forward and putting his hand on the 24-year-old's knee in a fatherly gesture said, "Well, Nick, does this explain the critical importance of your role in our intelligence work, and does it make you feel better about what you've been doing for your country?"

"Yes sir, it certainly does," Nick replied with a sigh. "I never knew why I was doing some of the things I was asked to do, but now I understand. Mrs. Samuels, I want to apologize for my rude remark on the phone earlier today. I plead temporary insanity." Everyone chuckled.

"You were under a great deal of stress at that particular moment, so your reaction was entirely understandable," she replied, smiling. "Of course you are forgiven."

"Mr. Butler," Special Agent Williams interjected, "please remember the telephones at your Century office and your apartment are tapped by the KGB. Also, I would like to meet with you on Monday to discuss certain aspects of the case. There are some loose ends that indicate there may be others in Walker's ring we have not yet identified. Please give me a call from a pay phone Monday morning," he said, handing Nick his FBI business card.

"Okay," Nick responded taking the card, wondering what this is about.

The meeting accomplished its purpose. Everyone read his lines perfectly. Butler was clearly back on board. Admiral Myers thanked Williams for his attendance on this rainy Friday night. As they rose from their seats, each person shook Nick's hand, thanking him again. Susan Samuels escorted Nick to the door.

"Come with me, Nick," she ordered. "I need to speak with you in my office."

Arriving at Samuels' office, she asked him to sit with her on the couch.

"The government owed you the explanations you received tonight," she began, "so you would understand—really appreciate—the importance of the role you played in capturing the Walker spy ring. I made a mistake not filling you in earlier. I apologize for that. I won't make that mistake again with the next phase of our operation. You clearly can handle the truth about what you're doing without revealing that information even inadvertently to anyone. You are a natural at spy craft."

"Thank you for that, Mrs. Samuels," Nick replied with a serious look on his face. "You're being honest with me, and now I'll be honest with you. I resented being in the dark—kept from knowing *why* I was doing what I was doing. I felt like a damned pawn in a chess game and I wasn't even a player— you were playing me. That's the reason I was so angry at you earlier today. Now that's past. I appreciate your confidence that I can handle the truth. I believe I earned it, and I definitely deserve it."

"You certainly did earn it, and now you've got it. The trust in you goes beyond what was said here tonight. I want you to know you are the single most effective clandestine agent I've worked with. I would like you to consider coming to work for the Agency on a permanent basis after you leave Columbia. You don't have to answer this now, but I would appreciate your serious consideration of it."

"I'm very flattered, Mrs. Samuels. Thank you for the offer. I certainly will consider it."

"Meanwhile, we have work to do in your role as Century's industrial spy, so I want to fill you in on the game-plan. The International Studies Association convention is coming up in two weeks at the Washington Hilton. David Hammond's speech is already generating a great deal of foreign interest. We know that from the advance requests for seating at that particular event."

"It will be a terrific speech," Nick said proudly, having worked on it.

She continued: "In addition to attending his speech, we suspect the KGB will attempt to get their hands on Hammond's classified report to the Air Force on how to employ stealth airplanes in combat situations. Getting that report must be Andropov's top priority."

Samuels paused for a moment then went on: "Of special interest to you is that Professor Jean-Pierre Capp of the Science Po will attend the ISA convention. He is coming mainly to hear Hammond's speech. He's bringing with him his recently-appointed Research Assistant, Nicole Girard."

"Nicole is coming to Washington?" Nick asked incredulously.

"That's right. Your recruitment of her as a Century industrial spy is working out quite well. Using her as a conduit, French Intelligence has transmitted false information to the KGB about various NATO combat scenarios Professor Capp is working on. Next year, just as you suggested, she will be hired by Thomson. In that capacity she will, without knowing it, pass bogus military electronic secrets to the other side. Your recruitment of her was a major coup for Western intelligence because she is a credible source for the KGB."

Nick enjoyed that compliment before asking, "Is the Baron d'Artois still involved?"

"Yes. He's her control at Century Aerospace's Paris office but she's really under the direction of the *Deuxième Bureau's* chief, Andre Devereaux, whom you met. I want you to get together with Girard while she's in Washington. As you resume your prior relationship you must keep in mind she is a KGB agent. And, while she's in Washington, continue in your role as her main contact with Century Aerospace. Will you do that?"

"Gladly," Nick replied enthusiastically.

"Next," she directed, "I want you to use your Century office telephone to call Professor Reynard at Columbia to ask if he will attend the ISA convention. He will say yes, and he will tell you he's learned Professor Capp will be there also, bringing his new assistant. You'll ask the name of the assistant, and he will say Nicole Girard. This script has been arranged with Reynard. Then from your apartment telephone, call Nicole in Paris and tell her you've just learned from Reynard she's coming to town and you're eager to see her again. Give her both your phone numbers and ask her to call you when she arrives in D.C. The KGB will of course be listening to these conversations, just as we intend."

"This is a pretty elaborate game-plan," Nick observed.

"Yes, it is, and it's been coordinated with French Intelligence. The main objective is to reinforce in Nicole's mind and the KGB's that you are Century's lead industrial spy. We don't want the KGB to think for one minute you work for the Agency."

"I'll keep up the act," Nick said, smiling.

"I have every confidence you will," she said as she rose from the couch. "Elliott Peterson, your driver, will take you to the Marriott Key Bridge Hotel. From there take a taxi to your apartment as though you just arrived from Dulles Airport. We don't want the KGB see you drive up to your place in a government car."

Returning to his Georgetown apartment through heavy rain, Nick unpacked and fell on the bed exhausted. It had been the longest day of his life—beginning with Natalie's arrest in her bedroom at 6:30, then the flight to D.C., this intense, high-level meeting at the CIA, a job offer to join the Agency, and detailed instructions for the next phase in his role as an industrial spy. His brain went limp. He planned to stay in bed all day Saturday.

Century Aerospace
Rosslyn, Virginia

Monday morning Butler walked to the Century office as usual. Stan Ebersol greeted him, asking if his week in L.A. had been productive. It had been, thought Nick, in more ways than one. Ebersol informed him Walt Gates' negotiations in Tehran last week were successful. The Iranians signed a contract for 144 F-11s, and the factory in California had started production ramp-up. Gates, Ebersol added, was on his way home but would soon depart for Taiwan to close that co-production deal for 300 F-11s.

After a while Nick went down to the building's lobby and dialed Special Agent Williams' number, as he requested at their meeting Friday night. Williams asked him to go to the Arlington Hyatt at noon and meet an agent in the lobby. The agent would escort him to his car, then would drive him to a secure location. Nick agreed to do this.

Shortly before noon he told Gladys he'd be out of the building for a couple of hours. Gladys wondered if the good-looking man was having a "nooner."

Nick walked the two blocks up Wilson Boulevard to the Arlington Hyatt. In the crowded hotel lobby an FBI agent spotted him and said, "Follow me, please." They took the elevator down to the garage and got in the agent's car, a blue Ford with Virginia plates.

U.S. Department of Justice
Washington, D.C.

The agent drove to the Department of Justice building on Pennsylvania Avenue, entering the imposing structure through a side entrance off 9th Street, driving down a ramp to an underground garage where he parked. He led Butler to an elevator, rode with him up to the fourth floor, and escorted him to a small windowless conference room. The agent left as Special Agent Lamar Williams rose to greet Butler. They shook hands.

"Nick," said Williams, "I'd like to introduce Ira Steinberg. He's the Justice Department attorney who's leading the preparation of the prosecution's case against the four perpetrators. Ira, this is the famous Nick Butler."

Nick shook hands with the distinguished looking middle-age lawyer. Williams asked Nick to sit at the head of the small conference table where a microphone was set up. The other men sat on his right and left.

Williams opened the conversation: "Mr. Steinberg not only wanted to meet you, but he also needs to better understand some of the background of the case to be able to prosecute it properly. Also, I want to close a few gaps in the time-line of the events. Your help will be invaluable to both of us. Our conversation will be recorded so we can go back over it in the future if need be. Is that acceptable to you?"

"Yes, that's fine," Nick said, feeling a little threatened.

"Thank you," Williams said. "First, to fill in the time-line, I'd like to understand the sequence of events when you first arrived in D.C. for your summer internship at Century. As I understand it from Susan Samuels, you arrived in Washington by train from New York on a Friday afternoon, checked into the Arlington Hyatt, and went to Georgetown where you had a drink at the bar at the '1789.' Correct, so far?"

"That is correct."

"While you were seated at the bar, Sonja Dahl entered the restaurant and took a seat next to you. Were other seats at the bar available at that moment, do you recall?"

"Well, the bar was pretty crowded. A guy had just gotten up from that stool when she came through the door. I noticed her enter right away."

"Why did you particularly notice her?"

"The truth is I went to the '1789' because I remembered it as a good pickup place and that's what I wanted to do—pickup somebody. Sonja was strikingly beautiful, and I hoped she'd sit next to me. And she did."

"Was it difficult to pick her up? I mean did it take a lot of drinks and conversation?"

"No. It was easy. She seemed to want to be picked up. We hit it off right away."

"Where did you go with her after the pickup?"

"We went to her apartment because it was nearby—closer than my hotel."

"Now, this is pretty indelicate, but I need to ask it anyway. Did you have sex with her at her apartment that night?"

"Yes."

"Going back earlier in the time-line," Williams asked, "who beside Susan Samuels and Steve Dyson knew you were coming to D.C. that Friday?"

"Professor Reynard and Anna Suzuki at the Institute knew. The Century Aerospace people also knew—Walter Gates and Stanley Ebersol."

"But did the Century people know you were arriving in D.C. on *Friday*?"

"Oh, maybe not," Nick corrected himself. "What they knew was I would report for work there on Monday morning. I don't think I told them when I would arrive in town."

"Did anyone else at the Institute know you were going to arrive on Friday?"

"Oh yes, my roommate Liam Erickson knew. He found a sublet tenant for my room on campus."

"Anyone else you can think of?"

"Not at the moment. I don't recall telling anyone else except my mother."

"Mr. Steinberg," Williams interrupted to say, looking at the lawyer, "Mr. Butler's mother is employed at NSA." Steinberg nodded in recognition of what that meant. "Now, Nick, when did you first go to the State Department?"

"The following Monday morning I went there with Graham Wolf and Walter Gates to discuss Century's request for an export license for Iran. Later in the day we went back to discuss our export license request for Taiwan and to pick up the Iran license."

"Did you see Sonja Dahl again over that first weekend, after the pickup on Friday night?"

"No, but I took her to dinner Monday night at Martin's Tavern."

"Did you have sex with her later that evening?"

"Yes."

"And that Monday you first visited the State Department—twice?"

"Yes. And Graham Wolf and I went there again on Tuesday to pick up the license for Taiwan."

At this point in the conversation, Williams turned to the attorney and summarized. He said the time-line established the fact that someone in New York City was also in Walker's network. Walker knew about Nick's arrival in D.C. on Friday before the KGB would have spotted him going in and out of the State Department the following week. Having been informed by the KGB that Nick was an industrial spy, Walker assigned Sonja Dahl to mark him that first night. Her willingness to have sex secured the relationship. That's a standard KGB tactic—easy pickup and easy, frequent sex. That keeps the mark on the hook. The open question is who in New York informed Walker about Nick's travel plans? It wasn't Reynard, who has a Top Secret clearance, and it wasn't Anna Suzuki, who's also cleared. Williams turned back to Nick.

"Do you have any reason to suspect Liam Erickson is not a loyal American?"

"I have no reason to suspect that," Nick answered feeling uneasy.

"Well, the evidence is pointing in his direction as Walker's informant."

"Please tell us what you know about your roommate, Nick," asked the attorney. "For example, who does he also work for at the Institute, where is he from, where did he go to college, that sort of thing."

"Liam," Nick responded, "just completed his second year at Columbia grad school in political science. He's worked at the Institute for a year under Professor Hazard who's a Soviet expert. To my knowledge Liam doesn't have a security clearance. He went to college at the University of Wisconsin in Madison where he grew up."

"What about his family?" Steinberg asked.

"His mother was born in Lithuania and is fluent in Russian. So is Liam. His father died years ago. That's about all I know."

"Thank you, Nick, for your patience with us and for your helpful information," Williams said. "You can return to your office in a few minutes." Williams then went to a telephone on a side table and made a call. Moments later the Attorney General of the United States entered the room. Everyone stood up.

"Mr. Attorney General, I'm pleased to introduce Mr. Nick Butler," said Special Agent Williams. "Nick, please meet Attorney General Mitchell Boark."

"Mr. Butler, I'm honored to meet you," Boark said, extending his hand.

"It's my honor, sir," replied Nick, shaking his hand.

"I'm fully aware of the vital role you've played in rooting out the Walker espionage ring. On behalf of the entire Justice Department I want to thank you personally."

"Thank you, sir. This is such an honor," Nick responded.

A minute later the Attorney General left the room and Nick's driver entered. Williams and Steinberg thanked him again for his help. The driver escorted Nick to his car, then drove him to the Hyatt's garage. Nick walked back to Century's office.

After Butler left the conference room, Williams and Steinberg began sorting out the information he provided. It was clear to both there is at least one more member of the Walker spy network—someone in New York City. Liam Erickson is the primary suspect not only because of the time-line but also because his mother's birthplace was in the Soviet Union. She may be a mole who gave birth to one and raised him for that role!

Williams walked across Pennsylvania Avenue to his office at FBI Headquarters to initiate an investigation in New York of Erickson and his mother in Madison, Wisconsin. He directed the FBI Manhattan office to request a court order for a wire tap on the telephones in Erickson's apartment and his office at the Institute of Defense Studies. Similarly, he asked for a tap on Mrs. Erickson's home phone in Madison. Williams began to consider a sting operation on Erickson.

Century Aerospace
Rosslyn, Virginia

After returning to his office at Century, Nick telephoned Professor Reynard at the Institute in New York, as Susan Samuels had ordered. The two recited the script exactly as Samuels dictated, all for the benefit of the KGB listening through their tap on Nick's phone.

"And so you'll be attending the ISA Convention in D.C.?" Nick asked the professor, just to confirm.

"Yes, I will. And you'll be glad to know your friend from Paris, Professor Jean-Pierre Capp, will also be there. He especially wants to hear David Hammond's speech you helped him with."

"It'll be great to see him again."

"Oh, and I should also mention he's bringing his new Research Assistant, someone Capp told me you also know."

"Who is that?"

"Her name is Nicole Girard," Reynard said.

"Nicole is coming to D.C. also?" Nick said incredulously.

"Correct," confirmed the professor.

"How great is that!"

Georgetown
Washington, D.C.

The next morning from his apartment Butler telephoned Nicole at her apartment in Paris. There was no answer, probably he thought because she was already at work at the Science Po. So he dialed that number. Madame Gardiner answered.

"*Bonjour, Madame Gardiner,*" Nick responded in French to her hello. "This is Nick Butler calling from Washington, D.C."

"*Ah, Monsieur Butler,*" she replied in French, and then switched to English. "How are you?"

"Very well, thank you. I'm calling to speak with Nicole Girard. I understand she is now Professor Capp's Research Assistant."

"*Mais oui,*" she replied cheerfully. "I'll connect you."

"Nick," Nicole answered, "how good of you to call!"

"It's great to hear your voice. Just yesterday I learned from Professor Reynard, my boss at the Institute, that you will be coming to Washington with Professor Capp to attend the International Studies Association convention. I'd really like to see you when you're in town. As you know I'm working in Washington for Century Aerospace this summer and I'll also attend the convention."

"How wonderful! I'd love to see you too," she purred in her Parisian accent. It was turning him on.

"Let me give you my phone numbers so you can call when you arrive— the office and the apartment." He gave the two numbers.

"I can't wait to see you," she said. "So much has happened since you left Paris."

"The same for me. Please call the minute you arrive in Washington."

"See you in two weeks."

The KGB monitored the call, of course. Anastas Kamarovski began to consider how to use this fortuitous turn of events. One of the KGB's top agents in Western Europe, Nicole Girard, was about to reunite with Century Aerospace's top industrial spy—in Washington, no less. He telephoned Yuri Andropov on a secure line to give him this new information and to begin thinking of ways to use it to best advantage.

Later that same morning on the walk to his office, Butler stopped off at the Marriott Key Bridge Hotel for breakfast and to use a lobby pay phone to update Susan Samuels on his meeting at the Justice Department and on his phone calls to Reynard and Nicole.

"By the way," Nick added, "while I was at the Justice Department Attorney General Boark came into the room to thank me for my work. That was a thrill, like the meeting last Friday night at your building."

"Everyone in the government who knows what you have done is very grateful. Those expressions of gratitude last Friday night were quite genuine, as I'm sure Boark's was."

"I'm grateful to you for putting that meeting together on Friday. I feel a whole lot better about what I'm doing because now I know why I'm doing it."

"I'm glad," Samuels said meaning it.

"What do I do next?"

"As far as I'm concerned you can relax until the ISA meeting when we'll have some things for you to do with Nicole Girard. I'm coordinating that right now with French Intelligence. There may be things Lamar Williams will ask you to do. If any of them impinge on your foreign role, I'll need to know about them."

"Okay, and thanks again for Friday night."

FBI Headquarters
Washington, D.C.

On Special Agent Williams' orders the New York City and Madison, Wisconsin FBI offices obtained court orders for wire taps on the telephones Williams requested—on probable cause of foreign espionage. The FBI field offices quickly installed the taps. Meanwhile Williams decided on a sting operation to test Liam Erickson's loyalty to the United States.

Williams doubted Erickson would have learned of Walker's arrest last Friday morning, and so he would naturally call Walker if he learned something important. The Special Agent decided to ask Nick Butler to phone Erickson to give him information to prompt such a call. This communication would be outside the KGB's channel—only in Walker's channel. Being behind bars,

Walker could not take the call, but the very fact of the call would expose a link between Erickson and Walker.

When Nick returned to his apartment that evening, he found Special Agent Williams parked outside his apartment building in a non-government car, a blue Ford with Virginia plates. Williams asked Butler to get in. They drove a short distance to the beautiful grounds of Dumbarton Oaks and parked in a visitor's space beneath a towering oak tree next to the stately mansion.

"Nick," Williams said, "I understand your loyalty to your roommate, but we've got to find out for sure if he's on our side or the Soviet's. I need your help to clear him—if he is a loyal American. Are you willing to help do that?"

"Since you put it that way, sure I'll help."

"Thanks. Tomorrow morning I want you to phone Erickson from a telephone in someone else's office at Century. Don't use your own phone. When you reach him, have a friendly conversation up-dating him on working with the Air Force at the Pentagon, on your trip to California working with Dr. Hammond on the classified report and his speech to the ISA convention, and that your old flame from Paris, Nicole, is coming to the ISA convention."

"I never told him about Nicole," Nick interrupted.

"Why not?"

"Because I didn't think he'd believe me. He'd think I made her up to make him jealous."

"I want you to tell him about her and suggest he come down to D.C. for the convention to meet her in the flesh. Of course do not mention she's KGB and she's also working as an industrial spy for Century. Just tell him she's beautiful and you'd like your roommate to meet her. Can you handle all that?"

"No problem."

Having settled on the plan, Williams drove Nick to the corner of Wisconsin Avenue and N Street and let him out in front of Martin's Tavern. Nick went in to have dinner, starting with a stiff drink.

Century Aerospace
Rosslyn, Virginia

Butler arrived early the following morning at Century. He located an empty office and dialed the apartment number in New York. Liam answered the phone. Nick repeated the speech Lamar Williams gave him—about all his high-level work over the past weeks.

"You went to California and worked with Dr. Hammond?" Erickson said in a disbelieving tone.

"Yes, I did," Nick emphasized. "It was more of the classified work I did for him at the Institute last summer, as well as a follow up to the Top Secret Air Force work I did at the Pentagon. It was quite a trip. The view from the beach in Santa Monica is really something."

"Well, Nick-boy, all I can say is I'm jealous. My work at the Institute this summer with Professor Hazard has not been all that interesting and I haven't had any trips."

"How about this idea for a trip," Nick segued. "Why don't you come down to Washington and attend the ISA convention with me to hear Hammond's speech and meet my girl friend from Paris, Nicole?"

"You had a girl friend in Paris? I don't believe it! You never mentioned her."

"I didn't think you'd believe me. But now you can meet her in the flesh. Seeing is believing! She's coming to the convention with Professor Capp as his Research Assistant especially to hear Hammond's speech. I'd like you to meet her."

"This sounds serious. Is it?"

"I like her a lot."

"Well, I'll just have to call your bluff," Erickson challenged. "I'll see if I can get Hazard to pop for the fare to D.C."

"Good deal. See you in two weeks."

FBI Headquarters
Washington, D.C.

Thanks to the cooperation of the New York Telephone Company and the tap on the apartment phone, Special Agent Williams enjoyed listening to his script being repeated so well by Butler. The roommate was obviously impressed with his activities. The jealousy factor came into play as Nick expected. Nick let drop any number of tempting pieces of intelligence any one of which should stimulate Erickson to make a call to Walker. It was only a matter of time, the Special Agent thought.

Williams phoned Susan Samuels to inform her Liam Erickson is the prime suspect in New York as a member of Walker's network and to fill her in on Butler's call to him. An FBI sting is underway, Williams stated, and he wants to be sure Erickson will receive Institute funds to make the trip to Washington. Samuels said she would take care of that.

Samuels telephoned Stephen Dyson at the CIA New York office to have him tell Reynard additional money would be provided to fund Erickson's trip to Washington. Dyson phoned Reynard and told him Erickson should be sent to the ISA convention on the Institute's dime. Susan Samuels authorized the money.

Institute of Defense Studies
New York City

After he hung up with Nick, Erickson left the apartment and walked to the Institute. When he had a chance to speak with Professor Hazard he told his boss he'd had a call this morning from Butler who urged him to attend the ISA convention to hear Dr. Hammond's speech.

"I'd really like to go to the convention, Professor Hazard," Erickson said to him. "I've never been to one, and Nick said Professor Capp is coming from Paris to hear Hammond's speech."

"Let me speak with Bill Reynard about this," Hazard responded. "He's in charge of the Institute's budget, and he may have funds available to pay your way. No promises, you understand."

"Thank you, sir. I really appreciate it."

Later that morning, Leland Hazard met with Bill Reynard to convey Erickson's request to go to D.C. Reynard, having already heard from Dyson, considered the request for a moment before giving his answer.

"Leland, I think it's a fine idea for Erickson to go to the convention. It will be good for him to meet some of our colleagues at other universities, especially Jean-Pierre Capp. After all, Liam was scheduled to go to the Science Po last winter, but Butler went in his place when Liam came down with the flu."

"Then I can tell him the Institute will cover his costs?" Hazard wanted to confirm.

"Yes, I'll authorize $2,000 for his travel and hotel expenses."

"Thanks, Bill. I know he'll appreciate it."

Hazard left Reynard's office on the second floor and climbed the stairs to his office on the third floor of the brownstone. He called for Erickson to come in.

"Liam, I have good news," Hazard said. "Bill Reynard agrees it will be good for you to attend the ISA convention, and he authorized $2,000 of Institute funds to cover your expenses."

"Fantastic!" exclaimed Erickson. "Thank you so much and please thank Professor Reynard for me. I'll call Nick tonight and give him the good news."

Later Erickson left the brownstone to go to lunch. He walked to his apartment where he planned to telephone his control to report about Butler's classified work and to tell him he would be in Washington in two weeks to attend the convention.

Erickson dialed his control's number. The phone rang a dozen times. There was no answer. Liam assumed his control was probably at work, so he'd try calling again in the evening. He made a sandwich and returned to the Institute.

The New York Telephone Company's equipment recorded the phone number Erickson dialed. It was to Harvey Walker's residence in Washington. To Williams, the pieces of the puzzle were falling into place. He informed Director Dean that Erickson is now a confirmed suspect as a member of Walker's espionage network. Dean phoned Admiral Myers and Dr. Singleton to report the same information.

When Erickson returned to his apartment after work, he proudly told his college friend he will be going to the ISA convention in Washington in two weeks, paid for by the Institute.

Then he telephoned Nick at his apartment in Georgetown to give him the same news.

"Tell me about this Parisian girlfriend," Liam asked Nick.

"Well, to start with, Nicole is beautiful. She's also extremely bright, having been hired by Professor Capp as his Research Assistant. And she's very sweet, not stuck-up like I expected French girls to be."

"Sounds to me like you've fallen for her," observed the former roommate.

"Not completely, but I'm leaning in that direction. That's why I want to get your expert evaluation of her," Nick said with a chuckle.

"From what I've seen of your lack of dating, you do need some help evaluating the field."

"I said you're an expert because you're the one who gets lucky every Friday night with a different girl from Barnard College. You have such depth of experience!"

"Okay, okay," Liam gave in to the taunting, "I'll meet her and check her out for you. Happy now?"

"Yeah. But the checking's only going so far," Nick warned, faking seriousness.

"We'll have to see about that. After all, you want a thorough evaluation—right?"

"I'll see you in two weeks," Nick said as he hung up laughing.

Listening through the wire tap, Special Agent Williams couldn't help laughing, too. Butler is a perfect actor, he thought to himself. He pulled off that conversation like two buddies having fun ribbing each other. Too bad, he thought, this is about treason.

Of course the KGB also listened to the conversation through their wire tap on the phone in Butler's apartment. Yet, because only Walker and Yuri Andropov knew Erickson's identity as a Soviet mole, this jocular conversation between the two roommates was discounted as meaningless to the *Rezident.*

A while later Erickson's temporary roommate left the apartment to go on a date. Alone now, Erickson dialed his control's phone number again. There was no answer.

This second attempt to reach Walker further confirmed Erickson's participation in the espionage ring. The final, solid nail in Erickson's coffin would be driven in during his visit to Washington at the ISA convention. Once again, Nick Butler would be the hammer.

Chapter 13:
The Spy Masters

New York City

The next day Liam Erickson again dialed his control's telephone number—once in the morning and again in the evening. There was no answer either time. His concern was growing that something may have happened to his contact. He was even more worried his sleeper status may have been compromised.

On the third day after talking with his former roommate he decided to pass Butler's information to his only alternate. He placed a call on the apartment telephone to his mother in Wisconsin.

Liam and his mother spoke in Russian. He told her what Butler said about his classified Air Force work at the Pentagon, his work with Dr. Hammond at NDAC, and about Hammond's up-coming speech at the ISA convention. He told her the Institute would pay his way to D.C. to attend the convention where he would meet Nick's French girlfriend who is flying in from Paris.

"The problem," he told her, "is my control is not answering his phone. I'm unable to pass this information along."

"How long have you been phoning him?" his mother asked in her Lithuanian-accented Russian.

"I've been calling twice a day for the last three days," Liam answered in his perfect Muscovite Russian.

"Hm. There may be a problem. I'll pass your information to my control and ask him to look into the situation with yours."

"Thanks, mom," Liam said in English.

"What's the French girlfriend's name?"

"I only know her first name. It's Nicole. She's Professor Jean-Pierre Capp's new Research Assistant at the Science Po."

"I'll see what I can find out."

FBI Headquarters
Washington, D.C.

"Jackpot!" exclaimed Lamar Williams out loud as he read the English translation of the Russian language conversation. Williams immediately went to Director Dean's office to report this breakthrough. The wire taps worked perfectly. Dean telephoned Dr. Singleton and Admiral Myers to relate the information. This recorded conversation confirmed Liam Erickson and his mother are both Soviet agents.

"The good news," Director Dean said to Myers, "is the FBI's sting uncovered another layer of the Walker network. We'll redouble our efforts in Wisconsin to investigate the mother to see where that trail leads. My suspicion is it will lead to the Soviet Embassy in Washington, but it may lead to the Soviet Mission to the United Nations in New York. We'll have to wait to find out."

"At our end," Myers stated, "we are pulsing our agents in Eastern Europe to learn what we can from them. I'm beginning to suspect Walker's network is an independent channel—independent from the main KGB—that Yuri Andropov set up to report directly to himself."

CIA Headquarters
Langley, Virginia

From a CIA mole in Moscow Susan Samuels received information that the Sukhoi Design Bureau is developing a next generation fighter airplane designed to achieve combat parity with the USAF's new F-15 Eagle, the American first-line fighter developed under the code name F-X. The Sukhoi's code name is T-10, but her agent reported it will soon be changed to Su-27. Two versions of that plane are under development, one of which is planned to have a swing-wing feature enabling it to take off from short airfields and achieve supersonic speeds up to mach two. Yet, the mole reported, Sukhoi's engineers have been unable to perfect swing-wing technology. Samuels saw this as an opportunity to plant more technical disinformation.

She knew Crayton Aerospace on Long Island had perfected the swing-wing for their new F-14, which recently began deployment on U.S. Navy aircraft carriers. She surmised that Crayton would likely have some flawed—but authentic-looking—engineering drawings of swing-wing technology that would drive the Sukhoi people up a blind alley. She began developing a plan to use Crayton's input for Nicole Girard to 'steal' from Nick Butler during her visit to Washington.

An even better idea came to mind when Admiral Myers informed her that the FBI had evidence Liam Erickson and his mother are both KGB moles. Samuels realized her plan could be modified to enable the FBI to nail Erickson. What if Butler allowed his roommate to discover film of Crayton's classified drawings in his possession and pass it to the KGB? That would be indictable evidence against Erickson and would also advance CIA's disinformation campaign with the Sukhoi people. Samuels presented this idea to Admiral Myers who liked it at once. He asked Singleton for a White House meeting to vet this plan that merged Stealth Gambit with the FBI's counterintelligence op.

The White House
Washington, D.C.

At 8:00 the next morning the attendees arrived at the White House Situation Room: Myers and Samuels, Dean and Williams, and Singleton and Garland.

Susan Samuels presented her idea for achieving the twin objectives: passing false Crayton Aerospace design data to the KGB using Liam Erickson to convey it, thereby obtaining evidence for an espionage indictment against him.

"Director Dean," Singleton asked, "what is your opinion of this idea?"

"From what we know about Erickson's contacts," he replied, "he only had Walker. We suspect he never knew Walker's name or his position at the FBI. With Walker behind bars, his only alternate contact is his mother, located in Wisconsin. So the issue is who could Erickson pass the technical data to once he has it?"

"Why not pass it to his mother?" Samuels suggested. "She obviously has a KGB contact somewhere she could pass it to."

"That would be a different kind of op from what you've used in the past," Dean said, addressing Samuels. "In the past film was lifted from Romeo, duplicated, and returned as though nothing happened. This new idea would not include duplication and return. It would be straightforward theft."

"It could include duplication if Mrs. Erickson is in D.C. and her contact is at the Soviet Embassy," Samuels responded. "But we don't know where he is, do we?"

"Correct," Lamar Williams answered, when Dean looked at him. "We don't know who her KGB handler is or where he is located."

"Then we must find him," Singleton stated. "I like the operation. The logistics will simply have to be worked out. Who's going to contact Crayton and ask for their cooperation?"

"Crayton's CEO, Chuck Stryker, is a classmate of mine from the Naval Academy," Admiral Myers stated. "I'm happy to make the contact."

"Okay with you, Director Dean?" the National Security Advisor asked.

"Fine with me," he replied. "Crayton will likely have someone attend the ISA convention which would be an appropriate time for a roll of microfilm to be passed to Romeo. If the Erickson part of the op doesn't work out, Girard could lift the film from Romeo, pass it to the Soviet Embassy for duplication, and return it unnoticed."

"That's a good back-up plan," Singleton declared. "Let's go with it. Phil, you call Crayton."

The meeting broke up with the main task falling to Lamar Williams to identify and locate Mrs. Erickson's KGB contact, which he hoped would be at the Soviet Embassy in D.C.

FBI Headquarters
Washington, D.C.

As it turned out he wasn't. When Mrs. Erickson telephoned her contact to convey her son's information, the tap on her phone recorded the number she dialed. It was in the 212 area code, which meant New York City. The number was at the Soviet Mission to the United Nations. The second after the call was connected a mechanism within the Soviet Mission scrambled the voice, masking the name of the person answering the call.

Lamar Williams phoned the FBI's field office in Manhattan to speak with the Special Agent in Charge, Neil Horner. It was Horner who had obtained the court order for taps on Erickson's phones at his apartment and the Institute.

"Neil," Williams informed him with urgency in his voice, "this is now your office's number one priority. We need to know ASAP the name of the

KGB *Rezident* at the Soviet UN Mission." Williams summarized the op to Horner who immediately assigned agents to begin an investigation.

Williams then called Susan Samuels who had returned to her office from the White House meeting to give her the information about Mrs. Erickson's contact. She offered to have Steve Dyson, the CIA Chief of Station in Manhattan, help Mr. Horner with his investigation. Williams accepted her offer. Inter-agency cooperation was turning out to be highly productive. After calling Dyson, Samuels phoned the CIA's COS in Moscow directing him to try to identify the KGB's top man in New York City.

CIA Headquarters
Langley, Virginia

Arriving at his office from the early White House meeting, Admiral Myers told his secretary to telephone Crayton's CEO in Bethpage, New York. Myers' secretary asked the CEO's secretary to have Charles Stryker stand by his secure phone for a call that would come in within minutes.

When the red phone rang in the Crayton office, Mr. Stryker said "hello." Admiral Myers said, "Hi Chuck. How are you doing?"

"Doing fine, Phil," replied his Annapolis classmate. "What can I do for you?"

"I need Crayton's help on an urgent matter. Is there any chance you'll be coming down to D.C. this week on Navy business?"

"Yes. We have an F-14 Program Review scheduled for Thursday at BuAir. Will that be soon enough?"

"Thursday is fine. I'll meet you at BuAir before your Program Review if that's okay with you."

"We're scheduled to begin the review at 10:00. If we meet at 9:00 will that give you enough time?" Stryker asked.

"That's perfect," Myers replied. "See you Thursday at the Pentagon."

The White House
Washington, D.C.

Dr. Singleton went to the Oval Office to report the recent developments to the President. He stated we now know the Walker spy ring is more extensive than was first believed. It includes Nick Butler's roommate at Columbia and the roommate's mother, a Lithuanian émigré living in Wisconsin. It now most likely also involves the chief KGB agent at the Soviet Mission to the United Nations. The identity of that individual is presently unknown.

President Reed directed his Assistant for National Security Affairs to brief Secretary of State Oscar Wasserman on the situation. The President wanted the State Department's help identifying the KGB agent at the Soviet UN Mission. After all, he said, our people at the U.S. UN Mission interact with their Soviet counterparts and may have some leads for the FBI.

"Moreover," Singleton added, "State's INR Bureau might also provide some insights."

"INR? What's that?" the President asked.

"Sorry for using an acronym, Mr. President. That's shop talk. It stands for the Bureau of Intelligence and Research. It's the State Department's intelligence agency."

"Good heavens," said Reed. "That's a new one on me. How many intelligence agencies do with have?"

"We probably have too many, sir."

The next morning, before his daily foreign policy briefing to the President, Secretary Wasserman was asked by Dr. Singleton to come to his office for a meeting. At the President's direction, the National Security Advisor needed to brief his former boss, who held his job before being promoted to Secretary of State.

Singleton gave the Secretary the essentials of the operation. He stated the FBI working with the CIA under a Presidential waiver discovered Harvey Walker, Deputy Director of the FBI for Counter-Intelligence, was a KGB double-agent. He even had his own KGB network working for him. Much of his network had been rolled up. Walker and three others are safely behind bars awaiting trial. Now another layer of the network has been uncovered, and the trail leads to the Soviet UN Mission where a KGB agent controls at least one sleeper agent, perhaps more. The President requests State's help in identifying the *Rezident* at the Soviet UN Mission.

"Of course we'll help in any way we can," the Secretary of State replied, marveling at the significance of this information. "I compliment the Bureau and the Agency for their success and especially for keeping this horrible situation confidential."

"Thanks for your help."

"Who's in charge of this operation?"

"The FBI's Special Agent in Charge of the Washington, D.C. Area. His name is Lamar Williams."

"How did we first learn of this treason?"

"It was by accident," Singleton replied. "CIA was running an op to pass aircraft disinformation to the Soviets through a graduate student intern posing as an industrial spy for Century Aerospace. A KGB female agent in D.C. passed classified disinformation from him to Walker, and another KGB female agent in Los Angeles lifted classified disinformation from the intern that was also passed to Walker, who put it in a dead drop. The Soviet Embassy's *Resident* picked up the package and later replaced it with a large sum of cash. That's the FBI's physical evidence against the spy ring."

"You say a graduate student played the central role? Who is this person?" Wasserman wanted to know.

"He's one of Bill Reynard's students at Columbia. Al Rubin at Penn, where the boy did his undergrad work, had identified him to Susan Samuels and to Bill as a promising candidate."

"Al and Bill are good men," Secretary Wasserman interjected. "Al's work on the Sino-Soviet split is exemplary. He was the first to identify there was a split back in 1960."

"The plot continued to unfold when the grad student participated in an FBI sting operation by communicating some high value information to his roommate at the FBI's request. The roommate tried to contact Walker, his handler, who then was in custody. So the roommate called his alternate contact, who happens to be his mother in Wisconsin. She telephoned her contact at the Soviet Mission. That's where the trail ended for us. We suspect her contact is the *Resident* at the Soviet Mission."

"I see," Wasserman said, shaking his head in wonder. "This has been a re-markable op. Its initial objective was to convey false aerospace designs when the op accidentally uncovered the Walker spy ring. I'm very impressed. At some point I'd like to meet this remarkable graduate student."

"That can be arranged on a confidential basis. The disinformation op is still running, you understand," said Singleton. The two men then left Single-ton's office and walked down the West Wing's corridor to the Oval Office to give President Reed the morning foreign policy briefing.

Thus, by early July the intelligence resources of the federal government were mobilized to identify the Soviet UN *Resident* to entrap Erickson and his mother.

Soviet Mission to the United Nations
New York City

When Mrs. Erickson dialed the main number at the Soviet UN Mission a scramble device blocked the FBI's voice wire tap on her home telephone.

She asked to speak with the Second Secretary. The operator connected her. The telephone on his desk rang, and Ivan Denisovich Markov, the Second Secretary of the Mission, answered, "Da." Speaking in Russian, Mrs. Estelle Erickson identified herself by her KGB code name and reported the intelligence her son had obtained from his former roommate.

"Why didn't your son phone his own contact with this information?" Markov asked.

"He tried to for three days, but there was no answer."

"I'll have to look into the matter. When does your son leave New York for Washington, D.C.?"

"The convention begins in two weeks. He's taking the train down from New York on Sunday week."

"Give me his address and phone numbers in New York in case I need to speak with him directly," he ordered. Mrs. Erickson gave the information.

Hanging up with Mrs. Erickson, Markov telephone his superior in Moscow, Yuri Andropov. The *Rezident* conveyed to the KGB Chairman the essence of Mrs. Erickson's call. The disturbing news is Liam Erickson's control has not answered his phone for three days. The good news is Liam Erickson will be meeting in Washington with Nicole Girard, a person Markov knew to be a KGB sleeper agent based in Paris.

"Yes, yes," Andropov said to this *Rezident*, "I know all about Girard's going to Washington. She and the greatest industrial spy I've ever known, Nick Butler, are lovers, and I expect she will find a way to gather more intelligence from him while she's there."

"What about the dead phone of Erickson's contact?" asked Markov, who did not know the identity of Erickson's handler.

"I'll have Anastas Kamarovski in Washington look into it."

KGB Headquarters
Moscow

Hanging up with his *Rezident* in New York, Andropov telephoned his *Rezident* in Washington.

"What's going on with 'inside channel'?" Andropov demanded. "He's not answering his telephone."

"I don't know, Comrade Chairman," Kamarovski answered. "I haven't had any contact with him for several days."

"I want you to find out immediately what's going on," Andropov ordered. "One of his agents has been unable to reach him by telephone for about three days."

"I'll look into it immediately, Comrade Chairman."

"That agent is in New York but he's coming to Washington soon. I want you to take control of him," Andropov ordered. "His name is Liam Erickson. He is the roommate at Columbia University of Nick Butler, the industrial spy working for Century Aerospace. I want Erickson and Nicole Girard to work together while in Washington to obtain any new industrial intelligence Butler may gather for Century Aerospace. When he arrives in Washington, we'll order Erickson to go to a dead drop to pick up your instructions. Let Markov and me know the location of the dead drop when you have decided on one."

"Understood, Comrade Chairman," Kamarovski replied.

Next, Andropov telephoned Alexi Mamanov, his *Rezident* at the Soviet Embassy in Paris. He ordered Mamanov to contact Nicole Girard and reconfirm the arrangement for her to meet in Washington with Nick Butler and now also with Liam Erickson. Tell Girard that Erickson is also a KGB sleeper agent and they should work together to lift from Butler any industrial secrets he may obtain.

Embassy of the U.S.S.R.
Washington, D.C.

Upon receiving these orders from his powerful superior, Kamarovski went to the embassy's garage and got in his Buick. He drove to the same dead drop in Rock Creek Park he and Walker always used. Though there was no chalk mark on the abandoned BBQ, he parked anyway and walked over to it. Opening the lid, he discovered the package of $110,000 was gone. This meant Walker had picked up the money or—God forbid!—someone else had.

Kamarovski decided to drive to Walker's home to see what he might learn. Driving slowly in front of the house, he noticed nothing unusual. He went to the end of the block and parked. Using his car phone, he dialed Walker's number. There was no answer, confirming what Walker's sleeper agent reported.

He drove back to the embassy on 16th Street. On the way he developed a plan. He ordered his secretary to have the most junior member of the embassy's staff report to him immediately. Within minutes a 26-year-old male arrived.

Kamarovski told him to change from his suit into a delivery man's uniform and return to his office. While the man was changing, Kamarovski prepared a package containing a book on American history. Inside the book's cover he placed a plain piece of paper on which he wrote two words: "call me." This was a prearranged contact signal between Kamarovski and "inside channel." The book was wrapped in brown paper and addressed to Harvey Walker, 2900 Tennyson Street, N.W., Washington, D.C.

When the agent returned in his delivery uniform, Kamarovski ordered him to take the package and deliver it to the front door of the address on the package and ring the bell. Wait for someone to appear. If Mr. Walker comes to the door, give him the package and get his signature on the receipt. If someone else comes to the door, say the package is for Mr. Walker only. If the person tells you Mr. Walker is not at home, ask when he is expected. Then depart with the package and return it to me.

The agent obeyed his orders. When he arrived at 2900 Tennyson Street, he rang the door bell. A maid answered the door. The "delivery man" said he needed Mr. Walker's signature to accept the package. The woman said he is not at home.

"When is he expected to return?" the man asked.

"I don't know," said the woman. "He has not been home for several days and I don't know when he'll return."

The agent departed with the package and returned to the embassy. He reported to Kamarovski what the woman said. The *Rezident* thanked the man and dismissed him.

The *Rezident* telephoned Andropov to report what he learned. The bottom line, said Kamarovski, is "inside channel" is missing. This is highly disturbing news.

The Pentagon
Arlington, Virginia

On Thursday morning at 9:00 Admiral Myers met with Crayton Aerospace's CEO, Chuck Stryker, at BuAir in the Pentagon. Myers took Stryker into an empty room in the suite of offices occupied by the Navy's Bureau of Aeronautics.

"Chuck," the Admiral said, "CIA needs Crayton's help with a sensitive mission we are undertaking."

"Just tell me what you want me to do, Phil," Stryker replied, cutting to the chase.

"We want to plant some disinformation in the hands of the KGB so they can provide it to the Sukhoi Design Bureau. Crayton perfected the swing-wing for the F-14, but the people at Sukhoi have been unable to do the same for their next generation fighter, the Su-27, one version of which requires a swing-wing. What I'm telling you is classified information. We want you to give them—through one of our agents—disinformation on swing-wing technology that will send them up blind alleys for a decade at least."

"So authentic-looking engineering technology that's deeply flawed—is that right?"

"Affirmative," replied the Admiral.

"When do you need it, Phil?"

"I'd like it in my hands early next week."

"Roger that," replied the Annapolis classmate.

Embassy of the U.S.S.R.
Washington, D.C.

Obeying Andropov's orders, Anastas Kamarovski needed to locate a dead drop where he could make contact with his new agent, Liam Erickson. Months earlier, after attending a memorial service at the Washington National Cathedral, he toured the building and noticed a location that might be useful in the future as a dead drop. He decided to check it out more thoroughly.

He drove to the main entrance of the Cathedral off Wisconsin Avenue and pulled into a small parking area outside the south transept of the imposing Gothic structure. Entering the massive building through its south door, he went down a flight of stairs to the lower level.

Along the building's south wall he came to the place he had only casually observed during his earlier visit—a space behind the tomb of Woodrow Wilson, the only President buried in Washington. No one was in the area so he stepped up on a marble ledge next to the sarcophagus to look more closely at the area behind it. There he found what he needed—a space about six inches wide and 12 inches deep between the stone wall and the marble tomb.

This was a perfect dead drop, just as he hoped. He relished the irony of using Woodrow Wilson, the only President who ever invaded the Soviet Union—at Vladivostok—to help the Soviet Union spy on the United States. Comrade Andropov would approve!

Returning to his office, he sent an encrypted telex to Andropov and Markov in New York. The telex described in detail the location of the dead drop. He asked the New York *Rezident* to direct Erickson to come to Washington on Sunday week to attend the 4:00 Vesper Service at the Washington National Cathedral. After the service, he should play the tourist role; go to the lower level to view the tombs. Instructions would be behind Woodrow Wilson's crypt.

Soviet Mission to the United Nations
New York City

When Ivan Markov received the telex, he decided to telephone Liam Erickson at his office at the Institute of Defense Studies.

"Hello Liam. Your mother in Wisconsin asked me to call," Markov said in his Russian-accented English.

"Hello sir," Liam replied hesitantly, not recognizing the voice.

"I'd like to have a drink with you this afternoon. Can you meet me at the West End Grill on Broadway at 5:00?"

"Okay, I can do that. How will I recognize you?"

"I know you," he responded and hung up.

FBI Field Office
New York City

"Bingo," Neil Horner exclaimed, listening to the conversation through the tap on Erickson's office phone. The vaunted, all-powerful KGB was tripped-up by a simple wire tap! How careless of them, he thought.

Horner dispatched two junior FBI agents to the West End Grill dressed in casual clothes—to look as much as possible like Columbia college students. One of them had actually gone there and had a Columbia T-shirt in his gym bag. The agents studied Erickson's photo from his Institute file and each took a camera to photograph the KGB agent, whose name was still unknown. One agent also took an audio recording device.

Horner phoned Lamar Williams to report this major development. He said photos of the *Rezident* would be on the wire to FBI Headquarters later that day. Williams informed Director Dean, who contacted the CIA and the White House. Excitement was mounting throughout official Washington in anticipation of this huge breakthrough.

At 4:30 the two FBI agents entered the West End Grill, across Broadway from Columbia University. The restaurant is deep and narrow with a bar on the left side extending from the front to the rear. On the right side are high-back wooden booths separated from the bar by a narrow walkway. The two agents took seats at the bar—one at each end. They ordered beers and waited. At that time of day the restaurant was practically empty.

At 5:00 Liam Erickson entered the restaurant and went to the middle of the bar. He ordered a beer. Shortly after 5:00 a middle-age man dressed in a dark suit and hat walked in. He quickly surveyed the room and recognized Erickson sitting at the bar. He walked toward a booth near the back of the restaurant. As he passed Erickson he said to the tall blond man, "Come join me." Erickson recognized the voice. After the man sat down at one of the booths, Erickson joined him, taking a seat across the table from the man, who ordered a Stoli on the rocks.

Both FBI agents clandestinely photographed the man. The agent with the recording device moved to the booth directly behind the Soviet agent where he could overhear and record the conversation. The other agent moved down the bar, taking a stool directly across from the booth and continued covertly taking photos from there.

"Liam, I understand your control is not responding to your phone calls," the New York-based *Rezident* said to him. "I am here to give instructions and to establish a link for you to a different control."

"Thanks for coming," Erickson said, feeling relieved. "I've been worried. Did my mother pass my information to you?"

"Yes. I am her control. Now listen carefully. You will go to Washington, D.C. on Sunday week. Arrive there early enough to attend the Vesper Service at the Washington National Cathedral at 4:00. After the service is over, look around the cathedral like any tourist would. Go to the basement level. Find the tomb of President Wilson. Hidden behind the tomb will be an envelope. Take it and read it later. It will give you further instructions. Your new control is located in Washington. Is this understood?"

"Yes, I understand."

"During your stay in Washington," Comrade Markov continued, "you will visit your roommate, Nick Butler. You do not know this but he is an industrial spy working for Century Aerospace. He has a network of agents working for him who are employees of various aerospace companies. He gathers critical engineering information from those companies on behalf of his employer. We take that information from him without his knowing it and use it for the Motherland's benefit."

"Nick's a spy!" Erickson exclaimed. "I had no idea."

"That's why he's so good at it. No one would suspect someone so young could be so effective."

"Well," Erickson bragged, "I did imagine someday he would achieve a high-ranking position—because he's so damned talented. I forwarded information about him to my control from time to time to build a file on him for future use."

"Your mother also provided me with the information on Butler you gave her. I am well aware of both dossiers, but now you must focus on the present assignment," the Russian cautioned.

"Okay. So I should take whatever information Nick gets and pass it to my new control?"

"Not exactly," Markov said. "Butler has a French girlfriend who will also attend the ISA convention. Her name is Nicole Girard. She's one of us. She is expert at manipulating Butler so let her do the lifting. She will pass the data to you, and you will pass it to your control. It is important the information gets back to Butler's location before he realizes it's been lifted."

"Does Nicole know about me?"

"She does. The two of you will be a team in Washington working together for the socialist cause," the New York *Rezident* stated. He paid the check for both drinks and left. Erickson walked out of the West End Grill a few minutes later.

The two FBI agents departed soon after Erickson left. They walked the half-block to the 116th Street station and took the subway to the FBI office in lower

Manhattan. The subway was faster than taking a taxi at that time of day. Arriving there, they handed their cameras to Neal Horner and began debriefing him on the conversation at the West End Grill.

The agent who had the recording device played the tape. He filled in the inaudible blanks. A stenographer took down every word. The photos were developed within an hour. The resolution was excellent. The face in the photos matched an FBI file photo of one of the Soviet UN Mission's employees. It was the face of Ivan Denisovich Markov, Second Secretary.

The photos and the transcript of the conversation were put on the wire to Special Agent Williams at FBI Headquarters. He took the information to Director Dean, who forwarded it to Langley and the White House.

By 8:00 that night responsible officials in the federal government had not only identified Mrs. Erickson's KGB control but also knew the KGB's game-plan for Liam Erickson.

"This is intelligence-gathering at its finest," Dr. Singleton said to the President, concluding his debriefing.

After that intelligence coup, the government's resources were focused on the up-coming annual convention of the International Studies Association when the remaining members of Walker's espionage network would be apprehended.

CIA Headquarters
Langley, Virginia

Early the following week, Crayton completed its package of technical drawings of bogus swing-wing technology. If built using these specifications and flown on an airplane, the plane would crash. Critical design flaws were imbedded in the drawings only the Crayton engineers knew about. This was exactly what Admiral Myers requested.

"Phil," Crayton's CEO said on a secure line, "I've got the package ready. How do I get it to you?"

"Thanks, Chuck, for the quick work," replied Philip Myers. "An agent named Stephen Dyson will come to your office later today and pick it up. Thanks again."

Myers phoned Dyson in Manhattan directing him to drive to Bethpage on Long Island to pick up the package Charles Stryker had waiting for him. This package would be the bait to catch Liam Erickson.

Dyson obeyed his orders. Returning to his office in lower Manhattan, he dispatched two agents to carry the package in a combination lock metal brief-case to Langley, Virginia. They flew out of New York on the next Eastern Airlines shuttle from LaGuardia to D.C.'s National Airport. An Agency car picked them up.

By early evening Myers and Samuels had the Crayton package. They ordered the CIA's photography shop to take pictures of the 20 drawings in the package using a mini-camera. Crayton had stamped each page top and bottom "Top Secret, Eyes Only" and put three red stripes diagonally across each page. When the roll of film was developed, it was taken to Susan Samuels' office.

The bait was ready to be used the following week at the ISA convention—the final act in Stealth Gambit and the final act in the FBI's rollup of Walker's spy network. Once again, Nick Butler would play the leading role.

Chapter 14:
The Spy Catcher

Hilton Hotel
Washington, D.C.

The Air France flight from Paris arrived at Dulles at 4:25 P.M. the following Sunday. Professor Jean-Pierre Capp and his Research Assistant, Nicole Girard, deplaned, took the mobile lounge to the main terminal, went through U.S. Immigration, baggage claim, and Customs, and then walked outside.

On this warm summer afternoon they welcomed the fresh Virginia air after being cooped-up for seven hours breathing what Professor Capp jokingly termed "manufactured airplane air." They waited their turn for an Airport Flyer taxi.

"The Washington Hilton Hotel, please driver—the big Hilton on Connecticut Avenue," Professor Capp emphasized which Hilton, knowing there are several in D.C. Capp and Nicole relaxed, enjoying the sights as the cab drove along George Washington Parkway next to the Potomac, entered the city across Key Bridge, and later turned north on Connecticut Avenue past the luxury shops to the hotel. After they checked in and went to their rooms, Nicole telephoned Butler at his apartment.

"Hello, Nick," she said. "It's Nicole. I've just arrived in Washington."

"How great is that!" Nick replied with his usual enthusiasm. "Where are you staying?"

"Professor Capp and I checked in at the Washington Hilton, where the ISA convention is being held. We'll go downstairs later and register for the convention. It starts tomorrow, as you know."

"Yes, I know. I can't wait to see you. What are you doing for dinner tonight?"

"Professor Capp and I already discussed that on the plane flying over. He wants to host you and Professor Reynard for dinner tonight at the hotel. He's calling Reynard right now to invite him. Are you free tonight?"

"You bet I'm free."

"Wonderful," she responded. "I'll meet you at 6:30 in the lobby."

Liam Erickson's train from New York's Pennsylvania Station arrived at Washington's Union Station at 2:00 P.M. the same day. Liam took a taxi to the Washington Hilton and checked in. Once in his room he telephoned Nick Butler to say hello. Erickson told him he was going to be busy most of the day. He suggested they get together tomorrow at the Hilton coffee shop for lunch. Nick agreed.

Washington National Cathedral
Washington, D.C.

Erickson unpacked, went down to the lobby, and asked the doorman to whistle for a taxi.

"The Washington National Cathedral, please," Erickson told the driver. This was his first visit to the Nation's Capital so he enjoyed seeing the sights on the way to the cathedral.

Arriving there, the driver pulled up to the main entrance of the huge Gothic structure. The front part of the building was still under construction, so Erickson carefully picked his way across the wooden planks leading to the temporary entrance.

On the way he stopped to hear a docent telling a group of tourists that the statuary—stone carvings of angels and gargoyles—stacked up on the grounds was waiting for the front part of the cathedral to be built so it could be placed there. These carvings were completed, she said, many years ago by sculptors and stone masons before they retired. This expertise no longer exists in the United States, she added sadly.

Once past the construction work and inside the gigantic building, the cathedral opened to a high, arched ceiling supported by parallel rows of massive stone pillars flanking the length of the structure. Huge flags of the 50 states hung from the heights along the length of the block-long nave. Above the flags he saw rows of leaded-glass windows projecting dapples of colored sunlight below onto the highly-polished marble floor. Turning to look back toward the entrance, he was dazzled by the enormous rose window above the doorway. The entire spectacle was breathtaking even for an atheist.

Enjoying this magnificent setting, Erickson walked forward about three-quarters of the way down the nave to take a seat amid the sparse audience. This was a good location to observe the Vesper Service that was about to begin at the high alter in front of him.

Anastas Kamarovksi watched Erickson from a safe distance. As soon as Erickson was seated and the Vesper Service began, he went down to the lower level and placed an envelope behind President Wilson's tomb.

Special Agent Williams and another FBI agent were already near the tomb secretly observing and photographing Kamarovski. After the *Rezident* left the area to return upstairs, Williams and the other agent went into action, knowing the Vesper Service would last only 45 minutes.

Williams rushed over to the tomb, climbed up on the ledge, and reached behind the tomb to pick up the envelope. It was sealed as he expected. The second agent stood guard while Williams ran up the stairs, went out through the cathedral's south door, and entered an FBI unmarked van parked outside the south transept.

The van contained a steamer device an FBI technician used to unseal the envelope. Williams opened the envelope and took out the contents: a photo and a single piece of plain paper. The technician photographed the words typed on the paper and the photo, put them back in the envelope, and resealed it. Williams quickly returned to the crypt, putting the envelope back where he found it.

When the Vesper Service ended, Erickson strolled around the cathedral's main floor looking at the side chapels and some of the ornate carvings. He soon found the stairs leading down to the crypts.

Arriving at the lower level, he quickly found President Wilson's tomb. Seeing no one in the area, he stepped up on the ledge to reach behind it. There he found an envelope. He pocketed it and climbed down. He cut short his tour of the lower level, went back up to the main floor, and left the cathedral through the front entrance. He had not seen the FBI agents watching and photographing him.

Erickson walked to the taxi stand inside the cathedral grounds off Wisconsin Avenue. He got in a cab and returned to the Hilton. Lamar Williams and the other agents drove the van to FBI Headquarters to develop the film. Williams had already read the message.

Kamarovski's orders to Erickson were straight-forward:

> Make contact with Comrade Nicole Gerard (photo attached) and develop a plan for Girard to lift any industrial secrets Nick Butler obtains. Top priority: get a copy of the classified report David Hammond wrote for the USAF on its operational plans to use stealth aircraft. After you obtain any material, telephone me at the number below. I will have it picked up and duplicated. Return the material to Gerard for her to put it back where she found it. Kamarovski

Lamar Williams sent copies of the message to Director Dean and to Langley. This was indictable evidence of Liam Erickson's conspiracy to commit treason.

Hilton Hotel
Washington, D.C.

Sunday evening at the ISA convention was festive. Nick arrived at the Hilton at 6:30 and amid the crowd of conventioneers found Nicole waiting for him near the reception desk. They rushed to each other and briefly embraced.

"I'd forgotten how beautiful you are," Nick said, holding her by the waist and admiring her face and figure. Of all the women he had known, Nicole was his favorite.

"I hadn't forgotten how handsome you are," she teased in her lilting Parisian accent. "Professor Capp is waiting for us in the bar. Shall we join him?"

"Sure thing," he responded, taking her hand as they strolled to the bar.

"Ah, *Monsieur* Butler," the dapper Professor exclaimed when they came in. "It's good to see you again."

"Good to see you again, *mon Professeur*," Nick replied. The two men embraced.

Professor Reynard then entered the bar and greeted his old friend and colleague, Professor Capp. They embraced. Capp introduced his Research Assistant, Nicole Girard, to Reynard.

"Enchanted, *mademoiselle*," Reynard said. She replied the same way.

"Good to see you again, Nick," Reynard said.

"Same here, sir," Nick responded as they shook hands.

Seeing the maitre d' approaching with menus, Capp asked, "Shall we take our table?"

They were led to a table for four next to a window overlooking the city. Capp ordered two bottles of fine French wine that were almost finished by the time dinner was over. The two famous senior professors and their two Research Assistants thoroughly enjoyed each others' company.

A couple of hours later Capp announced it had been a long day—beginning with the flight from Paris—and he needed his beauty sleep. Reynard said the same thing. The two older men excused themselves after Capp signed the check, charging the bill to his room.

Nicole and Nick remained at the table finishing their wine.

"Alone at last," Nick said the cliché with a chuckle, smiling at Nicole. "I've missed you."

"And I've missed you," replied Nicole, smiling back.

"Then why don't we do something about it?" he suggested. "This time you have the hotel room, and it won't have to be a 'quickie'."

They left the table and took the elevator up to her room. After Nick closed the door behind them, he took her in his arms and kissed her.

"I've wanted to do that all evening," he said, reprising his line from the Madison Hotel.

"And I've wanted you to do it," she replied, holding him close. "Why don't we get comfortable?" This time she said his line.

They quickly undressed and got in the king-size bed. They made love until about midnight when Nick left to take a cab to his apartment in Georgetown.

At noon the next day, Monday, Nick and Liam met at the Hilton's coffee shop for lunch. Nick had invited Nicole to join them. He wanted to introduce his lover to his roommate—to get his evaluation.

"Nicole," Nick said, "this is Liam Erickson, my roommate at Columbia. Liam, this is Nicole Girard, Professor Capp's Research Assistant." The two shook hands.

This might have been an awkward moment, but the two accomplished spies pretended not to know about each other. Liam realized Kamarovski's first assigned task—to make contact with Nicole Girard—had just been accomplished with Nick's help, no less!

"Didn't I tell you she's beautiful?" Nick said to Liam as they made their way to a table.

"You did, but 'beautiful' hardly seems adequate," the expert girl evaluator remarked.

They ordered iced teas and lunch. The three twenty-somethings had a raucous time regaling each other about bizarre happenings in grad school. As the meal ended Nick reminded them that Dr. David Hammond's speech is scheduled for Wednesday at noon.

"For me that will be the highlight of the convention," he remarked.

"Isn't that the speech you helped him with when you were in L.A.?" Liam asked Nick.

"Yes it is," he replied. "Hammond will be delivering an unclassified summary to the convention."

"Is there a classified version?" Erickson asked, attempting to carry out Kamarovski's second assignment.

"There is a classified *report*," Butler replied. "I helped write it, but I was not given a copy."

This information registered with the two KGB agents. Their main mission—to get the classified report—was not going to happen.

As they were getting up from the table, Nick said he was going to hear a panel discussion that was about to begin. Liam said he wanted to attend a different panel discussion. Nicole said she needed to return to her room to freshen up. Nick told Nicole he'd call her later at her room. He wanted to have dinner with her and resume their love-making.

The three separated at the coffee shop's entrance. Seconds later, after Nick was out of sight, Liam turned to follow Nicole to the elevator. They needed to talk. They took the elevator to her floor and went into her room.

"Well, Comrade Girard, it's good to meet you," Liam said after closing the door.

"It's good to meet you, Comrade Erickson."

"I've been given a dead drop location and a contact number here in Washington that we'll use if we get hold of anything useful from Nick," Liam said. "Based on what Nick said at lunch, it appears we won't get Hammond's classified report."

"You never know," Nicole said, as they sat down at her sitting area. "Nick is pretty amazing. He gets his hands on things that would astound you. He may have said that to cover his tracks. Does he have any reason to suspect you are KGB?"

"None that I know of. How about you?"

"He thinks I'm an industrial spy working for him and Century Aerospace. He can't have any idea I'm KGB."

"I think Wednesday afternoon and evening is the time to find out what Nick has managed to get his hands on," observed Liam. "Do you agree?"

"Yes, I do. After Hammond's speech will likely be the time Nick gets whatever he's going to get. Why don't we invite ourselves to have dinner at his apartment Wednesday night? After you leave the apartment, I'll get him in bed. You wait outside the door. After a while, he'll have to go to the bathroom. I'll lift the information and pass it to you, if there is any. You can bring it back early in the morning and return it to me. How does that sound?"

"It sounds like a good plan. I can get him to invite us over. That shouldn't be a problem," Liam said confidently.

Erickson left her room to go to a panel discussion. But first, at a pay phone in the hotel lobby, he reported to his new control the op would take place Wednesday night at Nick's apartment.

While Nicole was at lunch with Nick and Liam, the FBI planted a microphone in the sitting area of her room, having obtained a court order on probable cause of foreign espionage. Williams heard and recorded every word of Nicole and Liam's conversation. He telephoned Susan Samuels and told her the op would happen Wednesday night, saying the FBI would be prepared to spring the trap on Erickson. Moreover, he added, this recorded conversation is further evidence to indict and convict Erickson of conspiracy to commit treason.

National War College
Ft. Leslie McNair
Washington, D.C.

On Tuesday at noon Nick told Nicole and Liam he had to take care of some business at his Century office. The truth was Susan Samuels had instructed him to meet her at a secure location. He left the hotel and hailed a taxi. Remembering Col. Payne's instruction not to be overheard giving his destination, he waited until the cab was underway to tell the driver to take him to the National War College at Ft. McNair in Southwest Washington.

The cab soon arrived at the magnificent neo-classical building set amid manicured lawns on the peninsula formed by the confluence of the Potomac and Anacostia Rivers. Nick paid the driver, climbed the long flight of steps, and entered the imposing structure. Elliott Peterson, his CIA driver, was waiting inside. He opened the door for Nick to an office off the main corridor. Susan Samuels and Lamar Williams were seated at a small conference table. Samuels asked him to join them.

"Nick," she announced, "tomorrow is the big day."

"Yes, I know. That's when Dr. Hammond will give his speech."

"That's just the beginning of the events tomorrow," she declared. "As I promised, we are going to fill you in completely on the upcoming game-plan, knowing you can handle it."

"I'm glad you have confidence in me."

Samuels went on: "We know the KGB is hoping to obtain from you a copy of Hammond's classified report to the Air Force on how it intends to use stealth airplanes. We're going to let then 'steal' a bogus version of the report that we prepared. Our fake report will lead them astray for years. We'll put it in the safe in your Century office and let Erickson know it's there. Also, we're going to continue our aircraft disinformation operation you've conducted so well for us. This will accomplish two things: provide evidence of Erickson's treason and also send Sukhoi down blind alleys for years on swing-wing technology."

Samuels took out of her purse a roll of film and handed it to Williams, who continued to hold it so Nick could see it.

"We now know for certain," Williams said, "that Liam Erickson is a KGB spy—a sleeper agent. He and Nicole were ordered by the KGB to work together to lift whatever aerospace technical data you gather."

"Are you absolutely sure of that?" Nick asked, feeling betrayed by his roommate.

"Yes, we have proof positive," replied Williams. "Nicole and Erickson expect you to get your hands on something of value tomorrow afternoon after Hammond's speech. That will happen. It's this roll of film. They want to go to your apartment for dinner tomorrow night. After dinner, Erickson will leave you and Nicole alone. Nicole plans to have sex with you. After a while, you are expected to get out of bed and go to the bathroom. While you're in there, Nicole will lift the film and pass it to Erickson, who will be waiting outside the door. He will take it to his KGB contact for duplication. Nicole will spend the night with you. In the morning, Erickson will return to the apartment waiting in the hall by your door. When she can, Nicole will take the film back from him and replace it where she found it."

"What's on the film?" Nick asked.

"It's the same type of film you were used to handling at the Paris Air Show," Samuels told him. "It contains significant airplane technical data from Crayton Aerospace that the KGB desperately needs to assist one of the Soviet design bureaus. Yet, as before, the data is flawed and will lead the Russians down false trails for years."

"Now here's the tricky part," Williams added. "This roll of film will be given to you at the convention after Dr. Hammond finishes his speech. An FBI agent posing as a Crayton intern will discreetly pass it to you. He knows what you look like. We want the pass to appear secretive but at the same time we want either Nicole or Erickson to see it happen. Can you pull that off?"

"I'll think of some way to make that happen—they should see the pass but not be obvious about it, right?"

"Right," Williams agreed. "Also, you should invite Liam and Nicole to your apartment for dinner. Make it sound impromptu. Throughout the night we will have a stakeout watching the place to be sure they take the film. We want the KGB to get the film and we want to photograph Erickson giving it to them. This will be the physical evidence we need to indict him for treason."

Samuels added: "Also during the night, the KGB will break into your Century office safe and photograph our bogus USAF report with Hammond's name on it."

Nick said he understood the plan and would do his part.

"Before you leave, I have two pieces of news for you, Nick," Samuels said. "First, we've learned the true identity of Natalie Thompson, your friend from Santa Monica. Do you want to hear it?"

"I suppose so," he replied, feeling strange emotions welling up within him.

"Her real name is Brigitte Schaeffer," Samuels said. "She's an orphan born in East Germany and taken to Canada as a child, later brought to the U.S. She was raised and trained to be a KGB sleeper agent in this country. The KGB assigned her to the Walker spy ring. You helped expose another dangerous enemy of the United States."

"Are you sure of this?"

"Absolutely sure," she replied.

"Well, that settles that," Nick said, feeling much better about her arrest. After a pause he asked, "What's the other piece of news?"

"As you know," Samuels said, "Nicole Girard is also a KGB sleeper agent who is now employed for one year at the Science Po under Professor

Capp. Her employment there was at the direction of Andre Devereaux, whom you met."

"That's right; I met him at Orly Airport with Dan Murray."

"French Intelligence wants to keep a close eye on her and decided that could best be accomplished by her working in Capp's office. The professor was cautioned not to divulge any sensitive information to her. I wanted to clear your mind of any concern you might have on that score."

"Thanks," Butler replied. "I wondered about that, knowing Capp works with Top Secret NATO material."

At that point all three rose from their chairs and shook hands. Nick left the room first. Elliott, waiting in the hall, phoned for a taxi for Butler.

While waiting on the building's front steps for it to arrive, Nick turned to Elliott and said, "It's really heartwarming as a tax-payer to know the CIA and the KGB have arranged for me to spend tomorrow night with a beautiful woman." They were laughing when the cab pulled up in front of the majestic building.

Hilton Hotel
Washington, D.C.

Finally the big day arrived—Wednesday. The morning panel discussions were fairly typical, each academic trying to impress others with his brilliance. Nick went from panel to panel looking for one that might actually interest him—a practical topic related to the real world. Liam was doing the same thing, passing each other in the halls outside the meeting rooms.

At noon in the grand ballroom the plenary session was scheduled to begin with lunch, followed by the featured speaker, Dr. David Hammond. Tables were set up outside the ballroom for each pre-registered attendee to locate his luncheon ticket attached to his name badge, arranged alphabetically. Nick quickly found his: Nick Butler, Century Aerospace. He looked for a badge for a Crayton attendee, but there were so many he didn't see it.

Nicole came up behind Nick and said hello. He helped her locate her badge: Nicole Girard, Science Po. Liam soon showed up. His badge read Liam Erickson, Columbia University.

The three agents now ticketed and wearing badges entered the cavernous ballroom and found seats at a table near the front of the room. Nick spotted Professor Alvin Rubin at a table nearby and waved to him through the crowd. Smiling, Rubin waved back. Professors Capp and Reynard were seated at the head table with Dr. Hammond and the President of the International Studies Association, a professor from Stanford. Several hundred people filed in, taking seats at the tables of eight. Lunch entrées were served. Salads and desserts were already on the tables.

During the ISA business discussions and routine announcements, lunch plates were cleared away. Professor William Reynard, world-renounced Director of Columbia University's Institute of Defense Studies, introduced the featured speaker, Dr. David Hammond, Senior Political Scientist, National Defense Analysis Center.

In his introduction Reynard stated that NDAC was established as a nonprofit after World War II to work with the Air Force to explore alternative national security strategies and to offer practical recommendations, given the complexity and cost of modern weapons. Dr. Hammond, he said, is a leading member of NDAC's staff. Polite applause greeted Hammond as he took the podium.

Hammond's speech, Nick knew, would be a discussion of the impacts of technological innovations on military doctrine and strategy. Its focus, while similar to Professor Capp's lecture Nick attended at the Science Po, would be on the present time, examining impacts of recent technological advancements on the U.S. military, especially the Air Force.

Hammond began by discussing the technological breakthrough of the variable geometry wing, popularly known as swing-wing technology, allowing an airplane to takeoff from a short runway with its wings fully extended and once in flight sweep the wings back to enable the plane to achieve supersonic speed using an afterburner. The U.S. invented swing-wings in the 1960s for the USAF's F-111 program. The technology was applied in the early 1970s to the U.S. Navy's F-14.

He cited engine research that may enable sustained supersonic flight without using an afterburner—to increase the speed and range of aircraft so equipped. Vertical take-off technology is at the point where, he said, the U.S. will soon have attack aircraft that do not require an airfield, enabling forward basing. The British invented this technology, he acknowledged.

There will likely be innovations in ordinance as well as aircraft platforms, he opined. While hundreds of bombs had to be dropped during World War II to be sure some of them hit the target, in the future with "smart" weapons, Hammond foresaw, practically every weapon will hit its target because it will be guided with precision by the launching aircraft.

The ultimate technology breakthrough, Hammond predicted, would be stealth—the popular name for low observable aircraft. If stealth is achieved, he explained, it would have to be applied to an entirely new airplane design using a combination of reduced signatures: visual, radar, infrared, acoustic, and electro-magnetic. If, he foresaw, the U.S. Air Force were able to deploy at night aircraft virtually invisible to detection, the Cold War would be over. The U.S. would win it without firing a shot.

Why, he asked rhetorically, because state-of-the-art Soviet air defenses, recently put in place at a cost of tens of billions of rubles, would be nullified— they would be unable to detect incoming stealthy aircraft. Russia would be defenseless to such an attack, and they would know it.

This scenario of course assumes the Kremlin's masters are rational men. Hammond assumed they are, given that the Politburo fired Khrushchev after his reckless Cuban missile gambit when President Kennedy faced him down in that dangerous episode of brinkmanship.

Hammond was careful to put most of his speech in the future tense and frequently used the conditional "if." Nick knew the stealth part of his speech was in fact happening—it wasn't a matter of if, but when. But, Nick realized, for a public speech he could only say so much. Hammond left out all the operational scenarios Nick and Major Lawrence developed. No doubt they are in the classified report, Nick assumed.

When he finished his address, Hammond received sustained applause from the large, knowledgeable audience. Professor Reynard returned to the podium to thank Hammond for his insightful remarks. Then he dismissed the gathering.

As they were applauding, Liam turned to Nick at their table and commented that he, Nick, was privileged to have worked with Hammond at the Institute last summer and at NDAC this summer.

"I would love to see his classified report," added Liam, "especially the part about stealth."

"So would I," Nicole chimed in.

"Maybe in thirty years you might see it," Nick said chuckling.

Nick and Liam left the table to join the crowd rushing to the head table to congratulate Hammond on his speech. They waited their turn in line. Liam was standing directly behind Nick. A young man with a Crayton Aerospace badge nudged Nick on the arm to get his attention. Nick turned to him. Once

Nick saw his Crayton badge the man slipped a tiny roll of film into Nick's suit pocket then quickly faded into the crowd. Liam saw the pass.

When Hammond noticed Nick standing in line, he leaned across the head table and shook his hand. Erickson was now standing beside Nick.

"Well, Nick," Hammond said, "you had a big part in making this speech happen—thanks. Incidentally, I sent a copy of my classified Air Force report to your office. It's in your safe."

"Thank you, sir," Nick replied. "I can't wait to read it."

Nick and Liam then rejoined Nicole at their table.

"I feel like celebrating," Nick declared. "Hammond's speech was the highlight of this otherwise dreary convention. Why don't you two come to my apartment tonight for drinks and dinner, say around 7:00?"

"Sounds great," Liam and Nicole said at once, thinking how easy was that!

Nick gave them his address and the three separated.

Nick went to a pay phone in the lobby and dialed Susan Samuels' number. He told her the film was passed to him successfully and he believed Erickson saw it happen. She said Erickson did see the pass. Her agent, Elliott, was in the room and observed it. Nick then told her Hammond said in front of Erickson that his classified report is in Nick's safe and that he invited the two KGB spies to his apartment for dinner at 7:00. Samuels said she would inform Williams.

Liam and Nicole went to Nicole's room. Erickson phoned his new control. He informed the *Rezident* someone had passed to Nick Butler what appeared to be a roll of film and he and Nicole would be at Butler's apartment for dinner tonight, as planned. The *Rezident* told Erickson a white van would be parked outside the apartment.

"When Nicole lifts the film and passes it to you, take it to the van and get in," he directed.

"Even more important than the film," Liam stated to the *Rezident*, "Hammond told Nick his classified report to the Air Force is in the safe in Nick's Century office."

Lamar Williams listened to and recorded Erickson's half of the conversation. There was no tap on the hotel phone but what he heard was clear enough. The KGB op would be underway tonight. Minutes later Samuels phoned Williams to convey what Nick just told her about the pass—Nick now has the Crayton film.

"I know," Williams said, "my agent did a good job of dropping it in Nick's pocket. What's critically important is Erickson told the *Rezident* Hammond's report is now in Nick's safe."

"The op is on for tonight at Nick's apartment starting at 7:00," Samuels confirmed.

Georgetown
Washington, D.C.

Returning to his apartment that afternoon, Nick took the film out of his suit pocket and put it in the top drawer of the bureau. He changed into casual clothes and walked two blocks to the Safeway on Wisconsin Avenue. He bought steaks, Idaho potatoes, and greens for a salad. He was a good cook, but he wanted to keep the meal as simple as possible. He always had plenty of beer on hand in the frig but for tonight he went to a liquor store and bought a fifth of Stoli—to taunt his Russian agent guests.

At 7:00 Nicole and Liam arrived by taxi. They crowded into the studio apartment's tiny kitchen for drinks. Erickson played bartender. He poured Stoli on the rocks for himself and Nicole. Nick already had a beer working. Then the three settled down in the sitting area—a small couch and one easy chair. The single bed was on the other side of the room next to the bureau behind a bamboo room-divider. From where Liam was sitting next to the window he had a view of the street in front of the building. He noticed a white van pulling into an open space directly below.

There was no tension among the three spies, though they all knew the game-plan for the evening. Only Nick knew the entire plan, and he played his part perfectly. He was a gracious host, refreshing drinks before tossing the salad. The conversation centered on the convention, especially Hammond's speech. Nicole had not known about Nick's work with Hammond at NDAC in Santa Monica, which Liam told her about like a proud roommate.

Earlier Nick had baked the potatoes, and now he put the steaks in the broiler part of the small stove. Within minutes they were ready. The three sat down at the dinette table next to the kitchen and had dinner. Nick opened a bottle of California red wine and poured a glass for everyone.

Liam offered a toast: "To our gracious host!" They clinked glasses.

"Your cooking is fabulous," Nicole exclaimed as she took her first bite of sirloin steak.

"Thanks," Nick said. "Glad you like it."

"Nick-boy always did the cooking at our apartment in New York," Liam commented. "He's had lots of practice. This is really good, Nick. Thanks for having us."

"My pleasure."

By 9:00 they finished dinner. Nick cleared the plates, stacking them in the sink. There was no dessert. He brewed coffee, serving it in the sitting area. About 9:30 they finished the coffee. Nick offered to pour another cup, but Liam announced he wanted to sample the night-life in Georgetown. Nick, knowing what he meant, recommended Martin's Tavern down the street as a good spot.

Thanking Nick again for a great evening, Liam left the apartment. He went down the steps to the street, which by now was dark. He waited a few minutes then snuck back up the front steps into the apartment building. He sat down on the landing between the first and second floors to wait for Nicole to appear at Nick's door on the second floor.

Nick knew what he was expected to do next. His orders and his own instincts told him to hustle Nicole into bed, but he was in a taunting mood and delayed his own gratification. They continued to chat. Nick offered more coffee. Nicole declined.

After a while, she moved from the couch to the arm of the easy chair where Nick was sitting. Her hormones were taking over, and besides she wasn't going to waste any more time with her part of the op. Sitting on the arm of his chair, she put her hand on Nick's face and turned it toward her. She kissed him on the mouth. Continuing to kiss him she moved her hand down between his legs.

That did it for Nick's delaying tactic. He pulled her down onto the chair with him, sitting her on his lap. He kissed her repeatedly. Soon he said, "Let's get comfortable." They took off their clothes and dropped onto the single bed.

An hour later Nick got up and went into the bathroom, closing the door behind him. Nicole dashed to the bureau. There it was in the top drawer—a roll of film! She picked it up, closed the drawer, and rushed to the front door. She saw Erickson sitting on the landing. He saw her and jumped up. She tossed the film to him. He caught it, ran down the steps, and got in the van. It sped away.

Nicole silently closed the door and went back to the bed. Nick was still in the bathroom. He knew his part in the drama and wanted to give her plenty of time to steal the film without his seeing her do it, using the time to wash off parts of his body. He wanted to be fresh for what was coming next. Minutes later he left the bathroom, returned to bed, and relaxed, taking Nicole in his arms. They cuddled together silently for a while. Each was taking satisfaction in how well they performed their roles in this high-stakes drama.

Having done his duty, Nick was free to concentrate on Nicole's body until they fell asleep in the cramped single bed. His final thought before drifting off was of Natalie—the last girl he had slept with all night. She was arrested at dawn. Would Nicole be arrested tomorrow?

The FBI agent on stakeout standing outside Nick's apartment building photographed Erickson as he left the building carrying something in his hand and entered the van. He took a photo of the van's license plate. Another agent in a parked car pulled out and tailed the van to 16th Street, where it entered the gated entrance of the Embassy of the Union of Soviet Socialist Republics. The agent photographed the van entering the building. From his car the agent radioed Lamar Williams to report.

About two hours later the van came out of the garage and returned to Georgetown, parking on N Street in front of Butler's building. No one came out of the van. The FBI stakeout agent walked over to the other agent's car, got in, and relaxed until his watch shift was due to start in two hours. All anyone could do now was wait until morning when the lovers would wake up.

While Nick and Nicole were making love in Georgetown, across the river in Rosslyn two KGB agents broke into the Century Aerospace office suite. They went straight to Butler's office, found the safe, and opened it—the combination lock presenting no challenge to these pros. They removed the classified report:

Top Secret
Special Access Required

Applications of Stealth Technology to Military Aircraft:
Recommendations for USAF Roles,
Missions, and Operational Strategy

A Report to the Chief of Staff
United States Air Force

By
David Hammond
National Defense Analysis Center

The KGB agents photographed each of the eighty pages in the bogus report, returned it to the safe, and departed. FBI agents clandestinely photographed them through the glass door in Gladys' office. It had been a busy night for everyone concerned.

At 7:00 A.M. Erickson stepped out of the van. The FBI agent on watch duty poked his companion to rouse him to photograph Erickson. From the sidewalk Erickson walked up the one flight of stairs to enter the building. Inside, he climbed up to the second floor and waited beside Nick's apartment door. He hoped he wouldn't have to wait too long for Nicole to open the door. As it turned out he waited about an hour.

About 8:00 A.M. Nick woke up. He gently kissed Nicole's eyes to waken her. When she opened her eyes, he kissed her tenderly on the lips. She yawned as he got out of bed and padded barefoot into the bathroom, closing the door behind him. Suddenly she remembered her task and rushed to the front door. Erickson was standing there. Without a word he handed her the film. Quickly she put it back in the top drawer of the bureau and returned to bed.

Erickson went down the stairs and reentered the van which took him to the Hilton. The FBI agents followed him to the hotel where they reported to Special Agent Williams the mission was successful. Then the agents drove to FBI Headquarters, turned in their cameras to develop the film, and dictated their reports to a stenographer.

Lamar Williams phoned Susan Samuels to tell her Erickson had taken the Crayton Top Secret film to the Soviet Embassy. He will be charged with the crime of treason, but his arrest will be delayed until after the convention when Nicole leaves the country. He knew the CIA's disinformation op was running and Nicole was playing a big part in it. Samuels was very pleased. Once again Nick Butler had performed perfectly as the lead player in Stealth Gambit and in the FBI's counter-intelligence op.

Nick and Nicole showered and dressed. Knowing she would spend the night, he had bought bacon and eggs for breakfast, just as Sonja Dahl had done for him—it seemed an eternity ago. He prepared breakfast. Both were hungry after their night of enthusiastic love-making. After breakfast, they left the apartment and hailed a cab on Wisconsin Avenue to return to the Hilton.

Embassy of the U.S.S.R.
Washington, D.C.

Seeing the developed film Girard and Erickson had lifted from Butler, Anastas Kamarovski was at first disappointed. He was expecting to see David Hammond's classified report to the U.S. Air Force. Instead, he was looking at a stack of engineering drawings that made no sense to him. He called for his Soviet Air Force technical advisor to evaluate the photographs.

The Air Force colonel came in and as he studied the first three or four prints he began to realize what he was seeing.

"Comrade *Rezident*," he said with awe in his voice, "this is a major find. These are engineering designs from Crayton Aerospace that detail the swing-wing mechanism on their new F-14 fighter. This is truly a breakthrough for us. These drawings will enable the Sukhoi Design Bureau to complete the version of their new Su-27 fighter that also has the variable geometry feature."

"Have the Sukhoi people not yet succeeded in designing the swing-wing feature?" the KGB officer asked, surprised Russian technology was behind the Americans.

"No, Comrade, they have been stumped and a number of their tests have failed," the colonel replied. "These documents will save years of experimentation, quickly putting the Su-27 into the Motherland's service."

"Then we must not delay getting the documents to Moscow," Kamarovski said. He ordered the colonel to make copies of each of the 20 prints for the embassy's file and put the originals in the diplomatic pouch for the trip to Moscow on an afternoon flight out of Dulles.

He phoned Yuri Andropov to report this vitally important new technological input for the Motherland's defense.

"Once again Nick Butler has unknowingly handed the Soviet Union a priceless gift," he told the Chairman.

Later that day, when the film of Hammond's eighty-page report was developed and brought to him, the *Rezident* knew he had achieved an espionage masterstroke—the USAF's top secret operational plans for its future fleet of stealth aircraft. Its authenticity was unquestioned. This truly was the intelligence coup of the decade! He had fulfilled Chairman Andropov's order to get his hands on that all-important document. The report went in the pouch to Moscow.

Operation Stealth Gambit had achieved its purpose!

Department of Justice
Washington, D.C.

On Thursday afternoon Lamar Williams and Ira Steinberg met in a conference room in the Justice Department building on Pennsylvania Avenue. Williams reviewed for the attorney the evidence the FBI had gathered against Liam Erickson and his mother, Estelle Erickson.

He informed the lawyer their arrests will be delayed until after Nicole Girard departs the United States on Saturday afternoon because she is unknowingly participating in a remarkable disinformation operation begun by the CIA that is now being run by French Intelligence. Nicole must not learn about the arrest of her fellow KGB agent to prevent her suspecting her cover is blown and she is now a tool of Western counter-intelligence.

Steinberg informed Williams preparations are well underway at the Office of the U.S. Attorney for the District of Columbia for the prosecutions of Harvey Walker, Sonja Dahl (aka Angela Schmidt), Natalie Thompson (aka Brigitte Schaeffer), and the photographer/courier, whose name is Vladimir Bishoff, a naturalized U.S. citizen. The Grand Jury had already issued the indictments. In anticipation of the arrests of Liam and Estelle Erickson, the Justice Department's Criminal Division is assembling evidence obtained by the FBI against them for handoff to the U.S. Attorney.

Hilton Hotel
Washington, D.C.

On Friday evening Professor Reynard hosted a farewell dinner. He invited Professor Capp, Nicole, Nick, and Liam. In honor of the French visitors, he held the dinner at the most famous French restaurant in Washington—the Rive Gauche in Georgetown.

After a fabulous dinner, they left the restaurant and hailed taxis. The two professors shared one and the three research assistants shared another. Arriving back at the Hilton, Liam said he was going to find his date from the night before, hoping to get lucky again. Nick and Nicole went directly to her room.

They wanted to make the most of their last night together. Quickly they climbed in bed.

It was like their last night at the Prince de Galles—intensely passionate, almost desperate love-making. It lasted on-and-off all night with intervals of sleep between bouts of physically demanding sex. As dawn approached, the exhausted lovers fell into a deep sleep in each others' arms.

At 9:00 Nick woke up. He looked at the clock and realized they could sleep a while longer, but Nicole was beginning to rouse so he propped himself on his pillow and waited for her to open her eyes. A few minutes later she did. He smiled at her beautiful face. She smiled at him. Neither said anything. Nicole pulled him to her and held him tight. Then she kissed him and kissed him and kissed him again, her eyes welling up with tears. Never had Nick experienced such passion. He was brought to tears himself as he made love to her for the last time.

At 3:00 Nicole joined Professor Capp under the portico of the hotel's main entrance for their trip back to Paris. Their Air France flight was scheduled to depart Dulles at 4:50. Nick and Liam were on hand to bid them farewell. Professor Reynard had left for New York earlier in the day. Everyone gave a brief embrace. Nick did not want to embarrass Nicole in front of her boss by giving her the kiss he wanted to give. He did that a half hour earlier in private. As the taxi drove away, Nick shouted "bon voyage."

In his heart Nick realized he might never see Nicole again, given they are on opposite sides in the Cold War. That realization weighed heavily on him because he had come to love her like he had never loved before.

Liam and Nick went back into the hotel to the lobby bar for a beer. It was like old times for the roommates. Liam reported he had found his date from the other night. Nick wondered to himself what was going to happen to Liam if by now the FBI had the goods on him.

About an hour later Nick noticed two middle-age men in dark suits enter the bar. They took stools at the end of the bar near the entrance. One of them looked directly at Nick and gave a head jerk, as if to say get out of here. Nick instantly realized who they were and what they were going to do. They didn't want him present when it happened. He was grateful for that.

"Well, so long Liam," Nick said as he slid off the bar stool. "You've got to get going to Union Station and I've got to get to my apartment." Nick put money on the bar.

"Okay, Nick-boy," the tall blond man responded. "It's been a great week. And I highly approve of Nicole, by the way." The two young men shook hands. Nick walked out of the bar. He did not look back.

A few minutes later, the two agents approached Erickson, still seated at the bar finishing his beer.

"Liam Erickson?" asked one of the agents as he showed his FBI identification.

"Yes."

"Please step outside with us. We need to speak with you."

"What's this about?" Liam asked warily.

"We'll explain it to you outside. Please come with us."

Reluctantly, Erickson rose from the bar stool and walked out with the two men. When they came to a deserted part of the huge lobby, the lead agent said in a low formal voice: "Liam Erickson, you are under arrest for the crime of high treason against the United States."

The other agent recited his Miranda rights and asked if he understood them.

"Yes, but I don't understand what's happening," Erickson stammered.

"You will come with us. It will be explained to you at FBI Headquarters," the lead agent said. They cuffed him. Each agent took hold of an arm and led him to a government car waiting at the valet entrance.

At the same time in the Central Time Zone, Mrs. Estelle Erickson was arrested at her home by two FBI agents out of the Madison, Wisconsin field office. She was handcuffed and driven in a government car to the Federal Courthouse in Madison where she was held for the crime of conspiracy to commit treason against the United States. She was locked in a cell. The middle-age woman appeared to go berserk, pounding her fists against the bars while screaming at the jailers in a language none of them understood.

FBI Headquarters
Washington, D.C.

Special Agent Williams telephoned Susan Samuels to inform her Liam Erickson and his mother had been arrested and both are now in custody. Liam was in the same holding cell Walker had been in when he was arrested. Walker had subsequently been transferred to a cell in the D.C. Federal Courthouse.

Samuels phoned Myers at his home and gave him the news. Myers said the nation's indebtedness to Nick Butler had multiplied. Samuels agreed.

Director Dean, informed by Williams of the arrests, phoned Dr. Singleton who was working in his office at the White House that Saturday as usual. Singleton congratulated the FBI on their excellent work. He immediately informed President Reed who was in the residence part of the White House. The president asked his National Security Advisor to give some thought to how the government should express its appreciation to Nick Butler.

The President then phoned Director Dean and Admiral Myers to congratulate them on a job well done. He said to each of them: "The nation is a safer place thanks to you."

Chapter 15:
The Master Spy

The Department of Justice
Washington, D.C.

Two days later, on Monday morning, Ira Steinberg and a team of Justice Department lawyers were working with another team of lawyers from the U.S. Attorney's Office to prepare for the treason trials of the six individuals in custody. With so many defendants, this was a daunting undertaking.

The White House
Washington, D.C.

That same day Singleton was considering ways to acknowledge Nick Butler for his performance. Before making his recommendation to the President, he wanted to satisfy himself that Butler had truly played an indispensable role. He decided to phone Philip Myers. "What I want to understand, Admiral," Singleton asked, "is how important was Butler's performance protecting our nation?"

"First," Dr. Singleton, Myers replied, "Butler put disinformation in the hands of the Russians that will tie them up in engineering knots for years and years. This work was accomplished with the cooperation of the British and French governments, not to mention our own aerospace companies—General Aerospace, Wilshire, Century, and Crayton."

"I understand he played an important role in those operations, Phil." Singleton probed deeper: "But was he truly indispensable? Could others have done what he did just as well?'

"Dr. Singleton," Admiral Myers answered, speaking very firmly, "Nick Butler is a master spy. I know of no one else in our government or for that matter in the government of any of our allies who could have accomplished what he did in a matter of months. He is naturally gifted at our craft, making what he did look easy. But do not be misled by the easy-going style of this man or his boyish innocent demeanor. Inside, he's rock-solid. His love of our country motivated him to take great personal risks. To answer your question," Myers concluded, raising his voice, "Nick Butler was indispensable."

"Well, I certainly wasn't casting aspersions on the man's abilities," Singleton said back-peddling. "I simply wanted to confirm the importance of his work to determine how the nation should reward him."

"Here's another thing for you to consider, sir," the Admiral added, his voice thickening. "That very able young man blew one of the KGB's top spies in the entire world—I'm talking about Walker—and with him the KGB's espionage network that ranged from Paris, to New York, to Washington, to Wisconsin, and to Los Angeles. Do you think for one minute Yuri Andropov will sit by quietly if and when he finds out what young Mr. Butler did to him? Andropov is ruthless—famous for taking revenge. So this government not only has a duty to protect the false information Butler passed to the Russians, it also has a duty to protect Nick Butler's very life. That's how you can reward him! Good-by, sir."

Burk Singleton was shaken by those words from the distinguished admiral. He realized Myers is right. He was chagrined he'd failed to take into consideration the personal risk Butler would face for the rest of his life if the KGB found out he was the key player who rolled up their espionage network and that he was the lead player disrupting their aircraft industry for years to come.

The National Security Advisor decided that Butler's disinformation role should not be highlighted out of fear that might expose it to the KGB because its impact is continuing. The expression of gratitude, he concluded, should focus solely on Butler's counter-espionage role. That part of his activities is now finished and his role in it could be protected.

Later that day President Reed asked Singleton to recommend what should be done to reward Butler for his contributions to breaking up the spy ring and for planting the false airplane data in the Soviet's hands.

"I recommend we focus exclusively on his role breaking up the spy ring," replied Singleton. "That part of his work we can protect from exposure. The disinformation operation is so successful and so far-reaching in its importance to our national security that we should not risk exposing it in any way."

"Good suggestion, Burk."

"My thought is this, sir," Singleton continued. "I suggest we invite Butler here to have a private meeting with you in the Oval Office. Following that, I'll host a lunch in the White House Mess for him as guest of honor. Secretary Wasserman expressed a desire to meet the young man, being impressed with his performance. The lunch attendees will be Wasserman, the top CIA people, FBI Director Dean and his key agent, Mr. Williams, and my deputy. This is a secure setting, and it will be a feather in the young man's cap. Something he'll never forget."

"What about Century Aerospace?" the President asked. "They played a critical behind-the-scenes role from what you've told me."

"Oh, you're so right, Mr. President," Singleton agreed. "Martin Stark, Century's CEO, should be included. He has no idea the important role Butler played so this will be an eye-opener for him, telling him the skill his intern demonstrated. And it will be an appropriate way to thank him for providing Butler's cover story as Century's industrial spy."

"All right, Burk," the President concluded, rising from his chair, "let's do it. You've got your game-plan and your guest list. Have CIA send over Butler's personnel file for my background reading."

The National Security Advisor returned to his office and placed a call to Martin Stark at Century's headquarters in Los Angeles. He knew arranging for Stark's attendance would be the most difficult, given his office is in California. Also, Stark is the only non-government person on the guest list. He would have to be persuaded to attend.

After a preliminary chat, Dr. Singleton asked the Century CEO if he planned to be in Washington anytime soon.

"We have a contract signing ceremony in two days, on Wednesday, at the Taiwan Mission," Stark replied. "They've accepted our proposal to co-produce 300 F-11 fighters for their air force. I'll be there for that event."

"This coming Wednesday, you say?" Singleton asked to make sure he heard right.

"Yes, at 9:00 A.M. at their Mission."

"Very well," the National Security Advisor said. "Do you have any plans for lunch that day that cannot be changed?"

"No. I was planning to fly back to L.A. early afternoon. Why?"

"The President would like you to attend a special luncheon that day at the White House Mess. The event is to honor your summer intern, Nick Butler."

"What? Did I hear you right?" the CEO responded in a disbelieving tone. "The President is honoring my intern. I don't understand."

"Mr. Stark," Singleton continued patiently, "your intern has performed great service for the United States. It was not possible to inform you of this before now. This was a highly classified matter. It still is classified. Butler was the principal player in a vital counter-espionage operation. The President would like you to attend this casual lunch here at the White House also to express his gratitude to you for providing an indispensable element in this operation—Butler's cover story as your intern."

"Well, I'll be damned," Stark said in amazement. "I can hardly believe what you've just told me. I knew Butler would be performing some tasks for the CIA when Admiral Myers asked me to hire him as a summer intern, but I had no idea his work would be so important. Of course I'll be delighted to attend the lunch. Who else will be there?"

"The Secretary of State and the top leadership of both the CIA and the FBI will also attend. You'll be in very good company. Please come to the Pennsylvania Avenue entrance of the White House at noon on Wednesday. Tell no one the purpose of this visit. Simply say you've been invited to the White House for lunch."

Next Singleton summoned his deputy, Edith Garland. He informed her of the President's desire to honor Nick Butler with a special luncheon for his work uncovering the Walker spy ring. He gave her the guest list. Martin Stark had already accepted the invitation. She was ordered to close the Mess to the White House staff on Wednesday. This would be a highly confidential gathering. She should instruct the White House chef to prepare something special.

He directed her to invite the CIA and FBI attendees. He told her to have Susan Samuels send to the President Butler's file and to order Butler to her office at 11:00. She and Admiral Myers should bring him to the White House using the West Executive Drive entrance. They should arrive at the West Wing at 11:30, using one of the CIA vans with the heavily tinted windows. Butler must not be observed coming or going from the Executive Mansion.

"I will invite the Secretary of State," Singleton added, dismissing his deputy.

"Mr. Secretary," Dr. Singleton said on the telephone to Oscar Wasserman, "the President has directed me to invite you to a special luncheon at the White House Mess on Wednesday at noon. The lunch is to honor Nick Butler for his service in capturing the Walker spy ring."

"I will be happy to attend," replied Wasserman. "I look forward to meeting this remarkable young man. Please thank the President for inviting me."

CIA Headquarters
Langley, Virginia

"Nick," Susan Samuels said to Butler when he called the special number from a pay phone, "I want you to come to my office on Wednesday. I'll need you here at 11:00. So at 10:30 sharp please be at the Key Bridge Marriott parking lot, second floor, where Elliott will be waiting to drive you. Be sure to bring the roll of Crayton film you received at the ISA convention."

"Okay, I'll do that," Butler replied, wondering what this was about as he hung up. He knew from Stan Ebersol the signing ceremony for the Taiwan F-11 co-production deal was scheduled for that morning. Perhaps this has something to do with that. He would just have to wait and see. He decided for his second visit to CIA Headquarters he would wear his best suit. Last time he was in jeans and a T-shirt.

The White House
Washington, D.C.

Wednesday morning the players in the drama were assembling. Martin V. Stark was in Washington attending the contract signing ceremony for the huge F-11 coproduction program at the Taiwan Mission. Under the deal, Century will design and construct a factory adjacent to Taipei's airport to assemble 300 fighters. Airplane parts will be shipped from California. The contract value is in the billions. This is a great day for Century Aerospace and for Martin Stark personally.

After the contract was signed and a brief celebration ended, Stark was driven to Century's office in Rosslyn. He asked to see Nick Butler. Stanley Ebersol told him Nick left the office a short time ago. Stark could guess why.

Obeying Susan Samuels' orders, Nick left Century's office and walked to the Marriott parking lot, arriving there at 10:30. Elliott was waiting for him on the second level with the motor running. The two drove west on George Washington Parkway to the rear entrance of the CIA complex. Elliott pulled into the underground garage at exactly 11:00.

Admiral Myers and Susan Samuels were waiting beside the elevator. Myers was in his Vice Admiral's white summer uniform. Nick got out of the van, greeted his superiors, and handed the Crayton film to Samuels. She told Nick to get back in the van and sit in the back seat with Myers. She rode shotgun. The minute the van's doors closed, Elliott pulled out of the garage, doubling-back on the same route. Nick knew better than to ask any questions.

At precisely 11:30 the CIA bullet-proof black van pulled onto West Executive Drive off 17th Street. Elliott steered the van around the back of the Old Executive Office Building on the curved driveway, stopping in front of the West Wing's entrance. Nick's jaw dropped. Suddenly he realized where he was—The White House.

Admiral Myers said to Nick, "Let's go." The three got out of the van, climbed up the short flight of red carpeted steps, and entered the West Wing through the white French doors.

Waiting inside, Dr. Edith Garland clipped White House visitor badges on each of them. She led them down the center hall to the southeast corner of the building where they stopped at the desk of the President's secretary, who smiled and said, "Please go in."

Dr. Garland opened the door and told Butler to go in first. Nick stepped through the doorway, instantly recognizing the famous room. He was in the Oval Office! President Reed rose from his desk and walked over to Nick. Another man was with him.

"Mr. President, it is my pleasure to introduce Mr. Nick Butler," Garland said.

"Mr. Butler, it is my pleasure to meet you," the President said shaking his hand. "This is Dr. Burk Singleton, my Assistant for National Security Affairs."

"Mr. Butler," Singleton said, "we are pleased to meet you at last."

The President asked everyone to take a chair in the sitting area by the fireplace. Edith Garland left the room to attend to the other guests who would arrive shortly. Other than to stammer a greeting, Nick was tongue-tied. Looking around the historic room, he went to the chair the President indicated and sat down. Myers and Samuels smiled as they watched Nick being overcome by his surrounds.

"May I call you Nick?" the President asked.

"Yes sir," Nick replied, feeling a little shaken by what was happening to him.

"Well, Nick," the President said, "I asked your superiors at the CIA to bring you here today so I could personally express the thanks of the American people for your outstanding work in helping to capture the Walker spy ring. I understand you played the central role in that operation and I'm told you did it like a seasoned professional. The nation is grateful to you, and I'm personally very proud of you, young man."

For a moment Nick thought he would breakdown. Nothing had ever been said to him that resonated so deeply within him.

"Thank you, Mr. President," Nick stammered, choking back his emotions.

"Nick," the President went on, "in a few minutes Dr. Singleton will take you to the White House Mess for lunch. Other leaders in the government also want to express their appreciation for your outstanding contribution. This will be their opportunity to do so."

Dr. Singleton intervened at this point to add a word of caution. "Nick, this meeting with the President and the lunch that follows are strictly 'off the record.' I'm afraid you cannot discuss any of this with anyone other than those here today. The reason is your clandestine role is continuing, and we must take every precaution that it and you are not exposed to Soviet intelligence."

"I understand," Nick replied.

"Mrs. Samuels," the President asked, turning to her, "in your years of handling clandestine operatives, how would you gauge Nick's performance?" The President already knew the answer, but he wanted Nick to hear it from his immediate boss.

"Mr. President," she answered, "on a scale of one to ten, for being an effective espionage agent, Nick Butler is off the chart. He is so instinctively skilled he makes what he does look easy. He's a naturally-gifted agent."

"Admiral Myers," the President asked turning to him, "how important was Nick's role in uncovering the Walker spy ring—in your professional judgment?"

"Mr. President," Myers replied, "the Walker ring had been operating for some years. We don't know yet how long. We do know it did great damage to our national security. Some of our agents were assassinated because Walker identified them to the KGB. This ring was the single most destructive force working inside our own government, and we didn't know it even existed until Nick uncovered it in the course of his disinformation operation. Without Nick, Walker would still be in business harming our country even more. To answer your question directly, sir, Nick Butler's role was pivotal."

"Well, Nick," the President summed up looking at him, "I trust you're beginning to appreciate how much you did for our country and how grateful our country is to you."

"Yes sir, I'm beginning to grasp the importance of it."

"At lunch you'll be given more information on the significance of your role," the President added. Seeing that Butler was still ill-at-ease by what was happening to him, President Reed decided to calm him by raising a more normal topic. "Nick, I'm told you were the quarterback on Penn's varsity football team in your senior year. Is that right?"

"Yes sir," Nick answered proudly, feeling on firmer ground. "But I wasn't an All-American like you were at Michigan."

"Yet your team had a winning season under your leadership, if I'm not mistaken."

"Your information is correct, sir. Penn had an 8 to 2 season, but that wasn't good enough to win the Ivy League championship. Dartmouth won it my year with a perfect 10."

"Eight to two isn't anything to sneeze at," observed the President. "Congratulations." Seeing that Nick was feeling more at ease in this intense setting, the President concluded the meeting.

"Once again, Nick, I thank you on behalf of the United States for helping rid our government of this insidious traitor and his network." With these words the President rose from his chair, as did the others. Dillon Reed shook hands with Nick Butler and feeling an emotional bond the former All-American from Michigan hugged his fellow football player. Singleton, Myers, and Samuels applauded.

"Thank you, Mr. President," Nick said, choking back his feelings.

Dr. Singleton led the way out of the world's most famous office to the West Wing's center hall. Singleton put his arm around Nick's shoulders to steady him after the emotional moment with the President, leading him and the others to the stairs that go down one flight to the Mess.

As they descended, Singleton helped settle Nick by recounting a little history. He said when President Theodore Roosevelt built the West Wing he decided to put a mess hall in the basement for the staff members. In military tradition it was called a Mess. The stewards are all from the Philippines, keeping with the Navy's tradition since the Spanish-American War of having them serve food in the Officers' Mess aboard ship.

When they arrived at the foot of the stairs and entered the Mess, a small group of people was standing beside a large round table in the otherwise empty room. Nick immediately recognized the Secretary of State.

As they approached the table, Dr. Singleton introduced Nick to each of the five people waiting there: Dr. Wasserman, the Secretary of State; Samuel Dean, Director of the FBI; Lamar Williams, FBI Special Agent in Charge of the Washington, D.C. Area, whom Nick already knew; Dr. Edith Garland, whom he had seen earlier; and finally Singleton said, "and you know Mr. Martin Stark, Chairman and CEO of Century Aerospace." Each person shook hands with Nick and said a word of greeting. It was clear to everyone that the young guest of honor was a little bewildered at being greeted by such a high-ranking group of individuals.

Singleton asked everyone to take a place at the table. He seated Nick and put the Secretary of State on his right. Singleton was on Nick's left. When everyone was seated, the National Security Advisor announced that minutes ago the President had a private meeting with Mr. Butler in the Oval Office where he thanked him for his indispensable service to the United States. Everyone applauded.

"Director Dean," Singleton asked, "would you be good enough to relate to Nick and the others how important his role has been in ridding us of a KGB spy ring within our own government?"

"Gladly, Dr. Singleton," Director Dean began. "Mr. Butler was engaged in a CIA operation during which three KGB sleeper agents approached him at different times and places to obtain classified information from American aerospace companies. This data, provided by those companies at CIA's request, was bogus. It was used to entrap the KGB agents in a sting operation headed by Special Agent Williams that led us to Harvey Walker, the head of the spy ring. Mr. Walker is probably the most dangerous traitor in American history since Benedict Arnold. In his position as FBI Deputy Director for Counter-Intelligence he knew everything about the FBI's operations as well as American industrial secrets. He passed this information to the KBG for years in return for money. Special Agent Williams, please continue the story."

"Thank you, Director Dean," Williams said. "Through court-ordered wire taps and other surveillance of Walker's agents, we gathered indictable evidence against Walker and his network. That network was based here in Washington and also had agents in New York City, in Los Angeles, and in Madison, Wisconsin. Those agents were moles, planted on American soil years ago. All six of these traitors are now safely behind bars awaiting trial in Federal Court."

"CIA wants to thank you, Mr. Stark, for your cooperation with the aircraft disinformation operation," Admiral Myers said to Martin Stark. "Without your help, we would not have had Nick Butler's plausible cover story as your company's industrial spy and the bait we needed to entrap Walker and the members of his network."

"I am astonished to learn this," announced Stark. "Upon first meeting Nick at the Farnborough Air Show last year I judged him to be a serious and capable person. What you're telling me is he is much, much more than that—even recognized as such by the President."

"Mr. Stark," Susan Samuels interjected, "Nick Butler is the most capable espionage agent we have at the CIA. His instinctive skills and natural gifts at our craft are beyond compare. There are details of his performance I cannot share with you but if I could they would further astound you."

"Mr. Secretary," Dr. Singleton said turning toward Wasserman, "I trust this information about Nick Butler has given you new insights into his service on behalf of our country."

"I share Mr. Stark's reaction. I, too, am astonished at the depth and breadth of your work, Mr. Butler," said the Secretary of State looking at Nick. "I would like to offer a toast." Everyone rose, picking up their water glasses: "To Nick Butler, a truly great American patriot. It is an honor to sit at the same table with you, young man." Everyone said, "Here, here."

After that, Dr. Singleton went to the kitchen door to tell the stewards they could enter the room and begin serving lunch. The main course was Maryland crab cakes in honor of Nick's home state.

During lunch Nick was monopolized by Dr. Wasserman, inquiring about his professors at Penn and Columbia, especially Al Rubin and Bill Reynard. Wasserman knew both of them, having been a political science professor at Harvard. He was catching up on his colleagues. He was also testing Nick's knowledge of world affairs. Nick told him about his interest in working in the aerospace industry as a practical way to use his knowledge of government in business. He credited that idea to Martin Stark.

After the dishes were cleared away and the stewards left the room, Dr. Singleton turned to Nick, asking if he has any comments he would like to make.

"Yes, indeed," Nick replied. "I cannot begin to express my gratitude to each of you for your kind remarks and for being here to honor me. No words of mine are adequate. Suffice it to say, thank you very much. The work I did was at Susan Samuels' direction. She called the shots and I simply carried out her orders. Later on, Mr. Williams called some of the shots so he deserves the credit along with Mrs. Samuels. I was merely the foot soldier following orders. I thought I was participating in one type of operation, but it turned out two operations were going on simultaneously."

At this point Nick paused and took a deep breath. "My appreciation to President Reed for honoring me is beyond speaking. I have never been so moved. Please, Dr. Singleton, give him my thanks. I was overwhelmed at the moment and fear I inadequately thanked him."

With those words Nick fell silent. The entire room was silent. Then the room exploded with applause. Everyone stood up as the applause continued. Susan Samuels brushed back a tear. Admiral Myers was filled with pride for Nick. Singleton realized Nick had credited others for his achievements, taking none of it for himself. His respect for the young man deepened.

The gathering broke up. Myers, Samuels, and Butler returned to the van outside the West Wing, and Elliott drove them back to Langley. Director Dean and Special Agent Williams returned to FBI Headquarters in the Director's car. Martin Stark's driver picked him up at the Pennsylvania Avenue entrance and drove him to Rosslyn. Drs. Singleton and Garland went to the Oval Office to report to the President what Nick had said. Secretary Wasserman went with them to give his assessment of Butler to the President. He said Nick Butler is beyond first-rate.

Georgetown
Washington, D.C.

Nick returned to his apartment in Georgetown that evening. Everything seemed different. This day had changed him forever. He felt like he'd had an out-of-body experience. He knew the feeling wouldn't last, so he was going to enjoy it while he could.

He went to Martin's Tavern for a drink and dinner. To celebrate, he ordered a manhattan straight up. Sitting at the bar, he reflected on the remarkable events of the past year, especially the people who had been his friends and lovers, three of whom he had been instrumental in sending to prison—Sonja, Natalie, and Liam.

He realized his emotions were mixed. While he was proud he had helped capture Walker's espionage ring to safeguard the country, he nevertheless liked his good friend Liam and he genuinely cared for Sonja and Natalie, and especially Nicole. Bitter-sweet thoughts of them crisscrossed his mind.

Sipping his drink, it dawned on him that all three women he had known this year, beginning in January with Nicole, were KGB agents who were under orders to seduce him to gain classified information. This realization was a body-blow to the pride he always had in his pickup skills. That pride now seemed delusional. He hadn't picked them up. They had picked him up!

While absorbed in these thoughts, he noticed an attractive young woman enter the restaurant. She took a seat at the bar near Nick. She was alone. Nick smiled at her. She smiled back. Nick moved to the stool next to her and asked, "You're not a spy, are you?"

Epilogue

After a trial for each criminal defendant that lasted several weeks, the jury found all six members of the Walker spy ring guilty of the crimes as charged:

> Harvey Walker for high treason against the United States
> Liam Erickson for high treason against the United States
> Sonja Dahl for conspiracy to commit treason
> Natalie Thompson for conspiracy to commit treason
> Estelle Erickson for conspiracy to commit treason
> Vladimir Bishoff as an accessory to commit treason

Walker was sentenced to life in solitary confinement without the possibility of parole at the high security Federal Bureau of Prisons Penitentiary in Marion, Illinois. Liam Erickson was sentenced to 40 years to life at the same penitentiary without the possibility of parole and without visiting rights. Dahl and Thompson were sentenced to 20 years in prison without the possibility of parole and without visiting rights. Estelle Erickson and Vladimir Bishoff were sentenced to ten years in prison without the possibility of parole.

Nicole Girard continued employment for ten years at Thomson, unknowingly passing false and misleading avionics information to the KGB. Finally, the KGB concluded she had been turned, becoming a double-agent working for French Intelligence, because much of the engineering data she delivered proved unworkable. In 1985 she suspected she was in danger, and she vanished. She was not seen or heard from again.

Madam Gardiner, Jean-Pierre Capp's secretary at the Science Po, and Marie LeBlanc, the Air France stewardess, were arrested a week after Girard's disappearance. They were tried and convicted of treason. They are serving life sentences in a French prison.

Nick Butler graduated from Columbia University in 1980 with a Ph.D. in Political Science. The title of his award-winning dissertation was "Uses of Political Science in Business Management." Martin Stark immediately hired him to be Vice President in charge of Century Aerospace's Washington Office, succeeding Stanley Ebersol who retired. When Anastas Kamarovski informed him, Yuri Andropov was not surprised.

After the Berlin Wall fell and the Soviet Union collapsed in 1991, West German authorities entered East Germany and confiscated the documents at the Stasi Records Agency in Berlin. In those records they discovered the Stasi, under orders from the KGB, had artificially-inseminated two German women with Nick Butler's sperm. Both produced boys, now teenagers, whose identities were provided to the CIA. Susan Samuels, now CIA's Deputy Director of Operations, pondered whether she should inform Nick Butler he had unknowingly fathered two sons—one living in the United States and one living in Russia.

The Sukhoi Design Bureau's T-10 prototype of its swing-wing Su-27 was flight tested in 1978. It crashed. An improved model was flight tested in 1981. It also crashed. Sukhoi never built a successful variable geometry version of the Su-27.

Much later, Sukhoi successfully built a multi-role stealth fighter, the Su-47. Its first flight was in 2010—35 years after our story ended. It is being produced jointly with the Indian Air Force.

The U.S. developed and put into service three variable geometry aircraft: the F-111 in the 1960s, the F-14 in the 1970s, and the B-1B in the 1980s.

The U.S. developed five stealth aircraft: the F-117A in the 1970s, the B-2 in the 1980s, the F-22 and the YF-23 in the 1990s, and the F-35 in the 2000s.

About the Author

Wes Truitt was an executive at Northrop Grumman Corporation for 25 years. He was Executive Assistant to the Chairman of the Board and CEO, Corporate Director of Policy Analysis, and Vice President-Europe. Later he was Adjunct Professor at the School of Public Policy, Pepperdine University. He was Executive-in-Residence at the College of Business Administration, Loyola Marymount University, and Adjunct Professor at the Anderson Graduate School of Management, UCLA. Early in his career he was an Intern at the U.S. Department of State. He was a lecturer for one year at the U.S. Air Force's Air War College and a guest lecturer at the Naval Post-Graduate School. His B.A. is from the University of Pennsylvania, where he was elected to Phi Beta Kappa and was president of his fraternity, Theta Xi. His M.A. and Ph.D. degrees are from Columbia University. He earned a post-graduate diploma from the University of Florence, Italy, and he was a National Science Foundation Scholar.

CPSIA information can be obtained
at www.ICGtesting.com
Printed in the USA
LVOW04*2131240216
476535LV00013B/140/P